PRAISE F[illegible]

'Vivid, pass[illegible] my heart for a very long time to [illegible] Katie Marsh

'I cannot remember when I was last so touched by a story. *Tin Man* meets *Brokeback Mountain* – it really is that good. This isn't a book you just read, it's something you abso[illegible]. An incredible, poignant piece of work. Louise Beech had cemented her place as on[e of Br]itain's finest modern storytellers' John Marrs

'A b[ea]utiful, honest and tender love story that I won't forget for a long time. With wish[e]s, promises, betrayals, heartbreak and joy – Ben and Andrew's story spans time and [d]istance. Their love had me trapped in its spell, their tragic moments had me sobbing like a baby. The scenes in Zimbabwe had me right there, inhaling the heady scents and listening to the lions roar. This is Louise Beech at her very best. A triumph' Fionnuala Kearney

'Beech sets up the love story quietly and convincingly. And then – bang – something astonishing and completely unexpected happens to Ben and Andrew. This is where the narrative really gathers pace. I had read patiently until that point then I raced my way to the end. The book digs deep emotionally, but is funny and feel-good too' Fiona Mitchell

'Storytelling at its finest. Louise Beech is a beguiling wordsmith. Prepare to be hooked' Amanda Prowse

'The whole novel is skilfully woven together, with complex, utterly convincing characters and an impossible moral dilemma at the core. It's a compelling read through to the emotional final pages. I love the poetry, the wisdom, and the insights into life at a lion sanctuary, so vivid that the reader can hear and smell as well as visualise them. It's a stunning and very brave book' Gill Paul

'Louise Beech does it again. The setting alone makes this book worth a read, the lightly handled metaphor of a place where damaged beings go to recover provides a sumptuous backdrop that does its work on the reader's subconscious while they enjoy the action of the [s]tory. Love, complicated families and the hurtful things people say and do to one another out of fear, love and ignorance feature here, as well as messy relationships and the [m]istakes flawed human beings make while trying so hard not to. A moving read' S.E. Lynes

'H[e]artfelt and wry, this will transport you into a keenly observed world; secrets are hi[d]den, people are flawed, but humanity endures' Ruth Dugdall

'[Louis]e Beech is a natural-born storyteller with an elegance about her writing that [never f]ails to move me' Michael J. Malone

'[Thi]s real life, bruised, torn and coffee-stained, refusing to give up … simply stunning' Su Bristow

'There are times when you finish reading a book and know that part of it will stay with you always. This will be one of those books' Claire Allen

'It put me in mind of John Irving. It's that feeling of being in the hands of a master storyteller and just trusting him or her so completely' Laura Pearson

'Nothing about this story disappoints. The African setting, the excellent writing, and above all, the immaculate storytelling. It's a cleverly constructed book too. I loved the chapter headings which give us a glimpse of the story within the story. Another triumph. A beautifully crafted book' Carole Lovekin

'Again, Louise Beech has totally blown me away with her storytelling ability. I loved this beautiful but painful love story; which is also about coincidences, loss and difficult relationships. This is a story about the strength of love and what sometimes needs to be sacrificed for it' Madeleine Black

'Adored this beautiful and inspiring book' Kate Furnivall

'Already one of my favourites of 2018' Liz Robinson, LoveReadingUK

'There are books I love and books I will treasure forever and *The Lion Tamer Who Lost* by the superbly talented Louise Beech is the latter. She is the "queen" of storytelling. This novel was such a compelling and emotive read, and so beautifully written I'm not convinced anything I write will convey how truly wonderful this book was' The Book Review Café

'It was about the strength of love and the selfless sacrifices that people make at a time of crisis, and also having the maturity and courage to deal with life's setbacks if things don't go as planned … I knew this book would be a tearjerker as soon as I immersed myself in Louise Beech's story, with her poetic words leaping off the page like little sparks of light. Each one of her books is unique – nothing like her previous ones, but just as compelling and compassionate' Off-the-Shelf Books

'A very emotional read. Louise Beech, what are you doing to me? Your writing is lovely and evocative and you made me care for what happened to Andrew and Ben. Did not see the ending at all!' The Book Trail

'I've loved all of her novels. However, I think this one might be my favorite yet! I love Louise's books because I can't help but become completely captivated by the way she tells her stories and the beauty of her characters. Her books are always beautiful, poignant, and magical' The Misstery

'*The Lion Tamer Who Lost* is beautiful from the first page right to the very last page!' Have Books Will Read

'Louise Beech is able to find the extraordinary in the ordinary; to take a story that could easily happen anywhere and weave it into a magical story of love, life and heartfelt emotion that is nothing less than epic. Moving, honest, and heartbreakingly tender, *The Lion Tamer Who Lost* had me in tears more than once. A beautiful, poignant, stand-out book of 2018. I urge you to read it' Live and Deadly

'This book is a love story, a tale of secrets, guilt, confusion, bigotry and shame, beautifully woven together through the narration of Ben and Andrew. I was transported to the lion sanctuary in Africa through the author's stunning poetic and descriptive writing style' Compulsive Readers

'Louise's greatest skill is in her attention to detail. Her descriptions of the Zimbabwean savanna are quite beautiful. She is a writer of great perception and acuity. She writes with sensitivity, with a sharp ear for dialogue and for creating depth of character. *The Lion Tamer Who Lost* is a beautiful, thought-provoking and simply wonderful book. At its heart it is a tragic love story, but dig deeper and it is so much more than that. It is a look at the issues surrounding sexuality, acceptance, deception and the emotional fall-out from dealing with an earth-shattering tragedy' The Beardy Book Blogger

'Louise Beech's writing is exquisite. I'm not ashamed to say I cried. More than once. I cried at the relationship between Ben and Andrew a few times and I also cried over Will, the man who knew he had made mistakes and regretted them. An absolutely brilliant novel, told as always from the heart' Steph's Book Blog

'The writing is exquisite – every word carefully chosen, capturing the open skies of Africa with the same ease and beauty as those small moments within an intense relationship. This book was total perfection, beautiful, breathtaking, heartbreaking, and one of the very best books I've read this – or any other – year' Being Anne

'Beautifully and thoughtfully written' Trip Fiction

'I'm finding it difficult to convey how fabulous the writing is – as Louise Beech has left me, to quote her, "speechless, full of silent words" and not a few tears. A book that will stay with readers, and listeners, for a very long time' Linda's Book Bag

'A stirring novel, beautifully written, reminiscent of the early work of Maggie O'Farrell' *Irish Times*

'Quirky, darkly comic, heartfelt and original' *Sunday Mirror*

'This achingly sad story has wonderful characters' *Sunday People*

'A beautiful and compassionate read' *Prima*

'Fans of *Eleanor Oliphant is Completely Fine* will love it' *Red*

'With lilting, rhythmic prose that never falters, *How To Be Brave* held me from its opening lines … Wonderful' Amanda Jennings

'Two family stories of loss and redemption intertwine in a painfully beautiful narrative. This book grabbed me right around my heart and didn't let go' Cassandra Parkin

'An amazing story of hope and survival … a love letter to the power of books and stories' Nick Quantrill

'Louise Beech is a natural born storyteller and this is a wonderful story' Russ Litten

'*How To Be Brave* reminds us of the frailty of the human condition and champions that inner strength we all have when faced with adversity. Beautifully written and emotionally resonant, this will stay with you long after you turn the final page' Liz Loves Books

'Ms Beech has written an amazing story ... of unconditional love, the best cure for every pain and disease' Chick Cat Library Cat

'An exquisite novel. Darkly compelling emotionally charged. And I LOVED it!' Jane Isaac

'*The Mountain in My Shoe* is cleverly laced with a chilling and gripping storyline about a controlling, possibly psychotic husband. I couldn't put it down. Louise Beech is an author who writes with her heart on her sleeve' Fleur Smithwick

'Louise Beech proves with this incredibly moving story that the success of her debut, *How To Be Brave* – a 2015 Guardian Reader's Pick – was no flash in the pan ... A fabulous, exquisitely written novel that will stay with you for a long time after you turn the final page' David Young

'It is a brilliantly creative work of fiction, and a beautiful thank-you letter to the magic of stories and storytelling' We Love This Book

'This book will make you feel a plethora of emotions. It's funny, sad, dark, warm, chilling, moving, but above all, it is beautifully written. This will stay with me for ages. Pure class' Michael Wood

'Beautiful, poignant, funny, heart-rending, dark ... this book will stay with me for a very long time' Claire Douglas

'Captivating and haunting' Louisa Treger

'A story of pain and love ... moving and real' Vanessa Lafaye

'A dark, wonderful novel of self-discovery, of the things we hide inside ourselves and the bravery it takes to face them' Melissa Bailey

'Louise Beech effortlessly captures the grind of real life and infuses it with flourishes of subtle poetry to create a wonderful story' Matt Wesolowski

'Reading a book by Louise Beech is like a visit to the wrong side of the tracks with a friend to hold your hand. As you pick your way through an unfamiliar and unnerving landscape, she is forever saying "Look – here is beauty; look, there is goodness"' Richard Littledale

'*Maria in the Moon* is part psychological thriller, part love story and fans of *Eleanor Oliphant is Completely Fine* will love it' *Red Magazine* – recommended as one of September's best pulse-quickening page-turners

'Some books seem to fly under the radar and catch you completely by surprise, which is exactly what Louise Beech's *Maria in the Moon* did. Brilliantly written and incredibly moving, Beech captures the nature of memory and truth with an honest poignancy' *Culture Fly*

'Catherine has a gap in her memory. It's a mystery until she loses her home in a flood and a horrifying memory emerges' *Daily Express – Maria in the Moon* is recommended as a must read

'This is not a book to be rushed, but rather one to be savoured. Each word is important and I didn't want to miss a thing. Sometimes I went back and reread a sentence or paragraph. I needed to absorb it all. Louise Beech has such a lovely way with words. It's hard to describe how beautifully she puts across her characters' thoughts, fears and feelings. Her writing is insightful … It's a wonderful read and I absolutely loved it' *Nudge Magazine*

'Beech's exploration of the effects of childhood trauma keeps the reader intrigued until the end' *Booklist*

'Her writing is raw, beautiful and alive with emotions, and also full of fun. The finely balanced feelings of despair, hope, optimism and community spirit set up a rich background for the analysis of how to manage forgiveness and ways of coping with a painful, overwhelming past. This is not a typical crime-fiction story as it's quite possible to work out what terrible trauma has shaped Catherine's life, and how it has affected those around her, but nevertheless, the personal journey of the too prickly, angry, not-always-likeable but genuine character is worth following' Crime Review

'This is superb writing; a story that will stay with me for a long time and is extraordinarily written and presented. There are moments of unexpected beauty from richly complicated characters. It really is quite spellbinding' Random Things through My Letterbox

'*Maria In The Moon* is an emotional charged read and I defy anyone not to feel a tug of the heartstrings as Catherine's story reaches its climax. I cried as the book came to a close. But don't be mistaken, among all the emotion and angst of Catherine's life and those she listens to on the phone, there's suspense, but that's all I'm going to say #nospoilers. The book has been labelled as "Dark Drama" and it is definitely dark and dramatic' Crime Book Junkie

'The writing style is almost lyrical and you find yourself completely carried away with her words … *Maria In The Moon* made me cry, made my stomach knot, and made me realise the power and strength of the human spirit. An unbelievable read' Books of All Kinds

'*Maria in the Moon* is lyrical, magical, beautifully painful and filled with hope. It is emotions wrapped in paper, feelings trapped in the ink, life seen through the clearest eyes. Open the book and fall in love with a voice and a masterpiece' Chocolate 'n' Waffles

'Louise Beech has an instinctive understanding of her characters and delivers a story that will haunt you for weeks, maybe months after you finish it. Told with remarkable sensitivity and though difficult to read in places, needs to be read, if we are have any hope of understanding the frail hold Catherine and others like her, have on the reality of events long since buried … If you have not read her novels, then I recommend you do. Dark, poignant and moving, this new release will without doubt garner her many more fans and well deserved that will be' Books are my Cwtches

'This book portrays the power that memories can have, the good and the bad. Although quite dark in nature, there is always an underlying thread of hope ... The author has a natural storytelling ability' Reflections of a Reader

'I loved this novel, its uniqueness and how it captivated me with a whirlwind of emotions ... When I read the final sentence of the novel, I did so with a smile on my face. An incredible story, beautifully constructed. 5* genius' Anne Bonny Book Reviews

'Incredibly moving and quite literally breathtaking, this is a book that stirs all types of emotion in the reader and leaves you with a sort of wispy feeling of magical realism, one that makes you wonder if you dreamed the entire story or really did just read it. Excellent writing and highly, HIGHLY recommended if you're looking for a book that is many things all at once, as no single genre can confine this novel' The Suspense Is Thrilling Me

'This is such a beautifully written book, it's emotional, heartbreaking, tough reading in places but it also has some humour. I tried to slowly savour every word as I was reading but this is a story that had to be devoured. It's quite suspenseful and I just had to read on and on until I was satisfied. It was truly captivating. *Maria in the Moon* is definitely one of those books that will stay with me for a long, long time. It's haunting, captivating, raw, emotional and a book I will be highly recommending' It's All about the Books Blog

'This book deals with some very dark and difficult topics that are treated with great empathy and understanding. Louise Beech has a beautiful and lyrical writing style that really engages the reader, drawing them into the story and capturing their attention ... *Maria in the Moon* is a wonderful novel, it is poignant, heartfelt and utterly compelling. A real page-turner that will leave you with a book hangover, I highly recommend it' Book Literati

'It's an absorbing tale of loss and family, with the predominant theme being loss. Loss of your sanctuary, loss of your identity and loss of your innocence. I can see exactly why so many people adore Beech's novels' Damp Pebbles

'Filled with emotion and exquisite prose in Louise Beech's inimitable style, *Maria in the Moon* left me speechless and completely thunderstruck. Louise Beech hasn't just aimed for the stars, she's shot past them ... the very pinnacle of perfection' The Book Magnet

'I adored this novel; it is simply stunning and so powerful! I found I could really identify with Catherine. There are parts of her story that were really hard for me to read, coming a bit too close to my own experiences, but the writing is so beautiful that I had to keep reading through my tears ... This is one of those very rare and very special novels that will make you feel all of the feelings, it will take hold of you and it won't let you go' Rather Too Fond Of Books

'*Maria in the Moon* is stunning and has so many qualities that any review I write will never fully convey the beauty within its pages. I could simply just say "read it, you won't regret it" but that wouldn't be enough ... take the time to read it slowly in order to fully appreciate its exquisiteness and for the emotions to take hold but, when all is said and done, just make sure you read it' Bloomin Brilliant Books

'This is such a sumptuous, beautifully written book packed full of emotion and one that tugged at my heart strings as soon as I realised where the story was heading ... I loved being taken out of my comfort zone by such an extraordinary young woman. A breathtakingly beautiful story that deserves to be praised far and wide so that everyone can experience it' My Chestnut Tree Reading

'As *Maria in the Moon* progresses it becomes increasingly difficult to put the book down. While the reasoning behind the missing year may become apparent it is without doubt the skill of Louise's prose that makes this a riveting experience. I think this is a book that will take a little while to finally sink into my subconscious so I can wholly appreciate its beauty. I will probably read it again to fully savour every word because it's one that needs to be absorbed slowly' Ali – The Dragon Slayer

'This novel is a rollercoaster of emotions and hard to categorise or sum up neatly. It made me smile, laugh, cry and think. I was caught up in the storyline, the characters, the relationships and the backdrop of a real event but I was also mesmerised by the writing style and the powerful prose ... This book is actually very complex and multilayered in a way that is not obvious but the fact that the prose is so absorbing and captivating shows that this author has a real gift for language' Bibliomaniac

'It was emotional in the sense where you end up emotionally exhausted, heartbroken, powerless; all without shedding a tear. Raw, poignant and beautifully delivered, *Maria in the Moon* will emotionally destroy you in a way that you never thought possible. Allow yourself to feel the storyline. Allow yourself time to digest the emotion. It deserves patience and love, just like Catherine-Maria' The Writing Garnet

'I was moved to tears by the beautiful and sensitive writing. *Maria In The Moon* is a book about fear, love, hope and redemption. Louise Beech made me cry on my wedding anniversary and I love her for it; this is a very special book, insightful, empathetic, moving and so very real' Hair Past a Freckle

'Louise Beech writes with an emotional honesty and bravery that elevates her work from the crowd ... Very highly recommended' Mumbling About

'A novel that will test your senses through the very last page. A dark psychological thriller with complex and damaged characters. So beautifully written, this is a novel that will linger long after you have finished reading' The Last Word Review

ABOUT THE AUTHOR

Louise Beech is an exceptional literary talent, whose debut novel *How To Be Brave* was a Guardian Readers' Choice for 2015. The sequel, *The Mountain in My Shoe* was shortlisted for Not the Booker Prize. *Maria in the Moon* was compared to *Eleanor Oliphant Is Completely Fine*, and widely reviewed. All three books have been number one on Kindle, Audible and Kobo in USA/UK/AU. She regularly writes travel pieces for the *Hull Daily Mail*, where she was a columnist for ten years. Her short fiction has won the Glass Woman Prize, the Eric Hoffer Award for Prose, and the Aesthetica Creative Works competition, as well as shortlisting for the Bridport Prize twice and being published in a variety of UK magazines. Louise lives with her husband and children on the outskirts of Hull and loves her job as a Front of House Usher at Hull Truck Theatre, where her first play was performed in 2012.

Follow Louise on Twitter *@LouiseWriter* and visit her website: *louisebeech.co.uk*.

The Lion Tamer Who Lost

Louise Beech

ORENDA
BOOKS

Orenda Books
16 Carson Road
West Dulwich
London SE21 8HU
www.orendabooks.co.uk

First published in the United Kingdom by Orenda Books 2018

A catalogue record for this book is available from the British Library.

ISBN 978-1-912374-29-8
eISBN 978-1-912374-30-4

Typeset in Garamond by MacGuru Ltd
Printed and bound in Denmark by Nørhaven, Viborg

For sales and distribution, please contact *info@orendabooks.co.uk*

This is dedicated to my husband, my friend, my one and only Joe.

And to my dear friend Michael Mann, who said when I went to him for research help that I should change nothing because 'love is love, no matter who it's between'.

'Destiny has two ways of crushing us – by refusing our wishes and by fulfilling them.'

Henri Frederic Amiel

Bruises

Make a wish
on my latest bruise.
Boys like us
have nothing to lose.

Kiss them please,
every last one.
Will you still love me
when they are gone?

I'm not religious,
but if I were,
I'd kneel at your feet
and say a little prayer.

Here comes another,
to add to all the rest.
Count them please and choose
the one that suits me best.

Dean Wilson

PART ONE

BEN

1

ZIMBABWE

Home Is Always Near

> *Ben's Grandma said she had never forgotten Jenny, her best friend at school, even though she disowned her in favour of Linda Palmer. She said the friends who turned you away are often the most irreplaceable.*
>
> Andrew Fitzgerald, *The Lion Tamer Who Lost*

Morning is Ben's favourite time in Zimbabwe.

He has been here five days. Each of the mornings so far, he wakes before the other volunteers and stands on his hut's wooden decking in shorts, surveying what he secretly calls his: his sunrise, his land, his refuge. With only the hum of his roommate Simon's snoring, and the buzz of insects, at this moment it *is* his. No one else rises this early to watch the colours come to life; no one else witnesses the sky turning from ash into flame, or the trees from shadow into textured browns, like a tray of different flavoured toffees.

Ben enjoys the solitude of dawn more than the merriment of evening, when the volunteers prepare food and discuss the day's events around a roaring campfire pit, eyes orange in the glow. He enjoys it more than the two walks he has done with the lions in the enclosures.

The lions here look nothing like those he has seen in the circus or watched on TV documentaries. The first time Ben saw one pacing the enclosure fence five days ago – when he was dropped off with other new volunteers in a rickety bus – he thought it must have been the sun that lit his orangey fur with fire, or that the deep shadows had somehow inflated his size. But as he warily approached the high fence for the first time to look more closely, he realised that it was probably contentment that so increased him; being in a more natural environment than a circus ring gave him beauty.

Now Ben stretches, offers his skin to this new day, scaring a skittish split-lipped hare loitering by a thorny scrub. He laughs. The hare freezes for a second and then lollops off. Beyond them both, black against the dawn, tepee-shaped lodges zigzag like teeth. Behind it are the fenced grassy enclosures where cubs live before they are moved to the surrounding ten-thousand-acre park to learn how to hunt and return to the wild.

This is the Liberty Lion Rehabilitation Project. It is the kind of place Ben has wanted to visit since he was eleven. The kind of place about which he read endlessly before signing up. Just forty miles from Victoria Falls, the project site is parallel to the Zambezi River. The area was a hunting ground once, where warthogs and wildebeest were shot by cross-border trophy hunters. Now a national park, its riverbanks are a catwalk for elephant, buffalo herds, and lone antelope, which amble in the heat and dust, safe now from those guns.

This land is a temporary asylum for Ben.

He closes his eyes. The musky smell of hot animal fur drifts on the air. The muggy morning breeze seems to whisper something to him. He won't listen. He didn't come here to listen. Or to think. Or to remember. But the breeze tugs at his shorts, whispers in his ear. It sounds like *home, home, home*.

Suddenly the smells of England that have faded since he got here come alive in the air, merging with lion shit and heat. His father's cigarette smoke seems to rise from the parched ground. The stench of old beer has Ben opening his eyes again, sure there will be a pint sitting in front of him. He lets it in, just for a moment. He pictures the tiny bedroom; he sees the kitchen sink where he and his dad often argued; where they occasionally stood looking at the garden quietly; where Ben once dried dishes and talked about a future.

No. Shut it out.

He came here for the now. For *this*. He surveys again the new and beautiful land. Every day, every moment, he tries so hard not to think about...

The door creaks and Ben turns.

Simon emerges from the hut. Sniffing the air, he says, 'I slept like a corpse,' just as he has every morning since their arrival, and then breaks wind heartily. A solicitor from Essex, he's on a break from his tricky divorce. He said on the first day that he would stay here until the mess was sorted out.

Ben's ownership of the dawn is over.

'How long you been up?' Simon asks.

'A while. It's so hot I just toss and turn.'

'I noticed.' Simon breaks wind again. 'You're bloody lucky I don't knock you out of your bed, all the noise you make.'

'What do you mean? Do I snore?' Ben never has before.

'No. You shout out all kinds of crap.'

'Do I?' Ben's heart feels tight. 'Like what?'

'Can't tell. Doesn't make any bloody sense.'

Ben exhales.

Simon narrows his eyes at him. 'Might be something about...' he whispers, '...bury the bodies ... hide the evidence...'

Ben tuts. 'Yeah, right.'

Simon laughs. 'I'm off for a shower.'

Ben is sure he has never cried out in his sleep before. Certainly no one has ever told him he does. Shit. Time to eat. Time to forget the dawn. Time to start the day.

By the time he arrives for breakfast in the communal lodge, the thermometer reads twenty-five degrees and flies have begun their constant climb. Breakfast is cold meats, fruit, and muesli, and will precede the daily enclosure cleaning, the bottle-feeding of cubs, and lion walking. Volunteers groggily exchange pleasantries at long, bare tables and, as is now habit, bemoan the early hour.

Esther Snelling carries a plate of fruit and a mug of the thick coffee served from metal jugs and joins Ben where he sits alone at the far end of a table. A Newcastle NHS nurse who arrived two months earlier, she tells anyone who asks that she has come to care for animals instead of people, who swear at her and expect antibiotics for every ailment.

She nods at Ben and starts to eat her melon.

'Can't get used to this,' she says, hair unbrushed around her face, lips glossy with the juice, one hand fanning her face. 'They said December would be about twenty-five, but it's been thirty-five most days. A freak heatwave or something.'

'I can't imagine it *not* being hot now.' Ben stirs his muesli.

'To think I grumbled about the weather in England.'

'I bet you'll do the same again.'

'Maybe.' Esther pauses. 'I guess I'm a bit homesick today.'

'Understandable. You've been here...?'

'Twelve weeks.' Esther shrugs. 'Isn't it weird how quickly you forget home, though? I mean, when you first get here and it's all really mental and new, you just don't have room in your head for it. And then ... you have one of those days...'

'You do.'

It is as though, for the first few days, Ben has closed the door on England, but now it's open just a crack. He can see his dad's house today. And now – suddenly acutely vivid – the place he lived before he came here. The place that smelt of bread on Wednesdays and had a 365-new-words-a-year calendar on the fridge and books in the living room. He squeezes his eyes shut, tries to push it away, but sees a flash of silver, rusted slightly. A box. A lid. Too big.

'You okay?'

'Huh?' Ben realises Esther is talking to him.

'You were miles away.'

'Tired,' admits Ben.

'That all?'

He nods.

On the first night, while relaxing by the campfire, most new volunteers share their reasons for being here. It's almost a rite of passage.

Esther admitted to Ben that she had said it was to escape a nursing job she'd come to hate, but that really there was a boyfriend she had left at home. Greg. 'A knobhead' was her description. Most volunteers came out with clichés about wanting to make a difference. Some, like her, were more honest, and admitted they were getting over a break-up or escaping a tedious job.

When project leader Stig looked Ben's way that night, asking the question, Ben said, 'This place means freedom to me.'

Then he cringed. How fucking corny. Sounded like *Braveheart* or something. But he wanted to give a vague enough answer to avoid the truth. Maybe he should have just said that he'd promised his mum when she died twelve years before that he would do this one day. That was the truth, just not the *full* truth.

Stig had held his gaze, waiting perhaps for more.

No one knows Stig's real name. He has been Liberty's course leader for ten years and lost most of his left hand to a lion called Bertram. When he speaks, it is always as though he is addressing a full room, even when there's only you and him. It is like he sees *himself* as a lion when he puffs up his chest, shakes his long hair, and bellows facts.

He turned to the circle of new volunteers that night and asked them, 'What does freedom *really* mean?'

No one spoke, possibly not wanting to give a wrong answer on the first day.

'Freedom here,' said Stig dramatically, flinging out his arms as though to emphasise the vastness, 'is the lions being able to hunt and mate so that the next generation of lions don't need us at all. Some have said we're interfering with nature. And they're right. We *are*. I won't deny that. But the lion population has dropped by fifty percent in the last two decades, and we want to rectify that.'

'Even though we caused it,' someone near Ben murmured.

'As you probably all know, in the wild most lions don't live much longer than fourteen years due to injuries from territorial fights and a lack of prey. With our help, however, they often reach twenty.'

The new volunteers nodded and applauded this.

'So the lions *know* we're their friends?' asked a volunteer.

'Oh, no,' said Stig. 'They are predators, not your friends. *Never* let down your guard. You'll have to establish your position as leader of the pride; draw out the lion's natural survival instincts while suppressing their desire to savage you. Tame them without changing what they are.'

Ben shook his head at that; surely that *meant* changing them.

'You're nodding but you don't look sure,' Esther is saying now.

Ben snaps back into the present.

'I'm just *tired*,' he repeats more gruffly than he means to.

She finishes her fruit wordlessly. Ben tries to think of something funny to say to lighten the mood.

'This muesli is pure shit,' he says after a while. 'I reckon they use the sawdust from the enclosures.'

Esther doesn't say anything. Ben stares at the remaining mush, glad they are no longer dry flakes that he'll feel compelled to count.

'I read once,' he says, 'that lions used to roam the entire globe.'

Esther looks thoughtful. 'Even Newcastle?'

'Even Hull.'

'Jesus,' says Esther.

'There are a few pubs near me that they'd definitely liven up.'

Esther smiles. 'A few near me too.'

Stig arrives and plonks himself opposite them with coffee and a plate of ham, and says, 'Morning', in his voice that can be heard by all. Soon he is joined by sixty-year-old Arthur, on his tenth voluntary trip, and a young florist called Jenny, who cries at night for her mum. Then John, the project vet, slides onto one of the benches.

'We've had a call,' Stig booms, his voice quietening the room. 'One of our ex-volunteers lives not far from here and got word of two lion cubs chained inside a shack in a small village.'

A chorus of sympathetic *ahhh*s fill the air.

'He's been to investigate, and says they're being tormented by local village children. No one has anywhere to keep them safe, or any idea where their mother is. They're a brother and sister apparently.'

More *ahhh*s.

'The female is particularly vulnerable and won't let anyone near her.'

'So,' interrupts John, the vet, 'we need two volunteers who are up for a fifteen-hour round trip to rescue the cubs and bring them back here. We're gonna leave in an hour. Anyone?'

Somehow right, Ben thinks.

The words surprise him. They take him back to a library. To a mirror. A reflection. To a tapping foot. To the moment his life changed forever.

'Anyone?' repeats Stig.

The large room is surprisingly quiet. Perhaps volunteers prefer the relative safety of the project site and its daily routine. Tentatively Ben puts up his hand. This is the kind of adventure he has travelled here for, after all.

'Great,' booms Stig. 'Who else?'

Esther immediately attaches her own bravery with a raised arm.

'Nice one,' says Stig. 'Get a good breakfast inside you – you'll need it.'

In silence, Esther and Ben finish their meal.

'If this doesn't get me right in the thick of it, nothing will,' he says, as they carry their empty plates to the stacking area afterwards.

She nods. 'I'm nervous though. Never left the site.'

'Yeah. Me too.'

'We'll meet at the front gates in an hour,' calls Stig, on his way out. 'Pack whatever you might need for such a journey. We'll bring the camping gear and food and stuff, don't worry about that. We'll sleep a few hours there and return in the early hours.'

'This is it then,' says Esther.

This is it, thinks Ben.

2

ZIMBABWE

Lucy in the Sky with Diamonds

Ben could turn rubber balls into snow and frogs into rainbows, all from his wheelchair – but lion taming proved much more of a test.

Andrew Fitzgerald, *The Lion Tamer Who Lost*

Ben returns to his hut. For a moment, he regrets agreeing to go on the expedition. Is it too soon, after only five days, to be involved in such a huge endeavor? No. *It isn't.* It is exactly what he came here for. Beneath the trepidation, his excitement grows.

But what to take? A book? He didn't bring one, and anyway he will be too distracted to read. How about a pen and paper? Should he use the time to write his first letter home? No. He isn't ready for that, not by a long margin. But maybe he will want to record some of his thoughts on the journey; write up what he sees and experiences.

He throws a pad, a pen, and a change of clothes into a rucksack.

At the main gates there is an ancient jeep loaded with guns, medical supplies and a rusting cage. The engine throbs with worrying volume. Esther leans against the bonnet, wearing a green vest and shorts, hair plaited tightly, a pink rucksack at her feet. She picks nervously at her fingernails. Stig puts a hamper of food into the back seat while John checks the tyres.

'I'll take the first shift,' says Stig, and jumps into the driving seat.

John takes the front passenger seat, and Ben and Esther climb into the back.

They pull away.

The red soil road stretches for miles, like a lesion splitting the land, which is dotted with baobab trees and rounded mountains known as *kopjes*. Ben gives up tallying them after the first hour. Occasional purple jacaranda trees and scarlet poinsettias have passed their full bloom but still light the journey with occasional luster. The seasonal rains nourish the plants, drenching the jeep twice on the trip. Once the clouds pass over, the sun dries everything in moments, as though the water never even fell.

Esther sleeps at first. Ben is glad. He wants to concentrate on taking in this new land. He counts plenty of trees and mountains but only ninety-four other vehicles on the seven-hundred-mile round trip. Counting has always soothed him. The simplicity of ascertaining how many items there are – whether it is peas on a plate or cars on a road – somehow settles him.

'What are you doing?' Esther asks sleepily.

Ben realises he has been counting aloud, not doing it in his head. Embarrassed, he laughs it off. 'Nothing.' He pauses. 'You've missed loads.'

'Shall we play I Spy?' she suggests.

'I Spy?' Ben glances at the mostly repetitive landscape. 'Wouldn't be a very long game.'

'When I was a kid,' says Esther, vest strap falling off her freckled shoulders, 'we'd play it differently to how others do. Like you could spy things you can't actually see. So, I might say I spy a telephone box or McDonalds or the Eiffel Tower...'

Games without proper rules.

Ben has played these too many times.

'Wouldn't it take forever to get the answer?' he says.

Esther looks at her watch, then at the land cooking in the buttery sun, and says, 'We've got five hours.'

'Might be less,' says Stig. The smooth stump where his hand once was doesn't seem to stop him from doing anything. It rests easily on the wheel. John dozes beside him, occasionally burping and making them all laugh.

'Can't be bothered with I Spy,' says Ben.

'Let's see if this radio works, shall we?' says Stig.

It doesn't, but there is an ancient cassette player. Buried beneath empty water bottles, the only tape is a faded Beatles album, which they listen to ten times over. 'Lucy in the Sky with Diamonds' will forever take Ben back to the dusty road, to the smell of warm sweat and petrol and unfamiliarity.

'What can we expect?' Ben asks Stig.

'What do you mean?'

'Will these cubs be dangerous?'

'Depends if we've been given the correct age,' says Stig, 'but at three months they will be pretty hefty – bigger than a large housecat. And they'll certainly be able to give a nasty bite.'

'You know the ones we rear from birth?' says Esther. 'I understand the intention is for them to learn to hunt and then go free – but if we kept them, you know as pets, would they be safe? Would they ever attack us, or would they always know us, and know we were the ones who brought them up so to speak?'

'No matter what environment you raise a lion in,' bellows Stig over the music, 'you are *never* one hundred percent safe. They will still be wild and still act on their instincts. The need to hunt and kill never dies. No matter what. And if you get in the way of that...'

Ben exchanges a *yikes* look with Esther

'Still don't fancy I Spy?' she asks after a while.

'*Jesus*,' he responds gruffly, not quite sure why he feels so irritated. 'What's with you and that game?'

'Just takes me back to when I was a kid.'

'I don't want to play a fucking game.'

'What the hell's wrong with *you*?' snaps Esther. 'It was only a suggestion.'

'Nothing.' Ben realises he sounds like a petulant child and is glad the music gives them a little privacy in the back.

'Well, *something* is.'

'What's it got to do with *you*?' Ben regrets his harshness but being questioned about his sudden mood irritates him beyond belief.

'Nothing,' she says sadly.

'So drop it then.'

'You can be such a dickhead,' Esther hisses.

'*Thanks*.'

'Oh, get over yourself.' She crosses her arms. 'I bet half the people at the project have come away from some sort of shit back home. But none of them mope about like you do.'

Stig glances over his shoulder, so she lowers her voice, leans closer to Ben.

'You should be grateful I even talk to you. Seriously.'

Ben doesn't know what to say. Does he really mope? He knows he hasn't made as many friends as some of the volunteers with whom he arrived five days ago have. He just hasn't felt the need to. Esther is the only one whose company he enjoys and now he has been a complete bastard to her. He hates being this way. He wants to enjoy being here. Maybe he shouldn't have come. Maybe it was too soon.

Too late. He's here.

'You don't *have* to talk to me,' he says quietly.

'Okay then.'

For fifteen minutes they ignore one another, each looking out of the window. Ben tries to think of something light to say to show he knows he was a grumpy bastard.

Eventually Esther says, 'Do you know what Greg said when I told him I might come here?'

'What?' asks Ben, more pleasantly.

'He said, "What the fuck for? You'll probably get eaten or catch AIDS." Nice, eh?'

Sounds like my dad, Ben wants to say, but doesn't.

Instead he laughs.

'My family were dead happy about me coming here though,' Esther says. 'How about yours?'

'Mine?'

Ben doesn't want to think about it. He doubts Esther would believe it if he told her what happened back home. He still can't, even after turning it over in his mind, after taking it apart and putting it back together again a different way. It's like the stories he used to read in his mum's discarded magazines – tales he was sure they made up to shock.

'They weren't bothered,' he says eventually. After a pause, he adds, 'Okay ... I spy something beginning with ... b...'

Esther scans the landscape. 'Blackpool Tower.'

'Shit! How'd you know?' laughs Ben.

'I'm a total pro at this game ... Okay ... I spy something beginning with A...'

The game lasts an hour.

The sun is dipping low in the sky as they arrive at their destination. At the small village they meet Chuma Hondo, the man who has the two cubs in a wooden building behind his café. Though English is the primary language in Zimbabwe, due to its status as a British colony, only a small percentage of the population speaks it. Chuma tells his story in Shona, one of the country's dominant languages. Stig translates.

Apparently, the cubs were found after their mother was shot for stealing livestock from a local farmer, and though it's not ideal, Chuma has been keeping them in the small hut for their safety. Even as he speaks, children steal up on the other side of the slatted wall and push sticks between the gaps and yell what are clearly insults. Chuma wipes his hands on a filthy apron and shoos them away.

'Right,' says Stig. 'Let's get those poor buggers out of there and ready for their big journey.'

Ben has never physically handled a lion cub and now he's suddenly terrified. Perhaps sensing it, Esther puts a hand on his sunburnt arm. He looks at it and then her; she is beautiful in the golden light, almost a lioness herself.

'You'll have to get close to the cubs to do this,' says Stig.

He and John lead the approach to the hut.

'If they're only three months old they should be manageable. But only just. And they'll be mad as hell.' Stig looks at them both. 'Are you ready?'

They nod.

Stig opens the rickety door. The stench hits them all first. Clearly no one has cleaned up after the poor creatures. The two cubs are each strangled by a chain barely a metre long and make feeble attempts to climb the walls of their prison, then fall and swing their paws in rage and frustration. Ben follows Stig, with Esther close behind.

Tan-brown and gold, with flecked legs, the cubs are perhaps twice as big as a large house cat, and considerably noisier. Ben didn't expect their roars to be so powerful yet. They growl savagely at the approach of four more strangers.

'I reckon they *are* about three months old,' Stig says, bending down near the male, who growls and yanks on his chain. 'They're pretty small for their age, so they've probably not been fed well. But at least that means the journey back in that cage won't be too cramped for them.'

John adds that there's enough tranquiliser if needed – to give them a more peaceful trip.

Getting them into the crate that will transport them is not easy. The pair swing their paws, clawing at whoever comes near. Stig suggests two of them restrain the boy so they can first remove the girl, but he bites John – fortunately not puncturing the skin, only leaving marks – so they try to remove him first.

'A brother's love, eh?' says Esther. 'Just looking after his sister.'

Once they are safely ensconced, Ben kneels and peers inside. The lioness stares back, wary and desperate. The boy cub's growl is a low, rumbling warning that he will protect her, no matter what.

Ben recalls the balding lions he saw six months ago, in the circus back home. How can it be six months? They had barely responded to the lion tamer's cruel taunts, or the crack of his sharp whip. The fight had been knocked out of them. These two still have a chance to maintain theirs though.

'She's gorgeous,' says Esther, putting a hand on Ben's shoulder.

'Huh?'

'Look at her glaring at you.' Esther chuckles. 'Reckon you could tame her?'

I could be a lion. You could tame me. Think you can get me to lie down?

The words come to Ben softly, as though whispered in his ear.

The small cub growls.

'Isn't she best left wild?' Ben says quietly.

'Always so serious,' says Esther. 'I was only messing with you.'

'It was easier than we thought so we're not going to bother sleeping here.' Stig secures the padlock on the cage. 'John says he's fine to drive, so we're gonna head back. You guys ready?'

The small group departs, dust billowing like ghostly balloons in the jeep's wake. The village people clamour to spy the cubs one last time, tapping on the windows and waving, and then cheering at a last snarl from the now-sleepy siblings.

'What do you reckon we should call them?' John asks after a while.

The jeep bounces over the uneven road surface, its engine juddering occasionally as though it might die. Stig snores vigorously in the front passenger seat, and Esther has curled up in the back, her mouth sagging open as she breathes softly. The spittle on her chin catches the dusk light.

'I was thinking we should maybe call the boy Chuma after the guy who saved them,' John says. 'You agree?'

'Yes,' says Ben. 'That's a cool name.' He thinks a moment. 'Then I guess the girl has to be Lucy. You know, like in "Lucy in the Sky with Diamonds".'

'Nice one,' says John.

Ben settles back in his seat. He notices the pen and paper in his open rucksack and for a moment considers writing a letter. Who to? He certainly doesn't want to write to his dad. Doesn't know if he ever will. Perhaps he could write something and never send it? Perhaps if he does his moods will stop swinging so dramatically and his sleep will be less restless?

But nothing comes to him.

He is exhausted.

Instead Ben looks up at where the stars trail their trek home – the sky is an ebony blanket that they decorate with dots of happiness and sadness. A year ago, he would never have seen things in such a poetic way. He would have merely counted the stars or pointed out all the constellations he recognised, but he looks at everything differently now.

'Aren't they stunning?' says John, pulling him from his thoughts.

'They are.'

Ben doesn't think he has ever been as happy or as miserable as he is now. He is overjoyed to have come to the place he has always wanted to visit. He can imagine his mum watching him, knowing he fulfilled the promise he made all those years ago. But wrapped up in that is what happened back home.

When Ben thinks of the months before he came here, it makes him so sad that he is once again compelled to count the pieces of food on his plate, the maize and vegetables in his evening *sadza;* so sad that he once again thinks in what he has always described as mis-words; so sad that he almost wishes he had never come.

3

ZIMBABWE

A Name that Won't Be Forgotten

> *Ben wasn't sure he wanted to name his night-time lion, because then he might disappear.*
>
> Andrew Fitzgerald, *The Lion Tamer Who Lost*

Day seven begins as those before did and those after will; Ben on the hut decking in his shorts, watching his glorious sunrise, trying to adapt to the relentless heat, and to recover from another night of tossing and turning. This alone time he cherishes even more now because it is also the coolest time of day.

The temperature has definitely increased since he arrived and has him accidentally misnaming other volunteers and needing to shower twice daily. Even the gentlest activity results in damp clothes and a salty forehead. He is glad that this time of year is the rainy season; that the brief torrential downpour each afternoon cools the skin.

'How long you been up?' Simon makes Ben jump.

'Not long,' Ben lies.

He has become a great pretender; not so much a liar, more an evader. Since their reluctance to share that first night around the fire, even the quiet volunteers have opened up a little now. This place seems loosen them up after a few days, make them more honest about their private lives. Perhaps it is the vast space, the distance from home, or being among total strangers. Not Ben. He listens, fascinated, but says very little.

'You're an odd one, Roberts,' says Simon.

'Am I?'

'Always in a bloody world of your own.' He studies Ben. 'I have my theories.'

'You have?'

'Yeah. I reckon you're a serial killer. It's always the quiet ones. You've come here to avoid the police, haven't you?'

Ben laughs. 'This heat's making you delivious.'

'*Delivious*? What the hell does that mean?'

'I never said that...' Ben blushes. His old habit is back, full force. Mis-words.

'What then?'

'Delirious,' says Ben after a thought.

'Whatever.' Simon laughs again. 'Anyway, one of these nights you're gonna reveal all.'

'What?'

'In your sleep. When you talk.'

Ben's heart tightens. He wishes he had his own room.

'The *bodies*,' laughs Simon. 'Off for a shower, see you later.'

Simon goes into the hut and Ben heads off to the communal lodge for breakfast. Esther is already there, with a plate of fruit and a bowl of cereal in front of her. He wonders whether to sit with her or not.

The previous five mornings she has joined him as they eat the gritty muesli, and she always brings him coffee when they clean out the enclosures together. She saved him a space by the campfire last night, patting the spot on her bench. Ben sat with her. As Esther chatted about their adventure rescuing Lucy and Chuma, Ben's attention drifted as it so often does. When he looked up, she had joined the other volunteers to play cards. Ben knew he deserved it but didn't want to lose his one good friend. Esther looked over at him, eyes sparking in the nightly flames.

Did she seem interested in more than being just friends? Ben has never understood women very well. He wonders if his lack of interest fires her; that she thinks he's playing a flirty game. His university friend

Brandon – from what now seems like years ago – once had a theory about lack of interest being the best invitation.

Ben escaped the campfire then and walked the perimeter of the enclosure fence, the night hot with musky animal scents. Round and around he walked, until his legs ached.

'You okay?' It was Esther.

'Yeah.'

'You're really quiet tonight.'

'Just tired,' Ben said, his usual lame excuse for everything.

'Let's sit then,' she said, stopping at one of the many benches that line the fence. They did.

'Are you mad that I called you a dickhead?'

'What?' Ben laughed. 'When?'

'In the jeep.'

'God, no. I *was* being a dickhead.'

'You know something funny,' said Esther. 'When I came here I left my boyfriend Greg in the middle of the night while he was sleeping, just to avoid the fight that would happen if I'd told him I was going.'

'Shit. Bet he was shocked when he woke.'

'I left him a note,' she grinned. '*Dear Greg, remember to put the bins out and the tea towels are in the middle drawer.*'

Ben laughed.

'I bet he's left the dishes soaking,' she said.

'Thoughtful of him.'

Esther paused then. 'There's a bottle of wine in my room,' she said softly.

'Oh.'

'We could share it.'

'I'm tired,' Ben said again – after an embarrassingly long pause because he could think of no other way out of it.

Esther's disappointed face in the dimness made him feel lousy.

Now he wonders if it is wrong to join her for breakfast. He doesn't want to mislead her. He suddenly remembers Jodie Cartwright back home, and cringes. How wrong he got that. How unkind he was to her the night of his brother Mike's wedding. But Esther is such a gentle-natured yet feisty girl, always quick to befriend a volunteer who's being left out. There is a charm about her that grabs Ben's affection if not his sexual interest.

'Sit here!' Esther's voice rises over the din in the breakfast room.

He gets a mug of coffee and joins her.

'No muesli today?' she asks.

'Can't stomach it.'

'Ben' she starts, 'I just wanted to s--'

At this moment Stig, sitting on the bench behind them, speaks. 'I have bad news.' The room quietens. Sometimes only tragedy breaks the simple routine of the project; an animal found hurt and needing to be picked up or put down, an injury in the enclosure, or a lioness refusing to eat. Today it is thirteen-month-old Aslan, who was injured in a fight.

'John has operated on the scar,' explains Stig. 'But his face wound won't heal, despite two courses of antibiotics.'

The usual chorus of *ahhh*s fills the room.

'Emily,' Stig says, nodding at the nineteen-year-old art student on a gap year, who has moved closer to listen. 'I want you and a partner to separate Aslan from the pride. He won't be bloody happy as he's just begun to assert himself there. He's a feisty bugger too! I'm concerned about upsetting the balance in the group, but we risk further deterioration if we leave him with them.'

'Okay,' says Emily. She looks around the room for a partner and chooses Esther to go with her. Esther is popular. As they leave, she glances at Ben, clearly not altogether happy to be taken away.

'See you later?'

'Yeah, sure,' he replies.

'Okay, great.'

Ben is going to have to tell her *something* so that they can be friends. He could try the truth. The core of it is so simple. Just three words. But he is not sure he will ever say them. To himself. To anyone.

But he is glad now to be free to go and see Lucy for the first time since the rescue. Yesterday she and Chuma were given a thorough medical and then settled in rooms in The Nursery, so he stayed away. When Ben asked why they had to be separated, saying that surely the siblings needed one another more than ever since they had been orphaned, John explained that it was for their own good, as they would be separated anyway within the enclosure.

'Ben,' calls Stig as he tries to leave the breakfast room.

Ben's heart sinks. Is he going to be given some tiresome duty instead?

'You going to see Lucy?' Stig asks catching him up.

'Yes.'

'Good. That's what I want to talk to you about.'

'Oh.' Ben hopes it isn't bad news. 'She okay?'

'As far as we can tell,' says Stig. 'A little undernourished. They both are. But it's not their physical health we're most concerned with. As you know, their mother was killed. If she was around she would still be nursing them, be caring for them in general. She'd be teaching Lucy to hunt very soon.'

Ben nods. Poor Lucy. Poor Chuma.

'I want you to try and bond with Lucy,' says Stig. 'I'm going to ask Esther to do the same with Chuma when she gets back.'

'Okay.' The word comes out so softly that Ben says again, '*Okay*.'

'Bonding with a newborn cub is a long and slow process,' explains Stig. 'It usually begins at birth with bottle-feeding, so getting a three-month-old to accept you is going to be challenging.'

'Shit.'

'Yes.'

'How should I do it then?'

'In practical terms, milk. You'll feed her, and also we'll begin her on some meat.'

'But she attacked us,' says Ben. 'Won't she just fight me?'

'Probably. I tried yesterday, and she was so hungry she took it, but John had to help.'

'And you want me to do it *alone*?'

'Someone has to.'

'I'll try,' says Ben.

'You'll have to intimidate her. She must learn that you are superior, or she'll want to kill you.'

'Great.'

Stig laughs. 'No, not now. But when she gets older, if you haven't connected with her. Get her to trust you. As you know, our lions are taught from the start that volunteers are dominant members of the tribe. Lucy, however, won't accept this easily.'

'What if she doesn't at all?' asks Ben.

Stig ignores the question, which worries him.

'You must *make* her, and *fast*. This kind of thing can take months, but you need to do it in weeks. We need to move her in with the other lionesses as soon as we can, or she'll not learn to mix, and then she won't learn to hunt with them – and you know what that means for her survival in the wild.'

Stig pauses then, his silence as dramatic as his words.

'Do you think you're up for it, Ben?'

'I guess,' he says, not sure at all.

'Good.' Stig pauses. 'There's no time like now.'

'No. I suppose not.'

Ben heads for the place affectionately called The Nursery. This is a brick building where cubs requiring constant attention are cared for. Young girls come to the project for these babies – it is the job most applied to do. Older cubs able to eat prepared meat get moved into the fenced enclosures where they will hopefully form prides and then go into the reserve to learn to hunt in packs. By eighteen months, most lions can fend for themselves. But a perimeter fence still keeps them on the vast reserve, where they can be monitored.

Swatting tsetse flies and still not quite used to the overpowering smell of lion shit, Ben makes his way inside. He asks the first person he sees where Lucy is. Then he goes along the corridor, smiling at a woman bottle-feeding a cub in one of the rooms that he passes, her arms cradling him as though he is her own baby. Ben pauses at the fifth wooden door.

Then he opens it slowly.

For a split second he is walking through a different door. Into a flat for the first time. He can smell bread. See books. Feel breath on his neck. Feel the anticipation of what might happen within its walls. Then it is gone, and he is here again.

Here in a room with a lioness.

The light illuminates her tawny body sprawled against a back wall. As Ben enters the room, she stands up, haunches high, and growls a low warning. Her chains clank as she tugs on them.

'Lucy,' he says softly.

She growls again. Multihued fur ripples like a dirty river. Head dipped, she snarls, revealing tiny fangs.

'Don't you remember me?' asks Ben, kneeling with enough space between them to protect himself.

More growling.

'Don't you remember the journey?'

More growling.

'I *know*,' says Ben. 'You must hate being chained like up this but it's for your own safety, and for mine. Just until you get used to being here. Just until you and I form some sort of bond, I guess.'

More growling, even louder.

Shit. How is he going to do this?

'I bet you miss your brother,' he says.

Lucy tugs again on her chains again; the clanking sound reminds Ben of a silver box with a wonky lid that often fell off. He closes his eyes. He is back again in the flat that he so misses. He imagines hands opening the box. Hands that he knows as well as his own. Hands he longs to grasp. Ben sees the contents of the box. Sees tiny yellow Post-it notes. Sees tiny words written neatly there. Tiny wishes.

And a face.

That face. Those eyes. The gold-flecked irises he has tried so hard not to think about.

The face has a name. One Ben can only whisper when he is alone at dawn; a name that escapes his lips and floats over the burnt land to simmer with the heat. A name he has come here to try and forget. A name that he now realises will need more than physical distance and more than time to erase. The name rises in his throat.

Ben puts a hand over his mouth.

Shakes his head and lets out a strangled moan.

Lucy returns to her spot against the back wall and views him with narrow, distrustful, gold eyes.

Maybe if Ben says the name aloud he will finally sleep. Not toss and turn and cry out, not risk disturbing Simon and revealing all his secrets.

He closes his eyes.

'Andrew,' he whispers.

Lucy purrs her acceptance of the word.

Andrew.

4

ZIMBABWE

I'm Going To Lie Here

Ben slept, knowing the lions would wake.

Andrew Fitzgerald, *The Lion Tamer Who Lost*

For the next five days Ben concentrates mostly on Lucy. He is grateful for the challenge Stig has set him; glad to have something to occupy so much of his time.

Each morning – after his solitary sunrise, the usual banter with Simon, and a muesli breakfast – Ben and Esther head to The Nursery. Calling hello to Lois, a volunteer who seems to spend time with the newborns around the clock, they collect their bottles of milk and then part ways, each with their own ward to tend.

As soon as Ben enters the dimly lit room, Lucy is up on her feet, snarling savagely. He stoops low on the straw-covered cement floor, about six feet away, and talks to her in an even tone, ignoring her teeth-baring and swinging paw.

'Look, *milk*,' he says the first time. 'You know you want some of this lovely stuff. You must be bloody ravenous, girl.'

Most cubs her age would have already begun the process of being weaned off their milk, but Stig insists Lucy should have three bottles a day for now. She should also be winded like a human baby so she doesn't get tummy ache, but Ben can't get close enough to do that.

The first bottle ends up being hurled against the wall by her left paw. Thankfully, it's plastic so it bounces, and Ben retrieves it and tries again. Lions have a special organ on the roof of their mouths that picks up odours, so he unscrews the teat to let her smell the creamy contents more strongly, and holds the open bottle as near to her as he dares.

'Come on, you stubborn little madam. I reckon you want this more than you don't want me.'

She sniffs it. Growls softly. He screws the teat back on and holds it out, a little closer still, shaking it so that some drops spill on the floor to tease her. He has seen how most of the newborns are fed here. Volunteers cradle them closely, stroke their fur, whisper words of encouragement – giving them that feeling of being with a mother. The real mothers of these cubs are either dead or have abandoned them, so without the care at the project the babies would perish. Ben doesn't think Lucy will let him stroke her while she drinks, but for now he doesn't mind, if she will only take it.

In the end, he ignores her.

After a while, she approaches the bottle. Making no eye contact with Ben, she latches onto the teat. The noisy slurping as she drains the milk in minutes shows just how hungry she really is. Ben doesn't speak, not wanting to disturb her. He doesn't reach out to touch her, even though he longs to.

The hair on her back looks the coarsest, with dark little tufts dotted here and there like the bushes on the surrounding landscape. It appears softer at the sides, and particularly behind her ears, where it is most glossy and golden. Perhaps one day Ben will get to feel it under his fingers.

For now, he is just pleased Lucy has drained her first bottle.

'Good girl,' he coos. She snarls and returns to the far corner of the room.

His heart sinks.

After this, however, she takes her bottle at least. Each time Ben enters the room with one, she sits and allows him to feed her, the only sound her slurpy guzzles. Once done, she retreats. Ignores him. For hours in between these feeds, Ben sits about six feet away from her, talking gently, and crawling a little closer when she seems to calm. For this he receives just a clawy little scratch on his cheek as payment.

'Well, cheers for that, Lucy.'

Ben wipes the blood from his face and looks at the crimson streak on his palm. Flashbacks engulf him. The circus. Blood streaming from a fingertip. A bathroom. A new baby. Blood staining every surface. A hospital ward. A streak of red near a radiator.

The clanking chain dispels the memories. Lucy is getting comfortable for a snooze. Ben can try as hard as he likes to bury them – he can devote his energy to making the most of his time here – but he is powerless when some random sound or sight or smell evokes them. Maybe if he looked back on the happier moments before he came here then the past would not haunt him so much.

But he knows what those good days will lead to.

One evening, Ben spends some time with Esther. Sharing a large, rotten log that gives the best views of the long-shadowed savanna – a place she discovered and showed him – they compare notes about the progress of their lion wards.

'I know it's only been three days,' says Esther, excitedly, taking some chocolate from her pocket and giving some to Ben, 'but Chuma seems to be adapting. He actually let me stroke him today. Okay, he might have been busy feeding, but I got to tickle his tummy. Ben, it was so unbelievably soft. I actually melted.'

'Maybe it's because you're a nurse,' says Ben, a little jealous.

'How do you mean?'

'I guess you have to have a way with people? A bedside manner...'

Esther laughs. 'Doubt I've got that. Never got much chance. We were so overworked on the wards that there was no time to make any sort of connection with the patients.' She looks sad. 'That was why I wanted to be a nurse. And it ... well, it isn't what I hoped it would be. How about you?'

'What do you mean?'

'What were you doing before you came here?'

Hating my dad, comes to Ben, heatedly. *Hating him for what he did.*

'I ... I was at university ... then I...'

'You came here?'

'Yes. I came here.'

Quiet punctuates the evening insect song. There is nothing else. Just heavy darkness and the two of them. During a long, comfortable silence, Esther blows in Ben's ear – whether accidentally or intentionally he doesn't know – but it reminds him. Reminds him of Andrew's passionate breath. Of his soft snoring when he slept. Of him being *there*.

'Esther,' Ben says gently. 'I wanted to say ... about ... the other night ... the wine...'

'It's fine,' she interjects, moving away from him. 'Honestly. I just thought we could chat. That's all. I'm sorry. I tried to say that at breakfast the other day.' Her words are a nervous gabble. 'I just thought you'd seemed so grumpy and down that you could use a friend, and some wine.'

'You don't have to be sorry,' he says. 'Nothing to be sorry for.'

'I do. I gave you the wrong idea. The invite. It must have seemed like a come-on.'

'I didn't think that at all,' lies Ben.

'You did. But it's fine. It's all fine.' *She* clearly isn't though. 'Can we forget it?'

'Of course.'

'Good.'

There doesn't seem to be much else to say. He doesn't want an imbalance in feelings to get in the way of their friendship. Ben opens his mouth to thank Esther for putting up with his moods and distance, but she says goodnight and heads back to the huts.

In the middle of the night, while awake for hours, Ben realises what he must do. It occurs to him that it's fine going to see Lucy every day, but night is surely when she is more vulnerable. Perhaps therefore more receptive. Lions are territorial; this why a lion tamer always enters the ring first, establishing his ownership of the domain. The lion will jump and dance and perform for this master because *he* owns their world. Ben hasn't had the advantage of being there first with Lucy. He has been trying all week to own the space. To make her trust him, as Stig suggested. Now, he figures, what better way than when she's most defenceless: sleeping? If she dozes off and then wakes it will appear that Ben got there first.

That he was *always* there.

Ben sits up in his hammock, excited by the idea. He anticipates little sleep if he goes; he knows both he and Lucy will end up exhausted, but decides it's the only way.

Ben gets up. Doing this means he won't have to sleep, to dream, and then wake and toss and turn. He knows, as he puts a bottle of water and some chocolate into his rucksack, that Lucy will put up a fight. It will be him saying *yes* and her saying *no*; a game Ben has played before.

Swatting moths, blanket underarm, he makes his way through hot, woody blackness to the brick building and its nurseries. He says 'hi' to the three women doing night feeds in the room opposite, telling them that if they need chocolate he has plenty.

Then he opens the door.

Lucy stares at him. She stands up and growls softly. As always, her chains clank. Ben knows he will forever hear the sound in his mind and think of her.

'Hello, girl,' he says softly. 'You didn't expect this, huh?'

He approaches slowly.

'We're going to try something different.'

Lucy backs up towards the wall. This is something she has never done. Usually she glares, growls, haunches high, then launches, her chains tight. Is she submitting to him? Surely not so soon?

'I'm going to lie here too.'

Ben speaks firmly as though to a child, and Lucy bares her teeth and moves a little closer. No, he has not won her trust yet. It will not be as easy as that.

'You can complain all you want, but it's happening.' He scoops up straw to form a makeshift mattress, placing it a safe distance from Lucy. 'Think of it as a sleepover.' Ben gets onto his straw pile and covers his torso and legs with the blanket. 'You can growl at me all you like, but I'm staying. You hear me? *I'm staying*.'

Lucy snarls but doesn't move. Standing, she watches Ben, warily.

'Not exactly the Hilton, is it? No wonder you grumble all the time.'

Another snarl.

'You gonna stand all night? You'll be knackered.'

Snarl.

'Go ahead then.'

Snarl.

'Goodnight.'

As though understanding him, Lucy settles. Lies down. Glares.

'I can't be arsed with a staring contest. You win.'

Ben closes his eyes. After a bit, he half opens one and spies. Her gold eyes have dimmed. The lids grow heavy. Then she opens them, fights it. Perhaps he is cruel to disturb her like this? But if it means they bond, that means she will be able to join the other lions. If they don't ... Well, he won't think about that.

Eventually her eyes close.

'That's right,' he says softly. 'You sleep, girl.'

Throughout the hot, fidgety night Ben tells her each time she wakes that he's staying, and Lucy snarls and attempts to swipe him with her left paw. Nearby, baby cubs cry out for milk and love and attention. Doors open and close on the corridor.

Before it is light, Ben reminds Lucy he'll be back again with the dark, whether she likes it or not. This time her snarl builds to a savage roar that has Ben up against the door. Has he made things worse?

Was there any point in returning that night?

Ben rolls up his blanket and walks back to his hut, newly amazed by the flames of dawn burning the horizon. They should make him feel hopeful. But suddenly he has to stop and get his breath. Suddenly he can barely stand up. He falls onto a bench by the enclosure fence.

Inside, in the far corner, a pride of lions is slowly waking – yawning and stretching. Ben puts his head in his hands.

'Are you okay?' It's Esther.

Embarrassed, he nods, composes himself. 'Yes, sorry. Long night.'

'How come?'

'Oh. I spent it with Lucy.'

'You did?'

She sits next to him. Neither of them speaks for a while. Ben doesn't have to. Esther is very easy to be around.

'What happened?' she asks after a bit.

'I couldn't sleep. I'm so exaspalated that Lucy doesn't seem to be accepting me.'

'*Exaspalated*?'

Ben sighs. 'You *know* what I mean. Anyway, I thought perhaps it would help if I slept next to her. You know, to be more intimate somehow. Build that trust.'

'And?'

'She just growled even more when I left just now. I reckon if she hadn't been on a chain she'd have ripped my throat out."

'It was only one night,' says Esther.

'Maybe.'

'Don't give up with her.'

'I might ask Stig to take over,' sighs Ben.

'No. Don't be so hasty.'

'I'm not.'

'Stig hasn't got time to do it one on one like you. He must have asked you because he thought you could do it?'

'It's because we were there when they got rescued, that's all. I'll go and talk to him.' Ben glances at Esther. 'Don't look at me like that.'

'Like *what*?'

'All judgemental. Cos you think I'm giving in.'

'You have no idea what I'm thinking.' She looks straight ahead.

They sit in silence again.

'Why don't you tell me…?'

'What?' asks Ben.

'Why you're *really* here.'

Volunteers are now emerging from their huts. The gentle dawn warmth builds to its sticky heat.

'I...' he starts. But he can't finish.

'Wanna get breakfast?' She shoves him gently.

'Go on then. Because I just *love* that shitty gritty muesli and mud coffee.'

They head for the communal lodge. Ben looks back at the sky. The flames have died. Like a sea, it stretches for miles, all the way home, clear blue now.

After breakfast he returns to his hut and lies in his hammock just for a moment, just to rest his eyes.

He sleeps. He dreams. He dreams of the good days. He dreams of the moment he first saw Andrew. Of a library. Of a tapping foot. Of an essay he never finished.

Of feeling *somehow right*.

5

ENGLAND

Somehow Right

> *Ben's mum assured him that there are no wrong words, only the ones we really, actually, truly meant to say.*
>
> Andrew Fitzgerald, *The Lion Tamer Who Lost*

Andrew's reflection was the first part of him that Ben saw.

Ben had gone to pay off a library debt, and to start an essay that he wouldn't look at again for ten weeks – he was heading home from university for summer the next day. The library was full. But a computer in the far corner was free. As Ben took a seat in front of it, he saw gold hair in the mini squares of a mosaic mirror on the wall, like a pixelated photograph. The owner of the hair was hidden behind the computer screen opposite.

Ben opened the notes for his 'How Not To Lie with Statistics' essay and read them through. None of it made sense. The man opposite typed slowly and banged his foot against the chair leg: *tap, tap, tap*. Irritated, Ben peered around his own screen to glare at him, without success. All he was able to see of him was his reflected, pixelated hair in the mirror on the wall above them.

Tap, tap, tap. The rhythmic beat drove Ben mad. He banged his flat palms on the keyboard. The man peered around his screen, now, frowning. Ben caught his breath.

Somehow right.

These words came to him.

Somehow right.

Perhaps Ben had seen him before on the university campus; perhaps familiarity fired the odd feeling of knowing him. He had to be a mature student by the looks of him – unshaven, blond, pretty, but as though it had all happened by accident. His loveliness was at odds with a faded black shirt.

The man frowned, returned to his screen, and read his work slowly and softly aloud. It stirred something jittery in Ben's stomach. His dad had always mocked when he read aloud as a kid. He used to poke Ben's shoulder blades and say that only babies couldn't read in their heads.

Ben tried again to concentrate on statistics.

But the foot tapping continued to annoy him.

'That's aggregating,' he snapped.

The slow-reading man looked around his screen again, continued his involuntary foot dance, and said, 'Talking to me?'

'Yes.' Ben paused, sensing he'd said the wrong word again. 'I said that's fucking aggregating.'

The slow-reading man looked back at his screen. 'I think you mean *aggravating*. If I were *aggregating* you I'd be collecting you.'

Ben hated being corrected; his dad did it constantly: *Ben, how can a lad with half a brain think there's an l in chimney? It's not chimley! Even your bloody mother wouldn't have thought that! And it's scapegoat not scrapegoat!*

'I *said* aggravating,' Ben insisted. 'You heard wrong.'

'What, *twice*?'

The man continued reading softly aloud.

Ben couldn't think of anything to say.

He was sick of his dad's insistence that he wasn't applying himself to the degree. He looked around. At the next table four women read a fashion website and discussed whether handbags were bigger now than they had been ten years ago. None of them had looked at him when he came in. Ben wasn't interested in them, but it hurt. No one ever looked at him when he walked into a room.

But the slow-reading man opposite looked *somehow right*. Ben wasn't sure what it meant or why it had come to him.

Before he could think, he said, 'Do you want a coffee?'

The man raised his sandy eyebrows. 'I'm busy.'

'I mean from the machine in the hall.'

'Okay, thanks.'

Ben fetched two drinks and placed one next to the slow-reading man, who thanked him, barely glancing up.

Sipping his coffee, Ben asked, 'So what're you writing?' Something about this man made him feel bold.

The man sighed but then seemed to rethink: 'I'm writing about legs.'

'Legs?'

He smiled a sort of half-up, half-down smile and his face changed. *Somehow right*, Ben thought again.

'How they work,' he said. 'And how they *don't* work.'

'Why?'

'For a book.' He paused. 'It's a children's story so *you*'d be able to read it.' Ben knew he was mocking the fact that he looked so young. This man looked late thirties.

'You're doing a creative-writing degree?'

'I'm not a student, I'm a writer,' said the slow-reading man, 'I like this place. I also have a job in another library, but when I try to work there I can't concentrate.'

'But kid's stuff?' Ben realised too late that his tone was scornful.

The man looked back at his screen, making it clear the conversation was over. His foot resumed its rhythm. Ben's coffee tasted of rejection. He always got it wrong. This was how it went when he tried to flirt with girls in front of his best mate, Brandon; they would laugh at Ben's clumsy words, and look him up and down, clearly disappointed; so then he would be cocky and they would ignore him. Then they just talked to Brandon who knew how to keep smiles in place.

Was the slow-reading man indifferent too? Had Ben wrongly imagined the *somehow right* vibe? The thought of leaving without finding out for sure made his heart flip over. In his seat at the back of class he had secretly studied other lads, looked at thick necks, messy hair, broad backs, imagined what he might do with them. He wasn't really sure what type of man he would go for … if he ever had the chance.

But none of his classmates had made him brave like this.

'I'm going back home to Hull tomorrow,' Ben said.

The man continued typing.

'End of term,' said Ben.

In the mirror, the man typed right to left; in the real world left to right. His foot tap quickened. A black medical alert bracelet encircled his wrist. As he typed, a half-moon bruise peaking from beneath his sleeve was eclipsed, then revealed, eclipsed, then revealed.

Nearby the women laughed.

'Not looking forward to it.' Ben was unable to shut up.

The man's foot missed a beat.

'Can I *aggregate* you sometime,' Ben said.

The foot stilled.

The slow-reading man said, 'You don't even know my name.'

'Does it matter? Unless it's Tarquin.'

The left side of the man's mouth smiled. 'It's not Tarquin.'

'Well?'

'How *old* are you?'

'Why does *that* matter?' Ben plonked his paper cup on the table.

'Didn't your mother ever tell you not to talk to strangers?'

'Tell me your name and you won't be.'

'I'm busy,' said the man.

'That's a weird name.'

'Ha.'

'How long will you be busy for?'

The man smiled fully; it was still half-up, half-down, as though he wasn't quite sure yet. 'For the foreseeable.'

'Why, what's happening then?'

'I have to finish my book,' he said.

'What's it called?'

'I haven't got a title yet.'

'What's it about?'

'I'm not ready to share that.'

'Aren't strangers the best people to share stuff with?'

The man paused, sighed. 'Okay. So far, it's about a young boy called Ben who lost the use of his legs in a car accident. While he's recuperating this lion comes to visit him in the dark. He wishes for him, and he arrives. Well, um, that's about it so far...'

Ben was sure the man blushed.

'I'm Ben, too,' he said.

'*No*?'

'How weird is that?' Ben didn't say that he also loved lions.

'I'm Andrew.' Now Andrew held Ben's gaze, long enough for him to notice gold flecks in his irises, stubby eyelashes, widened pupils.

'I'm twenty-two,' said Ben. 'Is it your first book?'

'Third. I've not had much success with my first two. One of them was used in a school though. You might have read it,' he teased. 'I have to get on with it anyway.'

'Okay.' Ben smiled. 'You didn't answer my question.'

'I did.' Andrew started typing again.

'No, about me *aggregating* you. God, I'm embarrassed now.'

'You said you're going home tomorrow.'

He *had* been listening. 'I am. You live here in York?'

'No, Beverley.'

'I'm from Hull,' said Ben. 'We're close.'

Months later, when they first argued, Ben would insist that if it hadn't been for his autacity (*audacity*, Andrew would correct) they might never have happened. That if he'd not taken a black felt-tip from his jean pocket and walked up to Andrew and opened the book next to him and written his phone number across the first page and held it out until it dried, Andrew could never have called him. Andrew would remind Ben that he *hadn't* rung him because Andrew had accidentally added a surplus digit when transferring the number into his phone.

But when Ben snapped the lid off his pen that day by the mirror in the library, they knew none of this. Andrew looked at the numbers as they dried – five nines, two threes and a jumble of others – and then at Ben's face.

'That's a library book,' he said.

'Shit.' Ben gathered his things, suddenly sweating. 'Well, I guess if you want the number you can copy it.'

And he left without looking back, tense with shame.

6

ZIMBABWE

Cutting Chains

> *Ben's mum had always said that the sad stuff is balanced by the happy stuff. That a butterfly started out ugly.*
>
> Andrew Fitzgerald, *The Lion Tamer Who Lost*

On his fourteenth morning in Zimbabwe, standing on his decking, Ben feels even more alone. The fire in the sky doesn't transfix him. He is hot and flustered before the temperature has even begun its steady climb. After more vivid dreams about Andrew, he can't stop thinking about him. He glances at the beautiful flame lilies spouting intermittently near the other huts and wishes he might turn around, see Andrew emerging from his room, and ask him, 'So what do you think of this place?'

But it is only Simon who disturbs him.

'Where'd you go last night?' he asks, breaking wind with gusto. 'Woke up for a piss and your hammock was empty.'

'I was with Lucy.'

'She your bird then?'

'You *know* she's my young cub.'

Ben had been very close to not going for a second night. He went as far as knocking on Stig's office door to see if he would take over, and then changed his mind and had to pretend he'd forgotten why he had gone there.

He dreaded opening the door to Lucy's deafening roar.

But as Ben entered, she only softly growled her disapproval. When this was ignored, she settled. Her narrow eyes watched him prepare his straw bed and get into it. Sometimes he spoke to her; sometimes he just closed his eyes. When he was quiet she studied him. Ben wondered if the same indifference that piques the interest of house cats might work with these bigger ones. So he decided to ignore her altogether. She got on with her ablutions, watching him all the while. Ben smiled to himself. This was how he would do it. Didn't he know more than anyone how much harder you try when no one looks your way?

'Bet you've really been with some bird.' Simon laughs heartily now.

'What?'

'You and that Esther seem close. Now she's *hot*.'

'Don't talk about her like that.'

'I wouldn't say no to a bit of that. Can't see what she sees in you though.'

'Fuck off.'

Simon jabs him in the side. 'Only teasing, mate.'

Ben doesn't bother going for breakfast. He returns to Lucy. And after a morning with her, and a bottle that she easily takes, he has a quick nap and returns for the night. He *can't* give up on her. Esther was right. He should see it through. And, after all, he knows how it feels to lose a mother at a young age.

So he goes back.

For the first few nights she snarls as he enters, taking even longer than usual to stop when he ignores her. She pulls so hard on her chains that Ben fears she will hang herself, but doesn't dare try to stop her. It is torture to hear her in so much distress. Three times he leaves the room, thinking he won't go back. He walks the perimeter of the enclosure in the dark, cursing, and shouting at the night.

But he goes back.

Eventually, each time he arrives – blanket under arm and chocolate in rucksack – she barely moves when he opens the door. She merely looks up with an I-suppose-you-can-come-in sweep of her eyes and goes back to whatever she was doing. Ben tries to hide his excitement, not wanting to scare her, not wanting to dare hope she is beginning to accept him. He doesn't say a word.

Christmas comes and goes while he is lying with Lucy. In this heat, he can't quite believe it is the festive period anyway. Volunteers hang decorations and Stig puts a small green tree covered in lights by the main door. Snowy cards line the communal lodges. Esther excitedly shares goodies she receives from her family, doling out chocolates from a selection box and pulling crackers with anyone who wants.

'I have a little something for you,' she says, and gives Ben a small bottle of whisky, which he takes but knows he won't drink. He remembers the last time he was drunk and doesn't want to repeat that.

'I don't have anything for you,' he admits, embarrassed.

'Don't worry,' she says.

Since his rejection of her wine that night, and her insistence that she had only wanted to chat, Esther often studies him as though she can't quite figure something out. It doesn't make Ben anxious the way it previously has when women have appraised him. He doesn't feel ugly under her gaze. But he does sense that she wants much more than he can give.

Ben receives nothing from England, but then he hasn't sent anything either, and his dad has never bothered with cards. Eating breakfast one morning, he glances over at the phone on the wall and wonders about ringing Andrew. Whispering *Merry Christmas*. But what would be the point? He would only ignore him like he did back in England. And Ben can't take that again.

On Christmas Eve, while lying next to Lucy, he can't avoid thinking of home. Will his dad eat his Christmas dinner alone? Ben can't face this image, no matter how angry he is with him, and pushes it away.

Ben turns over in his straw to find Lucy staring at him, her eyes bright gold in the dimness.

'Merry Christmas,' he whispers, as his watch reaches midnight.

Now that Lucy no longer responds to Ben so savagely, and her chains have ceased their endless clanking, he talks aloud to her during their long nights together. He says the things that he just can't say to Esther, or to anyone. In a cracked voice, Ben describes his early moments with Andrew. Describes how each time they saw each other it was as though some hand bigger than his had guided them together.

'I never used to buy into that kind of fate stuff,' Ben says in the dark. 'I still don't know if I do.' He pauses. 'But Andrew always followed an accident. That was how it seemed.'

On their final night together – after eighteen days – Ben inches closer to where Lucy lounges. She is half asleep, in that in between place where dreams are close to reality. He moves so close that her breath, soft and uneven, tickles his ear. So close that he can smell the warm, furry heat of her tawny body. So close that she could tear open his throat if she chose to.

But she doesn't.

He has made good progress.

Then they both sleep for a few hours, undisturbed by slamming doors and mewling, hungry newborns. Ben wishes he might wake in the morning and find her rubbing her golden head against his. It doesn't happen. She just stretches and views him with sleepy, half-lidded eyes. Ben's disappointment fades; to have slept at her side and not be scratched to bits by dawn is enough.

In the morning he goes straight to Stig.

'I really think Lucy trusts me,' he says.

'That's bloody incredible, Ben. I have to admit, I didn't think it would happen. I've seen these things fail so badly.'

'Can we remove those chains now?' Ben asks.

'Of course. That's the easy part.'

'What do you mean?'

'Now you have to let her go.'

Stig picks up his empty plate and leaves. Esther joins Ben with her usual fruit and coffee. They nod at one another, but Ben is suddenly so tired he can't speak. He knows Esther is shattered too, that she has been spending her nights with Chuma.

'I got a letter from Greg,' she says after a while.

'Really? First one?'

'Yeah. It's actually quite well written. I was surprised. He's only semi-literate.'

'Esther!' Ben laughs.

Smiling, she says, 'I know. But you've never met him.'

'Why would someone like you be with someone like that though?' he asks seriously.

'Someone like me?'

'Yeah. Intelligent. Funny. Kind.'

'Oh, tell me more, Ben Roberts.'

'Well?'

Esther appears to think. 'You can't help who you love,' she concedes, sipping her coffee. 'I reckon you have to hope you get lucky and end up loving someone who's half decent. Anyway, it's definitely over between us. Me and Greg. I mean, I knew it was. It has been on my part for a while. I guess leaving in the middle of the night and going to another continent shows how I felt. But now he's accepted it too. Even admitted what a dick he was.'

Ben laughs. '"Dear Esther, I'm a dick."'

'Something like that.'

'And you're happy?'

'Yes,' she says softly. 'What you gonna do today?'

'I dunno. Sleep. Go see some of the bigger lions. I feel like I've missed a lot while being with Lucy. You?'

'Same.' Esther pauses. 'I'm glad we did it though.'

'What?'

'I'm glad we were the ones who rescued Lucy and Chuma.'

'Yeah.'

Esther shakes her head at Ben. 'Cheer up, gloomy face. It might never happen.'

But if it's meant to, he thinks. *It will. It really will. Even if it takes a mis-written phone number. Even if it takes a derailed train. Even if it takes a car accident.*

7

ENGLAND

The Train that Happened

Ben's dad came in dreams and whispered, 'Drop your toys on the floor and I'll always come.' And even though he had to travel such a long way, and in very snowy weather, he always did.

Andrew Fitzgerald, *The Lion Tamer Who Lost*

The nine forty-five train from York to Hull was fortunately travelling at low speed when it derailed near Doncaster. The impact damaged the buffet car roof, and one carriage overturned. Hand luggage, plastic cups and laptops got thrown around, and bags tore open, spilling out underwear.

Ben missed this train.

It was because of the black felt-tip pen with which he had defaced Andrew's library book. Halfway to the station he realised that he had left it in his room. It meant something to him now; so he *had* to go back and get it. When he finally got to the station a throng of discontented commuters were pacing the platform, peering over the yellow danger stripe as though contemplating suicide. A man in a leatherette jacket said he hoped they would reinstate a schedule quickly; in Ben's head the word *aggregate* replaced the word *reinstate*.

That's really aggregating.

He blushed; Andrew must have thought him an idiot.

He squeezed through the ticket gate, but an attendant stopped him, saying Ben couldn't use his ticket on the next train. 'It's non-transferable,' he insisted.

Ben stared at his left nostril, which sprouted eleven grey hairs. 'But that train crashed, so it didn't really happen,' he said.

The attendant narrowed his eyes. 'Didn't really happen?' He pulled a face like he'd tasted Marmite when he wanted jam. 'Look, you'd best take a chance with the next one to Doncaster and go from there.'

Ben didn't believe in chance. He boarded the ten-thirty to Doncaster, found a seat near poorly maintained toilets, and chucked his bag in the overhead rack. This train really happened; it left on time.

He checked his phone for the tenth time, just in case Andrew had called. Nothing. He put it back in his pocket; the disappointment stayed in his hand. His only escape was sleep. The train rocked and swayed and juddered and he shut his eyes and thought about Andrew, seeing the half-moon bruise on his arm, revealed as his sleeve moved, then hiding. He had awoken in the early hours to an image of Andrew's foot pounding the chair leg. There was a *thud-thud-thud* of music from some other student's room.

That's really aggregating.

I'm writing about legs.

Ben wondered how it would feel to touch Andrew's thigh, to trace a finger along its inner flesh. Was Andrew thinking about him? Had he smiled at the phone number scrawled across the library book or had he closed it and never looked back?

The train clattered and Ben opened his eyes. Looked down. Damn. The felt-tip pen had leaked black all over his pocket, forming a kidney-shaped stain. *Damn.* He stood, banging his skull on the overhead rack with a crack. Muffled within his jacket pocket, his phone started ringing. Ben scrambled for it. It might *statistically* be Andrew because no one else ever rang, and he had his number.

It wasn't.

'What do you want?' Ben asked his dad, dabbing at the ink with a tissue.

'Just checking you're not dead, lad.' Ben could tell by his unruffled voice that he'd had his first morning drink. Though he had not been home in months, Ben could picture him at the sink, whisky in a World's Greatest Dad mug and cigarette in hand. 'Heard there'd been an accident.'

'I'm still here.' Ben gave up on the now-shredded tissue.

'They said on the news it was a saturated track bed,' said his dad.

'What was?'

'What caused the accident.'

'I would have been on that train if it wasn't for this pen.'

'What pen?'

'Doesn't matter.' Ben dropped the pen in a bin and resumed his seat.

'So, you're okay.' Ben's dad's concern was rare.

'Yep.'

'Okay,' said his dad, 'I'll see you later.'

Ben put the phone in his pocket. Why had he rushed to answer it? Andrew wouldn't call, and Ben couldn't believe he'd thought, even statistically, he would. Of maybe ten girls that his friend Brandon had given Ben's number to, only one had ever called him: Steph from Cardiff. Ben had endured her drunken groping, and then she had rung him. Thankfully she was involved with a tutor, so he got out of anything more.

During a lecture once, Steph told Ben that while he could technically be defined as good-looking, something in the organisation of each feature on his face ruined it. She had whispered that his eyes were interesting, his mouth kind of childish, his nose robust, but that when combined, something didn't quite work. Ben never went to another lecture with Steph. But he did spend a lot of time analysing his face in his small mirror.

The train stopped in Doncaster. Ben waited for the stream of passengers to pass him, so he could escape and find a train home. He glanced out of the window. There, on a platform bench next to a kiosk, sat Andrew. Andrew from the library.

Ben tried to get closer to the glass. Squashed between a mother with two babies in a buggy and an elderly man smoking a pipe, Andrew had a brown satchel on his knee, and was staring into space. For a moment Ben wondered if he was imagining him; surely the odds were stacked against him appearing in this station at precisely this moment. But Andrew's soft hair lifted in the station's draught as though waving.

Ben pushed past the other passengers and stepped onto the platform. He was too late. Andrew had gone. Smoke curled from the old man's pipe and one of the babies in the buggy waved fat hands to reach it. Ben's thigh felt sticky where the ink had bled. Because of the pen he had missed a train that derailed and then got on one that stopped where Andrew was.

Where had Andrew been going? Had he seen Ben, too? Could there actually be such a thing as fate? No. Ben didn't believe in such stuff. And, anyway, what kind of fate brought two people so close to seeing one another again and then stopped it happening? A truly twisted kind.

Ben sat on the bench to wait for a train. Andrew was the first person he had ever given his number to. The first man. But what had been the point? He would *never* ring and if he did he would probably just cruelly analyse the features of Ben's face like Steph had.

But Ben wasn't good at forgetting people. He had tried to forget his mum. Forget the pain. She was just a statistic now anyway. One of those one-in-three. He thought of her in privacy, in the dark, where no one might observe his distorted face.

It would not be easy to hide Andrew there, but he would if he had to.

8

ZIMBABWE

A Lion Will Chase

Really, the lion is doomed to lose.

Andrew Fitzgerald, *The Lion Tamer Who Lost*

One morning Ben wakes late and misses his sunrise. The exhaustion of nights on a cement floor with a restless lioness has caught up with him.

Simon is shoving him, saying, 'Come on, lazy arse. Not like you.'

'What time is it?' Ben asks, groggily.

'Time you got a watch.'

He swings his legs over the hammock edge, feeling drugged because he has slept so deeply. Then he remembers. Today is a huge day. After a month of bonding, Ben and Esther are going to lead their now sixty-pound golden wards from The Nursery to the long-grassed enclosures, where they will meet the other lions for the first time. Last night Stig finally severed their metal umbilical cords. Ben stepped away as he did, but Lucy just padded around the brick room, curious about the parts she couldn't explore before.

Ben showers and meets Esther for breakfast and then they head to The Nursery where Stig is waiting.

'Ready?' he asks them, handing them each a stick. Volunteers use them when walking with the older lions.

'I guess,' says Esther, taking one.

'Not sure,' says Ben, taking his.

They go to their young lions' rooms. Ben opens the door, glad it will be the last time. Lucy studies him. She neither growls nor backs away, but is still wary. She eyes his stick.

'Come on, girl.' Ben's stomach turns at the thought that she could likely do him some serious damage now. 'Don't you want to explore the rest of this place?'

She ambles through the open door. Ben follows her down the corridor. It's best to walk slightly behind her so he doesn't appear to be a threat. Lucy makes several detours to run into the other rooms and then back out again.

Once outside, she is a new lioness. Her fur changes colour in the sun, from tawny to pure gold, and it is as if this affects her mood. She rolls and bounds and sniffs. When Chuma joins them, the two siblings rub heads. The cubs don't look back at the straw-covered rooms they have been in for five weeks.

The group can only walk so far together. As Lucy and Chuma enter their new high-fenced home, where they will hopefully attach to a pride, Ben and Esther must desert them. They watch with Stig from the other side of the fence, hoping these new members integrate. Ben wants to be at Lucy's side, but this is not a moment for him to share. This must be what it's like when a mother lets her firstborn child run into the school playground alone, he thinks.

But Ben still half hopes Lucy will turn and look back at him in her new freedom. Acknowledge their bond. Instead her tail swings with a dismissive flick and she views the new land with curiosity. She does not belong to him.

'She'll likely stick by her brother for now,' says Stig.

'I'm glad she has him,' says Esther.

The siblings rub rippled fur and play-fight a moment in the grass. Then they head for a soily mound in the field's corner, away from where the other lions group, each looking warily at the pride.

Ben has only walked in the enclosure with the older lions a few times; Esther has far more, having been here longer. The first time he went in with Stig and three volunteers, Ben wore the necessary padded jacket and assumed the erect stance of a ringmaster, hoping his abject fear would not betray him, and that his stick would deter them. Stig insists every day that, although they are accustomed to humans, these lions are still territorial predators. He told Ben when he first entered the enclosure that he must stand tall and that whatever happened he must never, *ever*, turn and run; a lion will chase and will always win such a race.

'Be aware of ankle-tapping,' Stig reminded him too.

Ankle-tapping is when lions try to trip up the volunteers. Stig insists it must be disciplined with a slap to the side of the face. It feels cruel to do this, but it is something a lioness will do to her naughty cub. Gabrielle, a frisky lioness, brought Joan, one of the more timid volunteers, to the ground last week and bit deeply into her thigh. It highlighted to the others the ever-present risk, but it upset Joan so much she left the sanctuary two days later.

Once the lions reach eighteen months they leave the fenced enclosure to roam the outer reserve. It is then unsafe for humans to walk with them at all. To witness their progress, the volunteers have to travel in the protection of a truck. Though Ben hopes this freedom will come to Lucy one day, he also dreads the moment when he has to let her go completely.

'Their bond will still be strong,' Stig preaches now, as they all watch the siblings sitting together. 'They won't have forgotten one another in the separation. But Lucy must seek out other females in the enclosure now and hope they accept her. Lionesses learn from their mothers, remember. They learn to hunt with them from as young as three months. Obviously, Lucy is just past four months now, so the sooner she bonds with the other females, the sooner she can join them on a hunt, or else...'

'Or what?' asks Ben.

'She might die when released.'

'*Why*?' asks Ben. 'Can't she learn to hunt alone?'

'Females hunt *together*,' explains Stig

'Why can't Chuma be Lucy's hunting complacent?' asks Ben.

'I think you mean companion,' says Esther.

'I *said* that.'

'Chuma will join his own pride,' explains Stig. 'I hope the lionesses that have already formed attachments let Lucy in. See, she's sniffing them out now. She knows what she has to do.'

Lucy has run up to the group, leaping playfully around them, brazen, insistent. *Look at me*, she says. *Accept me*. None of the lionesses acknowledge her. Ben holds his breath.

'Chuma will have to fight another male to assert his dominance,' says Stig. 'That's *his* challenge.'

'But he's so timid.' Esther purses her lips, swats a fly that lands on her forehead. She has tied her hair up and it swings like a tail. It is not dismissive though; one curl seems to beckon Ben. 'What a shame he can't just stay with Lucy. They don't have parents, so they *need* each other.'

'Siblings have to be separated before they're two and reach sexual maturity.' Stig walks the perimeter as they follow, poking the grass with his stick. 'Otherwise they'll mate. And this is best done outside their own family to avoid inbreeding depression.'

'What's that?' asks Esther.

Ben falls behind while Stig explains that it is reduced fitness in animals because of breeding with relatives. 'In some parts of Zimbabwe, the cheetahs are so inbred that a skin graft taken from one can be put on another with virtually no chance of rejection.'

Esther looks enthralled.

A rare cloud drifts in front of the sun and Ben thinks of saying that maybe this is a good thing. Maybe it means lives can be saved; such donations are sometimes necessary. Instead he watches Lucy. She gives up vying for the attention of the other lionesses and sits next to her brother on the hillock, rubbing her face against his, their coats now as glossy as blood-soaked grass.

'She's given up,' says Stig.

'She might not have,' says Ben. 'She might have a plan.'

'I agree. She may try again later. But…'

'But what?'

'Well,' says Stig. 'If she hasn't attached to the other girls within a few hours, it might never happen.'

'Maybe she's planning her next move.' Ben is angry at Stig. 'You ever think that what you're doing here is just interfering with nature?'

'Ben.' Esther softly shakes her head.

'It's true,' he insists. 'I read before I came here that some of these sanctuaries mean well but really do more harm than good.'

'You're right,' says Stig. 'Some do a lot of harm.'

'But not *us*,' Ben says.

'This is why we don't permit cub-petting by holidaymakers.' Stig sounds sad rather than angry. 'It's why we try to interfere as little as is possible with the lions before we set them free. Let them interact with one another alone. As we should maybe do now.' Stig looks at Ben. 'Watching Lucy won't help her. Go and find something else to do and let nature take its course.'

'Nature. That's a joke.' Ben shakes his head.

'Come back later and check their progress.' Stig heads off towards the huts.

Esther watches him and then turns to Ben. 'That was harsh.'

'So? Don't you ever think this is fucking wrong?'

Esther looks thoughtful. 'But the lions will die out without our help.'

'Which was our fault in the *first* place.'

'Yes.' Esther pauses. 'I know it's tough to hear, but Stig does know what he's talking about.'

'He does my fucking head in sometimes,' says Ben.

'Maybe we *should* leave them now – come back later. We might be hindering rather than helping by being here.'

Ben knows Esther speaks sense.

'Want to get coffee?' she suggests.

'Yeah. I could use that cup of mud.'

They get their drinks and take them to the rotten log overlooking the open land. For a while, they are silent. It is such a comfortable peace. Ben is aware of how rare it is to find anyone you can sit with so quietly and not feel you must fill the space with words.

Should he tell Esther he is gay?

The thought seems to have crept into his head without him noticing it. She would be the first person he has told. The only one who would know, aside from Andrew. This could be the perfect moment. It's not like anyone here will judge him. There are two gay couples – John and Paul, and Helen and Brigitte – at the project. But he can't say the words. Everything that has happened tells him that it will only bring him unhappiness. That he should turn his back on it. He hid it his entire life back home. Men have hidden it for years, so they could get married and have kids, to avoid being ostracised, to conform. It can't be that hard, can it?

Ben realises Esther is talking.

'Lucy will be fine,' she is saying. 'Far fewer male cubs survive into adulthood. Lionesses are tougher.' She grins. 'Just like the human female.'

Ben knows this is true. All lions face high mortality as cubs – for a variety of reasons, including injuries, lack of food, and being killed by adult lions – but when males reach sexual maturity, around age two, the older males within the pride kick them out. Lionesses typically stay behind.

'Isn't it cruel in the wild?' he says. 'The males get kicked out by their family for no reason. Imagine that? Must be so confusing. Being cast out into a world where he must make it alone or die.'

'Happens in the human world too,' says Esther.

'True.'

Ben is suddenly angry that, despite everything, despite what they had shared, Andrew would not speak to him before he left. Would not give him a chance. Give *them* a chance. That he simply cast him out. Ignored him when it all went wrong. And after all Ben did for him.

'I suppose at least in the human world we have our mates,' says Esther.

'Yeah. And alcohol.'

'Poor lions. No wine for them after a shit day, eh?'

'Sorry for being a grumpy bastard,' Ben says softly. 'I shouldn't take it out on you.'

Esther smiles, says, 'What else are friends for?'

Ben looks at her. The sun blesses her hair with gold. She has a good heart that shines in her face. He is still pissed off with Stig and his preaching. Sick of his endless voice. He wonders if he is just angry in general. Angry at life. Angry at Andrew. But none of it was really Andrew's fault. The blame for everything going wrong lies firmly at his dad's door.

He pictures that door. The kitchen. The sink.

And against his will, sitting on the log with Esther, he is there again.

9

ENGLAND

The Nine Lives of a Cat

Change is noisy and clanky; it squeals and smashes and scrapes. It rolls cars on ice like metal snowballs. It woke Ben.

Andrew Fitzgerald, *The Lion Tamer Who Lost*

When Ben had been home from university for a few days he tried to remove the black ink from his jeans with vinegar. His dad, Will, came into the kitchen where he was scrubbing them over the sink, and announced that he'd got him a girlfriend. Ben's first thought was that *girlfriend* was an inappropriate term for a sixty-three-year-old man to use. But then the girls he dated were usually half his age.

'What do you mean?' Ben had to ask.

That summer Will was drinking a glass of whisky before nine am, followed by a few beers in the pub with Brian before the betting shop, and cheap vodka at night before passing out to the *Question Time* credits.

'Well, Dad?' said Ben, when Will made no rush to explain.

The kitchen had not been updated since Ben's mother Heidi had barley twist units installed in 1987, with a leaded display cabinet that housed dust-coated mugs and forgotten family snaps. She died nine years after the remodel, when Ben was eleven.

Will rummaged in the cupboards for food. The sweet smell of cut grass lingered by the back door.

'Dad?' repeated Ben.

'Someone's got to sort you out.' Will heated fat in the frying pan and cracked some eggs into it. 'I thought you'd be home from uni to regale me with tales of debauchery, wild parties, protest marches and loose women.'

'I can't manage all that *and* get a degree.'

'Why not, lad?'

The fat spat like an unappreciative audience.

'Anyway, I've sorted you out,' said Will.

'I can sort myself out.'

Ben scrunched his jeans into an angry, soggy ball and put them in the bin. The stain, as black as a bad score on a maths test, remained. It just reminded him that Andrew hadn't called. Seeing him in the station last week had only reminded him how *somehow right* he had felt when near him. Being home and sleeping in a bedroom that time and taste forgot, Ben felt like he was being squashed. Squashed and suffocated.

'I told Jodie you'd take her out,' said Will.

'Who the hell's Jodie?'

'Jodie Cartwright. Dan-next-door's granddaughter. You used to play kiss chase with her in their garden, you great lop.'

Will flipped the egg; smoke filled the room. He rolled his shirt-sleeves up, found a cigarette in the drawer, and lit it at the gas, inhaling hard. Nicotine had stained his greying hair and yellowed his finger-nails, yet Will managed to remain somehow distinguished, with thick hair waving over his ears, eyes still rich with life, and a firm jaw.

'Jodie Cartwright?' Ben saw her momentarily, a ten-year-old skipping.

'Looks like butter wouldn't melt but I knew a girl like that once – Aileen.' Will grinned and Ben ignored him by pretending to look for something in the freezer. 'Looked like an angel but, oh, she could f––'

'She's not my type.'

'A woman doesn't have to be your *type* to be fun, lad.'

Ben slammed the freezer door shut.

'When did you last have sex?'

'Dad!'

'Well?'

'I'm not talking to *you* about this.'

'If you can't talk about it, no wonder you're getting nowt. You sure you're not a bloody shirt-lifter?' Will sat down at the kitchen table and savaged his sandwich.

Someone a few gardens along began mowing the grass and singing 'Come Fly with Me' with gusto.

'If I *was*,' said Ben, 'do you think I'd be able to tell a homophobe like you?'

Will laughed. 'Mike's got a woman and he's not even in the bloody country.'

Ben's older brother was on the frontline in Afghanistan, leaving behind his almost-eight-months-pregnant fiancée, Kimberley. He might not be back for the birth; war didn't permit such sentimentalities. Kimberley visited Will regularly, bringing him shortbread and sharing prenatal scan pictures. Ben had often seen them sitting close together on the sofa – too close; touching. It made him twitch and turn away.

'You having an egg butty?' asked Will.

'You know I hate eggs.'

Ben went into the living room. Pictures lined the fading walls; portraits of Mike in combats, poised for attack, and snaps with his army buddies. It annoyed Ben that his dad displayed these more prominently than pictures of his mum. Only behind the I Love Golf mug did she smile inside a rusting frame. Ben could still hear her soft accent, her silly words; and recall how his dad had mocked them.

Don't knock my statubes over, Will.

'It's statue, woman.'

What's a homosectional, Will?

'For God's sake, it's homosexual, a puff, woman, a bloody *puff*!'

They said it's olvarian cancer, Will, and it's advanced. How can we tell the kids?

'Ovarian cancer, Heidi. You want the kids to be a laughing stock when they tell their mates their mam has olvarian cancer?'

Will dropped his plate in the sink. 'Mike can keep a girl.'

'She's pregnant,' called Ben.

'How do you think I finally got your mother down the aisle?'

Ben's mum had been one of a huge sprawling Catholic family in Belfast. She met Will at a party at Hull University. He had, so his story went at every funeral and wedding, slapped the backside of 'this shy, funny-voiced thing', and because her brothers always told her to fight back, she'd smacked him in the face. Will had said, 'I'm going to marry you!' He never tired of this tale.

They married when she got pregnant a year into university.

He appeared in the doorway now. 'You think your mother'd want you to be alone, lad?'

'She'd want me to find the right person,' said Ben.

'Yeah, but you gotta go through a few wrong 'uns to get there.' Will laughed. 'You think your mother was my first love? I was thirty-five for God's sake – I'd slept with half of East Yorkshire by then. Your mother made me pure again ... for so long anyhow.' He fiddled with his cuff. 'You'd best get ready, lad.'

'For what?'

'Jodie said she'd come at twelve.'

'*What*?'

There was a gentle knock on the front door.

Will grinned. 'That'll be her.'

'Tell her I'm out.' Ben moved to the kitchen door.

'She can see you, you big lunk.'

At the window, a nose pressed between the dirty net curtains. Jodie had exactly the kind of pixie-like face his mate Brandon liked. Ben remembered her at thirteen, sunbathing in the garden, him knowing even then that the female form did not make him pant at the mouth the way it did his friends.

She came into the living room as though she was walking on a springy mattress. Will looked so intently at her that Ben ushered her out of the house.

Outside she said, 'You've not changed much, Ben.'

Not sure if it was an insult, he said, 'You haven't either.'

'You like my hair?' She touched the sun-kissed strands. 'Let's go for a drive.'

Ben got into the car next to her. He watched her move the gear stick and wished her skin was pale instead of fake-tan orange, that it was covered in bristly hair. The Piglet air freshener dangling from the rear-view mirror irritated him.

'I was surprised when your dad said you'd been asking about me.'

'He said that?' Ben couldn't hide his surprise.

'Don't be embarrassed,' smiled Jodie.

'I'm not.'

'Let's go to the park.' Jodie wriggled in her seat, exposing tan thigh.

Jodie glanced at him and then her thigh and smiled. 'You like it?'

'Yes. No.' Ben looked at the road. 'I don't mind.'

'You don't have to be nervous,' said Jodie.

'I'm *not*.'

She stopped to let children cross the road. A man in the street bent down to retrieve onions escaping from a torn carrier bag, gold hair covering his face for a moment; *Andrew*. Ben's chest felt tight, like new jeans. Then the man looked up, and he was no one.

'Do you like ice-cream?' asked Jodie.

'What?'

'We can get some at East Park.'

Jodie continued chatting in the same way until they parked near an expanse of grass where kids played football and dogs chased sticks.

'I'm not in the mood for the park,' said Ben.

'Oh.' Jodie had opened the boot and was pulling out a checked blanket.

'Let's get a beer on Holderness Road.'

'I'm driving.'

'Coke then.' Like she needed more sugar.

They joined the main street. Ben tried to walk out of sync with Jodie's clickety-clackety heels but couldn't; when she asked what he was doing, stopping and starting, he gave in to her pattern.

'I wouldn't think you'd drink during the day.' Jodie took his hand in hers.

'Why not?' Ben looked at his imprisoned fingers.

'Your dad's a bit of a boozer.'

A monumental smash interrupted them, a sound Ben would not forget for a long time. It was punctuated with glassy tinkles and car horns and squealing breaks. Jodie spun around, and Ben gratefully reclaimed his fingers.

A red lorry advertising champagne across its trailer had backed out of the avenue opposite the park, shoving the words *Champers Hits the Spot!* into the now-concertinaed bonnet of a car. Ben would later read that the mother (Ellen Lloyd, thirty-five) had been turning to tend her son (Jon Lloyd, seven) when the father (Grant Lloyd, thirty-seven) must have taken his eyes off the road too.

'Oh goodness,' said Jodie. 'We were just there!'

Ben walked towards the wreckage. The car's bonnet was as crumpled as used baking foil. The rear doors hung open, scattering glass and magazines and a black shoe onto the kerb. Furry dice hung from the rear-view mirror. Ben couldn't take his eyes from the four and six, knowing if he did he would see the two bloody heads shoved against the dashboard.

The driver involved had deserted his truck and was looking at the solitary black shoe; he moaned into his hands and backed away.

'Get him a drink,' said someone, and another someone went into a pub.

At first all the someones had remained distant, viewing from doorways and hastily parked cars. Now they closed in; elbowing for the best position. The flow carried Ben. Jodie held his arm, said it was too icky. But he was pulled closer. Through the yawning gap left by an absent door, Ben saw a small boy still strapped to his seat. The chairs in front had crushed up against his legs. The boy blinked over and over.

'Has anyone called 999?' asked someone.

Ben reached the front of the crowd. A woman knelt at the car, her heels sticking out like two blades. The boy inside said, 'Pete, *Pete*!'

The woman looked at Ben. 'He wants you.'

'I'm not Pete.'

'He *thinks* you are.' The woman stood. 'Talk to him, just until they come.'

Glass crunched under Ben's feet as he approached the vehicle. He crouched by the boy. His eyes shone with shock; his skin was waxen with hurt and the back of his hair stuck up.

'You're not Pete,' he said sadly.

'Who's Pete?'

'My brother.' The child's *b* came out like a bubble. 'He's on holiday ... I thought he'd come ... he's tall ... has funny hair like you.' Sirens sounded from afar. 'My legs hurt.'

Ben looked only at the child's face. 'What's your name?'

'Jon ... Why won't Mum talk to me?'

Ben remembered when *his* mum couldn't speak any more, when all her mis-words died, when they let her come home from the hospital and settled her on a put-you-up bed next to the Christmas tree in the middle room and let her watch reruns of *Lucky Ladders* as many times as she wanted. Three weeks after she passed away Ben found a note from her in his *Cats, Lions and Tigers* book.

Inside it said: *Ben, I love you and you must be there for your dad and your brother and for you. You are the only one that really evaluated me. Look after your brother. Do whatever makes your dad happy. But most of all what makes you happy.*

'I've asked Mum for my *Doctor Who* book,' said Jon.

Ben followed his gaze to the floor where the book faced downwards. The crowd disassembled, sirens blasted.

'I'll get it.'

'Make room for the paramedics.' A police officer touched Ben's shoulder. 'Come on, let them do their job.'

Ben moved away. When he looked back, a paramedic was putting a blanket over Jon.

Jodie appeared. 'You've got blood on your T-shirt.' She dragged him to a wall near the park gates, made him sit. 'You look terrible.'

What do you expect? Ben wanted to say. *I've just seen a child probably orphaned.*

'Don't know why people are still hanging around like vultures.' She exhaled. 'Do you want to come back to mine?'

Ben shook his head vigorously.

'Your top will stain if we don't clean it – let's find a café.'

He let himself be dragged again; let himself mimic Jodie's clickety-clacks. She took him to nearby café and marched to the counter, where a variety of stodgy cakes sat in a cooler. Ben pulled his bloody T-shirt away from his skin. More clothes ruined. The counter assistant appeared from the back, drying her hands on an apron and staring at the blood.

'It's not mine.' Ben realised how inane the explanation sounded. 'Can I have a bottle of water?'

'Is the coffee real or instant?' Jodie asked the waitress.

She ordered egg sandwiches (which Ben couldn't be bothered to argue about not liking) and carrot cake. They sat near the counter with their backs to the restaurant area.

'What are you counting?' asked Jodie.

Ben hadn't realised he was. 'Crumbs,' he said.

'Why?'

'Why not?'

While Ben dabbed his T-shirt with water she chatted about a party her friend was having tomorrow. He had to get out of this, go home. He rubbed his T-shirt so hard he knocked the water bottle over. He knelt down to mop the liquid with napkins. The water rose up his jeaned thigh, like wet flames.

Ben looked up then and saw Andrew.

Andrew.

One hand on the door, the other around the strap of a brown satchel, he must have seen Ben too and paused.

He came over. His feet were quiet. No jarring clickety-clackety heels announced him; he crept back into Ben's life with soft footfalls like a ruffle-haired ghost. Ben sat back on his heels, wondering if shock had made him hallucinate. He heard Jodie say she would complain that the carrot cake had very few orange pieces in it. Andrew said nothing; everything about him was silent. Ben thought if he blinked he would disappear again.

Andrew said, 'I was…' but the sentence trailed into breath.

'He thought I was his brother.'

'Who?'

'The boy in the car.'

'You were with him?' Andrew looked outside. 'I saw the aftermath. Is he okay?'

Behind them Jodie spat her words out like fruit pips, demanding an introduction.

'I think so.' Ben realised he was still kneeling and stood. 'You were in the station.'

'What station?'

'Doncaster,' said Ben. 'On a bench, the day after we met.'

Andrew paused, thought. 'I was going to see my publisher. I didn't see you though.'

'You'd gone when I got to you.'

'Give me your T-shirt.'

Ben stared at him.

'You need to get it in cold water before it dries.' He held out a hand. Three tiny freckles gathered like dust at his thumb.

Behind them Jodie asked whether Ben was listening to her because otherwise she was going. Andrew smiled the half-up, half-down smile that Ben remembered, and said, 'Give me the top.'

Ben peeled off his T-shirt and handed it to him. Andrew disappeared into the toilet.

'Who's he?' Jodie stared at Ben's naked chest. 'He's a bit weird.'

'A mate from uni. I didn't expect to see him here. Look, Jodie, you're sweet, but my dad … well, he had no right to interfere and tell you I was interested.' Seeing Andrew made him brave again.

Jodie grumbled that he could have told her before she wasted the petrol. Ben apologised again and said it was nothing she'd done. She shook her head, told him he was just plain weird, and left in a flurry of heels.

Ben didn't watch her for long.

Andrew returned from the toilet with the T-shirt squeezed and damp in his hands. They left the café together and bought a cheap top at a charity shop nearby and walked for a while through the park.

'You always follow an accident,' said Ben.

'What?'

'In the station; the train had derailed. And now, the car...'

'Odd,' said Andrew. He paused. 'I did try calling you. I must have copied it across wrong.'

Ben shrugged, like he'd never given it another thought. 'You're here now.'

'I am.'

10

ZIMBABWE

The Seductive Spell of Darkness

Friends are very much the best things in the world. Like socks that fit perfectly and keep your toes warm.

Andrew Fitzgerald, *The Lion Tamer Who Lost*

'You're miles away.'

The words jolt Ben from the past. He looks around. He is still sitting on the rotten log with Esther. How long has she been talking to him? The sun is much lower in the sky.

'Sorry. I *was* miles away.'

'You were. Where w––'

The sound then of light footfall; Stig approaches.

'I think you should come back to the enclosure,' he says.

Wordlessly, they follow him there. Lucy lies in the long grass near some of the lionesses. Though most of the females still ignore her, two appear curious. A slender creature with longer legs than the others shoves Lucy playfully; another glares at her up close. Lucy acts as though she doesn't care whether they engage with her or not. She swats her tail nonchalantly.

Ben smiles. She is clever. Did she learn it from him? That indifference provokes interest. Or is it purely instinct? Must be instinct.

On the soily mound, Chuma sits alone, watching his sister.

'Poor Chuma,' whispers Esther.

'Yeah,' says Stig. 'But I'm sure he'll be okay. He was probably waiting to make sure Lucy was okay first.'

'I know Chuma will be okay,' Ben tells Esther, even though he isn't.

A total solar eclipse dominates the end of Ben's third month in Zimbabwe.

March brings an eclipse across northern Africa. Quickly arranged safaris cash in on tourists wishing to view the event in full. Safety posters are displayed on roadsides, and in villages blindness-preventing glasses sell out. Then street vendors offer aluminium foil to crowds so they can watch day turn briefly into night through the safety of silvery paper. Many observers report an unusually beautiful eclipse. Further south, where the Liberty Lion project is, the darkness when the moon sits between the earth and sun is only partial. It lasts four minutes and seven seconds.

During which, Esther kisses Ben.

And he lets her.

Knowing the lions might be confused by the sudden change in light and temperature, the volunteers stay away from them. When the semi-blackness falls, some of the animals pace the fence. Others curl up close to their pals, growling softly.

Most of the volunteers gather in groups for the unique sight, sitting in the acacia trees' shade, sunglasses perched on their heads like holidaymakers waiting by a pool for cocktails.

'I know a better spot,' says Esther, watching them herd together.

She and Ben have been spending a lot of time together, united by their love of Lucy and Chuma. Each day for the last few weeks, once daily duties are done, they have watched their wards in the grassy enclosure. The two cubs are slowly settling in, separately, as was hoped. Chuma is finding it difficult still; his unwillingness to fight means he has trouble asserting his authority. A bloody brawl with a much larger lion, Gallant, has made him even more reluctant.

Lucy, though, is a keen leader in her group. She does not look over at Ben while with her lionesses, but when he feeds her she is receptive, and he is sure she remembers their nights together. Very soon, she will hunt. When she does, he can follow, far behind in a truck, observing.

'No one knows this place,' says Esther, leading Ben through the long grass to a rock jutting out like a bad tooth. It gives way to sloping land and provides a view for miles around. 'I found it the other day and sat writing my diary. It was so peaceful I felt like all my thoughts settled down.'

It is just the kind of thing Andrew might say – or have said. But he is past tense now; Esther is present. She is a great friend. Ben has opened up a little more recently, admitting he fell out with his dad before coming here. He tells her just enough – so that she feels he has confided in her, but remains his friend.

'Here we go,' says Esther looking at the sky.

They put on safety glasses, and watch the moon inching closer to sun.

'Stig said the locals think the eclipse is a harbinger of tragedy,' says Esther.

'Such a bloody Stig thing to say.'

Esther laughs. 'I hope they can see this in England. My little brother would love it. He's obsessed with the sky and space and faraway stuff.'

It's early morning, but the insects think it's early dusk and come out, buzzing in confusion. Light fades. Now an inky shadow, the moon turns the sun into a glowing iris, and it seems to Ben that an eye looks down on them. The world darkens.

Perhaps encouraged by this shroud of privacy, Esther moves closer to Ben and puts a tremulous hand on his knee. Should he stop her? Hurt her with another rejection? Hurt her the way *he* has been?

Now is the time to stop her before it starts.

But he lets Esther kiss him. She tastes of sweetness and youth – and something else. Something he cannot name. What is it? Femaleness. Though not unpleasant, it is strange. Their safety glasses clash. He tries to kiss her back.

Maybe life could be simple with her. No passion, maybe. But safety.

He shifts position so he can stroke her cheek. The moon has blocked the fire of day, but only for moments. Then the light returns, the moon moves on, and the sun rules again.

Ben pulls away from Esther and says, 'I can't.'

She frowns. 'But you *were*.'

'I just...' Ben holds his head. He thinks of getting up and leaving, but that would be unkind, and cowardly.

'You love someone else.' It is a statement Esther utters without looking at him. 'I'm not fucking stupid. You clearly had your heart broken back home. You've said your dad is the reason you're here, but there's obviously way more to it.'

Ben shakes his head.

'Look, I like you.' Esther pulls at the long grass near her sandaled feet. 'I know I denied it when you turned down my wine that night. But I felt stupid. Rejected, I guess.' She pauses. 'Who was she then? She must've *really* fucking hurt you.'

'They didn't hurt me,' he says carefully. 'It was something else. I'd never want anyone to think ... to think ... they did me wrong.'

'Sometimes it's as though – well, as though you're blocked or something.' Esther shakes her head. 'Sounds weird, but it's true. I've been hurt, too, you know.'

'I know. Greg was a bastard for treating you the way he did.'

Yesterday Esther stayed in her room all day with a tummy bug, and Ben sat with her. In that vulnerable, weak moment she admitted Greg had knocked her about. That when he'd had a few beers, he got jealous over every little thing she did. If she so much as spoke to another man, he snapped. She hid the bruises with long sleeves, and no one ever knew.

'Can't you get past it?' asks Esther now.

'Past what?'

'This thing beyond the two of you that ended it.'

'No,' says Ben quietly.

Esther throws a long blade of grass. After a while she says, 'Wish my little brother could see all this.'

Ben smiles. 'Bet he'd love it here.'

The split-lipped hare appears from behind a velvet bushwillow and lollops past the couple, perhaps feeling safe now the light is back.

'Maybe everyone should come here,' says Ben. 'Like National Service or something.'

'National Service?' Esther frowns.

'You know, in the old days when young men had to give a year's mandatory service to the army.'

'I'd like to see Greg have to do it.'

'Bet that would whip the bastard into shape.'

Esther looks at Ben. 'Whatever happened, your ex was lucky to have you.'

'I don't know.'

She reaches for his hand. She does it nervously and Ben can tell she fears his rejection again. He can't reject her. He *can't*. He knows how that feels. He knows what it's like to be ignored. Overlooked.

So he takes her hand in his.

They sit for a while. With the light back, Ben sees the golds and ambers of the landscape even more clearly. She kisses him again.

He lets her. The sun disappears behind a cloud.

Esther stands, keeping hold of his hand. She leads Ben wordlessly back to her hut. As she opens the door and ushers him inside, he remembers when he and Andrew first talked about wishes. When they were still counting their days. When they were thinking about the circus.

Ben asks Esther to close the shutters so it is dark. He lets her think he is just a bit shy, but he is afraid he might cry.

He closes his eyes and thinks of his small room back home.

11

ENGLAND

How Wishing Works

> *Ben slept as his world changed. Sleep lets change creep up and shake everything, like a plastic puzzle in a Christmas cracker.*
>
> Andrew Fitzgerald, *The Lion Tamer Who Lost*

On Ben's tiny bed Andrew first described his Wish Box.

Outside the morning rain died; the only sound in the room was the two clocks ticking out of sync. And then Andrew's words. Sprawled on Ben's duvet, he mentioned a *Wish Box*, stressing each word to make it clear that this was a proper noun. Ben watched his lips move over the capitals, listened to him describe how it was rusted silver with a wrong-sized lid that frequently fell off, and how Andrew wrote wishes on Post-it notes and placed them inside until they came true.

'Don't laugh,' Andrew concluded.

'Is this like that stupid Feng Shui stuff you once did to your flat?'

'It wasn't stupid,' snapped Andrew. 'It improved my sleep.'

'A *Wish Box*.' Ben said the pronoun with mockery. 'Weird. Even for you.'

'When I was little,' Andrew explained, 'I discovered wishing totally by accident. Scribbles I did in notepads somehow ended up coming true. Stop looking at me like that. Like, I wrote about these cool new Adidas trainers I loved and a month later someone at my mum's work gave her an almost-new pair in my size.'

'Doesn't mean it was cos you *wished* for them.'

'There was all sorts I wrote down that ended up happening. In the end I did it more actively. I wrote stuff down and kept it in a safe place until it came true. Now I put them in my Wish Box.'

'Don't the Post-it notes get stuck to the inside?'

Andrew ignored the scorn. 'I fold them in on themselves.' He moved his hands as though doing so. 'Don't give me that look. You asked about it, and I'm telling you. You have to be realistic.'

'*Realistic*?'

'You have to wish for something likely to happen.'

'That's cheating.'

The smell of damp grass floated up from the garden.

'It isn't.'

'Is.'

'Is this cos I told you about the peas?' asked Ben.

Last night he had admitted his obsession with counting all the peas on his plate before eating them. Now he counted their days together too; one day, two days, three, a week, a month, two. It made him feel they were less likely to lose one another again somehow.

'Wishing for something likely to happen is just cheating,' he repeated.

'I wouldn't cheat.' Andrew looked serious.

Ben couldn't believe he was thirty-nine, that a face so free of deep wrinkles and eyes so bright could belong to a man defined by society as almost middle-aged. A box with wishes stuffed in it had no place in the life of someone that old. Softly spoken and blond-haired, Andrew was as beautiful as the angels in those Botticelli paintings, something divine in Ben's shabby room. He had initially been embarrassed about his childhood bedroom, about the faded posters and the boyish collection of replica cars gathering dust on the wardrobe. Each time Andrew came over – when no one was home – Ben apologised.

'Give me more examples,' Ben demanded.

Andrew stretched out his legs and yawned. 'Say if I wished you were thirty-nine, it couldn't happen.'

'It will in seventeen years – at least I hope so.'

'But it couldn't happen *now*.'

'Tell me a *did* happen,' said Ben.

'No. You're laughing.'

Ben paused. 'So tell me *how* it works? I need the mechanics.'

'Okay,' said Andrew. 'First off, you have to be patient. Most wishes aren't likely to come true overnight. Then be realistic – make sure it's a thing that might possibly happen. And generally, only ever make one at a time. If one hasn't come true for a long time, it's probably okay to make anoth––'

'They don't *all* work then?' interrupted Ben.

'About eighty percent.'

'Not bad odds, I suppose.'

'Writing it down and putting it somewhere safe, like in a box, shows that you mean business,' continued Andrew. 'Then you're more likely to pursue it and make sure it comes true.'

'*Cheat*, you mean.'

Andrew ignored the jibe. 'Always make them positive,' he said. 'It's very important to be exact. If you're vague, it might not be the thing you want.'

Andrew was like no one Ben had ever met. Their differences filled the room; Ben's clothes in a neat pile on the bed end and Andrew's discarded T-shirt on the floor, his watch on top flashing gold lights at the ceiling. On their first date – two days after crossing paths for the third time in that café – they had been wearing exactly the same jeans. They had both spoken at the same time; they both said, 'I wasn't even going to wear these ones.' Now it was as if he and Andrew couldn't mirror one another if they tried.

And Ben couldn't get enough of him.

'*Why* do you do it though?' he asked now.

'Wish?'

'Yeah.'

'I suppose it compels me to make sure the thing I want happens.'

The breeze lifted a curtain away from the window sill. Only one of them was closed. Ben had pulled it, worried that Mr Cartwright next door might see them from his greenhouse. But Andrew had put his hand over Ben's belt, said, 'Who cares?' Ben had insisted they stay away from the window.

'I guess I've always done it,' admitted Andrew.

Ben pulled the duvet over his head. Within its folds, he smelt them, the deodorant Andrew wore, and fresh sweat.

'Did you wish for me?' he asked from inside the duvet.

Andrew turned the cover back. 'I wish you'd come to the circus with me next week.'

'Like a proper wish?' asked Ben.

'Yes.'

'Are you going to write it down?'

'I might.'

'Put it in your box?' Ben smiled.

'Maybe.'

'On a folded Post-it?'

'Maybe.'

Andrew fell quiet. Ben watched him drift into the distant place he went when all his thoughts had assembled themselves. The white landscape of his chest was broken by a single freckle. Andrew scratched it.

'Ever wish they'd find a cure for diabetes?' Ben asked.

'Didn't I explain how it works?' Andrew spoke gently, but Ben sensed agitation.

Andrew had had Type 1 Diabetes since he was a child. Ben had begun carrying glucose tablets, even when they weren't together, and had researched the condition for hours online. He'd studied Andrew's face endlessly for signs of hypo, for white cheeks or clammy forehead, until he shooed him away, impatient.

'Why the circus then?' The word circus knotted Ben's stomach, like ribbon just-too-tight around a gift.

'I need to research lion tamers.'

'Can't you just read about them?' asked Ben.

'Research isn't the same as seeing.'

'Have you been to a circus before?'

Andrew nodded. 'A long time ago; I can't remember.'

Ben propped himself up on a pillow and imagined reaching out to stroke the soft curve of Andrew's chest, but didn't. He was still too shy, afraid Andrew would push him away and say he'd done it wrong. Though everything about this felt right, it was new, and at times scary.

'Did you know that lion tamers remove the lions' teeth so they can't cause damage?' Ben clenched his fist. 'Isn't it illegal having animals in shows?'

'They're trying to ban it but this one still has big cats.'

Andrew looked at Ben while running his tongue over his own teeth. Was he imagining them gone?

'Come to the circus with me,' Andrew said.

'No.'

'I think you will.'

Andrew leaned closer, held Ben's gaze a moment, and then slid his tongue between Ben's lips. Then he unwrapped a bar of chocolate, took a huge bite, and kissed Ben deeply, sharing the sugar. Around Andrew's abdomen injection bruises and pinprick marks climbed like animal footprints.

'Seducing me won't work,' Ben mumbled into Andrew's mouth. 'It's cheating.'

'How long until your dad comes home?' Andrew asked.

Ben's stomach turned over. The thought of his dad returning out of the blue made his arousal feel wrong. His dad had already disowned a brother, Jerry, for being gay. It was the family tragedy no one talked about, at least never in front of Ben. Ten years ago, Jerry had hung himself. A neighbour found him in his garage. All Ben knew, from listening to snippets of hushed conversations as a kid, was that he never left a note. But he had often wondered if being ostracised by his family caused the suicide. Ben didn't want to imagine his dad's reaction if he walked in on him and Andrew.

'What's wrong?' Andrew touched Ben's face tenderly.

'You *know* what,' said Ben.

'Can I ask...?'

'What?'

'You don't have a great relationship with your dad.'

'No,' said Ben.

'So why the hell do you *care*? What the hell does it matter if he knows about us? I don't get why it's so hard for you.'

Ben didn't know how to explain it. His relationship with his dad wasn't the best, but Ben still longed for his approval. He remembered when he was four and his dad showed him how to line up dominos so they would fall in a circular pattern. When Ben's tiny fingers kept knocking them over too soon, Will had shaken his head, said he was useless and packed them away. He doubted his dad would even remember it now, but Ben did.

'Don't you ever think,' said Andrew when Ben didn't respond, 'that we come here because you *want* to be caught...'

'No,' said Ben. 'You've never invited me to yours. Where else can we go?'

'Come back under the covers then.'

'Damn,' said Ben. 'I think you just proved your theory.'

'Yeah?'

'I was wishing you'd say that.'

PART TWO

ANDREW

12

Trophies of Bravado

> *Ben fashioned a jacket from red velvet and sewed stolen buttons at the cuff. He told his grandma that in his magic coat he would be able to make lions lie down and purr. 'Not by hurting them,' he said, 'not by wearing their teeth as trophies of bravery, but by lying with them.'*
>
> Andrew Fitzgerald, *The Lion Tamer Who Lost*

As Andrew entered the circus with Ben, he looked down at their feet and smiled at the fact that their shoes were completely different – Ben's trainers were scuffed, his own boots were polished – but they walked exactly in time.

The marquee was turquoise and had six yellow stars near its pinnacle and a zigzag line like bared teeth encircling the lower sections. Dangling in the still air, the banner revealed only the words *Mr Jolly's B–*. When they passed the back seats, Andrew recalled his tenth birthday, and sitting there with his mother. She had bought the tickets as an apology for working every weekend. They were all she could afford, and she grumbled throughout the show that they could barely see anything from so far.

Andrew had barely been able to see because his vision was blurred. His tummy had somersaulted and his throat ached with raw thirst. Days later, Andrew was taken to the hospital in a neighbour's car, half conscious. After a blood test he was diagnosed with diabetes. Arriving from a double shift in a care home, Andrew's mother cried and told the doctor she'd had no idea. Andrew didn't tell her it had been easy to hide his symptoms from someone who was never there; then he assuaged his mother's shame with kisses.

This diagnosis led to daily injections and blood tests, a strict dietary routine and carrying snacks in pockets. Andrew accepted it with the resolve of a child accustomed to being alone for great lengths of time. What caused him far greater stress was never being able to grumble in case his mother again ran to the bathroom in tears and locked the door for two hours.

Almost thirty years later, with Ben, Andrew paid extra for front-row circus seats.

'Our twelfth date,' said Ben.

'I know.'

Andrew – with a life dictated by blood sugar readings – looked for the coincidences in numbers. His blood that morning had been 12.2, so he looked for ones and twos all day. Today he would find two lions, one fire-eater, two children, and one ringmaster.

'Where are we sitting?' Ben scanned the arena.

'Here.' Andrew pointed left.

Separated from the ring by bars, they were squashed close on benches. Andrew loved that each time Ben leaned forwards, their legs touched. He would happily have held Ben's hand but knew Ben would resist such a public display of togetherness.

Two boisterous children plonked down next to them and squabbled over who should sit where. The boy argued that *she*'d got the toy in the cereal box, so *he* should pick where he sat. Their father acquiesced.

'I always got the toy,' said Andrew, 'because I was the only one.'

'My brother Mike always got it. I remember this Spiderman web-blaster I wanted so much I cried. He got it and I sulked for days. He gave me it in the end.'

'You can have my web-blaster any time,' smiled Andrew.

'You were lucky having no siblings.'

'Not really.'

Andrew viewed the ring. Not fully lit it appeared plain, not yet magical. Shadows fell where lions would no doubt soon stride.

'Don't you feel sorry for the lions?' Ben said.

'Of course. But I need to watch the lion tamer.'

'I thought you'd been to the circus?'

'A long time ago,' said Andrew. 'I vaguely remember the trapeze artist because she wore gold sequins and had feathers in her hair. And I remember one of the lions.'

'What about him?' asked Ben.

'His fur was patchy. I waved but I knew he couldn't see me.' Andrew had wanted to say that he knew how it felt to be sick.

Ben said, 'I went the circus a lot with my—'

But he got cut off by the drumroll and the swell of theatrical music. Collar erect and whip in hand, the ringmaster strode into the ring and announced that he was Mr Jolly and that the clowns were here for everyone's delight: Tilly, Tommy and Toots.

'I hate clowns,' muttered Ben.

Tommy rode a tricycle, a grotesque multicoloured wig and white mask his costume, followed by Tilly with green pom-poms and Toots honking a horn repeatedly. They told the nearby twins they weren't sure who was who and could they swap seats so they'd be in the right place.

'I'm all muggled,' said Tommy.

'It's *muddled*!' called the red-haired boy nearby.

'Even *I* know that,' said Ben.

'Are you sure?' Andrew squeezed his leg to show he was only teasing.

'I hope the lions are next,' said Andrew.

'My mum once said they look allusive.'

'Allusive?'

He felt Ben stiffen. 'Don't correct her. I know she meant *elusive*.'

'You never talk about your mum,' Andrew said.

'I hate the circus. It reminds me of her.'

Andrew knew Ben's mum had died but didn't know how or when.

'I didn't know *that* was why you hated it,' he said gently.

Tommy the clown made a creature out of a long purple balloon. The nearby kids yelled that it looked like a snake; he assured them it would soon be a frog.

'We can go,' said Andrew.

'You need to be here.'

'I can watch lion-taming footage,' insisted Andrew.

'We'll stay.'

Suddenly, Ben kissed his cheek; Andrew felt the warmth of it for a while. He thought about last night, about his hasty undressing of Ben. About how much he had to have him, how fast.

Andrew had always gone for men he couldn't fully have; had always needed distance. He briefly loved Craig but couldn't have him because of an ex-wife, a woman he said he had left. But then she got addicted to painkillers and it turned out he hadn't left her after all. He loved Leo for four years, mostly because he travelled, and the world was his other partner.

Looking at Ben, Andrew thought there should be more words for love; the word love should mean total love. There should be another word for anything less – and that would have described what he felt with Leo and Craig.

Mr Jolly returned to the ring to introduce a fire-eater who risked her life to thrill the world. A crimson-costumed woman cartwheeled into the ring, spinning fireballs between her feet and hands. The audience went wild; men stood and whistled between their fingers. She plunged a flaming torch into her mouth. The smell of dead flame lingered for the rest of the show.

'How does she not get burnt?' asked Ben.

'She extinguishes the flame rather than eats it.'

'Cheating,' said Ben.

'Maybe more of a mis-word,' said Andrew. 'They're fire-*killers* rather than eaters. Watch how she lowers the torch to her lips, exhaling slowly to keep the heat from her face. Her tongue is stuck out wide and flat, see. She places the wick of the torch onto it and closes her lips and extinguishes the flame, quick.'

'But how?' asked Ben.

'She cuts off the oxygen.'

'It's kind of sexy,' said Ben.

Andrew moved his hand higher up Ben's thigh.

'If you want to stay,' said Ben, 'I wouldn't do that.'

Andrew decided to ignore him and bit his ear. He felt Ben's sharp intake of breath. The music and drumroll drowned out the sound of it.

Then it was time for the lions.

The lion tamer strode out, his twin-tailed jacket too snug, his belly distended over a shiny sash. The boy nearby stamped his feet. This was what the crowd wanted the thrills, the spills, the man brave enough to take on the king of the beasts. People stood for a better view. Two straggly lions ambled from the side. A hush settled over the marquee like a tranquilliser. The tamer shouted *Jump! Hey! Jump!* and waved a chair until the creatures climbed onto star-bedecked stools in the centre.

'Why the chair?' said Ben.

'It confuses them.'

'Because it's not a table?'

Andrew had to smile. 'The points of the chair's legs distract them from wanting to claw the lion tamer's face off.'

Three cracks of the whip and the beasts rotated like pathetic ballerinas. Their manes were thinning, their amber eyes glazed with indifference. Andrew saw the rows of eyes in the audience glinting in the stage lights.

Then the whip caught in one lion's mane. Gasps from the audience. As the lion tamer tried to tug it free Andrew expected attack.

Nothing.

A man behind them booed. An empty coffee cup hit the cage, followed by a handful of popcorn. 'It's all bravado not bravery!' cried the man.

For a dizzy moment Andrew thought maybe he was heading for a hypo and fingered the cereal bar in his pocket; when his blood sugar fell to less than four he could collapse if he didn't eat sugar.

Ben said, 'You're bleeding.'

Liquid streamed from his fingertip into his palm. The boy next to Ben told his dad the lion must have got the poor mister.

'My lunchtime test,' said Andrew. 'I cut too deep.'

'You're pale.'

Andrew turned to see Ben studying him in the endearing way he did when he thought he was about to pass out. During those moments Andrew enjoyed the nearness of his face, seeing the orange flecks in his eyes, his tongue when his lower lip drooped.

'I'm okay,' he insisted. 'I wasn't low.'

'Sure?'

He nodded.

The lion tamer now had the largest cat on the floor. He roughly rubbed its belly with his black boot. Andrew felt Ben snake a hand under his shirt. Andrew tried to focus on the show. The lion tamer punctuated each instruction with the whip. *Sit! Paws! Beg!* The audience hissed. Ben scratched Andrew's back. Gently at first, then harder. Andrew was excited by the sharp pain but repulsed by what he saw in the ring.

When Ben stopped, Andrew took hold of his hand.

Kept it tenderly held inside his.

'*Disgusting*,' he heard.

The father of the two children nearby was glaring at them.

'Beg your pardon?' said Andrew.

'My kids shouldn't have to see *that* in a circus,' said the father, motioning to their entwined hands.

'See what?' asked Andrew, but he knew.

'This is a *family* show!'

'Come on, let's go,' said Ben, clearly embarrassed.

'No,' refused Andrew. 'He thinks it's fine for his kids to watch those lions being tortured, but a couple of people holding hands is gonna scar them?'

'You're not *people*,' said the dad.

'Because we're men?'

Ben stood. 'Andrew,' he hissed. 'You're scaring the kids.' He started up the stairs to leave. The boy and girl looked intrigued rather than afraid. Their father shook his head and resumed watching the show, chiding them to do the same.

Andrew stayed for a moment, then followed Ben. He looked back as he stepped from the tent into dusk. The last thing he saw was lion blood seeping into the sawdust.

'He had no right to talk to us like that,' said Andrew, allowing his anger free reign as they walked to the bus stop. 'This is two-thousand-and-fucking-five.'

'We don't have to flaunt it,' sighed Ben. 'It's easy for you. No one knows about me.'

'Maybe. But if you think I'm gonna tolerate that kind of bigotry…'

They caught the bus into town and sat upstairs. Perhaps due to its emptiness, Ben put his head on Andrew's shoulder. When a gang of boisterous teenagers climbed the bus stairs Ben lifted his head and moved away. Andrew didn't care who saw, but he knew how nervous Ben was about their relationship. Maybe he should have just ignored the father earlier.

Ben dozed off.

Andrew thought about the first time they met in the library. How earnest and cute Ben had been. How he had smiled seeing so many nines when Ben wrote his number down – his recent blood test had been 9.9. He'd been disappointed when he dialled and got a dead line.

It had also been nine days later that Andrew saw Ben again.

Andrew had been in a café, sipping Coke, writing *Ben's grandfather appeared barefoot and saved him from the carnage* in the pad that always accompanied him. As the word *carnage* touched paper, real-life Ben had walked into the cafe with a girl and blood on his T-shirt. Andrew had put his head down, occasionally spying on them. His jealousy of the girl had been acute, a surprise. He viewed Ben with the sort of longing he put down to not being able to have him. Ben's distance – that it would seem he preferred women – intrigued him.

He decided to leave so he closed his notepad and started to open the door.

But he never managed to escape.

Now – on their twelfth date, after knowing Ben for thirty-five days

– Andrew put a hand over Ben's as the bus took a sharp corner. Ben stirred, sleepily opened his eyes, and kissed Andrew deeply.

'I think you should come to my flat tonight,' said Andrew.

Ben smiled. Kissed him again.

'Fuckin' benders!' yelled one of the teenagers.

Ben pulled sharply away from Andrew, cursing under his breath.

The other teenagers sniggered. A boy with spiked hair blew kisses at them and cried, 'Better watch out, lads. Don't wanna catch gay! Don't breathe their air!'

'Come on, you knobhead,' said a scrawny kid in denim, without looking at Ben or Andrew. 'It's our stop. Let's go.'

As the gang went down the stairs, whooping and laughing, the scrawny kid looked back, and Andrew saw in the moment their eyes met that he had realised this might be how it would be for him one day, and that he was hiding who he was.

'Jesus,' hissed Ben. 'This is such a mistake.'

'What? *Us*?' Andrew's heart sank.

'No.' Ben shrugged. 'Being out. In both senses of the word.'

'So come to my flat.'

'Really?'

'Yes.'

After copying Ben's number wrong, Andrew had been quite prepared to let him go. To create the distance that had always protected him. But now, he didn't know if he could ever let him go again.

13

A Private Place

Ben's friend Nancy, whose hair looked like custard, kissed his cheek after a game of Cheaty Chess (neither of them knew how to play Real Chess) and pinched him at the same time. Maybe without pain a kiss would be less.

Andrew Fitzgerald, *The Lion Tamer Who Lost*

Following their Saturday afternoon at the circus, Ben came to Andrew's flat for the first time.

They never went to Ben's at night because of his dad. During the day they spent time in Ben's narrow bed, making up for the dark hours they couldn't share. Clothes were discarded, frantic kisses sticky, clammy bodies joined, fast, impatient, hungry. They urgently undressed one another, taking no time to breathe. Now Andrew wanted to share time with Ben. Proper time.

Hardly anyone came to his flat. His friend Jill, a colleague from the library in Beverley, where he worked, sometimes visited on Fridays when they would drink gin and share gossip. But mostly, his home was where he wrote, where he reread *The Brothers Grimm* while making pasta, where he ate at the same time each day, tested his blood with a meter, injected insulin before meals, managed his condition. It was a private place; just his.

Now he unlocked the second-floor door and let Ben inside.

Ben stood in the hallway, looking nervous.

'Come in,' insisted Andrew, loving Ben's apprehension.

'I can smell fresh bread.'

'Mrs Hardy, always baking. Could be worse – she boils cabbage on Tuesdays.'

Andrew went into the kitchen and Ben followed, in step. It was a narrow, galley kitchen, the left wall bare while its opposite accommodated a colourful collection of cupboards, a worktop and tiles. Andrew watched as Ben studied his fridge magnets, the I HEART PARIS postcard, random photographs, and the 365-new-words-a-year calendar. That day's word was *patrocliny*. The small print, which Andrew had read while he ate breakfast that morning, said it meant the inheritance of traits from the father.

Ben picked up the red pot from the top of the microwave and turned it over, spilling small stones noisily and quickly scooping them up again.

'You hungry?' Andrew asked him.

'Not especially.' Ben leaned over the sink, looked out of the window into the overgrown shared garden. Andrew's back burned where Ben had scratched it during the lion taming. 'How about you?'

'Not really,' he said, 'but I should eat.'

Now Ben looked at him. 'Is your blood sugar low?'

Andrew had to admit it had been all over the place recently. He'd found it impossible to control that week.

'What might cause that?'

'Puberty.' Andrew grinned.

'Seriously,' said Ben.

Andrew loved how solemn he got over his condition.

'My numbers rocket if I'm coming down with a cold. I've been tired lately too. I'll eat, just to be safe.' Andrew took a cereal bar from the cupboard and opened the wrapper. 'You want a coffee?'

'No. I'm fine.' Ben still looked nervous.

'Come through.'

Andrew went into the living room; Ben trailing after him. Andrew never quite knew what to do when he had company. Accustomed to solitude, he felt odd with others in his habitat. He had always been quite private, never one for gay clubs, even as a youngster. Alone, he would turn on the computer, pull the curtains, read, moving his lips around the words. Tonight, he hardly knew where to stand. It wasn't that he wished Ben wasn't there, it was just how his presence affected him.

Andrew chewed the bar slowly.

'So where's this *Wish Box* of yours?' Ben emphasised the proper noun.

'It's in the northwest corner.' He motioned to the plant by the curtain where the small silver box with an over-sized lid sat on an occasional table.

'Where else would it be?' Ben gave him a mocking smile. 'What's this week's wish?'

'I can't remember.'

'You're just being devasive.'

Andrew ignored the mis-word. 'I'll tell you when it comes true.'

The wish that week was simple; *I wish Ben would introduce me to his family when he's comfortable. Just as friends is fine.*

'You only wish for what's likely,' said Ben, tone still mocking. 'So it should come true.'

He went to the desk by the sash window. Covered in folders and books, Andrew liked to think it was organised chaos. The Post-it notes that circled the computer screen like petals fluttered as Ben brushed past them. Andrew knew what they said: *Give Ben more reason. Titles for chapters? Voice, voice, voice.* Andrew loved seeing Ben with his things, loved how he picked up the soft butterfly his mother had left him and turned it over, how his boyish hands were careful.

'Why doesn't it fall apart?'

'It's been treated. You just have to be gentle with it.'

'And this is where you write,' Ben said.

'It's where I *type*. I write everywhere.'

Ben pulled a book out of the pile. '*The Early Gift*,' he read, '*by Andrew Fitzgerald*. How does it feel having your name on an actual book?'

Andrew had to think a little. 'Strange. *Good* strange. It's not a bestseller. That's what I'd love. One day. To see my own book in Waterstones or somewhere.'

'Can I borrow it?'

'Yes.'

'You must be proud.'

'I am.'

'What's it about?'

'It's about Elizabeth. She's being bullied at school,' Andrew explained. He had read it once to a group of school children on a mat; the boys had shuffled and poked one another; the girls had listened, slack-mouthed. 'She's got this huge birthmark on her face. At school the kids torture her.'

Ben shuffled like the boys in Andrew's reading session and put the book back on the desk. Then he moved the butterfly from hand to hand again.

'The woman next door is a bit magic and gives Elizabeth a gift to help her through it all.'

'What is it?'

'A photograph of Elizabeth's future.'

'How does that help her?'

'*Knowing* that she'll one day be a successful dancer. The *future* is her gift.'

'And that'd just make everything okay?' asked Ben.

Andrew decided to ignore the question. 'What do you want to do with *your* future, Ben?'

'I'd like to ... no, doesn't matter.' He put the butterfly back on the desk.

'Tell me,' said Andrew.

'It's silly.' Ben raised his eyebrows in a comical way, and Andrew knew he was trying to make light of it. Then he picked up the photo of Andrew's mother. 'You look like her.'

Andrew's mother, Anne, had been an only child too. His ancestry was a string of women who, for one reason or another, by death or circumstance, ended up alone. She married George in 1963. She never conceived during the four-year marriage. Then, just before Christmas, George admitted he was gay, which was still unacceptable in that otherwise-permissive decade. They divorced. Being unmarried and childless in her early forties was as frowned upon then as being married to a gay man. When Andrew came out ten years ago, she had merely shrugged as though it was nothing.

'I look like my mum too,' said Ben, pulling Andrew out of his memory. 'Better than looking like my dad. Aunt Helen says that my eyes flash like his when I'm pissed off. Glad I'm not *like* him though ... he's...'

'What?' Andrew moved closer to Ben.

'Emmoral.' Ben's eyes flashed amber and it occurred to Andrew that he messed up his words when he was emotional. The sparks in his eyes were his true language.

'Why's he immoral?' asked Andrew gently.

'Because he's sleeping with my brother's fiancé.'

'Is he?'

'He'd sleep with anything with a pulse. Probably if it didn't, too. He was unfaithful to my mum; there were women in the house when they shouldn't have been. Kimberley, my brother's girlfriend, has an...' Andrew saw Ben's twitch at the thought '...intense relationship with him. He's old and pathetic and thinks he's some Jack the Lad.' Ben shook his head. 'Sorry. Don't know why I'm telling you all this. Let's talk about something else.' He looked around. 'I really like your flat.'

'Would you like to see the bedroom?' Andrew said.

'I would.' Andrew noticed Ben's voice break a little.

Andrew led him there. He leaned against the doorframe while Ben looked at the abstract artwork on his walls, his ornate mirror, and the stack of writing magazines on the cabinet, before finally turning to Andrew. Even then he looked at his buttons, his hair, his hands.

Taking off his T-shirt, Ben put it neatly at the end of the bed, then kissed Andrew roughly, tugging on his belt. Andrew didn't move from the doorway.

Ben stopped. 'Don't you want to?'

'Why don't we take our time,' Andrew said.

'I'm ready now.'

'But what's the rush? We're not worried your dad might come home. There's no Mr Cartwright in the garden. It's just us.' Ben looked like he thought he'd done something wrong, so Andrew reached out and touched his cheek. 'Let's fight?' He kissed him, chastely, as a sibling might another sibling.

'Fight? I'd *never* hit you.'

'No, fight *with* me.' Andrew put a hand on his own top button and said, 'Undo me slowly.'

Ben carefully freed each button from its hole.

Andrew felt his shirt fall open like curtains on a show. 'I could be a lion,' he said.

Ben traced a patient pattern of circles over his chest with two fingers.

'You could tame me,' said Andrew.

Ben bit Andrew's bottom lip, tugging it away from his teeth.

'Think you could get me to lie down?' asked Andrew.

'Oh, I think so.'

When Ben tried to manoeuvre them towards the bed. Andrew stiffened against the doorframe, resisting.

'Let me,' whispered Ben, urgent.

'Let's just kiss,' said Andrew.

'But you're not kissing – *I* am.'

'Make me,' he said.

Ben studied him, breathing hard. Andrew could see the confusion in his tiny frown.

Andrew said. 'Be rough. Like you were in the circus today.'

'Like I...?'

'When you scratched me.'

'Did I?'

Andrew turned, shrugging his shirt off his shoulders to show Ben his back.

'I didn't mean...' Ben's pupils shone, but his face creased with concern. 'There are red marks. When did I...?'

'You dug your nails in each time the whip snapped,' said Andrew.

Ben's lips parted, moisture stretching in the tiny gap. 'I hurt you?'

Andrew smiled. 'It was too intense to be pain.'

'Your bruises never fade.' Ben touched the purple discolorations on Andrew's arms and stomach. He kissed the egg-shaped mark on his arm. 'Why not?' Ben traced a damp line with his tongue, joining Andrew's bruises like a puzzle.

Andrew didn't answer because he didn't know. The slightest knock or bump and his skin darkened; the clouds of black took an age to fade these days. He knew he should see his diabetes nurse about it. But he was afraid. Of what, he wasn't entirely sure. All he knew was that it had never happened before, and that he often woke in the dark from some nightmare, with a heavy sense of foreboding.

'I wish I could heal them,' said Ben.

'You are.'

Ben unfastened Andrew's jeans. He kissed his belly button, the red needle marks, the flesh, traced a damp line along the top of his shorts, and finally kissed his open mouth.

'Bite me,' Andrew urged. He buried a hand in Ben's hair, wrapping it around a clump and tugging on it.

'I want you,' Ben said into his mouth.

'Make me then.'

Ben pushed Andrew's shoulders. He resisted. He saw Ben bring his knee up between his legs – he was going to try and throw him, like a cowboy in a barroom brawl. Anticipating the move, Andrew managed to resist. Now Ben pinned his arm behind his back. Andrew twisted against Ben's strength, trying for a kiss. Then pulled away; offering, withdrawing, offering.

'I said no,' smiled Andrew.

Ben covered Andrew's mouth with his hand and whispered *yes* then undid his own zip and wriggled out of his jeans. He looked daft trying it with one hand occupied. Andrew bit his palm, pulled free, and repeated *no*. Ben fought back harder. They tussled until their bodies glistened with damp. When they were finally joined, neither was able to resist crying out.

14

A Nothing Father

Ben was not Benjamin. He was simply Ben. And he liked that.

Andrew Fitzgerald, *The Lion Tamer Who Lost*

Much later, Andrew put a heavy arm across Ben's chest. He was feeling sleepy. Ben asked if he should stay over and Andrew barely managed to say that he could if he wanted.

'Maybe I do like the circus,' said Ben suddenly.

'Huh?'

'It's why I'm here.'

'Thought that was the pen.' Andrew looked up, awake now.

'The pen?'

'Yeah. You said if you'd not gone back for your pen, you'd have been on the train that derailed.'

'No, I meant here. Now.'

'Yes.'

'I know you think it's all that fate stuff,' said Ben. 'But if you look at it mathematically, it's far more profound. If you work out the odds of you being at that station at the exact moment I was, and then in that café too...'

'And what are they?'

'Can't be arsed to work it out.'

Ben curled up a little and after a while, Andrew was sure he'd fallen asleep. He watched him. Smiled. He had never wanted anyone to stay quite so much. Andrew had never moved in with any of his previous partners, and he often hoped they would go home after sex. This was different. And the fact that it was completely overwhelmed him.

Andrew was about go and make some toast when Ben suddenly spoke. Had he not been asleep after all? 'When did you *first* wish then?'

'I told you – when I realised it worked.'

'How's that possible?' Ben asked.

'I was ten the first time I accidentally wished.'

'Accidentally?' Ben's sleepiness seemed to rest on the y.

'Obviously it doesn't work as well when you do it accidentally,' said Andrew.

'*Obviously*.'

'I wanted this dinosaur sticker-book I'd seen in the bookshop.' Andrew could picture the cover now, grey and black with an angry Tyrannosaurus rex on the front. 'I wrote in my notepad; *I wish Mum wouldn't be a mean old witch and would get me it, just for once*.'

'And did she?'

'Yes,' Andrew said. 'When I asked for it.'

Ben laughed and said it didn't count. 'You *asked* for it.'

'Ah, but she never usually got me anything I asked for.'

'Doesn't count.' Ben sighed. Andrew felt his breath against his skin. 'Go to sleep.'

'I'm not tired now. It taught me to wish properly though. Like I was going to wish for a bigger family – then I realised this was unlikely with a mother in her fifties.' Andrew paused. 'I wanted to be part of a family like the one next door. What *were* they called? Wish I could remember.' He glanced at Ben. 'There's a wish I made that's still in the box,' he said.

'Why is it still...?' Ben sounded sleepy.

'Because it never came true. I keep the ones that haven't. Still hoping, I guess.'

Andrew waited for a tired 'so what wish didn't come true?' but realised Ben was now really asleep.

Andrew felt alert though. Most evenings of late he fell asleep at the computer, waking with a stiff neck and a half-written word on the screen. It wasn't like him. Normally he could write long past midnight. Tonight, for the first time in weeks, he buzzed. Ben made him feel more alive than he had in years.

Andrew got up, careful not to wake Ben, made toast and took it back to bed.

'Mrs Robinson,' he whispered halfway through his third bite.

That had been his childhood neighbours' name. The Robinsons had been Andrew's ideal household. What he liked best was their arguments. He would put a glass to the wall and listen to the *But I had it first* and the *Play nicely or you'll get what-for*. Andrew's home was utterly quiet; the silence deafened him.

When Andrew asked about his father, his mother Anne always said, 'He was nobody; it was *nothing*.' Andrew asked and asked and asked. In his head, he gave this *nothing* father a name: Mr Bucket, after Charlie's dad in *Charlie and The Chocolate Factory*.

Ben stirred. Andrew stopped eating, watched, but he didn't wake.

Two years ago, Andrew's mother had finally told the truth.

She'd described how he was born of a four-hour affair with a man half her age. A man who made her feel young and alive again, if only for a moment. She had been forty-three; he had been the grandson of a patient in the care home where she worked. While on a cigarette break out the back of the home – crying over *nothing,* she said – he had asked if she had a ciggie to spare. She hadn't and so they had shared hers. He was in Anne's bed within two hours.

She didn't share the intimate details with Andrew but there was a wistfulness in her eyes when she said he had blown smoke rings and had loved her hair. Despite taking her telephone number and promising to call, the man never did. Andrew was the surprise eight-and-a-half months later. He was an extra burden for a spinster; she was a single parent at forty-four.

Anne passed away in her sleep, just weeks after sharing these details, without ever telling Andrew the name of his young, mysterious, cigarette-smoking father. He wondered if she even knew it. She had said she was worried that Andrew had paid the price for their wildness with his curse.

His curse, she called his diabetes; but Andrew always called it *just life*.

He finished his toast and put the plate on the cabinet.

Thinking about his mother, and his *nobody* father, made him melancholy so Andrew thought about the Robinson boys next door: Harry and Sam and Tom. Sam was Andrew's favourite. He knew how to fight. Andrew's mother didn't like him to fight. 'You'll have a hypo,' she always said. 'You'll fall and hurt yourself. You should do *nice* quiet things.'

Ben moved. Spoke again. 'You know I said earlier...'

'What?' asked Andrew gently, glad he was awake again.

'I said it was silly ... what I want to do...'

'Yes?'

'Well ... I want to go to Zimbabwe.'

Andrew waited for Ben to go on.

'When I was a kid,' he said, sighing sleepily, 'I watched this documentary about a lion sanctuary. I can still see dead vividly the closing shot of these two lions walking off into the sunset at the end. I told my mum I wouldn't go to the circus anymore. Told her I'd rather go to Africa and help set them free.'

Ben paused, for so long that Andrew thought he had drifted off again.

'The day before she died she pulled me close and whispered, "Go and free the lions, Ben, promise me!"'

'So are you going to go?'

'Yes.'

Andrew's heart contracted at the idea of Ben going anywhere. 'When?'

'Maybe soon.'

'What about university?' asked Andrew.

'I only bloody went because my dad went on about it. I wanted to make him think I was good at something. But it doesn't make me feel the way it does when I think about going and being with lions.' Ben paused. 'Would you come with me?'

'I don't know.'

'You don't know?'

'Well, I've not thought about it,' admitted Andrew.

The idea of going anywhere with Ben thrilled him though.

'It doesn't matter. I probably won't go. I'll just tear up the application form I got. My dad would just take the piss anyway.'

Moments later Ben was asleep again. Andrew turned off the lamp and closed his eyes. Ben snored sporadically. Soon the buzz of outside traffic died. Andrew slid further into the warmth of the bed and fell asleep.

He dreamed of the circus. A lion with bloody gums and patchy fur ambled into the ring. The little boy, Ben, from the book he was currently writing, sat on one of the stools. Andrew wanted to warn him of the danger. But Book Ben whispered, *He won't hurt me. I'm ill, you see. I'm injured. He knows this. He knows I've already lost.*

Andrew woke with a start. In the darkness, he smiled. He had a name. A name for his current as-yet-untitled book.

The Lion Tamer Who Lost.

Happy, Andrew fell back asleep.

15

The House of Things that Don't Belong Together

> *When he wasn't lion taming, Ben envied those who felt pain. He poked his useless legs with chess pieces and cried. But not because it hurt; because it didn't.*
>
> Andrew Fitzgerald, *The Lion Tamer Who Lost*

A week after their first night at Andrew's flat, Ben said brusquely, 'Since you keep saying you've always wanted a bigger family I reckon I've got the best deterrental to such a stupid wish: come and meet my dad.'

'What?' Andrew was too stunned to mention his mis-word. 'Come to your house when he's *there*?'

'Yeah,' said Ben.

'You're absolutely sure?' Andrew asked.

'No, but what the hell.' Ben paused. 'Come for Sunday dinner. See what an arsehole he is. I'll say you're just a mate from uni so you don't get fed much. My mate Brandon's been. They got on like a house on fire.'

'If you're really sure?'

'Shit, I'm not, but come anyway.'

Andrew had no idea what had brought this on. Then he remembered his recent wish. Ben would probably mock it if he told him.

On Sunday morning Andrew dressed smartly in a blue shirt. His head hurt, and he wasn't sure if it was nerves or exhaustion. He had fallen asleep at his desk again last night and woken in pain, his neck twisted. His blood sugars had crashed, and it took two cans of Coke and a cereal bar just to stop his hands shaking. He wondered again if he should make sure everything was okay; that maybe something else was causing these lows. They certainly had been happening a lot.

He bought a bottle of red wine on the way to Ben's house. When he knocked on the front door a crude voice inside yelled, 'Come around the bloody back.'

He found Ben at the back door. He ushered him into a steamy kitchen that had seen better days. Will was taking a too-crisp beef joint out of the oven, cigarette behind his ear, and feet bare.

Ben pushed his dad aside and shunted Andrew straight into the living room.

'He's doing my head in,' said Ben.

'I haven't even said hello to him,' said Andrew. 'He'll think I'm rude.'

'He won't give a crap.'

'The table looks nice,' said Andrew, trying for something calming.

Set for the three of them, the table provided mismatched plates and glasses and mugs in a cosy triangle. One plate had a flock of nine birds soaring over a moor; another was red and cracked; another floral green. None of the chairs matched either. The house was full of things that didn't seem to belong together. Andrew couldn't help but like it; the warm lived-in feel, the shabbiness.

'I secretly gave us the only identical forks,' whispered Ben, touching Andrew's hand and quickly moving away when the kitchen door opened.

Will came through with the joint.

'I'll open this then,' he said, taking Andrew's bottle.

'Great.'

Andrew could see that Will must have been attractive in his younger days. There was still a virility about him, even with his faded clothes and greying hair.

'Fuck knows why Ben set the table,' he said. 'We usually have it on our knees.'

'I thought we could be civilised,' sighed Ben.

While his dad was in the kitchen, he shook his head and apologised.

'No need,' said Andrew. 'This is fun.'

'Trust me – it won't be. I should *never* have bloody invited you.'

Will returned with three glasses of wine, his own the fullest. 'Sit,' he said. 'I'll carve the meat. You're not a vegetarian or owt, are you? I know what you bloody students are like.'

'I'll eat anything.' Andrew sat and got out his diabetes pouch. 'Just got to read my blood first, if that's okay?'

Will sat and swigged half his wine in one gulp. 'I don't care if you bloody shoot up.' He wiped his mouth with his sleeve. 'Ben said you're doing creative writing. Isn't that a bit gay for a man?'

Andrew squeezed a drop of blood from his fingertip. 'I *am* gay,' he said. 'So I guess I'm doing the right course.'

Ben glared at him. Andrew glared back. He might not want to be honest about it, but Andrew would not hide it. Will swigged more wine and started on his meat without further comment. Andrew read his machine display – he was 3.5, so it was a good job he was about to eat.

They ate in silence, until a creaking sound disturbed them. Ben looked towards the kitchen. The door opened, and a pretty, young girl came in, pregnancy stretching a polyester T-shirt into a balloon. She had bloated fingers, cheeks, and ankles, and hair stripped of shine, as though the baby had sucked it away.

'Kim,' said Will, his face lighting up.

'I didn't know you had company,' she said.

'This is my brother's fiancé, Kimberley,' Ben said pointedly.

She pulled out the chair next to Ben and lowered herself weightily into it. 'I'm starving; it all smells so good.'

'The smell's deceptive,' said Ben.

Andrew knew Ben had counted the twenty-nine under-cooked peas swimming in gravy on his plate next to a half-lump of mashed potato and four slices of beef. He had watched him. Their eyes had met for a split second, Ben's ablaze with a million things.

'Don't be rude, lad,' said Will. 'There's still a bit of meat and some roasties, Kim, if you like. Grab a knife and fork.' He waved his arm and said dramatically, 'Kim, this is Ben's *gay* friend from uni – Andrew.'

Andrew found himself merely amused. Somehow he couldn't be insulted by Will.

'Hi,' she smiled.

'You must be excited about the baby,' he said.

Kimberley grumbled that her back was killing her, said she had been getting shit-awful cramps all night, and she was going to have every drug on the planet when she went into labour.

'Ben, get the girl some food would you,' said Will.

'I'm eating.' Ben lifted his fork and shoved three peas with force into his mouth.

'Don't mind him, Kim. He's pissing off to bloody Africa anyway.' Will poured more wine. 'Reckons he might give up university and bugger off to Zimbabwe or some-bloody-where.' He glanced at Andrew. 'Christ, is *he* going with you?'

Andrew was surprised Ben had mentioned it to his dad after what he'd said the other night.

'Why would you go to a place like that?' Kim patted her tummy.

'It's just something I was talking about *maybe* doing,' Ben said.

Andrew could tell he was upset. Under the table, he touched his knee to comfort him, but Ben didn't look at him.

'Do I know you from somewhere?' Will said, opening another bottle of wine with a rude pop. 'I don't know many shirt-lifters, but I feel like I recognise you?'

Andrew shrugged. 'Doubt we hang out in the same places.'

'You're bloody right about that.'

'You don't know him from *anywhere*,' said Ben.

'Don't let him take you to any of those gay bars, lad. He might turn you.' Will laughed. 'Let that Jodie Cartwright keep you straight!'

'If he *was* gay,' said Andrew, holding Will's gaze, 'nothing would keep him straight.'

Ben glared across the table.

'Anyway, Ben's going to save all the world's animals.' Will went into the kitchen and came back with the last bit of gravy. 'It doesn't matter that he's a third of a way through an education *I've* mostly paid for. I grafted as a brickie for years to have a good pension and savings, and he's bleeding me dry.'

'I *love* animals.' Kimberley took a pea from Ben's plate and ate it. 'Used to want to be a vet as a kiddie but I'm allergic to cats.'

Ben dropped his fork onto the plate. 'You're always telling me I've got no gumption,' he said. 'Always saying Mike's the only one who's ever known where he was going in life. I only told you about it to shut you up. I knew you'd take the piss.'

Andrew felt his pain. He picked at his peas. It was hard when he had no appetite yet had to eat to get his blood sugars up again.

Kimberley tucked heartily into a second portion of food, pausing only to grimace and say, 'There goes another!'

Andrew frowned at her.

'Tummy twinge' she said.

'Who do you think's gonna pay for Africa?' Will asked, arms crossed.

'I'm not definitely going,' said Ben. 'I only mentioned it cos of you saying I'm epathetic about my life.'

'*Apathetic*, lad,' said Will.

'Anyway, I could get sponsored.'

'He should do what he feels like doing,' said Andrew.

His nine-bird-bedecked plate was still half-full of food.

'Who asked *you*?' Will took a cigarette pack out of his pocket and lit one.

'For God's sake, Dad.'

'Was it your idea that he goes? You writerly types are a bit artsy fartsy.'

Andrew looked at the cigarette pointing at him.

'How's your mate Brandon, Ben? Liked him. A proper lad's lad.'

'It was *my* idea,' snapped Ben.

'You're a writer?' said Kimberley to Andrew.

Andrew told Kimberley he wrote children's books.

'What are you writing now?'

Andrew described *The Lion Tamer Who Lost* and Ben's attempts to walk again after a car accident that had killed his parents. Though his legs were useless he found that from his wheelchair he could do things normal people couldn't. Lions came to his room at night because he didn't hurt them like other humans did.

Will flicked ash into a saucer. 'So you're writing about animals, Ben wants to go to Africa, and yet you didn't put the idea in his head?'

'Dad, drop it.' Ben pushed his plate into the middle of the table. 'I *can* think for myself. I only sent for the application form out of curiosity. Haven't even filled it in or anything. Mike's in Afghanistan and you think *that's* great.'

'Mike's doing something for his country, lad,' Will barked. 'You're talking about going to some backwards country to prance about with lions instead of getting a degree. Probably get malaria or AIDS.'

'Ooh!' Kimberley clutched her tummy and bent over.

'Are you okay?' Andrew started to get up.

Kimberley panted. 'Just Braxton-Hicks contractions.' She stood. 'I'll walk up the garden … makes it stop a bit…'

'Come on, lass.' Will stood too, hooking his arm through hers. 'I'll walk with you.'

They waddled into the kitchen and the garden beyond, Kimberley resting her head on Will's shoulder.

'When's her baby due?' Andrew asked when they had disappeared up the path.

'Soon.' Ben closed the door.

'Sure it's only these Braxton-Hicks things?'

Ben shrugged and said his father could deal with it.

Andrew whispered, 'Do you really think she's sleeping with your dad? Seems to me he's just being fatherly. Her fiancé is away, and it must be tough being pregnant alone.' He thought of his own mother.

'I've seen her leaving the house when I come back from the shop, kissing Will on the mouth. They often whisper in the kitchen. Anyway, I don't want to talk about *them*.' Ben exhaled hard. 'Why the fuck did you tell him you're gay?'

'Did I say I wouldn't?'

'No, but ... he's gonna wonder about *me*.'

'No, he won't.'

'He *will*.'

'Would that be so bad? I genuinely don't get why you're making such a big deal out of it?'

Ben shook his head. 'You don't have a dad like him.'

'No, I don't.'

Ben appeared to realise what he had said. 'Look, I'm sorry about how he spoke to you.'

'Don't be. It was fun being here. Being part of a bickering family.'

'But you see why I can't tell him?'

'I *can't*,' said Andrew. 'Yeah, he's a bigot, but his generation often are. He'll love you, *whatever*. He was crude, but he didn't tell me to leave. I like him. Can't help it.'

'He'd disown me,' said Ben.

'You don't know that for sure. And why do you care?'

'I *do* know for sure. One of his brothers – Jerry – came out, years ago. My dad never spoke to him again.' Ben paused. 'Then ten years ago he hung himself.'

'Jesus,' whispered Andrew. 'Poor guy.'

'I know. Dad never mentions his name. Never. So I don't. You think he's gonna be fine with his own son? Seriously? And I *do* care. He's a dick but still...' Ben exhaled. 'And besides...'

'What?' asked Andrew, trying to make his tone gentle.

'I promised my mum I'd make him happy.'

'At the expense of your own happiness?'

Andrew leaned in to kiss Ben, but he pushed him away. 'Not here.'

Will came back into the living room alone.

'Where's Kimberley?' asked Ben.

'In the toilet – she feels sick.'

Andrew looked towards the bathroom door. 'Maybe you should check her?'

Will resumed his seat. 'You go check – *you're* the feminine type. Door's on the left.'

Andrew went into the kitchen and knocked on the bathroom door. He could hear Kimberley groaning and panting, so much that she didn't answer when he asked how she was. Suddenly, as he turned to go back to the living room, he felt dizzy. When his sugar levels plummeted, he would feel disorientated. He held onto the nearby work surface. Surely his numbers couldn't have crashed again? What the hell was going on?

Ben appeared. He was fuzzy at the edges.

'Drink some Coke,' he said urgently.

Andrew could hardly respond. He saw Ben rummaging in his satchel, finding the bottle and bringing it to his lips; like magic, his vision returned. He unwrapped a cereal bar and ate while talking. 'Kimberley sounds like she's in pain.'

As though to prove it, a hearty grunt came from the bathroom.

'I can't go in there.' Will called from the living room. 'It's women's stuff. We should get the girl to a hospital.'

'He's had too much alcohol to drive her,' said Ben.

Andrew never drove; he had been told at his last appointment with the diabetes nurse that while he was having so many hypos he might pass out at the wheel. He knew Ben hadn't even had lessons yet.

'We'd better call an ambulance,' Andrew said.

Another cry from the bathroom compelled them to act fast. Will picked up the phone; Ben asked what they might need; Andrew said maybe towels. They knocked again on the bathroom door.

'Come in,' gasped Kimberley.

Lodged on the floor between toilet and bath, huffing and puffing, legs splayed, she said, 'It's right there. I can feel it.' She had pulled off her underwear and hiked up the roomy skirt.

Seeing how cold the tiled floor looked, Andrew helped Kimberley up and slid the threadbare mat beneath her. 'Breathe,' he said, trying to hide his fear. 'Just breathe.'

'We've called an ambulance,' said Ben.

Andrew had no clue what came next; he tried to remember all those hospital dramas he'd watched.

Will's arm reached around the door with warm towels from the airing cupboard, and Ben placed them near Kimberley. Andrew rubbed her feet.

'It's not gonna wait!' shrieked Kimberley, eyes wild. 'I need to push!'

Will called from the other side of the door that the ambulance was ten minutes away.

'Can't ... wait ... ten ... minutes!' grunted Kimberley.

'What do we *do*?' Ben asked Andrew.

'Just help,' said Andrew, trying to stay calm.

With no clue what he was looking for, Andrew peered between Kimberley's legs at the angry, stretched skin, the glimpse of fluffy hair differing in colour to that surrounding it. 'I think you're supposed to push on a contraction, so when you're in pain, just go for it.'

'Oh, God,' moaned Kimberley, chin on her chest. 'Here it comes...' She bore down, face crimson; the child's skull grew bigger within the circle of its mother's opening, but then retreated as Kimberley surrendered with a scream.

'Keep pushing,' urged Andrew.

On the wave of Kimberley's next tightening, in a rush of stained liquid and mucus, a head popped out, followed by a slimy body that Andrew caught in a towel. He was stunned. Moved and stunned.

'Is it okay?' Kimberley lolled about as limp as cooked spaghetti.

Andrew rubbed the baby gently.

'Why isn't it crying?' Kimberley tried to reach out.

Will tapped on the door asking why things were so quiet. As though to answer, the baby screamed. Andrew laughed; Kimberley laughed.

'What is it?' asked Kimberley.

'You should see.'

Andrew watched Kimberley open the towel and smile and whisper, 'Hello little girl – so you're the one who's been kicking me all this time.'

All Andrew could see when he handed the child over was blood staining Kim's skirt and the towels, and he thought, *Blood gets everywhere*. Blood means birth, it means life, it means death, and it means hurt. He saw his own every day.

'Should we cut the cord?' said Andrew.

'Leave it for the paramedics to do,' said Ben.

'She's Lola Heidi after your mum, Ben,' said Kimberley.

Will appeared in the doorway now, smoked cocktail glass in hand. Kimberley beckoned, and he leaned over to look at the bundle. Will trembled. He said that there had been no girls born in the family for a long time, the last being his sister who was now seventy.

'My mum's youngest sister is only fifty-four,' said Ben, clearly irritated.

'Still, it's a long time.'

Andrew had never seen a thing that was moments old, so much ahead, so little past. Never again would she be five minutes old. Already she was defined by numbers.

Ben walked out. Andrew followed and joined him at the window in the front room. Ambulance sirens wailed.

'That was pretty overwhelming,' Andrew said, trembling again. 'I just delivered a baby. A *baby*.'

The sirens grew louder. They looked for the ambulance. Eventually Ben said, 'You delivered my sister.'

Andrew insisted he was muddled up, that he was excited and not thinking quite right, and she was his *niece*, Mike's daughter.

'No, Andrew, trust me.' Ben looked at him. 'I have a *sister*.'

16

Nothing

When Ben was a baby, and had kicked the cot mobile onto the carpet, Grandad would come in, take off his blue slippers and put them on Ben's feet. They were too big and made him look like a clown.

Andrew Fitzgerald, *The Lion Tamer Who Lost*

Once Kimberley and her new daughter had been taken to the hospital with Will – who argued that as the grandad he should go – Andrew and Ben washed the mismatched plates and put them in the cupboards.

Feeling sure his blood sugars were low yet again, Andrew asked Ben if they had any Coke as he had drunk all of his. There was only weeks-old lemonade in the fridge. He made do, sipping as they tidied up. Andrew watched Ben rub the nine-birded plate until it squeaked and decided not to bring up Lola's parentage again unless he did.

Ben suddenly stopped and said, 'Do *you* want kids?'

'I don't know.'

'You must know,' said Ben.

'Why must I?' Andrew frowned. The lemonade was not having the same brisk affect as Coke did and he felt crabby.

'You're nearly forty.' Ben looked at Andrew, quickly adding, 'I'm not saying that's *old*, but you must know by now.'

'My mother was forty-four when she had me and never thought it would happen.'

'Exactly. Never say never.'

'She also said the fling that resulted in me was *nothing*,' said Andrew.

Nothing had baffled him as a kid. *Nothing* filled the room when Andrew's mother worked sixteen-hour shifts and he talked both sides of a conversation. Working in a care home, where she tirelessly toiled until retirement, she often said to him that she felt as old as those she catheterised. *I have nothing*, she would say.

'If we had a child, it would be *everything*.' Ben's eyes were serious.

'You're only twenty-two,' snapped Andrew. 'And you reckon you're going to Africa.'

'Are you okay? You look so pale.'

Andrew slammed the cupboard and looked outside. The room grew dark, but the sun hadn't gone, and the garden's shadows were not yet long. A brown moth bounced off the window as though drunk.

'I'm fine,' he mumbled.

But he didn't feel it.

Though he had never worried about his age, now he imagined a clock ticking past important moments faster than he could enjoy them.

This isn't nothing, it ticked.

'It's different for women.' Ben was stacking cups on the counter.

'How?'

'Women have a biological clock,' said Ben. 'I'm only asking cos of Lola. It makes you think, doesn't it?'

The brown moth gave up its dizzy dance and fluttered away.

Andrew finished his lemonade and dropped the glass into the washing up bowl. 'Do *you* want them then?' he said. When the glass sank into the bubbles he realised his vision had blurred again.

This isn't nothing, ticked the clock.

'I think one day, but not yet.' Ben was wrapping the tea towel about his wrist like a bandage, undoing it and then looping it again. 'That was incredible what Kim did. One minute she's pregnant and the next there's a living person. It won't be easy for us though, will it? I think I want one.'

'*One*?' asked Andrew. He went to the back door, needing air on his damp face. His heart was beating terrifyingly fast.

Ben approached him. 'We've only known each other two months, haven't we?'

'I'd never have *one*.' Andrew opened and closed the door like a fan, his gold fringe rising and falling.

'I get it, you *don't* want children.'

'No, I'd never have *one*. Do you have any idea what it's like to be *one* child?' Ben shook his head. 'Playing Scrabble on your own, making up the words for two people, playing cards against yourself. Getting a see-saw at Christmas that you can't use unless you have a friend over.'

Andrew's head swam.

This isn't nothing, ticked the clock.

'Are you okay?' Ben joined him at the door and they stood in the light for a moment before Andrew shook him off and returned to the sink.

'I'm fine! *You* brought up kids and dads and who they are!'

'I just feel for Mike not seeing Lola's birth – what he doesn't know. I'm sure my dad is that baby's blood father.'

'Going around saying it could fucking ruin lives,' said Andrew.

'Are you sure you're okay?'

'No! Stop asking me! I feel *shit*!' Andrew breathed hard. Held onto the table. 'I think I should test my blood again. Can you...'

He gestured at his bag for the blood meter, but when Ben had found it, Andrew saw he had run out of test strips. He started looking in cupboards, not sure what for. Everything was hazy. Words came out of him, words he knew barely made sense. Ben took his hands, stopping him pulling all the tinned mackerel off the shelf. He slumped against the doorframe.

'You need more sugar. Sit down. Stop moving about.'

'When a father doesn't stick around,' said Andrew, sitting on a chair, knowing he was babbling, 'when he barely appears long enough to impart that necessary essence of himself, he leaves a gap that is profound.'

'I know,' said Ben gently, kneeling at his feet. 'I know. We can talk soon, but now you have to eat this, *please*.' He held something out. His face was too close and elongated, like a ghostly mask. But his eyes were kind. His eyes. His golden eyes.

'I love your eyes,' said Andrew.

'I know. Eat this.'

This isn't nothing, ticked the clock.

Andrew reached for what Ben was holding out and it broke the fuzzy cloud. He could not get hold of it. He felt Ben open his mouth and try to force it in. He was talking but Andrew couldn't even hear him now.

This isn't nothing.

No, this was definitely something.

Something was very wrong.

Andrew feared that if he closed his eyes Ben would disappear forever. That he would never come around, never see his gorgeous face again. So he struggled hard to keep his heavy eyelids open. Or maybe he was scared that *he* would disappear, like when children play hide-and-seek and think they are invisible if they cover their eyes. Andrew didn't want to disappear forever – become *nothing* – but the dark dropped on top of the light, until there was only black.

PART THREE

BEN

17

ZIMBABWE

Something Must Die So Something Can Live

Ben knew he could never hunt. He did not truly have a lion's heart.
Andrew Fitzgerald, *The Lion Tamer Who Lost*

There comes a morning in Zimbabwe when even the sky's glorious flames don't lift Ben's spirits. When his sunrise, his land, his refuge does not comfort. It is early. Earlier than usual. He has been awake since it was dark. Isn't sure if he even slept at all. He wishes there was a chair for him to sit on outside the hut. Instead, Ben grasps the wooden railing and breathes deeply, tries to let the dawn infuse him with its usual calm.

Today, it is as if Andrew is with him. As if he can smell him, the soap he used, the deodorant he wore. The memories are flooding back now. Ben tried only to let in the good ones but doing that seems to have unlatched a door and let them all in.

Now Ben sees vividly the moment Andrew collapsed in their kitchen. Remembers the strange things he muttered before passing out on the lino at his feet. Ben injected him with his emergency glucagon pen, hands wobbling. It didn't work; he remained out cold. So Ben called an ambulance. It took an age to come; maybe it was minutes, but it felt like forever.

Ben thinks he should call Andrew today. He wishes for the first time that he hadn't thrown his phone away in England. He will use the communal phone here. It doesn't matter if Andrew hangs up or ignores him. No matter what happened, he has to make sure he is okay.

How could he not have done before now?

'Christ, Roberts, now you're talking to yourself when you're awake.'

Ben starts. It is Simon; he hasn't even heard him emerge.

'I was jus...' Ben can't think of anything.

Simon slaps him on the back. 'I'd have thought hooking up with someone like Esther you'd be *less* restless. I'd sure as hell sleep better if I spent an evening with her!'

'Don't talk about her like that,' says Ben.

'Only teasing. You ready?'

'For what?'

'The hunt?'

Ben had forgotten. Tonight Lucy will hunt for the first time, and he is going along.

'I'm coming too,' says Simon. 'Wouldn't miss it for the world. A gang of lionesses savaging something – *I'll* be there.'

Ben spends the rest of the day avoiding everyone, even Esther.

At nine o'clock, against a sunset waving on the horizon like the legs of an orange octopus, a now-eight-month-old Lucy heads out on her first hunt. Standing in the back of a dirt-covered truck with Stig, Simon and two other volunteers, Ben watches his young protégé lead the other lionesses.

Having bonded with a placid creature called Aurora and hot-headed Sheba, Lucy now asserts her innate leadership and takes the group towards a herd of impala gathered to relax by some smooth-barked fever trees. Nothing is more draining than sunshine when your fur is like a great winter coat and you must run at forty miles an hour to catch your dinner, so lionesses do most of their hunting at sunset when the temperature falls and the small animals grow sleepy, and at night where in the dark they can more easily approach their prey.

The group in the truck have two pairs of binoculars to pass around, but Ben isn't sure he wants to see a kill in close-up. Instead he views the action with the safety of distance.

'I almost feel like I should warn the impala,' he whispers to Simon.

'Better bloody not,' says Simon. 'Lucy might turn on *you* for dinner! Anyway, whose side are you on? Don't you want her to succeed?'

'I do ... but...' Ben feels helpless.

'Nature is brutal,' says Stig. 'Something must die so something can live.'

Fucking shut up, thinks Ben.

'I know,' he says.

One lioness always leads the hunt, often a mother, but there is no parent here. Aurora and Sheba prepare to attack from the side, unspoken agreements made before the quest. Lucy crouches low, camouflaged by long grass, and approaches the group of impala slowly. Her companions are some metres behind. She will know she must get close before charging; impala can run fast, and for much longer than a lion. If they get a good lead, there will be no meal tonight. However, if an animal spots a predator and stays very still, he might survive; a lioness's sense of smell is stronger than her sight or hearing.

But these antelopes are not still; they graze and shuffle and kick in the dying light. They are joyfully unaware of approaching danger. Ben feels sick for them. He loves Lucy but fears for the beautiful creatures she wants to rip apart. A very young antelope frolics about the legs of a bigger one, his tan and white tail swishing. Black patches above his feet look like socks. Ben wishes he would stop the dance. Save himself. Run while he can. Escape the inevitable.

But sometimes you can't.

Ben knows this more than anyone.

'Lucy's bloody ace,' Simon whispers to him. 'Look at her. You'd not think it was her first hunt. She'll have no trouble in the wild, mate.'

Ben should be happy; his cub is doing what she is supposed to, what will let her be free.

'She's definitely a leader,' says Stig. 'Look how the other two follow her, as slow as she is, trusting her totally.'

Engine throbbing quietly, the truck remains at a distance. The little black-socked antelope still leaps about.

Run, you fool, Ben thinks when Lucy is only feet away from the herd. *Run, and you might escape. How can you not sense her?*

'There she goes,' whispers Stig, the awe obvious in his voice.

Ben watches through his fingers, breath held, still refusing the binoculars. The lionesses attack. The impala don't stand a chance. In a flurry of panic, they leap about, hoping to confuse their foes, some jumping so high they look as though they have springs on their hooves. A few have the sense to escape, to run off into the grass. The black-socked antelope runs.

But Lucy runs too.

Her coat ripples like a golden sea. Her legs are fired by the heat of hunger and glisten with damp exertion. She leaps at the little antelope. It happens for Ben in slow motion. At first the attack looks like a loving embrace. Lucy wraps her front paws about the creature's neck and brings him roughly to the ground. She bites into his neck and crushes his windpipe. The antelope struggles – but not for long. The tussle is a desperate battle, and the small creature fights valiantly to survive. It is not that a lioness wants life more, or that she is the better animal, but she knows what she can have. Blood stains Lucy's jaws, the ground, and her paws.

And she looks utterly beautiful.

'Wow,' breathes Simon, almost speechless for once.

'I know,' says Stig.

Ben once read a theory that lions project calming thoughts into their prey, lessening their suffering as they die. If Lucy does this with her kill, the little impala gives no clue. He seems to succumb in misery. Though from this distance Ben cannot see his eyes, he imagines they flash with amber agony.

Simon nudges Ben, again offers him the binoculars.

'No thanks,' he says. 'It's horrible enough from this distance.'

Afterwards, the three cats lie down separate from each other, a preferred position to eat, and tear flesh from the stomachs of their prey, swallowing without chewing. The lucky antelopes who escaped death are long gone. The sun dies altogether. Blackness snuffs out the light.

The day is over.

'Dinner is served,' says Simon, grinning. 'Nice table manners.'

Ben ignores him.

After allowing the group sufficient time to eat, the truck then guides the lionesses back to the enclosure, and with some sadness Ben watches Lucy return to the rest of her pride. To her brother. She has found a way to have it all: her co-hunting lionesses, her sibling, and one day – no doubt – a mate. A lioness is the only feline who will mate for life. She will have to fight for him though, prove her worth by attacking and intimidating other females. But then he will accept her forever.

'Coming for a beer?' Simon asks Ben.

'No. I need to find Esther.'

'Lucky you.' Simon chuckles crudely. 'I'm all fired up by today and got no one to let steam off with.'

Ben ignores him and goes to find the woman who keeps him sane.

18

ZIMBABWE

A Hello So Very Far Away

> *The first time Ben met custard-haired Nancy, she was carrying a box of coloured rags. 'We're going to make elephants,' she said. 'In those colours?' asked Ben. 'Don't you think checked, spotted and multi-coloured elephants are the best?' she asked him. After that, he always did.*
>
> Andrew Fitzgerald, *The Lion Tamer Who Lost*

Ben finds Esther in the communal area.

In the month since the eclipse, they have been together. This relationship should be his hardest, being sexually the least natural, but in some strange way it has been easy. Ben has spent most of his life until now denying what he most wants. And then the man he finally met and wanted more than anything else is the one he can never have. If he remains with Esther, it will be simple. He will never love her so much that it's agony if she leaves him. He will never get so attached to her that her departure kills him. Never live in fear of losing her.

He is safe.

And she is fun. Even if he is not driven by physical desire for her, he loves being with her. They talk for hours, laugh at similar things, and she is intelligent and fires his mind with her sharp observations. She stimulates his brain if not his body.

She is waiting for him by the coffee machine, reading her journal.

As Ben approaches, she is unaware. He is the lioness; she is the impala. For a moment, he feels queasy.

Should he just tell her the truth *now*?

But he still can't say those three simple words.

So he sits next to her.

'How did it go?' She smiles and kisses his mouth warmly.

She always instigates any affection, leads into sex with a caress or a crude suggestion. Ben follows, never says no. He misses the fight; the *yes* and *no* game that he and Andrew so loved. They used to play it often, switching roles. It was dangerous, but they understood its power, and had a code word for when *no* really meant *no*. But the rest of the time *no* had meant *make me*. *No* had meant *I'm scared how intense this is*. *No* had meant *I trust you*.

Ben doesn't want to play it anymore. With anyone.

'She killed,' he says, not as excited as he had imagined he might be.

'Wow. On her first hunt.'

He nods. 'A small impala.'

'She is quite something.'

'She is.'

'What's wrong?' Esther speaks gently.

'It was brutal,' Ben admits. 'I knew it would be. But to see it ... so bloody vicious.'

'I love how sensitive you are,' she grins.

'Not really.'

'It's a good thing. I wasn't criticising.' Then after a moment Esther says, 'Let's go back to mine.'

As they depart, Ben spots a pile of new postcards on the side. Different ones arrive each week and they are free to the volunteers. One is a beauty. It's a picture of two lions next to a tree, side-by-side, manes thick and healthy, fur glossy and sunlit. He takes one.

'Aren't they gorgeous,' says Esther. 'The best ones yet. I sent one to my brother.'

'Maybe I'll send one to...' Ben hesitates.

'Your dad?' suggests Esther.

Ben will never be able to tell Esther the full truth about what his dad has done.

'Maybe to him.'

'A fling with your brother's fiancé is horrible, it really is,' she says.

Ben still feels sick about it. He has told Esther some of the details, if only so that she doesn't keep asking what it is that happened back home that makes him wake up in the night, covered in sweat. When they share a bed, she comforts him, begs him to tell her why he is so restless.

'Do you still love your ex-girlfriend?' she asked him one night.

'No, it isn't that. I'm getting over that,' he lied.

Then he told her it was his dad's infidelity with Kimberley, how it ripped the family apart.

'I'm really not trying to gloss over it,' continues Esther now. 'But I bet your dad would still like to know that you're okay here. Have you written to him at all? Called him?'

'No,' admits Ben.

'Do you think you should?'

'Stop hassling me about it.'

'Okay, okay.' She looks hurt.

'Sorry.'

Perhaps to appease her, he puts a postcard in his pocket and they head to her hut. In its privacy, she slowly undresses him, peeling off jeans and socks and shorts without a word.

'Let's turn off the lights,' he says, as always.

In the blackness, he can pretend Esther's skin is that of a sweetly fragranced man. Her face that of a well-shaved male lover; her hands small and patient versions of Andrew's.

'Let's keep them on this time,' she says, kissing him.

Perhaps he can just close his eyes. 'Okay.'

'Undress me,' she whispers.

Ben unbuttons her blouse, unfastens her shorts. He fumbles with her bra.

'Didn't they teach you at school how to unhook one?' she laughs. 'Thought it was part of the curriculum for teenage boys.'

She undoes it herself and puts Ben's hand over one breast, kissing him urgently. He shuts his eyes and kisses her back. When she puts her hand around his penis, he waits for his body to respond. Her greedy movement and his wandering mind finally cause the desired result. She leads him to the narrow bed. Here, in the full light, he turns Esther over onto her stomach. He has to have her that way. Andrew's long-ago *no* haunts him. Fires him. He wishes now that she might say it. But this is not a game they should play. He might hurt her.

Ben suddenly sees the tiny impala bloody and limp in Lucy's death grip.

'Kiss me.' Esther looks over her shoulder. Her hair fans like a mane. He doesn't want her to talk. If he can't have the dark, he needs the quiet.

'Shhhh.' He bites her neck, hard.

She moans but doesn't speak.

Ben closes his eyes and plunges into her. Esther cries out but doesn't resist. Jodie Cartwright comes to him in a flash. A memory. A moment together. Her tears. His behaviour. Ben has always feared that what had happened the night of his brother Mike's wedding might happen again. He pushes it away. Bites Esther again. Like Lucy's kill earlier, it does not take long.

Afterwards, he collapses against Esther's sticky body. When he realises she is fidgeting, and he must be heavy, he sits up.

'Wow,' she says.

'Wow *good*?' he asks, nervous now that he was too rough.

She smiles. 'Wow good.'

Ben studies her.

'You usually treat me like I might break or something,' she says. 'Not tonight.' She pauses. 'You're such a curious man, you know. What are your secrets, Ben Roberts?'

He shrugs.

'I love you,' she says.

'Do you?' Ben doesn't mean it to come out so bluntly. 'Sorry, I didn't mean that so...'

'It's fine.' She touches his face. 'You don't have to say it to me. Now or ever. But I *had* to say it. Because I do. I think I have since you first arrived here. Even though you were such a total pain in the arse. Still are, you moody so-and-so. But I do. I love you.'

Ben feels queasy. His chest is tight.

'Are you okay?' Esther touches his forehead.

'I think … it was today. The heat. That kill. Lucy. I don't feel like myself. I feel sick. Do you mind if I go back to mine? I need to lie down.'

'Do you want me to walk with you?'

'No, I'll be fine.' Ben pulls on his jeans. 'I'm so sorry.'

'Is it what I said?' Esther looks sad.

'No. God, *no*.' He touches her face, kisses her cheek. What a good liar he is. What a terrible, terrible person.

Ben stumbles through the dark. Before heading for his hut, he drops back in at the communal area. It is deserted.

Hand shaking, he picks up the phone on the wall and dials the England code and then Andrew's home number. What is the time difference? Will he wake him? Ben can't remember; can't work it out. Andrew's voice surprises him. Soft. Warm. So very far away. Ben realises it is a recording. Just a message.

Should he leave one?

He opens his mouth, not knowing what on earth he will say. Perhaps, *I miss you*. Perhaps, *Ask me to come home*.

Ben hangs up.

Is Andrew okay? Is he asleep? Out? Ignoring him?

Or worse?

No. If it were anything worse then surely the phone would have been disconnected altogether?

Ben stands with the phone in his hand for a while. Wants to redial and hear Andrew's voice again. His heart won't stop pounding. As he replaces the receiver, he wonders if he should call his dad too? At least let him know that he is okay here?

But that is one phone call he's not ready for.

Finally, he staggers back through the dark to his hut, hoping Simon is still drinking beer around the campfire. The room is empty. Ben drops into his hammock and puts his head in his hands. Tries to push away Andrew's voice.

And now Esther loves him. She *loves* him. This is huge. He should tell her they can't be together. Is it fair to lie when she feels so strongly? But it will hurt her. He knows this, and he can't bear to.

Ben realises the postcard is still in his pocket. He takes it out, strokes the glossy lions. Then he finds a pen and bites the lid while he thinks. Finally, he prints Andrew's address on the right. On the left, he simply writes, *I saw it and thought of us*. He does. Every day.

Still.

'Something must die so something can live,' Stig said earlier.

Though it irritated him, he can't stop thinking about it. Maybe the only way to stop thinking about Andrew is to send the card, a kind of last communication before committing to Esther.

But, as he drifts off into a restless sleep, his dad haunts him.

Ben hears his voice. Hears clinking glasses. Sees a pub. A confrontation.

The two of them.

19

ENGLAND

A Suitcase Full of Truth

> *Nancy thought there was a ghost in her wardrobe, a silver woman who jangled all the coat hangers when she was trying to sleep. Only Ben believed her. He did, after all, believe in most things that adult eyes overlooked.*
>
> Andrew Fitzgerald, *The Lion Tamer Who Lost*

Ye Olde Black Boy was Will's favourite pub. Ben had brought him here to confront him. Andrew had been saying he shouldn't keep suggesting his dad had slept with Kimberley unless he knew it for certain. Though this irked Ben, he knew Andrew was right.

The pub by the river, with wood panelling and tobacco-stained fixtures, had only been updated to add space. Dusty beer bottles, period adverts, and slave-trade artefacts lined the walls, telling visitors it was proud of its history. Once a smuggling den connected to the River Hull by underground passages, and a brothel for a time, it was allegedly haunted.

'Let's sit in the back.' Will nodded to the barman. 'Wish Mike was here to celebrate Lola.'

'I don't,' said Ben, unthinkingly.

Will ordered two pints. 'You'd rather your brother was in some desert shit-hole riddled with Taliban than at home with his new baby? Can you imagine what it's like there?'

Ben doubted his dad could imagine, having never left the country for so much as a European city break. It was easier to sit with his cronies in a pub and bemoan the hardship of life, with a beer in one hand and an opinion in the other.

'I meant … Oh, it doesn't matter.' Ben shook his head.

A phone call from Mike the Friday before had emphasised Ben's need to face their dad. Against an eerie silence that belied the war he was fighting, Mike had spoken of his sadness at missing Lola's birth.

Ben told his brother the baby was beautiful and that she looked like him. Mike talked about the lads sharing one bottle of beer to celebrate his fatherhood. Ben now wondered whether he'd tell Mike the truth if their dad admitted to the affair today. Could he be the one to ruin Mike's new family? He wasn't coming home for weeks and if Ben waited to tell him in person, he would have to carry it around like an overstuffed suitcase.

Will found a table, calling 'Afternoon!' to those in the back. Ben downed half his beer in one glug. That he needed a drink to speak to his dad irritated him. Will joked that he was just like him.

Will told Brackie, an old man with a wizened face, that he was a grandad now and they were wetting the little'un's head. Ben wished Brackie would fuck off; eventually he did, joining a group arguing the policy of some local MP.

Ben remembered Andrew's suggestion: *Tell your dad the truth about us*. Was exposing what his dad had done cowardly when he could not share his own secret? Maybe. Ben stared at the frothing liquid.

Finally, he said, 'Tell me about you and Kim.'

Will was momentarily at his best, having had one drink. He wiped his mouth on the back of his sleeve. Only his eyes moved, opening and shutting. The barman loaded glasses noisily into a washer.

Will stood, bought another beer and came back.

'Dunno what you mean, lad,' he said eventually.

'You do.' Ben was fortified now. 'You can bury the truth by pouring this stuff down your neck, but I'm not stupid. I've *seen* the two of you together. Are you sleeping with her?'

'For God's sake, the girl just had a baby and you want to talk all sordid.'

'Me talking about it is more sordid than you *doing* it?' said Ben.

'You think I'd sleep with my own son's fiancé?'

'You really want me to answer that?'

The barman slammed shut the dishwasher.

'I'm celebrating the birth of my first *grandchild*.'

Will merged the remains of his drink with Ben's as though to signal come sort of unity, like blood joined in a childhood game of true brothers.

'What the hell?'

'Have it, lad,' said Will. 'Look like you need it.'

The amber frothed in Ben's glass like the eye colour that had been passed down the generations. What had that word-of-the-day on the fridge in Andrew's flat been? *Patrocliny*; the inheritance of traits from the father. Would young Lola inherit them? Would those little eyes glow? Would it be her dad's or her grandad's flame they mirrored?

Will stared at his now-empty glass.

'Look, Dad,' said Ben, not unkindly. 'I've seen you with her. I may not know women like you do, but I know when they're *yours*. I see how they look at you. And Kim is one of them. So, you can either tell me or you can *not* tell me, and my mind will make it worse.'

A group of noisy students came into the back room. On the wall above where they sat down was a poster for a ghost-hunting night.

Will looked towards the bar. Ben told him a drink would help far less than just being honest and Will's shoulders slumped, like someone had let the air out of them.

'Okay,' he said.

'Okay, what?' Ben drank the pint that swam with both of them.

'I slept with Kim.'

'How ... *when*...?'

Between glances towards the barman, Will described how Kimberley had come over one day the previous winter, with shortbread her grandmother had baked for him. She was crying because she had broken the snowglobe Mike bought her in New York. They had chosen the ornament in Macy's for their engagement, and now it was wrecked.

'When women cry, I'm mush,' Will admitted. 'Jane was crying over her dead father when we met. Frances over ... I can't remember now.'

'It was Kimberley's fault for crying?'

Will insisted it was *he* who instigated the moment. He described how she'd wept on his shoulder that the crack in the glass globe was irreparable. He'd assured her he'd find a replacement so when Mike returned it would be like it had never broken.

Will said it happened by the sink, just once.

The sink was too real; Ben had argued with him there many times. He had washed dishes while his dad smoked with their neighbour Cartwright in the garden; he had talked to his mum about Africa there; he had daydreamed there; wondered why Andrew hadn't called him there.

Kimberley had kissed Will's cheek there and when he moved, so his lips were on hers instead, she'd been startled. But not enough to stop. The warmth of comfort had boiled over into the heat of curiosity. Kimberley had let Will push up her skirt and penetrate her against the sink.

'No details, *please*,' cried Ben.

'Sorry,' Will said, miserably. 'I'm always attracted to the pureness of a new woman. Then I have her, and it dies. She's flawed – grumpy or nagging or possessive.'

'Maybe *you* damage them,' snapped Ben. 'Ever think of that?'

Will sighed, said he had. He added that Ben's mum's death had cemented her purity, that she was eternally young, forever ideal. It was all Ben could do not to snap that his dad had treated her like shit, harping on about her mis-words, belittling her.

'I didn't think,' said Will. 'There's no excuse for what we did, but in that moment the feelings were real.'

Ben drained his glass. 'What was poor Kim's flaw then?'

'What?'

'You said it dies when you find women are flawed.'

Will looked at Ben's empty glass. 'Kim is flawless. She's cheerful. She's kind – she'd give you her last penny if it was all she had. And pretty as a flower.'

'She's deceitful,' said Ben.

'Yes.' Will moved Ben's glass to the opposite side of the table, leaving a trail of moisture, like damp footprints from a shower to a bed.

'So it's over?'

Will nodded; said it hadn't gone anywhere further than the sink. Kim had cried again afterwards and begged him to let her be, saying she loved Mike, that Will had been a comfort in his absence.

'Nowt else happened,' said Will. 'She's like a daughter to me.'

'Most fathers don't sleep with their daughters,' said Ben. He braced himself for the heaviest question. 'When did she find out she was pregnant?'

Will got up and went to the bar once more. The students laughed and flicked beer mats. Will returned, drank thirstily, and said he couldn't be exactly sure when she found out she was pregnant, only that she and Mike revealed it a month or two after his and Kimberley's union.

'Lola could be yours.'

'I doubt it.' Will finished the drink. 'She and Mike have been together three years. I'm old and he's young. Who do you think more likely to be the father?'

'But the *doubt*. Doesn't a kid have a right to know who their parents are?'

'Mike is Lola's father in every way that matters,' said Will.

Ben shook his head. 'I'm supposed to carry this around?'

Will asked what else he could do; surely Ben didn't think it right to hurt Mike when there was no point. He quoted the statistic he had seen in the weekend newspaper, that thirty percent of men had not fathered their own children.

Ben hated having numbers used against him.

The barman wandered over, took away the empty glasses.

Outside, in another world, the day went on, sun high in the sky, tide low.

'I won't tell Mike,' said Ben, 'but only because *you* should.'

'Why cause pain for something that's over?'

Ben felt guilty. It was an odd emotion, difficult to deal with alongside the host of others. Was his dad right to let things go?

And wasn't Ben the biggest liar of all, hiding who he was?

'You don't think he should know that his child might be yours?' he asked.

'You've never been unfaithful?'

'No.'

Will rolled up both sleeves as though preparing for battle and said, 'Only because you've never had a relationship. What the hell's wrong with you, lad?'

'Nothing,' Ben said softly.

The regulars laughed at Brackie's joke about two parrots and an Irish man.

'You've no experience,' said Will, 'so you've no room to judge.'

'I know I'd never be as dupricitous as you.'

'It's *duplicitous*.'

'Don't correct me.' Ben flushed with anger.

Will's voice was low. 'I'm only trying to stop you telling Mike something that will hurt him. Do you want to ruin his life on the *tiny* chance the baby isn't his? She'll look like him. What's the difference?'

'One day you're going to *really* mess someone's life up.'

Ben stood. The table hit his father in the knee. A couple of the students looked up and nudged one another.

'All these years you've picked up and dumped women. Maybe I don't know as much as you, but I know how to *treat* people!' Ben's outburst surprised even him. 'Thanks for the drink. I'm going.'

'Are you going to tell Mike?'

Ben didn't answer. He had been so sure that Mike deserved to have the full story but now he couldn't see straight.

He got so far down the cobbled street and realised he'd gone the wrong way and was heading for the river. He continued anyway. For ten minutes, he watched the murky brown water. Maybe some stories were not for sharing. Maybe some, like the ones he and Andrew shared in bed, were private.

Maybe his dad's should remain that way.

20

ZIMBABWE

A Letter from Home

> *Ghosts don't haunt people. People haunt people. Ghosts just wander into the wrong rooms.*
>
> Andrew Fitzgerald, *The Lion Tamer Who Lost*

Lucy reclines languorously by the one tree in the lion enclosure, relaxed in her full acceptance by the pride. She ignores Ben at the fence. Ignores a younger lioness who tries to play. Ben inhales the air, the putrid smell of shit and fur and heat. He wants to remember the intoxicating perfume forever. Never to forget standing here with the heat on his back, the wire fence to his front, and so many churning emotions inside.

He often stands here. It has become his second favourite spot after the deck at dawn. He prefers it alone here too.

The light begins to die. Shadows elongate. Summer is slowing now here, just as it is speeding up back home. Night will fall many times after Ben has gone. New lions will arrive; older ones will go free. In a few months, Lucy and Chuma will be released into the wild for good. Ben isn't sure he wants to wait around and see her disappear forever. But that means he will have to go home first.

Is he ready?

He has been here for more than five months now. How can it be that long? Where have the days gone?

He feels footsteps approaching. Esther. She nuzzles her cheek to his chest.

'Didn't see you at breakfast,' he says.

'Wasn't hungry.'

'Not like you.'

'No,' she admits. 'I just can't stomach that coffee at the moment.'

'You didn't eat much last night either.'

'No. My appetite has been really off. I just feel dead icky.'

'The heat?' asks Ben.

'Maybe.'

They have been a couple for two months, and have fallen into an easy, comfortable routine. Sometimes he experiences a curious homesick sort of feeling, except he doesn't yearn for England. He yearns for what he knows Esther can't give him. He tackles it by leaving her sleeping in the dark sometimes, and walking the perimeter of the enclosure, over and over. Only when his body is exhausted by the midnight trek does he fall back into bed, surrendering to the fact that nothing will satiate the wistful longing, and he will have to learn to live with it.

'Are *you* okay?' Esther asks.

'Yeah. You? Aside from your ickiness?'

She shrugs, doesn't respond.

Esther has not expressed her love for him again. Ben can't help but be glad. Though he is fond of her, he would never lie. He might live this lie, but he will not lie about love.

'This came for you,' Esther says, and hands him a letter.

Ben hardly dares look at the handwriting. Has Andrew received the lion postcard and responded? He sent it over a month ago. It's quite possible. Then Ben will know he's okay. Two more phone calls have only resulted in the answering machine.

'You sure you're okay?' Esther searches his face for answers, something she often does. He knows why; he knows how distant he can be.

'Yeah.' Ben looks at the envelope.

The scratchy scrawl is not Andrew's.

'Who's it from?'

'My dad.'

'Oh.' Esther pauses. 'Are you going to open it?'

'Not now,' he says. 'Maybe tomorrow.' He doubts it will be tomorrow. 'I just need to … I dunno. Prepare.'

'Have you still not rung him?'

'You *know* I haven't.'

'Maybe he's apologising in it.'

It will be for the wrong thing, thinks Ben. *He can't apologise for something he doesn't know he's done.*

'I'll read it tomorrow,' he says.

They stand in silence for a while, watching the animals. Soon it will be dark. The blackness here is different from that at home, lit only by the moon and stars, by the nightly campfire, and the small sun-powered bulbs hanging from huts. Chuma approaches Lucy. He playfully attacks her, pouncing and growling. She simply looks at him with disdain.

'She no longer wants him,' says Esther sadly.

'She's just showing him who's boss.'

'Maybe. She no longer bothers much with him at all. So much for blood.'

'She's just letting him know,' says Ben.

'Know what?'

'That she doesn't need him. That's got nothing to do with blood. She'll know it's kinder to let him go. He won't survive otherwise.'

'You sound like bloody Stig now.'

'Shit. I do, don't I?'

'But you're right,' admits Esther. 'I just wish Chuma was doing as well as Lucy is.'

'He will.'

Ben knows that in some ways Andrew turned him away so he would survive, too. So he could make a life in the world without what happened ruining anything. Ben realises that even his dysfunctional clan is better than having no one at all. Maybe even his adulterous dad is better than nothing. Family is family. Lions need one another, to hunt, to mate, to survive. Without it they die. How lonely Andrew must have been as a child; how much he must have wanted what Ben had.

'Do you reckon you'll ever come back here?' asks Esther.

'I don't know,' says Ben. 'Do you?'

She shrugs.

'To come back, we'll have to go home first,' says Ben.

'God. Newcastle is gonna seem like a shithole after this.'

'Hull won't look much better.'

'But I'm dying to see my brother.'

'I want to see mine, too,' says Ben.

Ben realises now that Esther seems different. Quieter. It occurs to him that she been this way for a few days. He is always so wrapped up in his own problems that he overlooks her and feels bad. It is dark now, but he sees her more clearly than he has for a while.

'You're not okay, are you?' he says, putting his dad's letter in his back pocket. 'I can tell. What is it?'

'It's nothing.'

'Esther, it's me. Tell me.'

'Let's go sit on our rock,' she says.

There is no hunt this evening, and Ben is glad. So they go to the rock where they watched the eclipse. Where Esther writes her journal, where now they often sit together, viewing the landscape. It's harder to find in the dark. Esther leads the way. They sit. It is much cooler now in the evening. He puts his hoodie around her shoulders. The stars spread above them, like glitter dust from a witch's wand. Ben puts a hand over hers, concerned.

'Tell me what's wrong,' he says. 'I've been so selfish, moping about my problems.'

'No, it's fine.'

'It isn't. Tell me, Esther.'

'I don't know how to say it,' she says.

'Why? Is it bad?'

'Well, no. But it...'

'You can tell me anything,' insists Ben.

'I'm pregnant.'

Ben hears the three words.

But all he can remember is a birthday gift and a promise *he* once made about saying three words.

A promise he would break.

21

ENGLAND

Three Things

In the books Ben read, the twists never surprised him. In real life, they turned his world upside down.

Andrew Fitzgerald, *The Lion Tamer Who Lost*

Andrew smiled, kissed Ben's cheek, and handed him a birthday gift. Then he flopped onto the sofa by his Wish Box. Dust settled on the ridged lid like grey snow.

'You remembered?' said Ben.

'Of course I did.'

Ben peeled away the gold wrapping paper so slowly that Andrew urged him to get on with it. Laughing, he took even longer on purpose. He took out a book: *Kingdom of Lions.* On the first page, next to a sleeping cat, Andrew had written simply, *For my lion tamer, happy birthday, Andrew.*

'Wow.'

'You like it?'

'I *do*.'

Ben kissed Andrew warmly and then sat on the floor, at his feet, looking up at him as he had that day in the café. He put his head in Andrew's lap. No matter what was going on around them, he had never been happier.

Eventually Ben said, 'I have three things to tell you and you won't perhaps like or agree, but tough, I've decided.'

There was a fourth thing – but Ben decided to keep to himself that he had secretly entered the first three chapters of *The Lion Tamer Who Lost* in a competition he'd seen online. If Andrew didn't place he would never be disappointed; if he did, it would be a wonderful surprise.

Surprisingly, Andrew didn't argue, as though all the things he had been asking Ben over the last few weeks had finally quenched some thirst. He pulled his hoodie around his shoulders, despite the room being warm with late summer's breath.

'Go on then,' he said.

'You can't argue.'

'I won't.'

'First thing is,' Ben began, 'I'm not going back to university. You can't expect me to. I want to be *here*.'

Andrew didn't speak, just watched him. Ben lost his way a little.

'Go on,' urged Andrew.

He didn't object to Ben's second suggestion. This was the one Ben had wrestled with most. The one he had feared Andrew would argue against. The sun edged across the sky, lingering like a child not wanting to go home for tea. They gazed at one another. Every shade of gold he viewed afterwards would take Ben back to his eyes in this moment.

'That's only two things,' Andrew said.

'And you're not dissipating them – you're fine?'

He nodded. 'The third thing?'

'I'm nervous.'

'Don't be.' Andrew smiled. 'I'm knackered, and I look like crap. Hit me while I'm vulnerable.'

'I know you like your distance.'

'I used to. But not with you. *Never* with you.'

Ben knelt up and put his hand over Andrew's. Andrew's was chilly. He warmed it.

'I love you,' he said, 'and I'm going to tell my dad about us.'

Andrew didn't speak for a long time.

'I'm going to tell him the next time I see him.'

Ben's knees began to ache, the joints nagging him to switch position.

The light left slowly. Then Andrew shuffled lower down the sofa, slid onto his knees so he faced Ben. He parted Ben's thin shirt collar, wider and wider, until the button popped and dropped to the floor where shadows won their game with the sun. He sank his teeth into Ben's neck. Their heads formed a circle, tipped towards one another. As they moved closer, the lid fell off the Wish Box. They left it where it was.

Ben hummed a low, aching song against Andrew's cheek as he felt his teeth digging deeper still.

'I love you, I love you, I love you,' he said.

Later, while Andrew slept, when his breathing evened out and the movement behind his eyes ceased, Ben stroked his hair. He wondered what the odds were of finding a man exactly like him, with hands that arched at the thumb like his did, with two fleshy mounds that pressed against his when he held him down, with one freckle nearer his left nipple than his right as though marking the spot for his heart, who believed in wishes and words and made-up games.

Zero.

The odds were zero.

22

ZIMBABWE

Here We Are

Nancy had a new sister. The family had a new baby. Ben longed for another sibling, but there was no chance of that now.

Andrew Fitzgerald, *The Lion Tamer Who Lost*

The savanna seems to quiet with Esther's revelation. The long, shadowy grass stills. The insect song ceases. The exquisite memory of Andrew fades. Has Ben heard correctly? He can't process the words.

Esther is pregnant.

'You're ... *How*?' he asks eventually.

She laughs. 'So you missed biology at school as well as the class on undoing bras?'

'No. Sorry. I mean ... I don't know what I mean. Are you sure?'

In the dimness Esther's face shines white. How can he not have noticed that she looks tired, washed out? How long has she been that way? Ben noticed every change when Andrew had hypos. He feels sick with regret. How can he have been so thoughtless towards her?

'I was suspicious three weeks ago,' says Esther, 'because I'm always so punctual, and I was late. I knew there'd be no way of getting a pregnancy test here, so I asked my friend Chloe to send me a couple. They came today, with the letter from your dad.'

'And you've done it?'

'Yes. I did both of them. They were both positive.' Esther sighs. 'I *know* it anyway. I feel ... different. It must have happened our first time.'

She looks at Ben and he realises she is nervous more about him, and his reaction, than she is about the pregnancy. 'Yes, I'm on the pill – you know I am – but I had that tummy bug, didn't I? Stupid, but I never thought I might not have absorbed it.'

'You're not stupid. *I* am. To not have known something was wrong.'

'You couldn't have known.'

'I'm usually good at...'

'What?'

'Nothing,' sighs Ben. 'Anyway, I'm sorry.'

'Don't be. I'm not.' Esther pauses. 'So, here we are.'

'Here we are,' Ben whispers.

'I don't expect anything,' she says.

'What do you mean?'

'I mean, we've only been together a couple of months. There's no pressure. But I want to have it. Crazy, but I do. It feels so ... *right*. That it was conceived here, in this glorious place. Doesn't that seem somehow extra special?' She puts a hand over Ben's. 'Look, you can be as involved as you want to, but I also understand if this is a shock and it's too much.'

'It *is* a shock,' admits Ben, 'but this is my baby too.'

He is sure she smiles in the dark. They have created a child. Here, in this wilderness, amidst fight and hunt.

'If you've made the decision to have it,' says Ben, 'I'll be there. For *both* of you.'

He touches his dad's letter. For the first time, he can relate a little to the man. He is going to be one too. A *dad*.

'Are you okay?' asks Esther. 'You're miles away again.'

'Yes. Sorry. Just thinking about my dad.'

'That's understandable.'

'Do you think you'll ring him now?'

Ben wants to say that he doubts it, but he doesn't. Esther doesn't need his outbursts and moods right now.

'We'll see.' Ben pauses. 'I won't be the kind of dad he is though. I can promise you that.'

'So you won't shag any of my female relatives?'

'Esther!' Ben smiles though.

'Sorry. That was bad of me.'

'No. It's fine. It's bloody true.'

Esther looks at him. 'What shall we do then?'

'Look, we can't plan everything now.' Ben tenderly moves a stray piece of hair from her cheek. 'This is all new, isn't it? But I guess we'll have to decide what we'll do about being here. I mean, you can't have a baby here, can you?'

'I guess not.'

'You must want to go back to Newcastle? Will you phone and tell your family?'

'No. I'll tell them in person.'

'Yes.' Ben supposes he should too. He can't think about that now. 'I guess we should get you to an English hospital as soon as we can, have everything confirmed, make sure you're okay.'

'I guess.'

'This changes everything,' says Ben, more to himself.

'It does.'

Esther leans against him, clearly tired. He lets her. It's time he did. It's time he grew up.

PART FOUR

ANDREW

23

A Story of Forty-Three Peas

> *When Ben said, 'save me' only Nancy understood. Ben's 'save me' didn't mean 'rescue me'; it meant 'put me aside until later'. Later was always better because the house got quiet and the moon rose and the animals came out.*
>
> Andrew Fitzgerald, *The Lion Tamer Who Lost*

The last time Andrew was hospitalised he slept on the children's ward, in a bed too short for a taller-than-average ten-year-old. That ward had been prettied with animal window-paintings and under-stuffed teddies.

The bed he now occupied was large enough but squeaked each time he moved; and this place was only decorated with blood. A splodge had been on the radiator since day one – it might have been there months, missed by exhausted cleaners. The food was tolerable and the nurses (particularly Sophie) cheerful, even after long shifts.

But Andrew felt guilty about having a bed when he felt better now. The other ward residents were needier than him; in the next bed an elderly diabetic woman, Lily, cried out that rats were getting in. She refused food so had to be drip-fed and disturbed the night with scrape-footed wanderings into the corridor. Even Kimberley, who had been admitted just hours before Andrew, only stayed long enough to be checked over.

He wanted to go home. To Ben.

The day before, on his morning visit, Doctor Amdahl had told Andrew they needed to keep him in to do further blood tests.

'Haven't my sugars stabilised?' Andrew had tested himself that morning, and was 9.9. 'What are you looking for?'

'The exact cause of your hypoglycaemic episode,' he said.

'Maybe I didn't eat enough that day.'

The statement was ridiculous; he had eaten an entire Sunday lunch at Ben's house.

'We're keeping you in.' Andrew wondered if the doctor always spoke so quietly when delivering what a patient didn't want to hear.

Now he awaited the day's highlight: Ben at visiting hours.

The previous day he had arrived with grapes and Andrew's notebook so he could write. Now he arrived bang on two. He pulled the curtain around the bed and kissed Andrew. His mouth felt cool. When their lips touched, Andrew didn't move for a moment, eyes open, studying Ben. He felt Ben slide a hand under the sheet, along Andrew's thigh.

'You'd better stop, or I won't,' smiled Andrew. 'It's been too long.'

'I've missed you,' said Ben.

Andrew put his hand over Ben's fingers, said, 'You'll get us thrown out for obscene behaviour.'

'Good.' Ben perched on the bed rather than the chair beside it. 'How are you?'

'Didn't get much sleep.' He leaned in close, whispered. 'The old dear over there was shouting about rats all night.'

As though to assert her existence Lily cried out, 'Hilda, are you there, love?'

'Do you think Hilda's a rat?' They laughed quietly. 'Is she diabetic, too?' Andrew nodded, and Ben asked, 'Don't you fear all those complications when you're old?'

Andrew insisted that if he ended up looking for vermin all night Ben should suffocate him with a pillow.

'Did you get the results of the blood tests yet?' asked Ben.

'Not yet.' Andrew avoided Ben's eyes.

'Are you worried something's really wrong?'

'No.' He paused. 'Okay, a bit.'

'To do with diabetes?' He sounded hopeful. Andrew found it

harder to face Ben's uncertainties than his own, to see them in his lined brow.

'What else would it be?'

'I miss staying at the flat.'

'Stay there if you want,' said Andrew.

He had given him a key. Leo, the man he had loved (or a word close to love) for four years had asked endlessly for one, but Andrew had never handed it over.

'It's the only place in the world I want to be,' said Ben. 'It'll be good to get away from home. Dad got so drunk last night he fell over in the garden and I couldn't get him back inside. Had to leave him on his back in the grass, shouting at the sky. I heard him at four this morning, staggering up the stairs, crying for Molly. God knows who she is.'

'It's sad,' said Andrew. 'Why do you think he drinks?'

Ben shrugged. 'When I ask, he says it's just a few, his only pleasure.'

'And how about the new baby?'

'She's good.'

'A lot for you to worry about.' Andrew squeezed his hand.

'More for you.' Ben squeezed his back.

Preceded by an unappetising smell, the lunch trolley arrived late. The curtain was wrenched open by a puffy-faced server. Andrew chose carrots, peas and chips, unable to stomach more. Pea skin floated like petals. Lily cried out for Hilda again.

'Eat more,' said Ben. 'They might let you go home.'

He ate one chip, pulling a pained face. 'Cold.'

Ben picked at the abandoned peas on the plate, grouping them, quietly counting each one.

'Why do you always count them?' Andrew asked, with no criticism, only curiosity.

Ben looked up, his mouth still forming the number.

He told Andrew the story of when his mum stopped eating.

He said that as she grew weaker and the cancer in her ovaries spread, her appetite diminished too. It was cruel that a woman who loved to bake apple pies with pastry that crumbled, and lemon meringue that stayed on your taste buds for hours, would lose not only her interest in food but her ability to eat it. Ben told Andrew he found comfort in the days when she ate forty peas; misery in the days she left that many on her plate. He'd sit with her and joke that if she ate just four more it would make her hair curl, and she'd tell him that was cauliflower, and her hair was curly enough. Or it had been once. Not much remained by the time she couldn't eat.

Near the end, when they all knew it was coming, Ben said, he ate what she didn't. An hour before she died he counted one hundred and fifty-eight cornflakes but couldn't eat them and poured them into the bin. Later her medication and stained bedding followed. Ben paused at the words *stained bedding*; Andrew sensed his reluctance to add anything unclean to his mum's story. He put his hand over Ben's, not wanting to interrupt. Even Lily ceased her cries for Hilda.

'Now *you* have to eat,' Ben said, his voice small. 'It's like some weird twist of fate, and you know I don't buy such crap. Like I'm here to count the food for you now.'

Andrew picked up the fork and ate his peas, Ben telling him there had been forty-three on the plate.

They didn't talk for a while.

'You must hate hospitals,' Ben said eventually.

'Not had much experience,' said Andrew. 'Just when I was ten.'

'You've never been in hospital since you were diagnosed?'

'I go to the clinic twice a year. Never had more than a minor hypo. Thank God for you. If I'd collapsed at the flat, I daren't imagine how long I'd have lain there.'

'It was nothing.'

Andrew looked up from his peas.

'Okay – it was scary. I heard someone say coma so when you finally woke my heart flipped over.'

Andrew wanted to press his palms to Ben's chest.

'Have you been up much?' asked Ben.

Andrew liked to walk around when thinking. At his flat he would pace the floor by the window. That morning he went to the main landing, where a floor-to-ceiling window offered panoramic views. It was a grey scene, dull to anyone else, with mostly flat landscape, the river and bridge beyond, but it was his home city. A poster advertised the circus with *the ferocious, man-eating cats!* Andrew wondered how it could be only ten days since they were there.

'A bit.'

'I've decided I'm going to confront my dad about Kim and him,' said Ben.

Andrew nodded and waited for Ben to go on.

'I owe it to my brother.'

Andrew asked what Ben would do if it was true; he said he would think about that when he had to.

'Maybe at the same time tell him about us?'

'Tell me again how old were you when you told your mum?' Ben asked.

'Twenty-nine. She just shrugged, said she had known.'

'Plenty of time for me yet then.'

Then Ben changed the subject: 'Can I ask you something?'

'Of course.'

'What is it you like about me?'

'What?'

'Just humour me.'

'How long have you got?'

Ben looked at the clock. 'Ten minutes and they'll be chucking me out.'

'It's not long enough,' said Andrew.

'Condensulate it – you're the writer.'

Andrew realised he was serious; this hospital and the imminent test had taken him to a long-ago time he now understood. Ben's last trip to a ward must have been when his mum was ill.

But how could Andrew tell him in minutes what he liked about him; describe in detail the times he watched him staring into nowhere, eyes narrowed, and how endearing it was. Say he loved the way Ben said his name, like a question. How no one had ever learned about the diabetes like Ben had. No one had ever kissed his stomach after injections, asking, 'Did it hurt?' and saying he wished he could take it away, without a trace of pity.

Andrew said simply, 'Your face. Everything you are is there ... the passion in your eyes when they burn orange. How your mouth curls up with humour. When you frown.'

When Andrew regained consciousness two days before, Ben's face was the first one he had seen. The crowds in the emergency room appeared as a mass but Ben stood out in that sea of strangeness.

'This girl at uni once said my face didn't quite work,' Ben said now.

'She must have been short-sighted,' said Andrew.

Ben left the chair with a fervent scrape, pulled the curtain around the bed again, and slid his tongue between Andrew's lips, like a game of tag. Catch me and I'll catch you back.

Andrew said, 'We could tell them I'm sleeping.'

It was when Ben whispered *yes* in Andrew's ear that Doctor Amdahl turned up. Ben sat back in the chair, his face flushed. Andrew pulled his hospital gown across his body.

The doctor spoke his news so faintly that Andrew had to lip-read. That was what he remembered most later; the strange drawl and unidentifiable accent.

'Would you prefer your friend stayed?' Doctor Amdahl asked Andrew.

'Yes.'

'We have some results.' Doctor Amdahl held charts, which he looked at now. 'They show that you have more white cells than red, and not enough platelets in your blood. It's an imbalance that we need to investigate further, to ascertain why.'

'Why *might* it be?' asked Ben.

Andrew put a hand on Ben's arm to shush him, but he ignored him.

'Isn't it just the diabetes?'

The doctor shook his head.

'You must know what *might* be causing it?' Ben leaned forwards in his chair.

Doctor Amdahl assured Ben that various things can cause the abundance of white blood cells and it would be unwise to even hazard a guess.

'The limited platelets in your blood are why you bruised so easily,' he said. 'We're going to test a sample of bone marrow cells.'

'How do you that?' asked Ben.

Andrew said Ben should just let the doctor talk.

'A sample is taken from the pelvis,' said Doctor Amdahl. 'We inject a local anaesthetic, make a small cut to insert a needle, and suck out liquid bone marrow – about a teaspoon.'

Andrew found it odd that the doctor talked as though he wasn't there, and then realised he was telling Ben.

'It'll be fine,' he told Ben, realising he was comforting him. 'I'll get this done and I can go home.'

'We'll do it tomorrow,' said Doctor Amdahl. 'Try and get a good night's sleep. Any questions?'

Andrew shook his head.

Afterwards the news sat between them like an unwanted Christmas gift. Ben got up, went to the window, resumed his chair. Andrew said it would be okay. Ben snapped that he couldn't *know* that – his mum had been Andrew's age when *she* died.

A nurse informed the ward sharply that visiting hours were over. Andrew was the only patient with anyone at his bedside.

'You have to *wish*,' Ben said.

'What?'

Someone in the corridor dropped something that sounded like glass.

Ben nodded like a wind-up toy. '*Wish* it'll be okay.'

'You don't believe in them.' Andrew tried to laugh.

'But *you* do. I'll get your Wish Box. I'll bring it tonight and you can write it down. You *have* to wish that the result will be good.'

Andrew shook his head and asked Ben to kiss him; he wouldn't.

'Don't you *want* to be okay?' he asked.

Andrew said he should go.

'What the fuck?' Ben shoved the grapes off the cabinet.

Lily cried out: 'Hilda come and stop the rats!'

'Right. I'll fucking go then.'

Green fruit squelched under his shoes and marked his departure across the tiled floor. Andrew counted the grapes as he left, just as he imagined Ben would: there were thirteen.

Andrew had only wanted Ben to go so he could cry. He did, soundlessly, in a toilet cubicle. He didn't cry about the test or for the heavy feeling that something was very wrong. He cried because he couldn't stand how Ben had looked when he wouldn't wish.

The wish formed for a moment in Andrew's mind; it tried to exist.

But he didn't believe it.

24

Running through Nettles

> *Mr Ellerington asked the class why a hungry crocodile might free an antelope caught securely in its jaws. Nancy said, 'Because his teeth are wonky?' Mr Ellerington explained that predators won't eat bad food, so the antelope must have been ill.*
>
> Andrew Fitzgerald, *The Lion Tamer Who Lost*

When a doctor twisted his fat needle into Andrew's bone, Andrew was surprised to think of Jonathon Edwards.

Aged twelve and a half, Andrew once ran through nettles because Jonathon said he was a coward if he didn't. Andrew wanted to appear brave. He ran bare-legged, in PE shorts, through the overgrown patch that separated the bike sheds from the hedge where the fifth years smoked at lunchtime. Jonathon had laughed afterwards, said only a total dickhead would have done it.

Andrew had already learned at this tender age that some hurt was necessary; after two years of diabetes he barely flinched at the five-times-daily puncture of needle and the prick of blood test. He found that his mood enhanced or decreased pain. Now – as a needle went in agonising search of bone marrow – Andrew pushed Jonathon's face away and saw only Ben. When he did, the pain disappeared like butterflies freed from a net.

Ben's kiss after a hypo had always soothed; his touch before a finger-prick test made it hurt less. And when they had sex, the exquisite pleasure of his touch had to be tempered by a simultaneous bite.

After the procedure, Ben was waiting by Andrew's hospital bed, eyes pale with concern.

'How did it feel?' he asked.

How could Andrew answer?

'It felt like ... just life,' he muttered.

'So now we wait?'

'Yes, now we wait,' said Andrew, and went into the bathroom to begin.

Sunday was Results Day. Like the Wish Box, this day was a proper noun. Andrew knew it was also the day when Ben planned to ask his dad about Kimberley. Ben had texted that morning to say he would visit him afterwards.

When Sophie, the cheeriest nurse, said the doctor would be coming that afternoon to talk about the test, Andrew resisted texting Ben. It wouldn't help his emotional confrontation with his dad. Also, he hoped the doctor would come before visiting hours because he couldn't bear the thought of Ben's face if the news was bad. At least if he got bad news alone, when telling Ben he could emphasise the positives.

'Hilda! I wish you'd show yourself!' cried Lily at one-thirty, after the lunchtime plates had been cleared.

'Hilda might visit tonight, sweetheart,' said Sophie, winking at Andrew as she took Lily's temperature.

'Don't talk crap,' snapped Lily. 'Hilda's been dead fifteen years!'

'Ah, well, she could come at any time then,' said the young nurse.

Andrew looked for Dr Amdahl between watching the clock hands make their too-quick rotations. He analysed passing footsteps. Women in heels clipped past; nurses too, their comfy shoes making hardly any announcement; squeaking wheels heralded walking frames.

But no sound foreshadowed the arrival of Leo after eighteen

months, sixty thousand miles, and still no word for love that wasn't love. Andrew's ex arrived with a small bunch of flowers. Andrew stared at them and then his face. It was just the same – tanned, half shaven, too happy.

'Leo,' he said.

'Andrew.'

'Hilda!' cried Lily.

Leo laughed and approached the bed, saying, 'She's in the wrong type of hospital.'

'It isn't visiting hours yet.'

'I sneaked in.'

The last time Andrew had seen Leo he had been holding a suitcase with a dangling label that read *Shanghai, China*. Andrew had said he should never come back, that he didn't want to share him with the world. Leo had yelled on his way down the stairs that Andrew was impossible.

'I'm back,' he said now.

He put the flowers on the cabinet. They smelt tart.

'How did you know I was here?' Andrew wanted to ask *why* he was here.

'Your neighbour said. Is it your diabetes?'

Andrew shook his head. He knew Leo wouldn't be interested in bone marrow; he abhorred physical weakness so much that Andrew had always been surprised he had dated him so long. 'It's how you handle it,' Leo had frequently said. 'You don't trouble me with it. I admire that.' Andrew had liked his lack of interest, never quite loving him enough to want him to fuss.

'Why were you at my flat?' asked Andrew.

'I wanted to tell you I've given travelling up.' He sat in the chair. 'I'm settling here. Gonna devote myself to writing – it's about time. I'll use my travel experience to have a go at fiction. You always said I should be more creative.'

Writing was all they had in common.

'I knew you'd want to know,' Leo said.

'But you love travelling.' Andrew pulled the cover higher, not wanting Leo to see the bruises.

Leo had been a hotel inspector for an international chain, mixing work with pleasure and taking full advantage of discount flights and free rooms. He made extra cash writing travel reviews for a newspaper. Many times, he'd invited Andrew along, and though they'd once gone to Prague together for a weekend, he much preferred the space afforded him when Leo was away.

'The world's all the same when you've landed in a thousand airports, spent evenings in bars that could be in any backstreet of any city. I think home could be exciting.'

'That's nice.' Andrew didn't know what else to say.

It was almost two o'clock.

'You think lots when you're somewhere else,' said Leo.

Andrew agreed: all he'd done on the ward was think.

'I thought about *us*,' said Leo.

I didn't, thought Andrew.

'It's good of you to come but this isn't a good time.'

'I hate hospitals,' Leo said. 'I made myself come for *you*. I could have left a note at the flat.' He looked like he wished he had. 'I know it's been a while, but we're still good, aren't we?'

Andrew could agree that they might have once been defined as *good*. Leo had been a generous if self-absorbed partner and Andrew had liked this. A man wrapped up in his own needs notices less that your love is a lesser word; they had ambled along in their mostly one-sided relationship for almost four years.

'Remember my Aunty Brenda out in Swanland?' said Leo.

Maybe if Andrew just let him say what he felt he needed to, then he would go.

'She died.' Leo's expression barely clouded. 'Long illness that I won't bore you with. Anyway, she left me her house. Great big place off a quiet lane, gravel drive, the works.'

Andrew watched the door.

'But there's no point without kids is there? I'm forty-two; you must be almost forty now. I've been thinking about it. We've had a long break. I know you like your space and we've messed about with me going here and there and everywhere, but what do you think?'

'About what?' asked Andrew.

'Us. Kids. You know. Together. Adopt.'

Andrew frowned. 'I've not seen you in over a year and you're asking me to have kids with you?'

'Get better first.' Leo laughed. 'Think about it for a few days.'

And then, at one minute after two, Ben walked in. Two men. One an unwelcome ghost from the past, the other a welcome one from the present, neither of them Doctor Amdahl with news of his future.

Leo looked Ben up and down as he approached the bed; Ben returned the study with equal fervour. They both turned to Andrew, the same question in their eyes. It was Ben he must answer ... calm the orange sparks.

'Ben.' Andrew patted the bed for him to sit. 'This is Leo. I mentioned him to you. He came to see how I am.'

'You're with *him*?' Leo heaped mockery on the word him. 'How *old* is he?'

Lily shrieked that the rats had parachutes now.

'What's it to you?' said Ben. He didn't sit in the spot Andrew patted, but squared up to Leo, eye-to-eye, assuming his full height.

Then Doctor Amdahl arrived, from the future. Stepping between them, he said good afternoon to Andrew and asked in his temperate accent if they might go somewhere less busy to discuss the results.

'Yes,' said Andrew.

Leo moved away from the bed, his flowers wilting in the overheated climate. Ben moved closer to Andrew. The doctor said there was a private room up the corridor and he could have someone present. Andrew said he wanted Ben there. He realised now that Ben was no child who needed life painted a pretty way.

'I'd best go,' said Leo. 'I only paid for an hour's parking. I'll call you Andrew, and you can update me.'

He left as quickly and soundlessly as he had arrived.

'Shall we?' said the doctor with a perfect voice for bad news.

They walked behind him down the sterile corridor.

'How did it go with your dad?' Andrew asked Ben.

'I can tell you later,' he said. 'Now is about you.'

'Did you tell him about us?'

Ben glared at him.

'Guess that's a no then?'

'Later,' snapped Ben.

'I was thinking,' Andrew said. 'I truly don't mind if you go to Zimbabwe.'

Ben leaned closer, so the doctor couldn't hear them. 'Like you wanted that fucking Leo to go travelling so you could be away from him?'

'Not like that at *all*. I just don't want you to feel tied to me.'

'I don't,' whispered Ben. 'We chose each other. I don't *have* to be here – and you don't *have* to have me. But we are.'

Andrew wanted to kiss Ben, but knew he'd pull away with the doctor there.

Now they were at the door to the room.

25

You Should Have Wished

Nancy didn't know what to say when Ben cried.

Andrew Fitzgerald, *The Lion Tamer Who Lost*

Doctor Amdahl opened the door and let them in first.

Andrew and Ben sat in the stiff sofa shoved up against the wall, and the doctor pulled up the chair and opened the folder on his knee. With the closeness of Ben and the warm air from a colossal radiator, it was hard to take in the doctor's words. He spoke as though telling a fairytale; the story of leukaemia ... that was how Andrew heard it.

In this story, leukaemia was a cancer of the blood-forming cells that began in the bone marrow and – if not treated – spread to the blood, brain and spinal cord. Andrew's story was one of chronic lymphocytic leukaemia, fortunately a slow-growing cancer that usually appears during middle age and affects white blood cells. The twist in the tale was that his diabetes had disguised most of the symptoms; the tiredness he had blamed on hypos and the bruises that wouldn't heal after his injections. Luckily the cancer did not appear too advanced, though further testing would determine the full picture.

Andrew looked at Ben.

He had kissed his bruises many times. Would he want to now?

'We'll start treatment immediately,' said Doctor Amdahl. 'The prognosis is good; we've found it early.'

Unlike before the procedure, Ben was silent.

'What *is* the treatment?' asked Andrew.

Doctor Amdahl explained that chemotherapy was the main remedy and it could be taken orally or through a needle. A hospital stay wasn't necessary; Andrew could recover at home. He said that radiation was another option, but they would discuss that. For now, they would proceed with chemo.

'The best treatment,' he said, 'is a stem-cell transplant, whereby donated cells rebuild a good supply and boost the immune system.'

Andrew frowned. 'Someone donating their own healthy cells?'

'Yes,' said the doctor. 'This would be from a relative where there's a good chance you'll be a close match. Unrelated donors are sometimes matched but it's rare to find one.'

Andrew thought about his lack of family.

'The success of a donation depends on the recipient's age and health. You're young in terms of cancer. Your diabetes need not cause problems if we monitor it closely. In all regards you're healthy. Is there a relative who might donate?'

Andrew shook his head.

'Can I donate?' asked Ben, animated at last.

'You'd have to be tested to see if you were a match,' said Doctor Amdahl. 'The procedure is pretty painful, and the chances of being a match are not high.'

'It's fine, Ben. I'll just have chemo.'

'What *are* the chances of someone random being a match?' Ben asked.

Doctor Amdahl said that there was a one in twenty thousand chance of someone matching a stranger. Ben's face fell.

Still he said, 'Then it's not *impossible*.'

Andrew looked at him. 'Ben, they're awful odds.'

'You won that writing competition last year and fifteen thousand people entered.' Ben seemed excited to have found numbers to justify his plan. 'Those were tough odds and you did it.'

The radiator clinked behind them, and the doctor uncrossed his legs. 'Do you have any more questions?' he asked. 'Would you like time alone?'

Despite Ben trying to hide it, Andrew knew the doctor understood their relationship.

'No,' he admitted, 'but I'm sure I'll have loads to ask later.'

'We have a great counselling team here for the questions I can't answer, and I can put you in touch with various cancer organisations.' The doctor stood. 'This is a lot to take in, so I'll leave you alone.'

The door closed after him with a heavy click. Andrew looked at Ben, more nervous now than he had been on their first proper date. He thought about it, about how they had met up at the pub near his home, both just looking at one another, wearing the same jeans and speaking at the same time and then laughing and telling the other to go first.

Now Ben said 'Andrew' at the same time as he said 'Ben'. Then there was nothing else to say.

Ben's voice was that of a boy when he said, 'You should have *wished*.'

Andrew put a finger over his lips and shook his head. 'That isn't how it works.'

'But you ... should have ... *tried*.'

Andrew couldn't speak. A strange thing filled his throat; not words, not air. Though with Jonathon Edwards he had been brave, now with Ben he could finally *not* be. Now he felt the pain of those biting, stinging nettles. Now he scratched where once he'd been determined not to.

Now he cried.

And Ben held him.

26

Dancing on Feet Bigger than Ours

> *Ben liked his wheelchair when it meant he could avoid dancing. At the Christmas school party, he watched the others sway and stamp and stumble. Nancy, however, danced like a ghost, flickeringly, swishingly, beautifully.*
>
> Andrew Fitzgerald, *The Lion Tamer Who Lost*

'Tell me a happy memory of you and your dad,' Andrew asked Ben during his second cycle of chemotherapy. The words rattled with ice cubes. Coldness numbed a mouth made sore by drugs. 'You've only ever grumbled about him. Pick something from your childhood and don't skip over any of it.'

For three weeks Ben had been recalling memories. At first he said, 'What am I, answers-dot-com?' Even his most resourceful answers had Andrew coming up with more questions. Just as Andrew sought physical pain in pleasure, now in emotional pain he sought Ben's happy days.

'I do remember dancing with him,' Ben said, after considering a while.

They sat on Andrew's bed, surrounded by pain-relief drugs rather than clothes and after-sex blankets, Ben at the top end and Andrew near the pillow, like reflections on either side of a mirror.

'Shouldn't we test your blood?'

Andrew shook his head vigorously, impatient. 'Ben, for fuck's sake they tested me *five* times at the hospital.' The diabetes meant he was monitored more closely than other chemo patients in case he needed extra insulin via a drip. He had been given anti-sickness drugs to help him eat too. 'You're avoiding the story.'

'I'll tell you. But shouldn't we talk about today first?'

'What's to discuss?' Andrew snapped. 'Chemo's fucking chemo and it'll go on until I'm better.'

It was the same every time – blood test, wait for result, hope white blood cell count was good so treatment didn't have to be delayed, chemo prepared, chemo taken.

'So where did you dance with your dad?' Andrew asked.

He wondered if his hunger for answers was a side-effect as powerful as the weight loss, as the strands of hair he stuffed in the bin when Ben wasn't there, and the nausea that made it hard for him to eat the so-necessary snacks. Or did he want to know as much as possible in case it was his last chance to ask?

'In the front room. Sometimes at Christmas when all the relatives came over. My mum had heaps of them, and they visited if there was a big celebration.'

Andrew loved the big-family stories best. Sometimes, when Ben talked, he made notes in his book. Now he rummaged in the bedside drawer for it and scribbled with a pen until it worked.

'Dad liked dancing with me best,' said Ben.

'Why you?'

'Because I was little,' said Ben.

'But he's quite tall,' said Andrew. 'Makes no sense.'

'He had me stand on his feet.' Ben moved his feet, left then right, as though dancing with a young child perched on each. His toes tickled Andrew's waist and he smiled. 'When he danced, I did too. He'd always had a drink, but it was one time I didn't mind.'

'And he just did that with *you*?'

'Mike's three years older and was chunky, whereas I was like a bit of string. Dad used to call me Stringy.'

'That's cute actually.'

'I suppose.'

'We all need to dance on feet bigger than ours sometimes,' said Andrew.

'Did you ever dance on anyone's feet?' Ben asked.

'No,' said Andrew, feeling a small prick of sadness. 'I'm tired now. Shall we play Cheaty Chess?'

It was a game they had created because Andrew had never learned to play chess; it was a mixture of snakes & ladders and chequers, with some random rules thrown in. He had no energy for their *yes/no* game, though on good days he still liked Ben to make slow, wordless, unwarlike love to him.

'You're tired but you want to play Cheaty Chess?' Ben nudged Andrew gently with his foot. 'I think you should sleep a bit first.' He moved across to Andrew's side of the bed and gathered up magazines and put them on the cabinet. 'Don't stay awake cos I'm around. I'm not here to keep you occupied, just to make sure you get better.'

'And I thought you were here to pleasure me.'

'Stop it,' said Ben.

'Kiss me and I'll go to sleep.'

'I'm not going to kiss you,' said Ben.

'Fighting talk.'

'No, it's *resting* talk,' Ben insisted.

Andrew was exhausted. He knew he should sleep, but he didn't want to admit he was scared that he wouldn't wake up again. Ben made him lie down, brought biscuits just in case, pulled the covers to his chin, and sat in the spot where he usually slept when he stayed over.

'Talk to me until I go,' Andrew said, feeling drowsy.

'No questions.' Ben moved a strand of thinning hair to the side of his face.

'Unless you have any.'

Ben only had one: 'Have you been wishing?'

Andrew should have known.

'I don't know what to wish for,' he said.

'*I* do.'

'But you have to be careful, you know that. I might wish to be well and there could be a price if it's not supposed to happen.'

'I'd pay any price,' said Ben.

Andrew sighed and closed his eyes. 'I wish for you to be here when I wake up.'

'That I can do,' said Ben.

And he was.

27

The Second Thing

If bad things came in threes, did good things? Ben wondered.

Andrew Fitzgerald, The *Lion Tamer Who Lost*

The next day Andrew handed Ben a birthday gift and watched him unwrap it far too slowly.

Then Ben told him three things.

First he told him he wasn't going back to university.

Last Ben told him he would tell Will about them.

The second thing Ben admitted he had struggled with the most.

'I'm going to take the test,' he said, and paused as though waiting for Andrew to object. 'See if I'm a match so I can make you well. I know the odds are ridiculous, but I can't not try. I *can't*. And you can't stop me.'

Andrew didn't want to. He was immensely moved that Ben would do such a thing.

The sun edged across the sky, lingering like a child not wanting to go home for tea. They gazed at one another. Andrew wanted to stay there forever.

'Dance with me,' said Ben later.

'There's no music,' said Andrew.

'You're the artist. Imagine some.'

'Ben, I'm too tired.'

'Dance on my feet then.'
'Ben.'
'Come on, it's my birthday.'
So he did; Andrew danced on feet bigger than his.

28

The Butterfly Effect

> *Ben dreamed that the car in which his parents died had wings. Snow whirled like detergent dissolving in a washing machine and they flew, over house and hedge and harbour. Wings are better than legs; they do not break so easily.*
>
> Andrew Fitzgerald, *The Lion Tamer Who Lost*

Andrew remembered a butterfly on his mother's wall.

The insect that once flew over meadow and stream, until someone caught it and killed it, skilfully preserving the long-tailed blue forever, had been passed down the generations. As a child, Andrew touched the glass-trapped butterfly, hoping to rouse it.

After his mother's funeral, he smashed the glass. He ran the rigid-winged creature under the tap until it softened and appeared to fly with the rush of water. Then he kept it where he wrote. He held it after Ben said a word that really meant love. When he was prepared to make the greatest sacrifice for him. Butterflies danced in his tummy, sending them spiralling up into his chest.

It was Ben now who suffered. After a test to check their blood types matched – which wasn't unusual, as they were both O Positive – the hospital arranged for a stem-cell extraction, preceded by a week of medication that moved Ben's cells from the bone into the blood. Ben was asleep when they inserted the needle, but Andrew knew it must have hurt him afterwards.

The scar it left bled at random moments.

'It's in the exact same place as that ink was,' Ben said.

'What ink?' Andrew asked.

'The ink that stained my jeans on the train. Why do I notice all this stupid shit now? What have you done to me, Andrew Fitzgerald?'

Andrew sank to his knees and kissed the wound. Then they switched roles, just like in their *yes* and *no* game.

'Don't be too hopeful,' Doctor Ahmed warned in his my-words-make-it-better voice. 'The odds are still stacked against you being a bone marrow match.'

They both tried not to think of it while they waited for the results.

Andrew was cranky. He knew Ben was sore, too, but Ben didn't have to write. He put on a cap to hide his thinning hair and opened *The Lion Tamer Who Lost* at the right page. It had been a good week, with the second course of chemo done and a pause before the next one to let blood counts rebuild, but Andrew's mood plummeted. Ben fussed him so much – making food and fluffing pillows – Andrew told him to go for a walk.

When he returned, Ben made cheese and pickle wraps and quietly put one next to Andrew. A moth was stuck to the sash window; its mushed wings had been immortalised by time and sun.

'I might explore what would have happened if Book Ben *hadn't* been in a car crash,' said Andrew. 'If one thing had been different. Like the butterfly effect – a *what if* scenario.'

'That term comes from Edward Lorenz's studies of chaos theory,' Ben said, counting his crumbs. 'He used a numerical computer to rerun a weather prediction and entered the decimal .506 instead of the full .506127 and the result was a completely different weather scenario.'

When he talked like this, Andrew felt guilty that he had given up university.

Ben shrugged. 'I don't like the phrase "butterfly affect" though.'

'It's *effec*t – and I think it's poetic.'

'What?'

'Poetic,' said Andrew.

'No, you said … *effect*?'

'Butterfly *effect* – effect is a noun, affect is a verb.' Andrew leaned back in his blue swivel desk chair, faded from hours of writing.

'Now you sound like my fucking dad.' Ben picked the plates up with a thick crunch. 'He's stopped criticising cos he wants to keep me quiet about Kim, and now *you* start.' Ben walked out of the room

Andrew felt bad.

'But sometimes a wrong word completely changes the meaning,' Andrew called after him. 'You know that the slightest change in a sum would have a huge impact on the result.'

'Don't speak to me like I'm fucking nine,' Ben shouted back from the kitchen.

'Well, don't *act* it,' Andrew snapped back. Then despite himself, he said, 'Grow up and tell your dad about us, like you said you would.'

Ben appeared in the doorway. Blood seeped through the pocket of his jeans. 'I *am* going to tell him. I haven't *been* there. I've been looking after you! Getting tests done, for *you*!'

'You're bleeding,' Andrew said, pointing.

'What?' Ben looked at the pocket. 'Fuck!'

He went to the bathroom and slammed the door. The lid fell off the Wish Box. Inside, a Post-it stuck to the rim. Andrew had finally wished. He took the new Post-it from its silvery bed and whispered it aloud.

I wish that Ben will be sufficient a match, so it makes it worth him enduring the pain, so I recover, and he'll know it was because of him.

He could hear Ben clattering about in the bathroom, running water, cursing.

Andrew only kept wishes that he still hoped would come true. There were two in the box, his latest and the one on a grey piece of paper, written in childish scrawl. He didn't need to read that one. He knew it by heart.

Perhaps it was time to let it go.

Perhaps after thirty years, wishes died.

He almost picked it up, prepared to finally tear it in two, when the phone rang. Ben came out of the bathroom and answered it, his voice too low for Andrew to hear what he said. Then he came into the room wearing only shorts. 'They want to see us at the hospital about my test.'

'Already?' Andrew's mood lifting at the sight of Ben's body, at the damp hairs trapping light on his chest.

'Aren't you nervous?' Ben asked.

Andrew shrugged.

Spying the Wish Box, Ben said, 'Did you...?'

Andrew put the lid back on. 'I did.' He paused. 'Will you believe in wishes if you're a match?'

Suddenly exhausted, Andrew closed his eyes for a moment and when he opened them Ben was right in front of him. He kissed Andrew with lips cold from splashed water and put a warmer hand inside his shirt.

'Remember the first day we took our time,' he whispered.

'Of course.'

Andrew bit Ben's lower lip and tugged it as though to steal his words.

'Do we have time now?' Ben asked.

Did they have time? Andrew gave the answer Ben always loved: *No*. His irises flashed traffic-light amber, the pause between stop and go. Ben hooked a finger under Andrew's belt, pulled him nearer and said, *Yes*.

And they made time.

Afterwards Ben said, 'I'm happy.'

'For now,' said Andrew.

'For now?'

'You're basking in a post-sex glow. Happiness that lasts is much rarer.'

'Don't you think we could make it last?' Ben frowned.

'I think you need to be ... *honest*.'

'I will,' said Ben. Andrew could hear exasperation in his voice. 'Let's just get these test results, and I'll tell him about us.'

'Then you'll be happy,' said Andrew. 'Because then you can really be yourself.'

29
The Biggest Mis-Word

Even on his worst day – and there were so many, often in painful succession – Ben could not regret what had happened, because then he wouldn't have slept next to the lions.

Andrew Fitzgerald, *The Lion Tamer Who Lost*

Andrew and Ben went to the hospital in a taxi. The dashboard clock said it was just after four. Andrew noticed because his last blood test had been 4.1 and he had eaten a bar of chocolate, despite wanting to throw up. The driver chatted to them non-stop; an official card said his name was Bob Fracklehurst. Andrew remembered that too because it was such an odd name. Andrea Bocelli was singing heartily in Italian.

'How can anyone listen to songs without knowing what the words mean?' Ben said grumpily, and Andrew knew he was nervous about the test results.

'It's the *way* Andrea sings them,' said Bob, clearly having heard.

'So what's this one about?' asked Ben.

'It's called "Canto della Terra",' said Bob. 'That means "Song about the Earth" – but it's really about love. Aren't all the best songs?'

Andrew glanced at Ben, but he was looking out of the window.

Over the soaring Italian lyrics, Bob whispered the English meaning – 'You and I are together briefly, for just a few moments, in silence as we look out of our windows and listen to the sky, and to a world that's awakening, and the night is already far away.'

'Isn't that beautiful?' Andrew said.

'Beautiful,' Ben replied quietly.

It was strange to not go for chemo; they almost went to the outpatient unit. Instead they headed for the general waiting room.

'Cross your fingers,' said Ben.

'I don't believe in silly superstitions,' said Andrew.

'How is wishing not a superstition?'

'It just isn't.'

Doctor Amdahl came to the waiting room for them and took them to a private room, but not the one where they found out Andrew had leukaemia. This was perhaps his own office because there was a desk with family pictures on it and a large mirror that looked like some sort of family heirloom. Andrew wondered if the doctor looked in it and checked his tie. It made him smile, despite the butterflies in his stomach.

'Please, sit,' said the doctor.

Andrew and Ben sat on padded chairs opposite the desk and Dr Amdahl stroked his tie. It was the same blue as the wall behind them. The room was warm. Andrew noticed that Ben's top was buttoned up the wrong way and remembered their frenzied kisses only an hour earlier.

'Well, the good news is that you're a match,' said Doctor Amdahl.

'A match? *Seriously*?' Andrew couldn't believe they had beaten those huge odds.

Ben grinned. 'A one in twenty thousand chance. Jesus. We did it. That's incredible.' To Andrew's surprise, even with the doctor there, Ben grabbed his hand. He squeezed it back. 'So does this mean we can do the transplant thing?'

'Yes.' The doctor paused.

Andrew realised he had said that the *good* news was that they were a match. Was there *bad* news, too? Andrew felt sick. Had they found something wrong with Ben? No. God, no.

'There's something else, isn't there? What is it?' he demanded. 'Is Ben okay?'

'Yes, yes, he's fine,' insisted Doctor Amdahl. 'Very healthy.'

'But there's something?'

Ben squeezed Andrew's hand more tightly.

'You're a close match,' said Doctor Amdahl.

'I know. You said. This is good.'

'For the transplant, yes. But your index numbers are too high to be merely incidental.'

'Can you say that in English?' asked Andrew, irritated.

'We need that taxi driver to translate,' laughed Ben. 'Sorry,' he said to the doctor. 'You had to be there.'

'HLA markers – or human leukocyte antigen – are these protein molecules on the surface of cells in the body.' Doctor Amdahl stroked his tie again. 'These molecules play a role in recognising cells that are your own from those that are foreign.'

Something warm and uncomfortable began to fill Andrew's chest. Something that made him frown and listen harder, try to understand faster, try to keep up with the words so they would explain the awful feeling of déjà vu, of sensing something before it comes, like the day he collapsed in Ben's kitchen.

'HLA markers are inherited,' said Doctor Amdahl. 'There are six HLA markers they look at for transplantation purposes, and we inherit three from our mother and three from our father.

Andrew looked at Ben. Remembered how thrilled he had been that Andrew so loved his face. Remembered Ben saying some girl at uni had said his face didn't quite work. And Andrew thought then that all the wrong things put the right way were perhaps better than all the right things in the wrong way.

Ben's face was all the right things in just the *right* way.

'You share three HLA markers,' said Doctor Amdahl. 'This means you must be related. Closely.'

Andrew felt as if he had become Ben now. He could not stop counting. The number of Doctor Amdahl's nasal hairs. The number of times he fiddled with his pen. The number of paper clips in the small box.

'It's highly likely you are brothers who share one parent,' said the doctor. 'Or perhaps first cousins. But definitely immediate family.'

Ben had said so many mis-words over the last few months. But the biggest mis-word was the one the doctor said now.

Brother.

That's what he was saying. He'd said something about maybe cousins, too, but that wasn't what Andrew heard repeating in his head. He jerked his hand away from Ben's.

Doctor Amdahl looked at them both. Said this was just an indication. For absolute results, they would have to test further. He said they were definitely related, closely, but a blood test between the two of them and whichever relative might link them would tell them how.

Andrew didn't want definite.

He wanted to say, *Thank you, but we'll get on with the donation ourselves and go home now, okay*?

But he couldn't.

Because he *knew*.

Dr Amdahl's phone rang, and he said he had to pop out, but could they wait, and he would explain what happened next with the bone-marrow transplant. The door slammed after him.

Andrew couldn't look at Ben.

'You're my fucking brother,' he whispered more to himself.

'We don't *know* that. Not definitely. He said cousins too. That's okay.'

'Okay?' Andrew shook his head frenziedly. '*Okay*? None of this is fucking okay!'

He felt sick. Put his head between his knees for a moment. Ben touched his back, and he pulled away as though his hand was hot.

'It isn't cousins – I *know* it's brothers. *Christ*.'

'How can you know?'

'I just do.' Andrew's voice was a high squeak.

He stood, paced the floor. Ben joined him, in step.

'Stop it!' cried Andrew.

He dragged Ben roughly to Doctor Amdahl's huge mirror.

'Look at *us*,' he hissed. 'Look at my eyes. Look at yours! I can see it now. Fuck, I can see it! Can't *you*?'

'No. I don't see it. The test could be wrong. That happens,' said Ben. 'Let's get them to do another. They probably mixed it up with someone else's. That's what it is.'

'So I'm some other fucker's brother?'

'Could be the *way* they did it. They miscounted those markers. Did something wrong in the lab. Why are you just *accepting* this? Hospitals make mistakes all the time!'

'Because I...' Andrew picked up Doctor Amdahl's plastic bin, thinking he would be sick.

'Those odds were too ridiculous. I see that now. So this result *can't* be true! The chances ... the chances are too great. It's maths...'

Andrew retched, but nothing came up.

'Look, even if we were related,' said Ben, 'we were us first. If we don't take any more tests, if we just ignore it, then no one need ever know.'

'*I* know,' cried Andrew. 'And that fucking doctor knows!'

He wanted to cry. This was his fault. His fucking fault. Ben looked so lost that he wanted to comfort him. But he couldn't. He *couldn't*.

'You reckon you know,' said Ben in a quiet voice. 'But *I* know they must have made a mistake.'

'You know fuck all,' whispered Andrew.

'It's just blood. Just these little HLA marker things stuck to our cells. Maybe it got stuck wrong. Maybe it's ... Maybe it's...'

Andrew reminded him that the doctor had said if they were siblings they only share one parent. 'Have you thought who *that* must be?'

Ben looked as though Andrew had slapped him.

'My fucking dad,' he said. The denial was draining away. The realisation was pale on his face.

'Yes,' said Andrew. 'Your fucking dad.'

'It *can't* be.'

'Who else is it? We definitely don't have the same mother.'

'I told him he would ruin someone's life one day!' cried Ben. 'I *told* him!'

Doctor Amdahl came back and said if they wanted to go ahead with it, they would begin the donation after Andrew's next course of chemo. They would filter Ben's blood with a machine and feed it directly into Andrew. Wordlessly, they both left the stuffy room. Along the corridor, they walked out of step, letting other patients pass between them. Bob Fracklehurst picked them up outside the hospital. Andrew was grateful for Andrea Bocelli. For words he didn't understand.

Back at the flat, Andrew tried to swing the door shut after him; Ben had to stop it so he could follow him inside.

In the living room, Andrew said, 'I won't take your blood.'

'Why not? It could save your life!'

'I want you to go.' Saying it was agony. It wasn't what Andrew wanted, not really, but he needed space. Time. To get his head around it.

'You want me to *go*?' Tears filled Ben's eyes. 'This is cos I haven't told my dad about us, isn't it? That's what this really is!'

'Yeah, right,' said Andrew, cruelly. 'You gonna tell your dad *now*?'

Ben looked stunned. 'Why do I have to *go* though?'

'I write children's stories,' Andrew said, knowing fully how nasty he was being but unable to stop. 'And nowhere in those do brothers fuck each other and then live happily ever after.'

Ben kicked over the coffee table. Books went everywhere.

'Now I'm just a *fuck*?'

Ben moved closer to Andrew, put his hand over his mouth. Andrew covered it with his. Their two same hands.

'No,' said Andrew.

Ben kissed him.

'*No*,' Andrew said again.

Ben carried on kissing him.

'I won't stop you.' Andrew didn't move. 'But I'll never fight you again. That game is over. It *has* to be, Ben.'

'But that's not fair,' sobbed Ben. 'This is a fight I don't know *how* to fucking win!' After a moment he demanded why. 'After everything we've been through, you just want me to *go*?'

Andrew went to his Wish Box and picked it up.

'Yes,' cried Ben, 'I know about your wish for us to be a match! That bloody came true, didn't it? You were right! Be careful what you fucking wish for!'

'No, that isn't it.' Andrew removed the lid. For the first time ever, it hadn't fallen off when he picked it up. 'There's a wish I wrote when I was a kid. The one I said never came true.' He took out the faded sheet of paper with childish scrawl barely visible now. He could remember writing it. He had been proud to have a proper ink pen.

Now he couldn't bear to look.

'What is it?' asked Ben.

'*You* read it.' Andrew held out the paper.

Ben took it. He looked at Andrew.

'Go on. Out loud.'

'*I wish*,' said Ben slowly, squinting at the washed-out script, '*I had a brother and I wish him to have messy yellowy hair like Darcy's brother and to know how I like to fight and we can play Scrabble when Mum's not here.*'

Ben looked up. 'Jesus,' he said.

'Tear it up,' said Andrew.

'No. It's your ... wish...'

'Well, *I* will.' Andrew snatched it and ripped it into tiny pieces. He dropped them at Ben's feet. Then he said quietly, '*This* is not what I wished for.'

'No, but you *did* wish for us to be a match. And I had that horrible test, so at least let me give you my blood? And then we can talk about this. Work it out. You're in shock. I am too. I get it now. I had no idea about the other wish.'

Andrew headed towards the bedroom. 'We can do the donation if you really want to but then I don't think we should see each other again. Lock the door when you leave.' He closed the bedroom door after him.

When he heard the front door slam, Andrew sagged to the floor. He cried until he vomited all over himself. He hated what he had done.

The wish. Turning Ben away. He got up and grabbed the phone to call him. To say sorry. To beg him to come back and hold him. But then he would only have to turn him away again because they couldn't be together. They couldn't. And his heart couldn't take that.

He finally knew who his *nobody* father was. Not just some elusive, cigarette-smoking stranger. Not Mr Bucket from *Charlie and the Chocolate Factory*. He was Will Roberts. But there was no joy. There would be no emotional reunion. No making up for lost time. Getting to know one another.

Andrew's father was also the father of the first – the *only* – man he had ever loved.

PART FIVE

BEN

30

ZIMBABWE

A Missed Sunrise

When Ben couldn't figure out the lyrics to songs on the radio, he just made up his own words.

Andrew Fitzgerald, *The Lion Tamer Who Lost*

Music drags Ben from a dream. It is a vaguely familiar song. The words fill the stuffy hut, pulling him from images of the Wish Box and Doctor Amdahl and a large mirror with him and Andrew side by side, so alike. What are the lyrics? Why does he know them and yet they make no sense? They are Italian. What was the singer's name in that taxi, that terrible day?

Ben opens his eyes. Sharp sunlight blinds him. The other hammock is empty, the door open.

'You overslept,' calls Simon from outside. 'But I finally managed to get a station on this bloody transistor radio we found. It's not exactly Radio One, but still. Think this is what they call classical, isn't it?'

It's the second time Ben has overslept. Missed his solitary sunrise. He sits up, his head aching from another restless night. His stomach knots just as it did when the realisation of what those long-ago test results meant had sunk in.

'You gonna get up then, lazy arse?' calls Simon. 'Thank God, I'm going today – you had me up more than ever last night, ranting and yelling.'

Ben's dream was so intense. He was back there. In that blue-walled office. Wishing he had never offered to take the blood test. Wishing he had sensed what he and Andrew were to one another. He should have known that such an intense bond was due to far more than random chance. He should have seen the physical similarities so obvious afterwards – their eyes, their hands, their feet. If he had, he would never have given his blood, and they would still be together.

But that togetherness isn't *right*.

This he has battled with the whole time in Zimbabwe: a desire to have what he simply can't, mixed with repulsion at himself for wanting it, mixed with a love that feels too absolute to be wrong.

It is that love that makes Ben glad he was able to donate his stem cells so Andrew might have a chance to recover.

But *has* he recovered?

Ben doesn't even know.

He must try calling again. He'll try today.

'I'm off for breakfast,' calls Simon. 'You coming? Might have a beer since it's my last one.'

'You go without me.' Ben sits up.

Simon comes back into the hut, the music increasing in volume as he brings the radio with him. 'I'm actually gonna miss you, Roberts.'

'W*hat*?'

'Oh. Sorry.' Simon turns it down. 'I said I'm actually gonna miss you, you restless freak.'

Ben laughs. 'Yeah, me too.'

'Still wish you'd told me where you buried all the bodies though.'

'What bodies?'

'Doesn't matter. Right, I'm off for brekkie.' Simon slaps Ben on the back and heads off.

Ben turns off the radio and goes onto the deck, but he has missed his sunrise. It bothers him more than it should. The day is now set to be bad, in his mind. He throws on some fresh clothes and heads for the communal lodge.

Esther is already there, eating her fruit and looking around for him. She can't stomach the mud coffee now; nausea plagues her on and off all day. Yet despite this, happiness has radiated from every gesture and word since Ben promised he would be there for her and the baby. It seems that with his acceptance she is free to be the mother she was destined to be. Her cheeks and eyes glow, even away from the evening campfire.

Sometimes she has almost said in front of the others how excited she is; Ben had to gently remind her that until they get official confirmation from a doctor, they're not telling people.

'But we *know*,' she gushes each time he says it. '*I* know. I can feel it.' And she puts Ben's hand to her still firm stomach. 'We don't need a doctor's yes.'

Only Stig knows about the pregnancy. They had to explain the reason for suddenly requesting that they leave in the next month or two. Esther didn't want him to think it was anything that had happened here. Stig didn't seem surprised, and warmly congratulated them.

'I think it's the first Liberty Lion pregnancy,' he smiled. 'At least between humans anyway. Will you send us pictures when it's born?'

'Of course!' Esther smiled.

'We like to keep up with the volunteers who've left as much as the lions who have,' said Stig.

Ben suddenly didn't mind Stig so much. He could be preachy and annoying, but his heart was in the right place.

'Our own little cub.' Esther stroked her tummy.

'How soon do you want to leave?' asked Stig.

'A month or two will be fine,' said Ben, at the same time as Esther cried, 'As soon as there are flights.' She looked at him, asked, 'You okay with that, Ben?'

'I thought we said...'

'I'm ready to go,' she admitted.

He nodded. It was different now. He was connected by blood to Esther. It didn't matter what *he* wanted. It was about *them*. This child. He was going to be a father. It would be his priority. They would go home together. He had made his choice to be with her weeks ago, and now this new life had further cemented it.

But if he could be a father, couldn't he be a brother to Andrew too?

'Yes, I'm ready' he said to Esther. 'Let us know about the next flights that come available, would you, Stig?'

Now Ben approaches Esther, still upset about his missed sunset, still with those Italian lyrics and the dream of that blue-walled room haunting him.

'Morning,' she says, her face bright.

'Morning.'

'You look knackered again, Ben.'

'Yeah. Bad night.'

'Good practice,' she laughs, and when he looks confused she says, 'For the sleepless nights ahead.'

'Won't faze me.'

'Have you told your family you'll be coming home yet?'

'No,' says Ben.

'*No*?' Esther pauses. 'Not read your dad's letter yet?'

Ben shakes his head. She could never understand the kind of pain Will has caused him. And she can never know about him and Andrew, what they were, and what they are now.

What the fuck would she think? What would *anyone* think?

'I'll read it on the flight home,' he says. At her frown, he adds more gently, 'I *will*. Esther, you've got to let me do it in my own time. Okay?'

'Okay,' she concedes.

Stig arrives then, sits opposite them with his muesli. 'I have news,' he says, his voice not the booming one meant for all ears. 'There are two cancellations on a flight to England.'

'Already?' Esther holds her face. 'We only told you three days ago! When?'

'Tomorrow afternoon.'

'*Tomorrow*?' Ben panics. It is too soon. He isn't ready for it all.

'You should take them,' says Stig. 'They're all full for another three weeks.'

'We will,' gushes Esther.

'Great. I'll go and reserve them for you now.' Stig stands and assumes his usual commanding tone. 'Everybody, listen up.' The room quietens. 'I'm sad to say that we will be losing two of our favourite volunteers tomorrow – Esther and Ben. But tonight, we'll have a bit of a party to wish them luck, so make sure you come!'

Ben can't eat any more muesli. Everything is happening way too fast. Like he has no control over it. Like he's sitting on the sides watching his own life passing by. Like a car just before it crashes.

Later in the afternoon Esther and Ben go and sit on their favourite log. The day is hazy, so the view is limited to nearby mounds and dry grass.

'You sure you're okay?' she asks. 'You've been ... distracted.'

'It's just ... well, it's all so big. These changes.'

'I know. But we'll be going through it together.'

'Yeah. You're right.'

Ben feels a sudden surge of protectiveness. He should make sure Esther is okay. That she has all she needs. Is safe. He holds her hand.

'You look tired too,' he says. 'Should you have a nap?'

Esther smiles. 'Only if you join me.'

'Sex could hurt you. Could hurt the baby.'

Ben realised as soon as she told him about the baby that it was a way to be free of his obligation to join her at night. He won't have to hope she will dim the lights.

'Don't be silly.' She pushes him playfully.

'I'm serious. You know I can't sleep with you until you've been checked over at home and it's all okay. I *mean* it.'

'We can at least hold each other,' she says.

That he doesn't mind.

They go back to Esther's hut. It has always been easier to be together there, away from Simon with his crude comments. Esther undresses and climbs into bed first. It reminds Ben of when he entered the brick nursery to lie next to Lucy. Esther, however, is not reluctant. She kisses Ben, clearly hoping to seduce him. But he says a kind no. She relents and quickly falls asleep in his arms.

When he is sure she is totally out for the count, and the light is beginning to die, he sneaks out and heads for the communal lodge. A group of volunteers play cards in the corner but don't even look up. Ben picks up the phone and dials Andrew's number. What will he say if he answers this time?

He doesn't. It is a recording again. But the message is slightly different. He has changed it. Ben frowns. So he *is* there. He *must* be okay. Should he leave a message? Say he is finally coming home. Say he gets it. Why Andrew did what he did. Say he thinks he can be a brother to him now. He really does.

But Ben says nothing and hangs up.

Is he ready to go tomorrow?

He doesn't know.

Lucy, he suddenly thinks. *Lucy*.

He must go and see her now. There won't be time in the morning to say goodbye properly. He and Esther will probably have to wake early to be picked up and taken to the airport, and lionesses are not naturally early risers, enjoying more than eighteen hours sleep a day.

He goes to find Lucy. She is not in the enclosure. She is leaving for a hunt. Darkness is beginning to swallow the landscape, but the lights from the truck illuminate the insect dance and the glossy, graceful movement of three hungry lionesses as they head out for the kill. Ben remembers all the times he has watched her. How it has soothed him during these challenging months: her languorous movements; the way her rippled fur changes colour with the weather; the way she completely ignored him most of the time.

'Want to come one last time?' calls Stig from the back of the truck.

Ben shakes his head. He does not want his final memory of Lucy to be a bloody one. Though he knows it is part of nature, he doesn't want to see it.

'I'll be back in an hour – for your farewell party,' calls Stig.

Ben waves them off; Stig and the two volunteers wave back. Lucy leads the group into the reserve. She doesn't even turn around.

Ben wills her to.

Just this time.

'Goodbye, Lucy,' he says aloud.

He remembers when he thought of her as his child and was sad to let her go from the nursery to the enclosure. Now he is going to have his own baby. Stig has promised to keep him updated on Lucy's eventual release into the wild, assured him that he'll send plenty of pictures. Ben is sad not to be able to stay long enough to see it for himself, but their baby will be born before that. There is no way of being there for both of them. He has to choose his own child.

'Goodbye Lucy,' he says again.

The small party slowly disappears into the wilderness, fading in the fake light. Lucy leads the other lionesses, her golden head and tail low, pace steady but confident, fur like damp sand in the headlamps.

'Turn,' hisses Ben. 'Just once.'

Why doesn't she? And why does he so *need* her to? Why does he need recognition for what he has been to her? He gave Andrew his blood happily, wanting to help him live. Knowing he had done so was enough. Surely knowing he has been part of helping Lucy overcome a difficult start should be enough.

Don't I mean anything to you? Ben wants to cry.

Didn't he ask the same of Andrew? Yet now – with time – he knows he meant *everything* to him. That Andrew had done the right thing in not looking back.

Lucy has gone now. Devoured by the night. Doing what she was designed for. Without looking back.

'You *do* mean something to her, you know.' It is Esther. He's not seen her walk up beside him. She puts a head on Ben's shoulder. How did she know what he was thinking?

'The fact that Lucy didn't need to look back is down to you.'

'You're just trying to make me feel better.'

'Stop being sulky.' Esther laughs, and shoves him. 'If she *had* turned, it would mean you'd failed – that she is dependent on you. And that kind of weakness would mean death in the wild. You *know* that. Remember what Stig said way back?'

'No.'

'We have to tame them without changing what they are.'

'He was talking his usual crap,' snaps Ben.

'You freed her.'

'I didn't. *She* did that.'

'With your encouragement,' insists Esther.

'But it's because of *us*, isn't it, that she needed me. We've been killing lions for years. So how can I congratulate myself for helping free her when my species caused the deaths of hers?'

'Because you're helping undo the bad we've done. And hopefully soon the lions won't even need us to do that.' Esther pauses. 'At least you know she's okay. Chuma still isn't fully part of his pride. And I don't know if he ever will be. I have to go home without knowing he's okay.'

Ben puts an arm around her.

'Anyway,' she says. 'I reckon I tamed *you*.'

'What?'

'I was in bed the other night and I realised you hardly ever get your words mixed up anymore.'

'What do you mean?' asks Ben, already knowing.

'I used to love when you said some words just slightly wrong. Oh, don't look so put out, you big chump!' She laughs and kisses him. 'You never do it now. I reckon I taught you all the words. Come on. Let's go. We've got that goodbye party and then an early start.'

Glancing one last time into the darkening reserve, Ben walks Esther back to her hut before returning to his. It is the last time he will ever see Lucy. And all Ben can think of is the last time he saw Andrew.

He understands better now.

But it still hurts like hell to remember.

31

ENGLAND

Turn

If you look back, you'll only bump into everything.

Andrew Fitzgerald, *The Lion Tamer Who Lost*

After the final session of the stem-cell donation, Ben wanted to say something to Andrew that would make him open up.

But he had run out of words.

A nurse removed the apheresis machine tubes from Ben and Andrew's veins. Ben drank plenty of liquids to replace those he had lost, and watched while Andrew ate glucose tablets and biscuits to up his sugar levels.

Then, together, they left the room.

Outside, November's breeze was full of cold promise; the airless warmth of the treatment room had ill-prepared Ben for this sudden new season. In silence, they walked along the main hospital path and then down the street, Ben dreading that different buses beckoned, different routes, different homes.

A solitary leaf followed them like a butterfly.

Andrew finally spoke after weeks of silence.

Ben was delighted and turned to hang on every word.

'You should go to Zimbabwe like you've always wanted,' said Andrew, simply.

'But I don't want to go without you.' Ben felt sick. 'Come with me, *please*. We can go as friends. Friends travel together ... friends could work...'

'I can't.'

'You *can*.'

'Ben, I'm doing this for you. I've had to ignore you … or I … I'd have given in.'

'So *give in*!'

'*No*. To be with you now only delays the pain. Can't you *see* that?'

'No,' said Ben. 'No one needs to know.' He knew he sounded like a child, insisting reality could change, but he still believed they could bury it if they really wanted to.

'*I* know,' said Andrew. 'And how long before it *would* matter? When we argue? If we want kids? When you want to tell your dad we're together? He's *my* father too.'

'I looked after you,' said Ben, tears on his face.

'And I'll never forget it.'

'You won't be calling me, will you?' Ben said it like a statement. But he wanted it to be a question. 'When I get on that bus you'll never get in touch with me again, will you?'

Andrew didn't respond.

'How will I know you got better?'

'You'll know,' Andrew said without looking at him.

Their footsteps were in perfect unison. They always had been. Ben watched their feet. His own trainers with one lace tied differently to the other contrasted Andrew's boots with zips like uneven teeth. They couldn't walk out of sync; they never had. Would they still walk the same way if Ben was in Africa, hundreds of miles away?

Ben lingered by Andrew's bus stop; his was the next along.

'This *can't* be it,' he said.

Andrew wouldn't look at him.

'What harm is a hug?' asked Ben.

'Then hug me like a brother,' said Andrew.

It was an excuse to be near him one more time. An excuse to hear that lion heart beating. Andrew put his arms around Ben, and Ben put his head against Andrew's chest. Buttons dug into Ben's body.

He snaked his hand under Andrew's top. He moved his mouth to Andrew's. But Andrew pulled free.

'This is why we can't.' He held his face in despair, the amber flash in his eyes so like Ben's own. 'I wanted a brother. But I want you as we were, as lovers. And I can't have *either*!'

'You fucking wished for it,' cried Ben.

Andrew nodded. 'I know.'

'Sorry. Please don't go.'

Andrew's bus rounded the corner. He turned back to Ben before alighting; Ben felt a flush of momentary hope.

'I hope one day you forgive me.'

The door hissed shut.

Ben watched as Andrew found a seat. He didn't turn to look out the window as the bus departed.

'Turn,' whispered Ben. 'Just once.'

The bus pulled away. Ben walked to keep up with it. Andrew didn't look.

'Don't I mean anything to you?' cried Ben.

The bus disappeared into the rest of the traffic.

Ben sat on the curb and cried.

32

ZIMBABWE

Goodbye Lucy

The mother felt sad; her cub looked sad. Because we all want to stay in the place we're loved. But love goes with us – it is light and has easy-to-grip handles and needs no passport. The mother knew this secret.

Andrew Fitzgerald, *The Lion Tamer Who Lost*

Just as he did on his first morning in Zimbabwe, Ben stands on the wooden decking in shorts, viewing what he has secretly called his sunrise, his land, his refuge, for six months. It is June. Winter is here and it's too chilly for shorts at this early hour. But Ben perseveres. It has been his routine to wear them and he doesn't want to deviate from it on this last day. He missed his sunrise yesterday, but today he was up and waiting long before it rose.

Today he and Esther go back to England.

Simon left yesterday, so there's no hum of snoring to contend with the buzz of insects, no breaking wind. Curiously, Ben misses him. But the moment is his alone; only he witnesses the colours come to life, the sky turning from ash into flame, the trees from shadow into textured browns.

The skittish split-lipped hare joins him, loitering by a sparse bush. Beyond them both, the sun rises. And behind them, in the grassy enclosures, the lion cubs will play before being freed to live in the wild. Ben is going back to the wild; to England, his wilderness. This place has been a haven.

He put the few things he brought with him into his bag last night. Then, around the campfire, he and Esther said goodbye to the volunteers they have grown close to. For Esther, it was a weepy affair. She has made many friends and promised to stay in touch, to go and visit people once home, her tears glistening in the light of their final fire. Ben has not been quite so sociable.

Now, standing on the decking, he remembers England. He lets it all in. He sees Lola being born. Sees his conversation with Andrew about children, before watching him collapse on the kitchen tiles. Sees the room in which he gave him his stem cells. Sees the flat he can still smell. It is one year since they first met in the university library and the memories flood back as he watches the sun, hoping it will lift the chill.

Soon Esther will be here with her luggage, and then the taxi in an hour, at ten. Then they will leave. He can't quite believe it. The last six months has felt more like six years.

But he is ready now.

He turns and sees Esther approaching. Her cheeks are pink in the chill air and her hair is plaited, though one wisp flies rebelliously free. Ben's heart sinks; his throat feels tight. He feels cruel at the reaction. So, he buries it and smiles. She is what he has chosen. This is what he has chosen. This is what he will live.

Esther is not smiling. She looks white.

'Are you okay?' he asks, genuinely concerned.

'It's Lucy,' she says.

'*What's* Lucy?'

'Last night ... another hunt ... later on ... after we went to bed...'

'What?' Ben feels sick.

'She was gored by a male buffalo. Out on the reserve. Stig just told me at breakfast. He's coming to find you soon ... but I wanted to...'

'Is she okay?'

'She should be, yes. Don't worry they—'

Esther is interrupted by Stig's approach.

'What happened?' cried Ben. 'Will she be okay? Where is she?'

'She's recovering in the enclosure.'

'I need to see her.'

'She won't want you near her when she's hurt like that. Nor will the other lions. But you can see her through the fence.'

Ben heads that way. Esther and Stig try and keep up.

'What happened?' demands Ben.

'She went for a huge buffalo, the feisty girl, and his horn almost ripped her leg off – her lower left flank is severely injured. We called in emergency vets and they tranquilised her and cleaned and sutured the wound. It was pretty successful, only took two hours. Now we'll just keep an eye on her, make sure it doesn't get infected.'

They arrive at the enclosure fence. Lucy is lying by the one tree in the grassy area. An angry red gash joined by black stitches cuts the back of her body in two. Now and again, she roars softly, and licks her wound. Chuma paces nearby.

'See,' says Esther. 'She's okay. She has her brother. This is definitely something he's good at. Taking care of her.'

But when Chuma tries to rub heads with his sister, Lucy growls at him, swings a paw at his face. He backs away and views her from a safe distance.

'Shit, poor Lucy.' Ben feels sick. 'It looks... Jesus, it looks ... How is she even *okay*?'

'It looks worse than it is. The surgeon did a great job. It looked shocking before he fixed her up, trust me.'

'What does this mean?' asks Ben. 'She won't be able to hunt, will she?'

'Not for a few weeks,' says Stig.

'What if it puts her off for good? What then?'

'It needn't.'

'*Needn't*?'

'Look, you two are going home today.' Stig pats Ben heartily on the back. 'Go and get your breakfast. Let us do what we do here.'

'How *can* I? How can I go home?'

'Ben,' says Esther. 'You couldn't do anything anyway. You heard Stig – she wouldn't let you near her right now. Our taxi will be here soon, and we've got a long journey ahead of us. You should eat.'

'I can't.'

'At least let's get you a cup of mud?'

Ben shrugs.

'Go on,' says Stig. 'I promise we'll keep you updated with every bit of progress she makes for the rest of the day and once you're back home.'

Ben panics. 'Shit. I don't have a phone.'

'I do,' says Esther. 'Message me, Stig.'

'I'll get one as soon as we land,' says Ben, 'and send you the number.'

'Goodbye then, Chuma.' Esther goes to the fence. Her young ward doesn't even acknowledge the farewell.

Ben realises this is sad for her, too. He puts a hand on her shoulder. 'I'm proud of you,' he whispers.

'What do you mean?'

'I've been a pain in the arse for most of my time here,' he admits. 'But you've never complained once. You've put up with me, with your morning sickness, with all of it.'

'I wasn't *putting up*,' she says. 'I've been happy here. Haven't you?'

Ben doesn't respond.

'This isn't how I wanted it to end,' he says eventually.

He remembers Andrew helping him fill in part of his application form before he came. One line comes to him now: *I hope you'll give me a chance to see my favourite animals, being released into the wild where they belong.*

He has not been able to see that. Lucy is only nine months old, so not ready to leave the enclosure permanently yet.

And it's time for him to go.

33

ENGLAND

An Ideal and Restriction-Free Candidate

Ben joined the school Chess Club and hated the new rules and that Nancy would no longer play their made-up game.

Andrew Fitzgerald, *The Lion Tamer Who Lost*

When he got home from watching Andrew leave on the bus, Ben got out the Liberty Lion Project application form. He had kept it inside the book that Andrew had bought for his birthday. All he had to look forward to now was his dad, his drinking, the burden of secrets, and an empty future.

Ben read through the segment about why they should consider him, a section Andrew had helped him fill out while he was ill.

It has been my lifelong wish to see animals run free in their own habitat, something I promised my mum I'd see one day. I would love to be part of a project that helps give them back what we humans have taken away from them – freedom. I'm twenty-three, have no commitments, and hold a full passport. I hope you'll give me a chance to see my favourite animals, being released into the wild where they belong.

He and Andrew had argued over the *no commitments* part. Ben had said he *did* have a commitment – Andrew. Andrew insisted it was better to appear an ideal and restriction-free candidate. He won.

And now Ben had no ties at all.

He sent it that afternoon.

With frost topping spiky trees like cake icing, St Mary's Church on Sculcoates Lane wasn't sufficiently heated for a November baptism-stroke-wedding-blessing. It was two weeks after the stem-cell transfusion; two weeks since Ben had sent off his application form. His brother Mike had been home for a week, and he and Kimberley had grabbed a cancelled slot when it came up.

Ben wondered if Kimberley's dress – which was as pink as a guilty face – had been influenced by her fling with Will. Her flushed face seemed to thaw the shivering guests as she trounced down the aisle, and her crimson flowers somehow added warmth to the air too. Mike had said they wanted the day to be one of joyful colour. He wore his with pride; that morning Ben had polished the Afghanistan service medal he had recently earned.

'Now, polish my shoes, lad,' Mike had joked.

Ben did it – to avoid looking at his brother, afraid that what he knew would show in his eyes. Looking at his father was just as hard. Ben could hardly be in the same room with him, and now they must unite in celebration.

They sat side by side in the front pew. Uncle John was on the other side, blowing his nose with gusto, and Aunt Helen next to him, sobbing into a tissue. Jodie Cartwright sat four rows behind with her parents. She had looked Ben up and down on the way in.

Will had asked that morning the real reason why he hadn't gone back to university.

'I'm going to Zimbabwe,' Ben had said, curt.

'I understand, lad, if it's what you really want.'

Will had disguised his vodka with fresh orange, but Ben knew.

'You're not gonna mock it now?' Ben said, knowing that the fact he was keeping his dad's secret was what made him kind.

'I never should've,' said Will softly. 'How come you've not been staying at that puff's house these last weeks?'

'*Don't* call him that.'

He had told his dad he was house-sitting while Andrew was in Spain, that when he returned he'd pay rent and stay in the spare room. Ben realised that subconsciously part of him had hoped his dad would guess what the situation really was. Now he was relieved he had never told him.

'I hope you're making the right decision.' Will's words were not harsh. 'Think I'd rather you went to bloody Africa than live with some rent boy.'

'For fuck's sake, Dad.'

Ben wanted to say, *Do you realise who you're talking about*? He wanted to grab him by the throat. Scream that he had ruined his only relationship. He looked at his dad's hands around his mug. *Those fucking hands*, he thought. Not just who they had touched, but the actual hands. The fat arch near the thumb. Like Ben's. Like Andrew's.

Now the priest blessed Kimberley and Mike, and called the godparents to the altar. Because of Mike's pleas, Ben had reluctantly agreed to be godfather. Lola wailed at the water blessing. Ben held a candle; it fluttered in the draught.

'That's that done,' said Will afterwards.

'Another tot safe from the devil,' said Uncle John.

'Too late for us,' said Will.

Ben stumbled for a moment as they walked outside, had to gulp so he would not sob.

By the gravestones, Jodie joined him.

'Like my hair?' It had been teased as stiff as cocktail sticks. 'I shouldn't talk to you after you dumped me that day, but I don't hold grudges. Wanna ride with me to the party?'

'I promised I'd look after the baby while they go in the wedding car.' Ben was glad of this obligation. 'I'll see you there,' he added.

'Something's different about you.' Jodie squinted at Ben. 'In a good way.'

I'll never be the same again, thought Ben.

She smiled. 'Still single?'

Not only single, but apparently an ideal and restriction-free candidate.

'See you later, Ben.' She winked and was gone.

In a sports-centre function room, the party commenced. Scuffed tables camouflaged with cloths and made pretty by lilies and heart-weighted balloons offered hot and cold buffet food. After an hour or so, with half-eaten food and empty cups cluttering the tables, Kimberley and Mike enjoyed their first dance. Then mismatched couples took to the floor, shuffling and swaying to the Take That tribute band.

Ben sat with Uncle John and Aunt Helen and watched. He hated dancing; his feet were clumsy. By the speaker a girl danced on her father's feet, giggling when he tried to jump.

Ben would never let anyone dance on his feet again.

'Don't you fancy that Jodie lass?' asked Uncle John. 'I'd have snapped her up in my day, lad ... Your dad's having a good time as usual.'

Will had his arm around Mrs Cartwright, while her husband glared. Lola slept in a buggy, oblivious to the question mark hovering over her head. Kimberley threw her bouquet. Ben drank beer to forget Andrew's face.

Jodie came over and put the bouquet between her and Ben on the seat, like a peace offering.

'Did you manage to get the blood out?' she asked.

'The blood?'

'Your T-shirt was covered in it last time.'

'I threw it away.'

Ben thought of the cheap one he and Andrew had bought; how the sales guy had stared at his naked chest. Andrew had tugged on the sleeve to straighten it after Ben slipped the T-shirt over his head. It was first time he had touched him; he could still feel it now.

'You're not weird, just interesting. Are you flattered?' Jodie puckered her over-red lips.

'About what?'

'Me still talking to you.'

Ben finished his beer and shrugged. Uncle John and Aunt Helen went to dance. Mike came over with a whisky chaser for Ben, and gin for Jodie.

'Not spirits,' said Ben. 'I'll pass out.'

'Ah, it's a wedding.' Mike took a pack of cigarettes from his pocket. 'Off for a ciggie.'

'We should get pissed,' said Jodie. She put his hand on her knee.

Ben needed air but there wasn't any. The room was spinning. Its centre was a circus ring, colourful, blurred, hot. The dancers were clowns with oversized feet and gaudy costumes.

'I don't feel so good.' Ben stood, dizzy. 'Give me a minute.'

He approached the doors to the car park, where smokers huddled against the chill. Mike's rich laugh warmed the cold. His tie had come undone; he was reminiscing with his pals about rebuilding a mosque with the Afghan army so children could learn to read instead of sitting outside.

'Remember the kid with the pack of cards covered in women's tits,' said Mike. 'What was his name? Played a sharp game.'

Like a backing track, laughter emanated from the nearby women's toilets: Kimberley.

'Hey bro,' said Mike as Ben appeared.

'Hey, yourself.'

'You okay?' Mike frowned.

'Just needed to get away.' Ben motioned to the toilets. 'Kim sounds happy.'

Mike inhaled on his cigarette and nodded. 'Just glad to *make* her happy. Where's Lola?'

'With Dad, so I'd not leave her long.'

Mike shook his head. 'Is he still getting pissed all the time?'

Ben couldn't say that it was guilt that probably made him drink half a bottle of vodka to sleep.

'So, you've left university,' said Mike.

Ben couldn't take his eyes from Mike's mouth, how his lips moved in such a similar way to Andrew's. Andrew would appear now every time Ben saw Mike, every time his dad cocked his head a certain way. Strange how things can be there all along but until you know you don't see them.

'I'm going to Zimbabwe,' he said.

'You should. Get out of the house. Why do you think I went away so young?' Mike let the smoke filter slowly from his mouth. 'What a shame Mum's not here, eh? She always cried at a good wedding. Remember when Dad put Bacardi in her fruit juice and she did the can-can with her sisters and they fell on the buffet table?'

Mike stubbed out the tab end with his foot and they headed inside.

At the women's toilets, he paused.

'Wait,' he said, putting his ear to the door.

'What're you doing?' asked Ben.

But he knew – Mike got into trouble so many times as a kid for listening to things he would then share with Ben. He would ascertain their dad's mood, then say, 'Dad's gonna be drinking today, we can miss school' and they were free to roam the field behind the house.

'You know how *dirty* women talk when we're not around,' he grinned. 'Told you – Becky just said she might do that Sam from number fourteen. Wonder what plans Kim has for me tonight.'

'I don't want to hear.' Ben wished his brother would give up the childhood game.

Mike pulled him to the door. 'Just listen to Becky – she slept with half the local footie team in one night.'

The function-room doors opened, and music briefly filled the lobby. When it closed again they could hear Kimberley and Becky talking, voices lower, serious.

'They're whispering,' said Mike. 'This could get juicy.'

Ben's chest tightened. 'We shouldn't be listening.'

'Shhhh.'

Kimberley was crying now.

Ben tasted ham and pickle sandwich, and beer. He opened his mouth to protest but Mike put a hand over it. Beyond the door Becky said Kimberley should forget what had happened and enjoy her day. That stupid mistakes were just that. The function-room doors swung open and song words – *In the corner of my mind I celebrated glory but that was not to be* – filled the lobby.

'Close it!' hissed Mike at the drunken woman staggering through.

'Mike probably has a few secrets of his own anyway, being a man,' said Becky.

'But it was his *dad*,' said Kimberley. 'I'll never forgive myself.'

She emerged from the toilets, Becky behind. Seeing Mike, she stopped and the colour they had so insisted on – that stained every flower and dress – drained from her face. Ben wanted to rejoin the festivities, but his feet were cemented to the ground. The doors swung open again and song words – *My heart is numb, has no feeling* – escaped.

'*What* was my dad?' Mike's voice was low.

Kimberley began to cry without covering her face. Becky made excuses and returned to the party.

'Tell me what it's best I don't know.'

Kimberley ran outside, sobbing.

'Mike.' Ben's feet moved now, and he put a hand on his brother's back. 'Why don't you talk later? I bet it's nothing.'

'Yeah, right.'

Mike marched outside.

Ben made it to a sink just in time to throw up. He went back to the party. Jodie spotted him at the bar and joined him. Will was flirting with a girl squeezed into a satin frock. An abrupt end to the music drew Ben's eyes to the stage, to Mike. He provoked cries of: *Speech, speech, speech*. Instead Mike asked Will to come forward. Thrilled, their dad stepped into the spotlight, grinning at those who patted his back.

'Friends, this is my dad.' Mike's tone was even. 'I'd like to thank him for this special day.' Some cheers. 'And I'd like to thank him for *fucking* my new wife during my absence.'

Silence. Then a chair scraping.

'Yes, folks, while I saw mates lose limbs and some their lives he was sleeping with my fiancé. Thanks for everything, Dad.'

Lola made a *gah* sound. Mike gave the mic back to the stunned singer. The drummer dropped his sticks with a clatter as Mike hit their dad in the face.

Will fell to his knees and was helped up by the priest.

'I just wanted to fix the snowglobe,' he said.

'What?' Mike's face glowed with exertion. 'It's not broken. What are you rambling about, you fucking drunk?'

Will looked at Ben by the bar.

'You told him,' he said. 'Today of all days.'

Halfway to the doors, Mike stopped. Frowned. Looked towards his brother, eyes pale. 'You *knew*?'

Ben had no voice.

'You *knew*?' Mike appeared not to understand. 'You let me get *married*?'

Ben attempted a sentence, gulped and tried again. 'I thought I was … I…'

Mike approached him and raised a hand. Ben closed his eyes to the unavoidable. It didn't happen. When he opened them, Mike had gone. Will wailed in a chair and was fussed by relatives.

He called out, 'What should I do?'

'Go back in time and don't do what you did,' yelled Ben.

Jodie handed him a whisky and he downed it.

He bought another. And another.

Then she invited him outside.

It was dark.

The Piglet air freshener in Jodie's car dangled like a bad luck charm.

How the hell was he here?

'Let's kiss,' she said.

Headlights from a passing vehicle illuminated her face.

Warm mouths open, warm tongues touching.

'Say no to me,' he mumbled.

'But I want to, Ben.'

Jodie's arms were above her head; Ben's teeth buried in her neck.

'Ben, stop, you're being dead rough now!'

An open door then, cold air. Jodie was cursing.

As the fog lifted he saw Jodie bathed in lamplight, smoking a cigarette, telling him he was presumptuous.

Piglet was immobile.

Ben was saying sorry.
He staggered home.

In the house of mismatched objects, of forks with no similar knife, unpaired plates and solitary saucers, Ben saw himself, his brother and his father as merely existing without their partners. They woke at varying times of the day, ate without appetite in bedrooms, passed one another on the stairs as though they were ghosts.

Mike needed space from Kimberley before returning to Afghanistan at the end of November. Ben had no choice but to reside there until he received a response to his Liberty Lion application.

At night, he would wake to a branch tapping on the window; just like Andrew's foot tap-tap-tapping. He would cover his head to block out the noise. He had tried ringing Andrew. He never answered, so Ben left messages. Message after message, asking why. Asking him to call back and talk to him. Just once.

But he never did.

At first Mike, wouldn't speak to anyone. After blacking his eye at the party, he had given six words to their dad – *Stay the fuck away from me*. And Will did; he shuffled off to the shed with a cigarette when his eldest son entered the kitchen, or upstairs for a nap when he came into the lounge.

Whenever Ben entered the room Will loitered like a bad schoolboy, humble and pathetic, clothes scruffy as though he had slept in them for a week. Despite everything, Ben couldn't ignore him entirely. He just couldn't. Pity mixed with repulsion and rage. It was exhausting.

Six days after the wedding, Ben found Mike by the kitchen sink, head in his hands. The picture of their mum had been moved there; plates were piled up in the sink; the ashtray overflowed.

Mike asked, 'What am I supposed to do?'

They were his first words.

Ben couldn't answer. What did you do when circumstances

outside your control changed everything? He had mauled Jodie in an encounter he could hardly recall. He had gone next door to apologise, mortified he'd upset her. Mrs Cartwright warned him to stay away or her husband would kill him. Ben had never hurt anyone before.

Who *was* he now?

'What should I do?' Mike repeated.

Ben leaned against the adjacent cabinet. 'I think that if Kim's sorry, you should forgive her. Not *him*, but her. The closeness she had to Dad was fatherly. She was lonely and he took advantage. She's not a bad person, is she?'

Mike shook his head and took out a cigarette and lit it. 'It must have occurred to you that Lola might not be mine?'

Ben couldn't lie. 'It's a slim chance, surely?'

Mike admitted to Ben that he too would have struggled with whether to reveal the affair if it were the other way around. 'You were trying to do what you thought right. But *him* – how can I look at him again?'

Ben didn't say that he too found it agonising.

He realised suddenly that it didn't matter now who knew he was gay. He could tell Mike. So what if Will found out? So what if he had disowned Uncle Jerry? So what if he disowned Ben? He was leaving anyway. So why didn't he just say it? Those three words.

'I thought about taking a paternity test.' Mike blew smoke rings. 'If Lola is mine I can get past what she's done. But what if she isn't?'

'Don't take the test.' Ben spoke more urgently than he intended.

Never underrate not knowing, he thought.

'Maybe.' Mike stubbed out the cigarette and dropped it into the sink as Will had done time after time. 'She has my blood and that's what counts, yeah?'

Ben shrugged.

'Doesn't mean it'll be easy, though. I doubt we can come here for Sunday dinner and be a normal family.'

In the end Mike moved back into the flat with Kimberley and Lola for the rest of his leave, beginning on the sofa, and finally returning to their bed. Mike had to make his choices quicker than most; time was a luxury not for him. With only days left on leave he had to accept Kim or wait another three months. When he flew back to the war zone, she stayed away from the Roberts house. Ben visited her and the baby but didn't tell Will.

Will cried at night. Ben heard him. Even a pillow over his head didn't block out the moans.

Escape came. A last-minute place on the Liberty Lion Project came up; someone had dropped out due to a family death. Ben showed his dad the letter.

'You go next week,' said Will, his hand shaking.

'Another placement might not come for months.'

Will scratched his neck. 'You'll not be here for Christmas?'

'What does that have to do with it?' Ben's mouth tasted of a mixture of pity and revulsion. 'I'm just telling you.'

He left his father mopping up spilt orange juice with a stained tea towel.

Ben tried to prepare. He had given up calling Andrew. Was tired of leaving messages. He had heard nothing. He still believed they could ignore the result, go somewhere no one knew them, even if it meant being merely friends. Ben felt ashamed of the desire that still fired when he thought of Andrew. But he couldn't stop wanting him, despite what they were. The conflict was deafening.

So he had to go to Zimbabwe alone.

On his final night in England, Ben stood outside Andrew's flat at midnight. All the lights were out. Was he home? Did he sleep? Did he wake over and over, wishing they had never taken the test? Did he wrestle with longing that both tugged at his heart and choked him?

Ben still had a key but wouldn't dream of intruding without an invite. The moon slipped behind a cloud, darkening the street. He threw his mobile phone in the gutter. If he was going to Zimbabwe, he was going completely. Turning his back on England. Turning his back on Andrew. On who he was.

He would go and free the lions, so he could bear being forever caged.

34

ZIMBABWE

Will's Letter

Ben felt bad when he missed his father more than his mother. It wasn't that he loved him more, but that he had not loved him as much as he should have when he was still alive and nagged about crumbs on the duvet and the light still being on past midnight.

Andrew Fitzgerald, *The Lion Tamer Who Lost*

As Ben and Esther board the flight home, he looks back. But there is nothing to see; they are miles from the reserve. Esther touches his arm, maybe sensing his concerns.

'Stig said he'd text me if there was anything to tell us about Lucy,' she says again as they take their seats, 'and he hasn't. I'll check again when we stop in Johannesburg.'

'I'll get a new phone when we land,' says Ben. 'Jesus. Nineteen hours. Why such a long flight? And two bloody stops.'

'Beggars can't be choosers. Just be glad there was a cancellation.'

After they have eaten their tepid airline meals, Esther asks Ben, 'Are you just gonna surprise your dad then?'

'What do you mean?'

'Well, you haven't called him.'

'I don't even know if I'll go home,' sighs Ben.

'Where else will you go?'

Ben thinks of Andrew's flat. Of the soft butterfly on his desk where he wrote. Of the Wish Box. But he knows he can't just turn up there.

He will have to call him. See if he will talk to him now. What will he say? Ben has no idea.

'Why don't you read his letter?' asks Esther. 'No better time than now.'

'His letter? Oh, my dad's. Yeah. Maybe.'

'Hours stretching ahead of you.' Esther tries to get comfortable, closes her eyes. 'Wake me if by some miracle they come around with chocolate. I've got such a craving. Can't wait to buy some in England.'

Ben asks the air hostess for a beer. Sipping it, he takes his dad's letter from his inside pocket and reads it.

To Ben,

I haven't written a letter since I wrote to the council about the wheelie bins. That was a one-off and anyway they never wrote back and the bin men still don't take away the ones that aren't pulled right to the kerb. The green one has been near our gate for two weeks and if we get rats I'll box them and send them to the bloody council.

I'm a man of speaking words not writing them, so this is hard. I talk out loud to you and Mike all the time like a soft sod. My life is dead empty with you gone but I know I've only got myself to blame for that. I've written to Mike too. Told him stuff I'm going to tell you. It isn't to make excuses or to make you think such and such. Just to say.

I should ask how your trip's going. I hope you come home when you're done. I hope Mike will come here too when he's next home. Maybe we could do the place up and decorate cos it's a shithole really. I admire you for going to Africa and doing something. I've not been much of a role model. I'm proud of you.

~~*Excuse me you'll have to give me a moment.*~~

Maybe being away has given you a break from me. Me and your mum drove each other mad and she'd go back to Ireland and see her sisters and when she came back we'd be like newlyweds for a week. I should've been a better husband but by the time you learn stuff it's too bloody late.

What happened with me and Kimberley is not something I'm proud of. I was wrong to sleep with her. I've always loved women. Probably the understatement of the century. Kim has a quality I've always loved – sweetness. I've never been happy unless there was some woman. I've told Mike in his letter that she shouldn't be blamed. I took advantage of her tears and I hope he'll forgive her. She's about the age that Molly would have been. Who's Molly, I know you're asking. I'll tell you in a mo.

I don't think Lola's mine. I think Mike can be sure she's his. I can see you tutting like you do and asking how I know. I just do. I hurt girls. I'll try and explain it. I can't make girls that survive. Maybe those X and Y things are faulty in me and maybe it's why I love them so much. I know it's best I never had a daughter. I'd only have hurt her too, no doubt.

When Mike was just two and before you came along your mum got pregnant. We never told Mike. I don't know if we sensed something or it was just cos he was little, but we decided to wait until your mum was near the end. When she was six months she started bleeding and having pains while she was picking tomatoes in the greenhouse. At the hospital they left her in a room to miscarry and then cleaned her up and disposed of the little thing and said we could go home.

It was a girl. We called her Molly. I never saw her. I said to you when Lola was born there'd been no girls in the family for years, but that wasn't entirely true cos there was Molly. I suppose she didn't want to come into this mess of a family. Can hardly blame her.

We almost never had another baby cos Heidi didn't know if she could go through it again, and even though I said we should talk about it she never wanted to. She'd sit in the room where the baby would have gone and rock in the chair and look like she'd died too. I started drinking more. I've always liked a drink, but it became more than just something I did with my mates.

When Heidi got pregnant with you she didn't dare get out of bed. She said she wanted a boy, but I wanted a little girl because it seemed such an impossible thing and I knew I'd be so glad I'd stop drinking.

When you were born, your mum loved you so much. Sometimes I think you got some of the feminine qualities of that girl. Like they were left in your mother's womb and you stole them from our daughter. I resented you so ~~fucking~~ much.

God, it's not that I blame you. I don't. I'm just explaining why I was always so critical of you. Why I treated you worse than Mike. I'm not writing this for you to say oh that's fine Dad and have it all good cos it isn't. I'm saying it cos it's true. I remember the time I tried to show you how to line up dominos and you were dead clumsy. And I lost it with you. I've never forgotten that. I'm sorry.

I haven't been drinking. I was going to, so I could write, but I want clarity. I feel like a drink now I admit. Can't lie and say I won't later.

I don't expect you to respond but it would be great if you'd drop by here when you're back. Maybe if you do Mike will too. Don't know how long letters take to get to places like Africa. People email now don't they, but I can't get on with that. I'd have rung you, but I don't know the number of your lion place. Anyway, it's better that it's all written down and you can look at it again if you want to.

~~*I think of you when I stand at the sink you know*~~.

I'm going to stop before I start rambling and go and find a post box.

Hope you come home.

Love Dad

Ben reads the letter twice. Then he folds it and puts it back in the envelope. Esther, snoozing quietly besides him, stirs a little.

'Go back to sleep,' says Ben. 'We've still got ages.'

'You read it?' she asks, drowsily.

'I did.'

'Okay?'

'I don't know,' admits Ben. 'I still don't know.'

But he decides he can go and see his dad.

35

ENGLAND

A Lifetime of Letters

And he signed, Love, Ben.

Andrew Fitzgerald, *The Lion Tamer Who Lost*

As Ben and Esther rush through Heathrow Airport to make it to their train and coach home, Ben is captivated by a stack of beautiful gold books outside an airport shop. He tries to pull free from Esther's hand, so he can look more closely. She resists, holding more tightly and reminding him her train is leaving in twenty minutes. Ben stops anyway.

He picks up one of the books. Exhausted after the nineteen-hour flight, he wonders if maybe he is imagining the title. The so-familiar words in looped shiny letters. The name he knows so well written at the top in a similar font. The final T is wrapped around the tail of a playful lion cub; in front a small boy sits cross-legged; behind them both, chess pieces float against a blue sky.

Ben whispers the words aloud: '*The Lion Tamer Who Lost* by Andrew Fitzgerald.'

'It's pretty,' says Esther. 'But I have to go.'

'I *must* buy it,' says Ben.

'Why? It's a kids' book.' She pauses, then smiles. 'Our little one won't be able to read for a long time, you know.'

'I...' Ben turns over the cover. Touches the glossy yellow spine. Looks at the black-and-white picture of Andrew. It is the first time he has physically seen his face in so long, and it's like a punch in the chest. He looks tired. Sad. 'I *know* the writer.'

'Really? Wow.' Esther looks at the time on her phone. 'Look, I can't wait if I'm going to get my train. There's a huge queue in there.'

Ben looks but knows he has to buy it.

'You don't understand,' he says. 'This is by my ... a really good friend.'

'Shall we say goodbye here then,' she suggests.

Her hair is plaited, as she has often worn it on hot days with the lions. Her mascara is smudged. Travellers push roughly past with suitcases. Ben feels a surge of affection and touches her cheek. They have seen each other almost every day for six months. Now they will part to each go home – her to Newcastle, him to Hull – and then decide where they will live as a couple.

'Give me a hug,' she says, her voice breaking.

She is tiny in his arms. Ben kisses her forehead.

'I'm going to miss you,' she says.

'It's only two weeks,' says Ben. 'I'll buy a new phone today and text you.'

He can tell she doesn't want to go and feels bad that he is more eager to look at *The Lion Tamer Who Lost*. So, he decides to say he loves her. To make her feel special. But the words catch in his mouth. He can't do it.

They simply part with another hug.

And he buys the book.

In seat seventeen of a National Express coach Ben carefully opens the first page. He wonders when it happened, *how* it happened. Did Andrew win that competition he entered him in before they broke up? Maybe a publisher simply read and loved it. He isn't surprised. How *happy* Andrew must be. And he must be okay if this has happened.

On the first page it simply says, *For Ben*.

He puts the page to his chest, overwhelmed. Then he opens it where Book Ben first sees lions under his bed. Then to where he gets them to lie down next to him. Then to where they leave him. He opens a random page and reads the words aloud, but softly.

'Ben liked his wheelchair when it meant he could avoid dancing. At the Christmas school party, he watched the others sway and stamp and stumble. Nancy, however, danced like a ghost, flickeringly, swishingly, beautifully. This was perhaps the only time Ben wished his feet could move too.'

Ben remembers when Andrew danced on his feet.

It seems a lifetime ago.

Impatient drivers honk horns, pulling him from the memory. Outside, black clouds trot across the sky like sheep looking for a funeral. The motorway traffic moves more lazily, each car nudged up against another. Two children in the seat behind squabble over who's had the window seat longer; their mum says she'll get the driver if they don't behave, and the boy says, 'If he comes back here we'll crash and blow up.' Ben smiles. He sounds just like Mike did as a kid. Mike voicing the worst in the back seat of the car, Mike pointing to abandoned wheels in laybys and foxes squashed flat on the road.

Suddenly he misses him. Longs to see him.

But he is nervous about seeing his dad. The letter helped. When someone opens up like that – especially someone like Will – it is impossible not to feel some compassion. Ben feels sad about the sister he never had. Now that his dad has shared the truth about a long-ago daughter, should he tell him he has a long-ago son too? If he can see Andrew as a brother, is it time to let him have the family he always wished for?

Ben turns back to the book. A wool-haired woman in seat nineteen puts down her knitting and leans across the aisle, says her name is Betsy, and that she has nine grandchildren.

'What are you reading?' she asks.

Ben holds up the golden cover and she oohhs at the lion cub.

'My Eleanor would love that,' she says.

Ben buys some dry cheese sandwiches from the coach assistant. He offers Betsy half.

'So where are you going?' she asks him, cheese stuck to her wrinkled cheek.

'Home,' he says, simply.

'Where have you been?' Her dentures clack together.

'Zimbabwe,' says Ben. 'For six months.'

'Heck, you must have missed your family.'

Ben nods. 'My brother mostly.' He means Mike, then realises the word should be plural.

'I've six brothers,' says Betsy. 'Eh, the fallings out we had – used to fight over who got the biggest bedroom and the most lemon meringue pie, and then when we grew up we chuntered on about who got more attention. But we always made up.'

Ben wishes he and Andrew had such simple things to solve; lemon meringue pie could be cut more equally, and bigger bedrooms won with a coin toss.

'Did you write to your brother?' Betsy asks, knitting now.

'I sent a postcard,' says Ben.

He realises now how thoughtless he was not to have written to Mike. But then they never exchanged letters while he was England, so why would they now?

'Letters get all your thoughts down without interruption,' says Betsy, knitting needles dancing. 'You don't have to be on holiday.'

Ben has a lifetime of letters in his head.

Betsy eventually falls asleep and he reads another excerpt from the book.

'*Ben joined the after-school chess club and hated the new rules and that Nancy would no longer play their made-up game. She won the end-of-term tournament because her king defended her queen and covered all Ben's escape squares. If they had played at home, he was sure she'd have surrendered.*'

Ben remembers Andrew and him playing Cheaty Chess. There are so many other curious similarities in the book; so many words that he knows their relationship inspired. He finds a pen in his rucksack. With no paper, Ben writes on the blank pages at the end of the book.

Dear Andrew,

I'm on a coach. I just got back from Zimbabwe. I don't know where to start. What to write. Your book is beautiful. It was the first thing I saw when I got back to England. I've read most of it now. I see so much of us in it and all that was going on when you were writing it. The words seem more real somehow inside it than they were on your screen. You must be so happy.

I thought of you all the time when I was away. I thought of your questions. Remember, during chemo? You asked me to tell you a happy memory of me and my dad. We didn't know you were asking about your own father, did we? I was giving you ~~your~~ our family history. I should call him our dad now, shouldn't I? I was so angry at him then about the Kimberley thing and I refused to find good memories for you. I picked the dancing on his feet thing because it was all I could think of.

But there's another thing I remember.

How are your blood readings? I think of them when I'm reading the time. Are you well now? I'm guessing you are because the book is out and inside the cover it says you live in Beverley. You look so sad in the picture though.

Ben looks up, pen poised. Rain spots the window as though it's a dot-to-dot puzzle asking to become something; as a child, he always counted the bumps in his woodchip wallpaper, seeing patterns, forming shapes. Andrew does the same with words. They are as alike as they were different when together.

The rain increases, drowning the dots.

I'm still mad at my dad. That might never go. But he's told me some stuff that makes me see him a little differently. I refused to find good memories for you that day. I wanted to deny there were any. But I can't. Just as I can't deny us and what we are. You were right to end it. I totally understand how that must have been for you.

I want us to be what we are.

Andrew, I met someone. A girl. I know you'll think I'm lying to myself.

I know that I am too. But I won't ever love another man. And I do love her. It might not be how we loved. Nothing ever will be. But she's kind and she's fun. And she's going to have our child.

Yes, I'm going to be a dad. That's why we're home.

'Do you want a mint éclair, lovey?' asks Betsy, leaning across the aisle with a green crinkly packet.

Whatever she is knitting is taking shape.

He unwraps the sweet. The taste takes him back to school trips and long car journeys to the coast, squashed up against tents and bags in the back with Mike. He wonders whether Andrew's childhood holidays were squashed and doubts it. He never talked about them. The best holidays were the squashed ones. Tents that wouldn't stay up, shared sleeping bags that made hellishly loud rustles as you turned over, breakfast a battleground of who got the few rashers of bacon first.

I've thought a lot about telling Dad the truth about us. Telling him he's got another son. He lost a baby girl before I was born. He sent me a letter while I was away and told me. Really, he lost two kids, didn't he?

Andrew, I can be your brother.

I can. I'm with Esther now. I understand why you had to let me go. How important having a family is to you. If I'm your brother, then you'll have a dad. You'll be able to get to know him, and Mike. No one need ever know what we once were, only that we were friends and that this curious coincidence has happened. They don't even have to know about the wish.

The hiss of doors opening interrupts him; the coach has arrived in Leeds and it's the end of Betsy's journey. She gathers her wool and needles and bags, and gives Ben a thumbs-up. A guy with headphones pounding some bassline gets on and takes that seat. The coach pulls out of the station. The rain stops. The window dries, ready for a new puzzle.

So the other thing I remember about Dad...

It's another happy one like the dancing on his feet. We used to do newspaper sudoku puzzles together. I was maybe twelve and Mum hadn't been dead that long. I know he asked me instead of Mike cos I was in the top maths group. Mike was grounded that day for stealing penny goodies from the corner shop. But I still felt proud that he needed me for that half-hour after our Sunday fry-up. He ordered this ridiculous pamphlet once from the bookstore about how to do brainteasers properly and I just told him that the point was to figure it out for yourself.

Dad had this pencil he always used cos then he could rub out wrong answers. We did the easy sudokus at the start. The ones where they give you more numbers in each box. But they bored me. It was like cheating. Like when you picked wishes that had good odds. There were three levels of sudoku in the Sunday paper. Piss-easy, mid-level and hard. Dad liked that in the piss-easy ones he could just go along the lines to see if that row already had a two or a three or a five and eliminate that way.

Anyway, that memory makes me smile. Maybe you can make such memories with him one day.

The ink is beginning to fade and Ben scribbles on a napkin until it flows again. His fingers are stained black. The sign for Hull passes the window. Almost home.

Ben finishes the letter.

Andrew, I'm not who I was when I left England six months ago. I was selfish then and wanted you how I wanted you. I still love you. I always will. But it's more important to me that you're happy, and if that means being a brother to you, I can. Remember when we talked about being happy that time, just before we got the results. You said I'd be happy when I could really be myself. But I'm happy now. I am. Knowing I'll be a dad. Knowing it's the only way we can ever see each other.

You said that last time at the bus stop that you hoped one day I'd forgive you. I do. There's nothing to forgive.

PART SIX

ANDREW

36

No More Questions

When Ben could finally walk a little stiffly, like a matchstick man, the lions left. He put snacks by the bed and wondered if he should pretend his twig legs still didn't work.

Andrew Fitzgerald, *The Lion Tamer Who Lost*

In a hospital room, Andrew and Ben were joined again. They were attached to a machine that would pass Ben's life-giving stem cells into Andrew. The white apheresis machine was no larger than a photocopier and sat between their beds. Andrew had looked up *apheresis*; it was Greek for *to take away* and meant the omission of letters at the start of a word. Like some of Ben's mis-words.

No omission of letters could change the word they were now.

Brothers.

'How many times do we have to do this?' Andrew had asked the doctor at the start of the treatment.

'Three times this week,' said Doctor Amdahl, 'and three the next should do it.'

Then he described again how Ben's donated stem cells would enter his bloodstream and travel to the bone marrow, where they would hopefully produce new cells in a process known as engraftment. Andrew pictured Ben's cells seeking his, merging, their almost-identical blood swimming together. Ben would always be inside him now.

'We'll monitor all of this by checking your blood counts on a frequent basis,' Doctor Amdahl added.

So for two weeks a sterile needle took blood from the vein in Ben's left arm, passed it through the machine to remove the required white cells for Andrew, and then returned to Ben the remaining red ones. Each session took four hours.

Andrew hadn't seen Ben since he asked him to leave the flat. Their first eye contact was awkward, and they had to swap beds because they had picked the wrong ones. A nurse prepared the device and then left them alone.

As soon as she had gone, Ben asked Andrew with soft desperation, 'Don't you love me anymore?'

Andrew wanted to put a hand on his cheek. He wanted to tell him of *course* he did, didn't he *know* he did, didn't he know that his refusal to see him was *because* he did, that he was letting him go *because* he did. Andrew wanted to pretend they had never taken the test but knew if he pulled the needle out of his arm and touched Ben he would never leave him. He knew what they now were to one another would slide between them in bed, like the snake tempting Eve.

The last few weeks, since the revelation, Ben had filled Andrew's mind. He found his mismatched socks in the linen basket, his favourite chocolate bars in the fridge and his spare toothbrush in the bathroom. One of his CDs randomly sprang to life when Andrew powered the machine. Ben's late-night phone messages punctuated the solitude. Torment cracked his otherwise perfect non-mis-words. Andrew ignored them. He wrote furiously, of Book Ben's despair when lions ceased their midnight visits.

Now, when Ben asked if he loved him, Andrew turned away. He couldn't look at him. He wasn't strong enough.

During their third session, Ben said, 'I miss your questions. My favourite was when you'd ask what I thought. Why won't you talk? I've no clue what you think but you've always asked me. So ask me now! Ask me something – *anything*.'

We have all the answers now, thought Andrew.

He smelt Ben's hair gel sometimes, cloying in the windowless room. When they were still together, he had tasted it once during sex. Now it followed Andrew everywhere; it washed over him in bed, where in the dark he almost succumbed to phoning Ben, thinking he couldn't give him up. Perhaps they *could* be together, even just as brothers.

No.

How could he go to Ben's home and see his own father and not be able to say who he was? How could he be around the man he had liked despite his rudeness? This man who had existed all along, nearby. And how could he meet Mike, his other brother? Meet Lola, the niece or sister he had seen born. Ben could never understand what it felt like to finally have a family, and not be able to meet them.

Andrew would have to choose nothing.

In choosing something he would take away Ben's chance of a normal future. Ben was young enough to move on and find someone else. Much as the thought of him with another man hurt more than any medical test, Andrew knew he must sacrifice what he wanted for Ben's sake, too.

'Why did you accept my blood, but you won't even talk to me?' asked Ben during their fourth session, his voice loud and angry.

It was a question Andrew had asked himself, one he couldn't answer. Perhaps it was so he could have some part of him without judgement. Perhaps he was just a coward, afraid to die.

'Do you know what I'm going through?' Ben demanded. 'I'm losing my fucking mind.'

Andrew knew the medication Ben had taken to coax stem cells from the marrow into his bloodstream caused him muscle aches, headaches, and insomnia. He shivered frequently and complained of numb lips.

'I gave up university for you!' he cried.

You gave that up for a boyfriend who never asked you to, thought Andrew.

'Why can't we overlook it?' Ben continued. 'Talk to me! How the fuck can you ignore me like this?'

With great difficulty, thought Andrew.

'Let's get the proper DNA test done,' said Ben, more gently. 'It might not even be true.'

A test will only confirm what I know, thought Andrew.

A nurse came in then, read some print-out papers, asked if they wanted tea, and left to make a sugary one for Ben, who then seemed to run out of words.

He had more at their fifth session, though.

'We could run away,' he said, scratching where the plastic line had pierced his skin.

He wore the jeans Andrew loved, ones that had never been ruined by blood or ink. The ones he had too. The ones they had both worn on their first date. Andrew remembered the last time Ben wore them. They had been drinking lattes in the coffee house near his flat, an autumn day like any, a good day when his blood reading was 7.7, when he was between chemo, when they were still in that place called *not knowing*.

'We could go where no one knows us,' insisted Ben. 'Away from my dad.'

Our dad, Andrew wanted to say.

Ben's pause said he had thought of this, too.

'Come with me to Zimbabwe.' Ben's voice broke. 'You love lions too. You can do all the research you want for your book; I can do what I promised my mum. It's perfect. We could stay there.' He paused. 'No one would know.'

We'd know, thought Andrew for the hundredth time.

And then it was the last session. They left the room together. On the way to their bus stops their footsteps were in perfect unison. Andrew watched their feet. He tried to walk out of sync with Ben.

But it was impossible.

37

Two Phone Calls

> *Ben decided, after another boring English lesson, that in the future he would write all his own books.*
>
> Andrew Fitzgerald, *The Lion Tamer Who Lost*

When Andrew unlocked the door to his flat an hour later, the phone was ringing. Anticipating Ben, he stood by the machine, hand over his mouth, heart hammering. Instead an unfamiliar voice said she was Tara Smith from Black House Books, a publisher Andrew had heard of.

He picked up the phone.

'Hello,' he said in a voice that didn't sound like his.

'Hi,' she said. 'Is this Andrew?

'Um, yes.'

'How are you today?'

'Great.'

'I'm really pleased to tell you that you've shortlisted in the Best First Three Chapters section.'

'In the *what*, sorry?'

'The Best First Three Chapters section – for the children's book category. It's our annual competition. Congratulations! Only twenty of you went through. You must be thrilled. We had over five thousand entries.'

Andrew wondered if his sugar levels had dropped or if the emotion of leaving Ben was responsible for his confusion. 'What did you say?' He sat on the sofa edge like an unruly child waiting to see the headmaster.

'We invited entries to our annual competition earlier this year. Hang on a moment; I have your letter here.'

While Andrew waited he scanned his desk as though a clue might be there. His latest chapters sat on the growing pile. The photo of his mum faced the wall though he couldn't remember moving it; he got up and turned it to face the room again.

'Here,' said Tara. 'It says you've had two books released with a small publisher ... one was used by a primary school ... and that *The Lion Tamer Who Lost* is not yet published and almost complete...'

'That's all true,' said Andrew, 'but I didn't send it.'

'Ah, yes, the letter's from your agent. I guess he decided to surprise you.'

'My agent?' Andrew frowned.

'Yes, Ben Roberts.'

'*Ben*?'

How on earth?

Andrew tried to think back. He frowned. Recalled that there was a time when Ben had asked unusually incisive questions about the book while they played Cheaty Chess. He had thought Ben was distracting him from what had been a bad day, one when Andrew's hair had come out in the sink. Ben had put his arm around him, joked that he would buy a new rug for him.

He must have pretended to be an agent and submitted the chapters secretly.

Tara interrupted his thoughts. 'Thank him for us, won't you? We enjoyed your novel so far.'

'I...' Andrew felt like the room got smaller. 'He's not my agent anymore.'

'Oh dear. Well, we can just deal with you from now on; it's not a problem. So, can you make it to our award ceremony in London in four weeks?'

While Tara explained how the winner would be published and receive a ten-thousand-pound advance, Andrew walked the length of the lounge. He looked at the chair where Ben often sat watching him type and wondered what he was doing.

'How long have you been writing?' asked Tara.

How long had it been?

Ever since he had been in the back of his mother's car on a trip to Ireland, no older than three, and thought the clouds looked like mean ghosts. He had given them names and relationships to one another.

'At least your agent submitted it before you parted ways,' said Tara.

Ben had been there for the whole book. He had listened to Andrew read chapters when he required feedback. He had massaged Andrew's shoulders, moving hands lower with every word.

Andrew closed his eyes; he couldn't think of those things now.

'If you go to our website,' Tara continued, 'you'll see who else shortlisted. I'll send out your ticket for the ceremony today and if you can attend we'll book you a night at the hotel where it's held. It's November the thirtieth. Can you come?'

'I don't see why not.'

Andrew's mind raced; would he be well enough? It was four weeks away.

'Yes,' Andrew repeated, more firmly.

'Great, we'll see you there,' said Tara.

Afterwards Andrew sat in silence. Had he really shortlisted out of five thousand others? Had Ben assessed those odds when he sent it? Twenty shortlistees in five thousand was better than the one in twenty thousand odds of their test being a match. Ben had done so much for him; given blood, cared for him, and now this. What had he done in return? He had not even given him the chance to try and be a brother.

The phone rang again. Now it would be Ben. The machine didn't pick up and it rang and rang. In the end, Andrew answered.

'I was bloody worried for a minute there!'

It was Leo. The past was chasing him, and he was too tired to run.

'Thought you might be dead.'

Andrew sighed. 'You won't have to fake tears at a funeral.'

'That's cold,' said Leo.

'You've caught me at a bad time,' Andrew replied.

'A bad time?' He laughed. 'I know you've been having chemo, but you must have heard?'

Andrew wandered to the window, touched the brown moth still stuck to the glass. 'How did you know I'd had chemo?'

'I called your place about four weeks ago and spoke to – what's his name? He said you were ill; I should leave you alone. But I had to ring you about this.'

Leo had spoken to Ben. Ben never said.

'Ring me about what?' Andrew asked.

'The competition,' said Leo.

'How do you know? *I* only just found out.'

'I shortlisted too, you divvy.'

Andrew went into the kitchen for a cereal bar. 'You?'

'Sure did. Saw your name at their website too. Not surprised. You've had practice. I just scribbled out something about a group of kids who go pirate hunting. Is what's-his-name going with you?'

'His name's Ben.'

'Is he going with you?'

'No,' said Andrew softly.

'I'll drive us then,' said Leo.

'No, I'll get the train,' said Andrew.

'Stubborn as ever. Why spend the money when I can take us?'

'I like the train.' He crunched on the oaty biscuit.

'For God's sake, I'm not gonna try anything. Is what's-his-name possessive? Doesn't he trust you?'

'Leo, I'm tired. I'll see you there.'

Andrew clicked the red button on the receiver and Leo's voice died.

He returned to the living room. Ben had obviously entered the book in secret. Andrew half anticipated the phone ringing again, expecting Ben to try and reconnect. He didn't.

He had nothing again. Nothing he knew, understood well, was familiar with.

But nothing is so much harder after you've briefly had something.

Andrew got better.

Doctor Amdahl – glancing intermittently at the empty second chair – told him a few weeks later that after evaluating the results of various blood tests, he could confirm that new blood cells were being produced, and the cancer was in remission.

Ben's blood had healed Andrew. He might be able to live a long life because Ben was his brother. He could finish the book because he was his brother. Andrew would become who he was, who he should be, because Ben was his brother.

But he could not have *him*.

38

The Lyrical Chambermaid

Ben hated reading aloud in class.

Andrew Fitzgerald, *The Lion Tamer Who Lost*

The awards schedule flapped next to the hotel reception desk, lifting at the breeze from the revolving doors. Andrew had never attended one before. He thought of school assemblies, of never getting a certificate for being the best swimmer or earning a thousand house points. 'Too busy daydreaming,' Mr Wood always said, forgetting that low blood sugar could lead to such distraction.

Andrew read the day's schedule. At noon writer Lynne Lowell – whose novel, *Playing with Fire,* had been a bestseller – would talk about getting that first draft shipshape. Children's writer Paul Stock would sign copies of his book after that. Then the Black House editors would give talks throughout the afternoon. And finally, before the evening meal, the shortlisted writers had to read their work aloud.

Andrew hated public speaking. He had only read in local schools to children, which he hadn't minded. Kids were so eager, so easily pleased.

A receptionist appeared behind the desk and asked, 'Can I help you?' in a haughty voice. 'Breakfast is down the corridor.'

'Thanks, I've been.'

Andrew lifted the schedule page and read the evening's highlights: the prize-giving ceremony. There would be ten thousand pounds for the winner and five hundred for two runners-up.

'It's only for those with invites,' said the receptionist.

'I know.' Andrew showed his.

The receptionist smiled as though a puppeteer had lifted the corners of his mouth. 'We'll see you later then, sir.'

The revolving doors sent in another gust that tugged the schedule pages from Andrew's hand. Leo pulled a familiar case into the lobby, his shoes clicking on the wood.

'Andrew.' He always said his name as though to remind him he existed. 'Didn't think you'd be here yet – did you stay last night?'

'I thought it'd be good to prepare.'

'I worked until late, slept a few hours, then got up at five and came.'

Leo gave his name to the receptionist. Then said to Andrew, 'Your hair,' and raised a hand towards it.

'It was the chemo. It'll grow back again.'

'How come what's-his-name didn't come with you, then?' With Leo's wanderlust sated, the year-round tan had faded, leaving dry skin about the eyes and a spattering of freckles.

Andrew shrugged. 'He's busy.'

'Too busy for something as big as this?'

'I've got stuff to do. See you later.'

'Want to get a coffee?'

'No.' Andrew felt unkind but wasn't in the mood.

'What's up?'

'My health's not the best and I don't want to push it.'

'Guess I'll find something to do.' Leo dragged his case towards the bar.

Andrew headed for the stairs.

'Don't you think,' called Leo as an afterthought, 'that maybe something more than our books brought us both here together?'

Andrew was surprised. Leo was never so profound.

'No,' he said. 'Never occurred to me.'

Andrew knew, however, that it *was* more than his book that had brought him to this London hotel with a room overlooking Covent Garden and five types of tea on the condiment tray. He had Ben to thank for being here.

Andrew thought for the hundredth time of writing him a letter. Of explaining exactly why he had done what he had. Of saying his love had never died. That it was because of the strength of it that he had known he must let him go. Give him a chance to find love that didn't break such laws. But Andrew knew Ben was probably in Zimbabwe now and he didn't have the address.

A beautiful voice disturbed his thoughts.

Andrew stopped halfway down the corridor to his room. It must be one of the writers reading somewhere nearby. But only his door was open. Just outside a chambermaid trolley piled with towels and toilet rolls was parked. The words continued. He looked into his room. Inside a woman in a too-big striped smock sat on the bed and read from a magazine. Her red hair was pinned up with a clip. Andrew listened to the lovely voice, not wanting to move in case he startled her.

Eventually she saw him. She flushed as bright as her hair and apologised profusely. 'Oh, sir, I'm sorry. Please, I'll get out of your way.' She was Irish. A lilac name-badge spelt *Cora* in faded script.

'No, it's fine. You read beautifully.'

'I'll be in trouble if Sheila catches me slacking again.' Cora hugged the magazine to her chest. She looked no older than twenty. 'Please don't report me. I got caught reading the other week when I should've been ironing. Listen to me going on! You're going to report me, aren't you?'

Andrew laughed and said he had no intention of doing any such thing. He just wanted to know if Cora had been taught to read like that. 'You must be an actress,' he said.

She shook her head, said she had only been able to read at all for two years and now couldn't stop doing it aloud. Andrew knew he also moved his lips when he read – a curious quirk Ben shared.

'What time do you finish?' Andrew asked.

Cora emptied the bin and stared at him like he'd asked her to undress.

Andrew realised she might think it a come on. 'I wasn't propositioning you.' He paused. 'Can I ask a small favour? ... And in return you can be my guest today.'

'Your guest, sir? I don't understand.'

Cora unhooked the open door, ready to leave. Andrew explained how he was there for the award ceremony and could take a companion.

Cora let go of the door and it hit her in the head.

'You're one of the writers?' She rubbed her temple. 'We had JK Rowling stay here once and I was so excited I didn't sleep!' She paused. 'What's the favour though?'

Andrew thought quickly; if he missed Tara Smith's three o'clock talk he'd have an hour before he had to read with the others at four. 'Would you read some of my story to me, so I can figure out how to do it best?'

'*Me*?' Cora leaned on the trolley. 'That's all – I read a story to you and I can come to your big posh do?'

Andrew nodded.

'Maybe.'

She smiled and pushed her trolley on to the next room.

'Meet me here at three,' he called after her.

Later, Andrew joined the other writers in the Regency Suite for the first talk. Lynne Lowell read an extract from her novel and answered the questions fired afterwards. Paul Stock followed with seven pages from *Jason's Magic Pencil.* He then signed copies on a table in the corner. Reeking of alcohol, Leo heckled Paul, asking why a child with a magic pencil would paint puppies when he could have had a Nintendo Wii.

Andrew was glad when Paul thanked the audience for listening, so he could sneak away to wait for Cora. At ten past three he thought she wasn't coming. Eventually she knocked. She had changed into a polka-dot dress. Aware of how peculiar this meeting was, Andrew asked if she would like one of the five flavours of tea.

'I've tried them all,' Cora admitted. 'The yellow is best. I shouldn't tell you this, should I, sir.'

'Call me Andrew. I feel like a school teacher when you call me sir.'

'Oh, sorry, sir ... *Andrew.*' Cora looked at the shampoos scattered about the bathroom, the pyjamas on the floor. 'I ought to be cleaning.'

Andrew laughed. 'I'm messy, I know.'

He took the printed copy of *The Lion Tamer Who Lost* from his case. In some ways, it was a memoir. Every page had been influenced by Ben – every rewrite by his thoughts, every plot development by their relationship.

'When you read earlier, how did you make it sound so...' Andrew wasn't sure what word he wanted; '...hopeful?'

Cora sat on the bed and fiddled with her strap. 'I just think about...'

Andrew sat on the adjacent bed. 'About what?'

Cora's voice assumed its lyrical quality as she talked about a father who disappeared when she was five. She said she later left school at fifteen with no qualifications. When she finally learned to read she felt if she did it aloud her father, somewhere, somehow, might hear and come back one day.

Cora said, 'Stupid, I know.'

'No, it isn't,' insisted Andrew.

He handed her the manuscript.

'You wrote this?' Cora touched the pages. Andrew nodded. 'Wow.'

'Will you read it to me?'

She did.

'*"Here comes the Stick-Man!" they cried. In the chorus, no voice was louder than the next. "Hey Ben! You walk like you got one leg shorter than the other!"*'

Those lines Andrew had written while Ben was sleeping.

'*Like a pride of hungry lions, they circled Ben. But he knew they would soon tire of teasing a creature who could not outrun them. He knew when the girl in 6G who wore an eye-patch appeared with a skipping rope he would be forgotten.*'

Andrew had typed these words knowing Ben would be waking soon.

'*Nancy headed for the lunchtime club with a stack of chess set boxes.*

She turned away from Ben. Perhaps she hadn't seen him. Perhaps the sun got in her eyes. But Ben didn't think so.'

Andrew had edited those lines after Ben had gone.

Cora stopped. 'Is that enough?' she asked. 'Oh, sir, I didn't mean to upset you.'

'No, these are good tears. I guess I just have to read it as though I'm reading it to someone special, like you do.'

'And who would that be?'

Andrew paused. 'Ben.'

'Who's he?' Cora asked.

'My brother. He's away.'

Until now he'd never said *brother* aloud. There was curious relief in sharing it with a stranger. He could say it, as though he really had one, without judgement.

'Read it to him then.' Cora paused. 'So what happens tonight?'

Andrew gathered up his pages. 'I only know it begins at eight. Shall we meet in the bar five minutes before?'

'Do you think you'll win?' asked Cora.

Andrew hadn't thought about it. He could barely think beyond having to read in front of an audience.

'Just being here is a win,' he said.

Then he thanked Cora again and walked downstairs with her, saying 'If only we could swap places,' before heading back to the Regency Suite.

Andrew was the fifteenth of sixteen readers. He wasn't sure if it was worse seeing the others perform first but there was little he could do except wait. Most of them gave long lists of credentials, catalogues of university MAs and competition wins. Leo took to the podium ninth and read confidently, looking up frequently to engage with the room. Andrew wondered if he should fake a migraine.

When it was his turn, he climbed the steps, heart hammering, and launched straight into the chapter after a shaky breath. An elderly woman suggested that he move closer to the microphone and he lost his way. The audience were deathly quiet. He resumed and tried to read it as though Ben were listening but that only made his throat tight. He was glad when it was over.

Questions followed.

'Your first time?' a woman with red lips said, and Andrew nodded.

'Your first book?' asked a bespectacled man, and Andrew shook his head.

'Reckon it'll win?' asked Leo, and Andrew left the stage.

Later, before the prize-giving, the finalists occupied four oval tables in the restaurant for watercress and crispy duck salad, pan-roasted halibut, and sticky ginger parkin. Leo was at Andrew's table. *Two Hundred Blue Skies* author Geoff began the meal with descriptions of all the writerly retreats he had stayed in. This led to Leo describing how prostitution was an esteemed profession in China. Gladys, the woman who asked Andrew to move nearer the microphone, said prostitution was not suitable table talk.

Louisa, the red-lipped woman who asked Andrew earlier at the reading if it was his first time, said, 'Travelled much, Andrew?'

He opened his mouth to speak but Leo butted in. 'He's diabetic. He always preferred it when I travelled. Second-hand travel I call it.'

'You two know each other?' Geoff shovelled halibut into his mouth.

'We dated for four years,' said Leo. While the others continued chatting he leaned closer to Andrew and said, 'So what is it you like so much about what's-his-name?'

'He's called Ben and you know it.'

'Can't be going that well if he's too busy to come to something like this with you. He was like a devoted little puppy in the hospital.'

'Can we talk about something else?' Andrew couldn't eat any more.

'So something *is* wrong?'

'No.' Andrew found himself counting the remaining morsels on his plate.

'Your face says otherwise. You never were any good at hiding your feelings. Talk to me. Christ, we were together four years.'

To shut him up, Andrew snapped, 'We split up.'

'Shit. Why?'

'It's complicated.'

'Isn't it always?'

Andrew stood, said good luck to the others, and headed for the door.

Leo followed, catching up with him at the stairs. 'Sorry if I was rude.' He paused. 'Come on. Why'd you really split with what's-his-name?'

Andrew glared at him. 'It's Ben. And it's none of your fucking business.' He continued up the steps.

'So you *do* know why,' Leo said gently, dropping the rude persona. He was suddenly the man who had long ago attracted Andrew, unmasked as though at a fancy-dress ball. 'Come and have a drink? We'll talk.'

Andrew shook his head, suddenly exhausted. 'I wish you luck though.'

'Luck?'

'Tonight.'

Andrew returned to his room and slept for an hour. He dreamed of hungry lions. One was hungrier than the others. He snarled long and low. He crouched as though to attack.

I'm hungry again, he said.

Andrew moaned in his sleep.

39

The Lion Tamer Who Lost

Ben never won, but he played as though he had many times over.
Andrew Fitzgerald, *The Lion Tamer Who Lost*

Cora waited for Andrew in the hotel bar. He spotted her on a bar stool, swathed in black silk, hair dotted with sparkling jewels.

'I keep nodding at the guests like we have to when they pass in the corridor,' she said. 'Only they don't know who I am so they stare.'

'No wonder,' smiled Andrew. 'You look wonderful.'

Cora blushed and confessed she and her flatmate shared the dress, each wearing it when they had somewhere to go.

'So, are you ready?' asked Cora.

'Not really.'

Walking into the Royal Function Suite, where a stage with promotional plaque and ceiling spotlights dominated, Cora chattered to Andrew about the pervy guest in room 342, and he was glad he had invited her. She would distract him. Rows of chairs sheathed in velvet faced the podium, none yet occupied. Guests and judges moved about the room, taking canapés and glasses of champagne from waiters. Leo chatted with red-lipped Louisa by the fire exit but looked over when Andrew entered. Andrew pointed out who was who and who had written what to an overexcited Cora.

Leo came over and handed Andrew some champagne, looking smart in a dark grey suit. 'Who's your guest,' he asked.

Andrew introduced Cora, said she had been helping him read.

Leo laughed. 'You've written three books and you can't read?'

Louisa swept up to the group. 'Five minutes and they begin the announcements,' she said. 'My money's on that *Two Hundred Blue Skies* guy. Of course, I hope it's me though.' She paused, studying Cora as though she were an insect beneath a microscope. 'Don't I know you? I *do*. You cleaned my room this morning. Not very well I might add – you left stains in the bathroom.'

'But there were so many,' Cora whispered to Andrew.

He smiled behind his champagne glass.

Louisa went in search of more fitting company.

Cora asked Leo how he thought Andrew had done at the reading earlier.

'Not bad,' he admitted. 'He was a bit quiet. Needs to project the words more. But I guess it was sincere.'

Cora looked pleased at the word sincere. 'That's because he read it for his brother, Ben,' she said.

Champagne bubbles popped in Andrew's mouth.

'His *brother*?' Leo shook his head. '*Ben*? You must be mistaken.'

'No, he told me,' said Cora. 'Ben, who's gone away...'

'But he doesn't have a broth—'

Tara Smith's magnified voice requested that guests please take their seats for the prizes. Louisa came over and took Leo's arm, insisting he sit with her at the front, and dragged him away. He looked back at Andrew, frowning. As they all sat, Cora studied Andrew with concern, said he looked white as the lilies in her mam's garden.

What had possessed him to tell her?

And then bring her here?

Christ. He felt sick.

An insect buzzed about the back row, an unwelcome wasp in winter. It hovered in the spotlight that elongated the lines in Tara's face, so she looked like a sketch in a children's book. Her hair was golden. Since the chemo had thinned his, Andrew noticed hair more than usual. Sickness killed it. The balding lion in the circus years ago had been dying. Leo twisted in his seat to stare at Andrew. His hair met in a point at his neck's nape.

On stage Tara spoke, holding a package like the Wish Box.

'We commend you all for making it this far.' Several people cheered. 'You can be very proud – to have shortlisted out of all the incredible books we received means this is only the start of your careers. Well, you must be impatient, so here we go.'

Andrew wasn't thinking about the winners' names.

Only the word *brother*.

'I am delighted,' said Tara, 'to announce that in third place is Louisa Thompson with her charming tale, *Midnight*.'

Louisa's hair fell snake-like about her shoulders as she went up for her prize.

'And the second-place prize,' said Tara, 'goes to Thomas Gibbs for *Peter and the Golomoth Grasshopper*.'

Thomas had black locks that curled tightly about his ear.

'And finally, the moment you've all been waiting for.' Rapturous cheering. 'It gives me immense pleasure to award the first prize, an amazing ten thousand pounds, to Geoff Summer for *Two Hundred Blue Skies*.'

Ripples of applause, then. Deflated faces and forced congratulatory smiles. Geoff, whose thinning hair screamed sickness, went to receive his prize. What was his sickness? Diabetes? Cancer? Incest? Had he married a woman only to discover she was his sister?

Andrew tried to escape.

'You stay,' he insisted to Cora. 'I've been feeling ill all day. Tell me about it tomorrow.'

Leo caught up with Andrew on the stairs. 'Hang on. Andrew, *wait*. What the hell are you running from?'

He reached his room but Leo blocked the doorway.

'What did that Cora mean?' he asked. 'Ben's not your *brother*.'

Andrew slid his key card along the slot, but the light flashed red.

'She was just mixed up.' He tried the key again.

'She seemed pretty sure,' Leo insisted. 'And you're acting weird. You're hiding something. What's going on?'

'Nothing.' Flustered, Andrew dropped the card and tried again. Green. Escape. He opened the door, but Leo blocked his way.

'*Is* Ben your brother?' he asked.

Andrew couldn't answer. He was no liar. But this truth stuck in his throat. He pushed past Leo and slammed the door on him.

'Why would that girl think you said it?' asked Leo through the door. 'Brother isn't something you would accidentally say.' A pause. 'You said it was complicated. Earlier. Is that what you meant? But... *how*...? Jesus.'

Silence.

Then questions through the wood: What the hell happened? Is it true? How did you find out? Is this why you split up?

Andrew put his hands over his ears. When Leo finally left, he dropped into the chair by the dressing table. He looked in the finger-print-streaked mirror. He saw Ben. When Ben once said he loved Andrew's half-up, half-down mouth he probably never realised that he had it too. They would always be together – in Andrew's own face.

In the morning, Tara found Andrew as he was checking out and commiserated with him on losing. Commiserate sounded like the word misery, and made Andrew think of Ben's random mis-words.

Keen to depart before Leo appeared and interrogated him again, Andrew thanked Tara. 'Sorry to rush off,' he said, 'but I've a train to catch in twenty minutes.'

'I really liked *Lion Tamer*,' said Tara. 'But Geoff Summer just blew us all away. He had that X factor. Good luck anyway.'

'Thanks. For the opportunity.'

Andrew hurried away. He wished he had never have gone to the ceremony. He just wanted to get on the train, go home and resume his nothing life.

40

Dark

When they were reunited at the Maths Makes Magic! club Nancy asked Ben how many zeros made infinity. 'Enough,' he said, and she smiled because he always had a more interesting answer than Mr Dobbs, even if it was probably wrong.

Andrew Fitzgerald, *The Lion Tamer Who Lost*

A few weeks after the London ceremony, Tara surprised Andrew with a phone call, inviting him to her office for a meeting. Contrasting with the lemon shades of her room, Tara wore a black suit befitting a funeral. Her walls were lined with front covers –*Antichrist*! by Jack Shane: Best First Novel; *Playing with Fire* by Lynne Lowell: two million copies sold – and four Andy Warhol prints.

'We've had a slot suddenly come free for a new book in April,' she said, after the usual pleasantries. 'The writer of the book we were planning on releasing had an accident.'

You always follow an accident.

The words came to Andrew hard.

'So we're delaying that one for now. We want to release *The Lion Tamer Who Lost* alongside *Two Hundred Blue Skies*. We think they will complement one another nicely. What do you think?'

Andrew didn't know what to say. He had been recovering at home. After not placing at the awards, he had convinced himself that it was over for his book.

'Yes,' he said. 'I think ... yes.'

'Great. Things will have to move fast though,' Tara said. 'Plenty of editing to be done. We'll have to work around the clock. Are you up for it?'

'I am,' he said.

'We'll go through it properly soon, but I had an immediate thought the first time I read it.'

'What was that?' asked Andrew.

'I don't think *both* of Ben's parents should die.'

'Oh.'

'Don't be hasty and consider it if you will,' said Tara.

Andrew felt protective of Book Ben and his story.

'How about this ... how about only *one* of them – let's say his dad – dies and Ben is only crippled for a month or so and when he does recover it's fully, not walking like a – how did you put it – ah, yes, like a stickman.'

This was new to Andrew. He didn't know how much control he would have over his book. He hadn't signed anything yet.

'You can be honest,' smiled Tara. 'It's *your* book. That was just my initial gut reaction. That one parent dying is surely enough.' She moved in the chair and it squeaked as though wanting to reject her. Behind her, the window overlooked London's unsymmetrical skyline.

Andrew spoke carefully. 'But if Ben walks again that soon the lions won't visit him for long, and he'll barely get to know them. I worry then that the reader won't care?'

'Maybe. But *both* parents dying? That's dark, Andrew.'

'Is it?'

'How about just his dad?'

Andrew couldn't speak. If he did this – if he handed his book over – it wouldn't be his anymore. And it was all he had left.

Tara clasped her hands together on the desk's polished surface. 'Andrew, we love your writing style – this is why we decided to take a chance on you when the slot came free. I just worry that it's too ... bleak?' She smiled, her eye corners creasing.

Andrew shook his head. 'It's weird because I see it as hopeful. How Ben rises above everything that's thrown at him.'

Tara's phone buzzed. She clicked it off and put it in the drawer.

'I think you have a good point,' she conceded. 'Ben's motivation is fired by his great loss.' She nodded as though agreeing with herself. But Andrew sensed there would be future battles if he accepted Tara's offer. 'Perhaps your next story can be a little gentler – some stuff is just too dark for kids.'

'Not all children are afraid of the dark,' said Andrew as the sun moved behind the BT Tower, separating them with a long, sneaky shadow.

The editor pulled her sleeve back over her charm bracelet and said, 'I guess we'll see.'

When Andrew first saw the illustrator's impression of Book Ben a few weeks later on a computer screen he faltered again. As a child, he had hated illustrations in books; what an artist interpreted from the prose was never what he envisioned while reading. Narnia's lion, Aslan, he had seen as graceful and giant-clawed. So, when he opened the book and found a creature no larger than a donkey he had slammed the pages shut in annoyance.

Now here was Book Ben, actualised.

Andrew couldn't deny the beauty of the image. Meryl had been an artist for thirty years and had brought Book Ben to life. Even in the black-and-white sketch his eyes glowed and his hands were refined, befitting someone with useless legs. Unruly kinks messed his hair. He actually looked like Ben. It reminded Andrew of his favourite Roald Dahl book, *Charlie and the Chocolate Factory*, and the pictures found there.

'Since it's for eight to twelve-year-olds, there will be around one picture per chapter,' said Meryl, 'and I'll draw whichever scene most stands out. You can be honest,' Meryl added when Andrew stared at the image. 'It's your story. What do you think?'

Andrew said he thought he was perfect.

Black House released *The Lion Tamer Who Lost* in April and it turned out that Tara was wrong about some things being just too dark for children; they embraced the dark.

Andrew read a newspaper piece describing how, in their thousands, with their pocket money and with birthday money, children had bought the book. Something about Ben's story must have resonated. In the reviews he read, parents described how their children had told their friends who told their friends who told their friends. How they had tidied bedrooms and done homework on time and put shoes away properly, just so they would be rewarded at the weekend with a trip to the bookstore.

Andrew took part in a whirlwind of promotions, interviews and signings. A lot was expected; no sooner had he returned to his flat than a call came from Tara about a radio host who wanted him for a show about the demise of classic children's books, and a journalist who would give a rave review in exchange for an exclusive chat with the diabetic recovering from cancer who had got lucky with his overnight success.

Andrew kept a bag permanently packed at the end of his bed.

Everyone wanted to know about forthcoming books and new ideas. Tara expected either a proposal for a sequel or something new by July, which she wanted completed by the next spring. The hard work, Andrew learned, was not the writing but the promoting. He understood why a lot of the successful names on Black House's list lived in or near the capital, where most events took place, but he couldn't imagine moving there. For all his absence of family, and having no one to leave behind, Andrew clung to Beverley – the place he knew.

Early in May, between a book fair and an appearance on a local news show, Andrew's phone rang before he woke. Expecting it to be seven o'clock he found the day had rushed on without him, that it was already nine-thirty. He rarely slept so long. He did a blood test: 6.9. A good reading. Andrew thought about looking for the sixes and nines in the day, but he hadn't done that in so long.

Recently, his readings had been more erratic though. He put it down to being so busy. Rushing from train to tube, office to bookstore, he had struggled to eat as regularly as when he had the luxury of a routine at home. Hypos caught him unaware. In a bookstore toilet in York, a warning *LO* had flashed across the blood meter's screen, meaning his sugars were so low a number couldn't be provided. Andrew had forgotten his glucose tablets and asked the store manager if she might get him some Coke. She had looked him up and down and said she would see what they could do. Andrew laughed later to think how she might bitch about the stuck-up writer with incessant demands.

Now the telephone continued ringing.

Andrew answered it.

'Do I get a signed copy then?' It was Leo.

'How are you?' asked Andrew.

'Why didn't you tell me?

He had not seen or spoken to Leo since the awards ceremony. Leo had called and left messages, but he never returned them.

'Tell you what?' Andrew's chest tightened.

'About the book. You must be delighted. How did that happen?' Leo paused, seemingly aware of the bitterness in his voice, and then said more evenly, 'I'm happy for you. I suppose you deserve it. You've been writing longer than me.

'Tara contacted me after the event and things went from there.'

'Great. Listen, I've been calling you for weeks – is your machine broken?'

Andrew sensed the reason for Leo calling was not only because of the book. He waited for him to get to the point, which never took Leo long.

'Are you and Ben still separated?' And there it was.

'Yes.'

'Is he seriously your *brother*?'

Andrew couldn't speak. This again.

'If he isn't, why would have you ignored me then? Ignored me since?'

Andrew got a cereal bar and bit into it. A moth flew into the window, seemed stunned and fluttered off.

'I can tell this is hard for you,' said Leo. 'Why not talk to me?'

Andrew still couldn't.

'Who else you gonna talk to, for fuck's sake?'

'Okay.' Andrew sat on the sofa. 'It's true. We're brothers.' It felt good to unburden himself. 'Ben offered to donate stem cells when I had cancer. That's how we found out.'

'Jesus.'

'Yes. Jesus.'

'But if you didn't *know* then there's no reason to feel disgusted is there?'

'Of *course* we didn't know,' Andrew cried. 'You think I'd have begun that kind of relationship with a man I *knew* was my brother?'

'Does his family know?'

'No.' Andrew scrunched up the cereal bar wrapper. 'Why would they?'

'They're *your* family now. You always wondered about your father.'

Andrew didn't tell Leo that he had seen Will a week earlier in Morrison's, the first time since he and Ben split. Will hadn't noticed him. How strange it was to view him with knowing eyes – his father. He wore a checked jacket that had seen better days and his basket bulged with meals for one and bottles of alcohol. Andrew had hidden behind a tower of cereal boxes, wanting to approach but afraid. Scared Will would somehow recognise their new relationship in Andrew's expression and turn him away. This all ran through his mind in a flash. Will approached the cashier before Andrew could intrude; before he could suggest he not have those awful packet meals, that he'd cook something for them.

Andrew thought about the one Sunday lunch he'd had with him, the mismatched crockery, the undercooked peas. He wished there was a way to have a relationship with Will. To say, *You're my dad*. But he was afraid that the truth about him and Ben would somehow end it all.

'Shit, you've had some bad luck,' said Leo. 'Diabetes, cancer, and this.'

'It's ... just life.'

'Can't you two be friends?'

It was the question Andrew had asked himself over and over. If they could be friends, then they would be able to be brothers.

'Could you be just friends with someone you've loved more than anyone you've ever known?' Andrew asked Leo.

'Yes,' said Leo. 'I'm your friend, aren't I?'

Andrew didn't know quite what to say.

'Why don't we meet up?' Leo said. 'Maybe this sibling thing happened for the best? Maybe we could make a go of it.'

'I'm not around much,' said Andrew sadly.

'And if you were?'

Leo deserved the truth, didn't he?

'Thank you for listening,' Andrew said. 'But I don't think we could work now.'

Letters arrived at Black House and got sent on to Andrew. Children wrote notes full of mis-words and exclamation marks and drawings. They wrote: *I think lions knock on my door at night too* on paper that smelt of wax crayon and bedrooms. They enclosed their photos and collectable cards and dead daisy chains and their own short stories in jiffy bags, which Andrew put into a folder to keep forever.

To the lion tamer mister, said one notelet, each word carefully printed. Andrew pictured a girl of eight chewing her lip as she painstakingly put down her thoughts in joined-up letters, just as he had once written the wish that changed everything. He made sweet tea because his blood sugars had dipped again and sat with the note, moving his mouth quietly around the syllables.

I were leg brases because i have an old person diseese and i walk one up one down like ben and i love him because he never worrys too much. I sometime wish to walk write but ben makes me happy to be wrong.

Andrew responded to every letter he got. He would wake up at three in the morning slumped over his desk, having passed out on the pile of notes. As a kid, he had written to his favourite authors and never once heard back. Waiting by the letterbox, he made up excuses for his heroes and heroines – they had such *important* things to do and book-writing was so very time-consuming. He knew now that many of these writers had died long before he got out his pen.

Andrew would stumble to bed after waking at his desk, waking again hours later ravenously hungry, one of the signs his blood sugars were low. He would pass out halfway through a chocolate bar, dream vividly about starving lions, and come to with the wrapper stuck to his cheek.

Then one morning before returning to London for another book event, Andrew received a postcard. Sometimes the postman had to knock now to hand over all the letters he got. Something fell from the bundle as he carried it to the living room. He knew immediately when he picked up the glossy card and saw two lions curled together by a tree that this was not from one of his young readers.

It was from Ben.

Judging by the date and various countries' stamps it had taken almost three weeks to travel from Africa to England. Andrew put the other letters on his desk with a twinge of guilt at preferring the postcard, then carried it to the bedroom. The bed squeaked gently beneath his weight, an accepting sigh. He sniffed it first as though even after a month it might carry some remnant of Ben's essence. It hadn't; the card smelt dry, emotionless. Next he analysed it for fingerprints or some other link.

Finally, he read the words.

Just his name and address and *I saw it and thought of us.*

Andrew felt sick.

He had turned his back on Ben for something that was not his fault, something with which he too was struggling to come to terms and had also just discovered. Had this denial made the sibling relationship not exist? No. They still were what they were. But what they *hadn't* been was two children who had grown up side by side, two children who had shared a bath or a bed, who had fought and argued, who had bonded in innocence within a family unit. He and Ben had been two adults who met in a library, who went to the circus, and who listened to a soft-voiced doctor say one of them had cancer. Only the blood pulsing through their veins made them brothers.

Nothing more.

Sitting on the bed they had once shared – with the postcard in his hand – Andrew realised that Ben was not the brother he had wished for. It had not been his childhood wish to find and sleep with and fall in love with and then lose a brother. Ben was the lover, the love of his life, who he had *failed* to wish for.

The telephone rang. Andrew dropped the card.

'It's me,' said Leo. 'I've been worried about you.'

'No need to,' said Andrew. 'I'm fine.'

'Listen, I read this article in yesterday's newspaper about a brother and sister who slept together from being fourteen. Remember that novel that came out in the eighties – *Flowers in the Attic*.'

'I can't talk, I've got to catch a train in a few hours.'

Leo continued anyway. 'I think your story would make a great adult novel. Worked for Virginia Andrews. Can I interview you if I need help?'

Andrew snapped, 'No! We're not like the two you read about. We didn't grow up together! Don't you dare write about us.'

'No, it'd be fiction,' said Leo. 'But what a tragedy it could make. I've been thinking about it ever since you told me. I've been reading all these tragic tales of adolescent girls finding comfort with an older brother. Read this student survey where ten percent admitted to sexual experience with a sibling'

'Don't even thinking about using my name in any way.'

Andrew hung up.

Felt dizzy and had to breathe deeply for a while.

Then he propped Ben's postcard on the dresser and left for London.

41

This Isn't Nothing

It took ten attempts for Ben to first walk. Each time he fell, he was more determined to get up.

Andrew Fitzgerald, *The Lion Tamer Who Lost*

Andrew felt safe when he was surrounded by books. His customary nerves at having to face the public were lessened somewhat by the fact that they would be children. Kids were always so receptive. Nonjudgemental.

Andrew looked around the store, the biggest in the UK, and couldn't quite believe he was here. The store manager, Stella, showed him to a table covered in heavy grey felt, where piles of his books had been propped in one corner and a selection of pens sat to the left. He still smiled each time he saw the cover of his novel. The words *The Lion Tamer Who Lost* were flowing gold letters. The final T wrapped around the tail of a playful lion cub. On the front, Book Ben sat cross-legged. Behind them both, chess pieces floated as though free of their rules.

Stella put a welcoming hand on Andrew's shoulder. 'Coffee?' she asked. 'I suggest a strong one judging by the huge queue outside.'

'Can I possibly have Coke?' he asked. He didn't have time to do another blood test and felt queasy, so wanted to make sure he could last the morning.

'Of course,' she said. 'Sit down. Get comfy. We open in ten minutes.'

Andrew sat in the chair behind the table. He was exhausted. Had been for days if he was honest. No matter how much he slept or how well he ate he felt lousy. No time now to think about it though. Or

Leo's idea for a novel. He only hoped the sugar would get him through the day.

A nearby board advertised that Andrew and some other authors were appearing that week. He thought he looked confused in his picture, like an actor who had forgotten his lines. It was the same image they had used in the back of his book. Black lines were etched beneath his eyes.

But I'm here, he thought. *I'm in Waterstones. Like I always dreamed.*

There was no one to whom he could say it aloud. He had no one with whom he could share the moment. No Ben. All that wishing and here he was, alone.

When the doors opened, children varying in age and size and colour tumbled through them. Some came with parents, some with grandparents, some with friends. But some were alone too. As a child Andrew, had gone to so many places by himself, spent hours in a dark library corner while his mother worked. He wandered the shopping precinct, then went home and drank hot chocolate next door with Mrs Robinson. Andrew knew his mother wasn't to blame; life had been unkind to her. Will had played a bigger hand than her in his solitary childhood.

Andrew wondered now if his mother had ever wished for anything. Had she hoped Will would come back to her?

'Will you sign it to Alfie, mister?' A boy so freckled it appeared his face was scalded jolted Andrew from his thoughts.

'Say please,' chided his equally freckled mother, with a firm nudge.

'Oh, *please*, mister,' he said.

'Of course I will, Alfie.' Andrew turned the book around and wrote in loopy scrawl over the first page. 'Did you read it already?'

'Not yet,' said Alfie, hugging the book to his chest. 'My friend Carl read it though and he said it's dead good.'

Alfie's mother reminded him to say thank you to the kind man.

And so began four hours of signing. Andrew lost count of how many times he wrote his own name. Halfway through the session he almost forgot how to spell it and had to look at the book cover for help.

'I forgot how to spell *the* once,' whispered a chubby girl who noticed Andrew's momentary confusion. 'I just couldn't remember, so I put in a better word instead.'

'Good idea,' said Andrew.

Stella brought him a coffee and he ate two cereal bars. This event felt somehow like a conclusion; like the destination after a long, long journey. Something urged him to enjoy it. *This isn't nothing*. The phrase came to him. Like déjà vu. Wasn't that what he kept thinking that day in Ben's kitchen? *This isn't nothing*. Yes. The ticking clock. Ben's kitchen before he collapsed.

'Can I get a photo?'

Andrew looked up. A boy gave him a mostly toothless grin.

'Of course.'

Andrew stood up. The room spun for a moment. He gripped the desk. Once steady, he posed with the boy. Others then asked to have pictures taken too. Andrew realised he might be forever immortalised in albums he would never see.

Halfway through, Andrew took a break. He read his blood, surprised that he was low despite the Coke and cereal bars. He ate another one, his last. He would have to buy more. Back at the table he felt dizzy again and wondered if he'd have to stop.

When he looked up he saw Ben.

No. Something not quite right. Ben, but shorter.

Ben, but with darker hair.

Not him.

The non-Ben held the book to his chest with crossed arms, like his heart was reading the blurb on the back. He came to the table. A child somewhere began to cry.

'What do you think?' he asked.

Andrew felt queasy. 'What did you say?' he stammered.

'Look at the ink.' The man pointed to the pen.

It had leaked all over the felt.

'Damn,' said Andrew.

Stella brought another pen and dabbed at the stain.

'It's the best book I've ever read to my son,' the non-Ben said. 'You got him into books. He was never bothered before.'

'Thank you.' Andrew opened it at the title page. 'What's your son's name?'

'Elliott. He makes me read every night. It's truly beautiful. You have a real way with words.'

Andrew was touched. 'Thank you.' He wrote a dedication to Elliott.

'Who's the real-life Ben then?' asked the man.

'Sorry?' Andrew blinked.

All the edges were blurred. He could see two of everything. The bookstore swam.

'You dedicated the book to Ben.'

Of course. He had. No one else had asked who he was.

'He inspired some of the story,' said Andrew. 'He's my...'

Andrew looked at the page. The words misted. He remembered again that day at Will's home. His *father*'s home. Collapsing in the kitchen. Andrew had feared that if he closed his eyes Ben would disappear forever. He had struggled hard to keep his heavy lids open. *This isn't nothing*, he'd thought. He felt dizzy, now as then. He could hardly keep his eyes open, now as then.

'Are you okay?' The voice came from far away.

There was no real Ben now to catch him if he collapsed.

Andrew wished he could see him again. Tell him that he might have cruelly turned him away, but every time he passed the hospital and every time he ate peas and every time the spellchecker underlined one of his misspelt words, he thought of him. Every time he saw posters for the circus and every time he felt low and every time he saw the number nine, he thought of him.

A crash. What was it? The table. It had fallen. Books scattered.

How?

'Get help,' cried someone.

Who for?

Then Andrew realised he had turned the table over. He was on the floor, next to his chair. Feet surrounded him; children's colourful plimsolls, lace-up boots, high heels. Where were Ben's trainers? Gone. They walked elsewhere now. Zimbabwe. With the lions.

The last thing Andrew saw before passing out cold was the first page of his book.

For Ben.

PART SEVEN

WILL

42

The Woman Who Cried

Nancy gave Ben a colour-by-numbers picture for his birthday, already complete. She said it wasn't very good. Ben shook his head and insisted it was proper art because she'd gone over the edges and painted green where there should be red.

Andrew Fitzgerald, *The Lion Tamer Who Lost*

The living room needs cleaning.

Johnny Cash and John Denver records obscure the cigarette-burned floor near the old stereo with a turntable that rotates one second too slowly. The cover to Cash's Best Of album is torn in half, splitting titles 'I'll Still Be There' and 'What Do I Care?' Will tried fixing it once with masking tape but gave up.

He can't remember listening to the old collection last night, but the evidence is there. Now he returns the LPs to the shelf and wonders why bad memories never fade. The record covers are washed out now, yet regrets tumble into Will's head so clearly each morning. Does the drink wash away only the good? How he would enjoy vivid memories of swearing at Cartwright or of Heidi in her healthy days. Instead, every morning he sees Mike's face at the wedding, and Ben's as he left for Zimbabwe.

In the kitchen, Will lights a cigarette at the gas hob and stands at the sink. His hand is so unsteady that ash falls each time he inhales. On the table, folded, a newspaper sudoku's few blank squares beg for answer. They have been waiting since Ben left. That's six months ago now.

Will inhales hard and the cigarette's tip crackles like a dying bonfire. He won't finish the puzzle. He probably knows the answers, but Ben always helps him put the numbers where they belong.

He sent a letter to Ben but can hardly remember now what he wrote. Though he was sober at the time, he has been drinking too heavily since. There's been no response. Will checks the post every day. He has no clue when Ben will be home – *if* he'll even come home. He is sure Mike has leave in a few weeks, but doubts he'll come here.

He longs for a drink.

It's a thirst he has little strength to resist.

Did he finish the bottle last night? He rummages in the kitchen cupboard, then returns to the living room where he feels down the sides of the now-stained sofa. An indistinct tapping disturbs the search. Will frowns. Where's it coming from? He parts the dirty nets, looks out front. No one. The tap, tap, tap continues so he goes to the back door.

Outside the light is blinding, the glory of late June.

No one there either.

Then a voice comes from the side of the house. Hesitant footsteps. A man appears. Will is momentarily confused. He knows him but can't place him. Realises then that it is Andrew, Ben's friend.

'You said to come around the back,' he says.

'What? I didn't say nowt.'

'No, last time.'

'It's a bit bloody early, lad,' says Will.

Andrew looks up the garden as though surprised to be here. 'It's eleven o'clock,' he says. 'I'm…' He pauses as though trying to recall what he is. 'Walking. I was just walking by here and I had to knock.'

'Walking? Here? It doesn't go anywhere.'

Will realises why he couldn't immediately place Andrew. He doesn't look well. He must have lost weight since that Sunday lunch, and his cheeks are hollow. His face is scrunched up like an old newspaper.

'Ben's not here,' says Will. 'Thought you knew? He's away.'

'I know.' Andrew's face softens. 'I came to see you.'

'*Me*?'

'Yes. Can I come in?'

'Not sure about that,' says Will.

'Why?'

'You might be, you know, *after* me.'

Andrew shakes his head. 'No.'

Will doesn't step aside or open the door any wider. 'Do you have news about Ben? He's okay, isn't he?'

'I haven't spoken to him. Please, I just have to talk to you and we can't out here.'

Will stares at this man, wondering what to do. Finally he moves aside. Andrew steps over the threshold, clumsy and awkward. He surveys the room. Will wonders if he's looking for Ben; Will does every morning and last thing at night. He slept in Ben's narrow bed the first three nights he was gone, thinking how the childhood die-cast replica cars were now so caked in dust it might never wash off. Andrew studies the sink, the cupboards, the sudoku puzzle on the table, and then looks at Will with eyes full of knowing.

What is it he knows?

Suddenly Will sees clearly the moment he undressed Kimberley – exactly where Andrew now stands. Why does it come to him now? He isn't sure. This is not a bad memory. It should be; its effects have been bad. It comes to him in a photographic flash: untied straps and undone hooks that won't easily free, giving time to go back, to not, to go, to not; his mouth on her neck, tasting youth and bitter perfume while she moves a hand shyly over his zip as though assessing how much he'll hurt her; shortbread – a gift from her grandma – sitting on the counter where Will lifts her by the waist so he can bury himself between her thighs; the happy family on the shortbread box not covering their eyes when Will thrusts into her; her crying out as he moves, clearly not knowing what this does to him.

'Are you okay?' It's Andrew.

He's still here.

But why?

'Yes,' says Will. 'Just ... nothing. So, what do you want, lad?'

'I…' He looks like he might faint. 'I don't know where to start.'

'Just say it.'

Will wonders if Andrew has a secret crush on Ben, and wants to unburden himself. But why would he come to *him*? Will knows he was rude at that Sunday lunch. Isn't he the last person Andrew is likely to want to talk to?

'I need to sit down.' Andrew holds the sink.

'Okay, okay, come through.'

Andrew follows Will into the living room. He sits in the single armchair and Will moves a pile of newspapers from the sofa and sits there. The ashtray on the coffee table is full. The packet next to it is empty. He needs a drink. He remembers now where a bottle might be.

'Do you want a drink?'

Will opens the cabinet, gets a half-empty vodka bottle from behind the photo of Heidi and pours some into a tumbler. Who is he even hiding it from now?

Andrew shakes his head. 'It should be a nine,' he says.

'What should?' asks Will.

'Top left. The sudoku puzzle, in there.'

Will gulps vodka. 'This is just weird, lad. I hardly know you. Why d'you want to talk to me? You didn't come to talk about fucking puzzles.'

'Did you know I had cancer?'

Will shakes his head, even more confused. 'Why would *I* know?' He drinks more. 'And why do I need to?'

'I collapsed again, last week.'

Will doesn't speak. What can he say?

'I got better though, thanks to Ben.'

'Thanks to *Ben*?'

Andrew nods. His eyes say there's more, but his mouth takes its time. Eventually he says, 'Ben had this blood test to see if we were a match and gave me his stem cells. He's probably why I'm alive.'

'*Ben* did? Why *him*?'

'Because … we're good friends.'

'Didn't you have any family who could do it, lad?'

Now Andrew looks distraught, and Will regrets being so blunt.

'I shouldn't have let him do the test,' he says.

'Why?' asks Will.

'Because it changed everything.'

'I'm lost.'

Andrew takes a deep breath and exhales slowly. 'Do you remember a woman called Anne?' he asks.

Will wonders for a moment if this is something to do with the sudoku puzzle again. Did Anne Someone invent them? The vodka relaxes him, as the first glass or two always does, and takes the edge off any irritation.

'Anne who?' he asks.

He realises a surname will not help. He only knew one Anne, long ago, but Andrew can't possibly know her or know that. Anne was his first lover. She was probably forty years old to his twenty-three. Anne was the woman whose tears began a lifelong need to comfort women who wept.

But he never knew her surname.

'Anne Fitzgerald,' says Andrew.

'I remember a woman called Anne, but I can't know if she's the one you mean. Hell, there are a lot of Annes around. I've known a few bloody women.'

Andrew reaches into his pocket and takes out a photo. He hands it over. Will looks at it. At Anne, in black and white. Soft curls fall onto shoulders, ringlets that once reminded him of the Greek goddesses in his mother's hallway pictures. Her mouth is an upside-down curl too, as though when she laughs she wishes to be sad and when she frowns she wishes to be happy. He gasps at the memory. He has not seen her in so many years.

'It's my Anne,' is all he can say. 'But how? Why do you have this?'

'I'll tell you. But tell me first ... did you care about her?'

Will drinks. He sits back in the chair, closes his eyes.

'I promised I'd never forget her and I never have,' he says, happy to talk about her. 'You never forget your first, do you? And she was my first, in all ways. In love, in sex. I was a late starter at twenty-three, would you believe? Made up for that, I bloody know.'

Andrew moves to the edge of his seat. 'Your first – so she wasn't *nothing*?'

'God no, she was anything but nothing.'

Will enjoys remembering. He almost forgets Andrew is there, that he is talking aloud. The vodka warms and lulls and encourages.

'I'd never seen a woman cry until her,' he says. 'In our house, when I was a lad, fuck, you didn't cry. Crying was for wusses, for the weak. Stiff upper lip and all that. So, when I saw Anne on that bench alone, her breath in the cold air, I'd never seen anyone so vulnerable, anything so erotic.' He exhales slowly. 'I grew up in about two hours. She was out the back of the care home. My grandfather was in there, getting closer to death by the hour. She was crying and smoking. I asked if she had a spare ciggie and she let me share hers. The last in the pack. Her hair had fallen from its bun, I remember. I never did ask why she was crying. We went back to hers. It was only one afternoon, but...' Will looks at Andrew, realising these are intimate moments he's sharing. 'Look, she was special. But why do you want to know? How do you know her?'

'She was my mother,' says Andrew.

'Your...?' Will drops his glass, curses as the liquid wets his lap.

Andrew nods, his eyes sad.

'I felt like I maybe knew you,' says Will, studying him. 'That Sunday. You look like her. You do. But I don't ... How? And how did you know *I'd* known her? She only knew my first name, never had my picture...'

'I know because of Ben.'

'You're really losing me, lad. I've never talked to him about her!' Will pauses. 'Wait, you said *was* my mother...'

'Yes. She died a few years ago,' says Andrew. 'It was peaceful.'

Will nods. Doesn't know what to say.

Taking another swig, he eventually says, 'I think you'd better tell me about Ben. How is he any part of this?'

He suddenly remembers finding a single-paged confession by Heidi once, hidden in a bottom drawer after she died. A page of mis-words and regret: *At Mona's Christmas party I kissed Gary under the misseltoe. He's only nineteen. A proper kiss. That means I'm a terrible terrible wife.* Will had merely smiled and whispered to himself that they were all terrible, terrible people, they all did terrible, terrible things, and he loved her even more with the confession.

'It's going to come as a shock,' says Andrew.

'For fuck's sake, lad, just tell me.'

'When Ben did the blood test, we found out that we were probably brothers.'

'Huh?'

Will can't put the words together in his head. They are so alien. Make no sense. Is it the vodka?

'We had all these markers in our DNA. It is very probable we are brothers, maybe cousins. But I knew brothers. I just *knew*, because I...' Andrew shakes his head. 'That doesn't matter. You've confirmed it. You were with my mother when she got pregnant.'

'Brothers.' Will whispers the word. 'When did you...?'

'End of September.'

Then Will realises. Looks at Andrew, slack-mouthed. 'So you're my...'

'Yes,' says Andrew. 'I am.'

Will stands. He feels his knees giving a little. As he staggers, Andrew comes forwards to rescue him, but Will waves his arm, says, 'No, I'm okay. Just need a ciggie.'

He goes into the kitchen, Andrew following behind. He lights the cigarette at the gas flame, then opens the door, letting in the light. Somewhere faraway a lawnmower buzzes.

'I don't know what to say,' admits Will.

'I understand. It's a hell of a lot to take in.'

Will then realises and says, '*Ben*. Ben knows. Of course. Is that why he went away? But why would he go? Why wouldn't he come and tell me? This isn't so bad, is it, lad?' He looks at Andrew. 'A shock. And a hell of a strange coincidence. But not *bad* news.'

Andrew turns away from him as though he might leave but then he seems to think again. He is so pale now he looks close to collapse. Will remembers the diabetes.

'You okay, lad? You need some ... sugar or something sweet?'

Andrew shakes his head. 'It's not that,' he says.

'Is this why Ben hasn't written to me?' asks Will, frowning.

'He was angry about ... you and Kimberley. Yes, he told me once we knew ... our link. He was angry that the ... you know, *moment* with Kimberley and the moment you had with my mum has affected others. Him. Us.'

Will nods. 'I've been an idiot.'

'You miss Ben?'

'Yes. I do.'

Will studies Andrew. Sees him anew. The eyes, the mouth. Familiar. Like Ben. Like Mike. Like himself. Another son, after all this time. Affection floods his alcohol-stifled mind. This is his son. How on earth did life happen this way? Is this some vodka-fuelled dream and he'll wake on the sofa? No. Andrew, Ben's friend, a man he met once and made quite unwelcome in his home, is his son. He wants to make some gesture to show acceptance but doesn't know how.

Instead he says, 'I still don't get why Ben volunteered his blood or whatever to a mate?'

'Maybe we somehow *knew* we were more,' says Andrew softly. 'You admitted earlier that you felt you knew me that Sunday. Maybe we always know.'

'Maybe.' Will pauses. 'What should we do?'

'I don't expect anything,' says Andrew. 'This is new to you, whereas I've had months to come to terms with it. But I had to come and tell you.'

'Why now?' asks Will.

'What do you mean?'

'Why not last month or the one before?'

Andrew shrugs but there is clearly something more to it. 'I'm really exhausted now. I should go.'

'Okay.' Will drops his tab end in the sink. Faraway, the lawnmower stops. 'So you haven't spoken to Ben since he left?'

Andrew shakes his head and goes to the open door. The light there softens his shadows.

'How come?' asks Will. 'Isn't he glad you're brothers? I mean you're such good mates and all.'

Andrew steps over the threshold. 'I think maybe it was all too much for him,' he says.

'Come back sometime if you want, lad,' Will calls after him.

Andrew turns. 'Really?'

'Yeah. I'll take you to the pub.'

'Maybe.'

'I didn't mean to be rude that Sunday,' says Will. 'I got my opinions, I know that, but I'm just a brusque old so-and-so. I can accept what you are. You know ... being a shirt-lifter and that.'

Andrew smiles. Will sees his eyes are teary.

And then he is gone.

Later, in the afternoon, Will goes upstairs and puts clean sheets on the bed.

He thinks of Anne.

Her sheets were fresh; covered in daisies like a meadow and yet smelling of talcum powder. She apologised for the pile of clothes by the bed end and he thought only of taking hers off, of undoing her crisp care-assistant's smock and seeing for the first time a woman who wasn't his mother or aunt.

But she undressed herself; not like a stripper, not teasing but shy, back turned, still crying.

'Don't cry,' he whispered, aroused by the salty flow.

Will sits now on the corner of his urine-soaked mattress. Anne is one of the few pure memories that's stuck. One of the rare good memories that's clear. Even though their union has influenced every woman he has chosen since, he hasn't thought of her in so long. But Anne has shone in Heidi's waved hair, in Kimberley's sadness, in the tears of every female since.

He had dared to touch Anne's cheek when their cigarette lay dying in muddy water by the care-home garage; she had gasped as though cut and put her hand over his and kissed him. At the thought of that first touching of tongues, desire uncoils in Will's groin. On a filthy bed, aroused and miserable, he weeps.

Why didn't he go back to Anne?

She gave him her number afterwards. Didn't his mother wash his trousers with that scrap of paper in the pocket? Hadn't he wanted to go back to the care home and explain that that was why he hadn't called? Walked past hoping to see her? Maybe.

He isn't sure.

Can't remember.

Into sleep Will drifts; into dreams; into Anne's bed again.

Don't cry, he whispers, burying his face in those thick ringlets while fingers hungrily explore her. *I can't not*, she says. Anne lets him clumsily move between her legs, as eager as he is afraid. She holds his face as he does. Hers is still wet with tears. She says over and over, *Don't forget me, don't forget me*. Will promises he never will.

They made a son.

They created Andrew.

After all these years, it isn't over. Anne is still with him, through Andrew. And he is maybe here for a reason.

But why? And why now?

Will wakes to evening's yellow light, knowing he must bring the family together. He must get them together, under this roof, and assure them that things will change. *He* will change. He has done wrong, but he can put it right. His actions forty years ago have brought them all here and can unite them. His response to Anne's weeping has flooded the future of his own children. Ben. Mike. Lost Molly.

And Andrew.

PART EIGHT

BEN

43

ENGLAND

Putting the Numbers in the Right Squares

Ben liked that his grandma found only seven candles for his tenth birthday cake. 'Make a wish,' she said. 'But don't tell anyone.' His grandma insisted then it wouldn't come true; Ben argued that it was more likely to if he put it in the hearts and minds of as many people as possible.

Andrew Fitzgerald, *The Lion Tamer Who Lost*

The evening light dies.

Ben looks through the back door at his dad. Nothing has changed. It is as though he never left. If he didn't have luggage and aching knees from hours on the coach, Ben would feel like he'd just been to the shop for milk. Will stands by the table, studying the sudoku puzzle, cigarette in hand.

Ben watches for what feels like minutes before going in. Will doesn't turn straight away; Ben thinks he senses it's him. Who else would it be? Mike probably hasn't come by. Kimberley likely stays away now, too. Ben's eyes are drawn to the sudoku puzzle. One of the numbers is wrong.

Will puts the newspaper down.

'You've got an extra nine,' says Ben.

Will turns, seems surprised. 'Oh. I thought...' The words die.

'Expecting someone?' Ben dumps his holdall on the floor.

'No. Yes. Maybe.' He pauses. 'You're home.'

'Stating the bloody obvious, Dad.'

'You never said. I'd have … well, got ready for you. I'd have got some shopping. Got nowt in really.' Will goes to the cupboards, opens them, showing bare shelves.

'You must have teabags?'

'Yes.'

'Make us one then.'

Will switches the kettle on. 'I'm dead glad you're here, lad.' He hardly looks Ben in the eye. 'I am … Bit surprised, mind. Did you fly in today? Did you get my letter?'

Ben nods.

'Was it good? You like the place?'

'Yeah, loved it.'

'Great. Was it hot?'

'Sometimes.'

Will nods. The water in the kettle bubbles. 'I understand,' he says and finally looks at Ben.

'Understand what?' Ben is confused.

'Why you left England. I mean, I knew it was because of me. My behaviour. Kim. The rest of it. I was an arsehole.' Will rummages in the drawers, and failing to find what he wants, goes into the pockets of his coat hanging by the door. 'But I know everything else, too.'

Everything else?

'I don't…' Ben frowns.

'Andrew was here,' says Will.

'*What*?'

Ben's legs give, and he collapses into a chair at the table. The newspaper falls, scattering pages at his feet. In the black-and-white images, he sees moments he and Andrew shared: the kisses, the fights, the *yes* and *no*.

'I know,' says Will.

'*What* do you know?' Ben can hardly get the words out.

Will makes tea in the old brown pot and puts the lid on with a soft clink.

'Don't look so worried. It's fine. I had to get my head around it, too. I've only had a few hours to think, but trust me it's all I've done, lad. It's not s--'

'A few hours? I don't understand.'

'Andrew was here this morning.'

'This *morning*?'

Once again, their paths almost crossed.

Will nods. He pours tea into the mugs and adds milk.

'I was pretty gobsmacked. Thought it was gonna be you, which is ironic now. Then I thought maybe something had happened to you and he was here to tell me. God, it was all going through me head. I had him standing on the step for ages. And then he came in. He told me. Now I'm just surprised he waited so long to come.' He hands Ben a mug. 'Why didn't *you* tell me, lad?'

Ben can't believe his father is okay. How much does he know? What exactly did Andrew tell him? Why did he come? Andrew. Andrew was *here*.

Ben can't speak.

So, Will does: 'I suppose I know why,' he says, standing at the sink with his mug and another cigarette found in his shirt pocket. 'You saw that moment as another indiscretion of mine. But it wasn't. Not this one. I was a young lad and she was my first. But I've never forgotten her.' He sighs. 'I still can't believe we made a child ... and that he ends up being your mate all these years later. What kind of bloody coincidence is that? I guess that's why you two had lots in common. Genes can be a weird thing.'

Ben sits up. Did Will call Andrew his *mate*? Is he unable to say another word?

'So, he just told you about Anne?'

'Yes. And the test.'

'What did he say?' Ben tries to remember to breathe.

'Just that he has no family and you offered.' Will puts out his cigarette. 'I did think it was odd you'd offer to do such a thing for a mate, but with hindsight, maybe that connection was there. That DNA link.

Somehow you sensed it? Wanted to make sure he got better. Must've been awful seeing him ill. And then you found out. He said it seemed to be all too much for you and you left for Zimbabwe.'

'That's all he said?'

'Yes. Not much more, lad.'

Ben exhales slowly. So, Andrew mentioned nothing about their relationship. Will is still in the dark about Ben's sexuality. But he knows they are brothers, that he has another son.

'How do you feel about it all?' asks Ben.

'Still shocked. But not unhappy. No, quite chuffed.'

'Even though he's gay?'

'Ah, I know I was a bugger that Sunday to him. But I'm not bothered about him being bent really.'

'Don't say it like that! Not bothered? You were fucking awful to him. Fucking *awful*. And what about Uncle Jerry? You never spoke to him again when you found out *he* was gay. And then the poor man killed himself! How bad you must have made *him* feel!'

'*What*?' Will shakes his head. 'What the hell are you talking about, lad? Uncle Jerry was a bastard for stealing from our mother, but I didn't care that he was *gay*. I know that *anyone* can rob off you, doesn't matter if you're gay, straight or one of those multi-sexuals. Yeah, we ribbed him like hell as kids, cos you did that back then. It was our way. But that's not why I never spoke to him all them years. Took thousands from our mam he did.' Will pauses and then adds, 'And I was devastated when he died ... That's why I can't ... don't often talk about him...'

'Oh.' Ben's head hurts. All this new information.

'Is that what you thought?' It seems to tickle Will; he laughs heartily.

'It's not funny,' snaps Ben. 'You're a fucking bigot. You know you are! You're always judging things and making people feel small!'

Will studies him. 'You're right. What can I say? Sorry. I've always been that way. I guess I ... I tear apart what I don't understand. But in truth, I couldn't care less who shags who.'

Ben suddenly wants to cry. His dad would never have cared after all.

But this is instantly followed by the realisation that, had he come out sooner, and announced Andrew as his partner, then he could never have come to the house and met his long-absent father without shame and humiliation. Somehow, Ben's ill-judged understanding of Jerry's banishment means things might be okay now for them all.

'Look, lad,' says his dad. 'It's been a funny old day. Andrew comes, then you. And I'm glad. About both. His news was a shock, yes, but it already feels ... well, normal.' He pauses. 'You must be dead tired. Long trip, eh? How was the sanctuary place? Everything you hoped?'

'Yeah, good.'

It seems so far away already. So unreal. Like it never happened. How quickly this life grips Ben, floods his senses. What did his hut smell like? The air? The grass enclosures? All he can smell now is the old frying pan and cigarettes. What will Lucy be doing now? He remembers her injury. The horrific gash on her leg. He bought a new phone before getting on the coach. He should message Stig to find out how she is. Soon. He can't think straight yet.

Outside, the sun is almost gone; the garden is shrouded in shadow. Will switches the light on.

'Guess you can tell me tomorrow?' he says.

Ben shrugs, takes the new phone from his rucksack.

'Are you back for good then?' asks Will.

'Yes.'

'What brought you home now?'

For the first time since stepping into the house Ben remembers Esther. The baby. He sent her his new mobile number on the coach but hasn't heard from her yet. She seems like a distant dream already. Andrew has filled his head again. Esther deserves better than a liar like him. But it's late now; he is exhausted. He hasn't the energy to tell his dad everything that happened in Zimbabwe now.

'Another time,' he says.

'Will you stay here – or at Andrew's place again?'

'I'll stay tonight, for now.'

'I'll have to make your bed up.' Will collects the mugs, puts them in the sink. 'And your room might be a bit dusty. Breakfast'll have to just be tea cos the shop's shut now.'

'Doesn't matter.' Ben picks up his holdall to go upstairs.

'You wanna talk some more?' asks Will. 'Guess we've lots to discuss.'

'Not yet. I need a shower.' He heads for the stairs.

'He didn't look well,' says Will.

'Who?' asks Ben, not thinking.

'Andrew.'

Ben stops. Lets his bag drop. 'What do you mean?'

'He was thin,' says Will. 'Very pale. Tired looking.'

'Maybe he was low? Needed Coke?' Ben's instinct to make sure he's okay floods back.

'No, I remembered about the diabetes and asked him. Said it wasn't that.'

'So, what was it?' Ben's voice is shrill.

'I don't know. It didn't feel like the moment to ask. I was taking everything else in remember. He was ill last year though, wasn't he? Cancer...'

Maybe Ben's stem-cell donation *didn't* work? Maybe Andrew still has cancer? How could he not have known? *Felt* it? How could he have not tried even harder to find out? But Andrew ignored all his calls before he left England. Was *that* why?

'I should go now, see how he is.'

'Ben, it's late. I bet he's asleep. He looked so tired. Wait till morning. You can't do anything now. You've been travelling all day.'

'What if the cancer is worse?'

'Well, you won't help him if you go and wake him, will you?'

'I suppose.'

'Get some sleep yourself and go tomorrow. Bet he'll be glad to see you.'

How little Will understands. Ben wants to say that he doubts Andrew will welcome him, that he never said goodbye when he left for Africa. But he came by today. Did he hope Ben would be here, too? Did he want to see him? Ben loves him enough to be able to be a brother to him now, but Andrew doesn't know that.

Everything is different now.

'I'll go tomorrow,' says Ben. He pauses. 'Did Andrew ask where I was?'

'No, he seemed to know you wouldn't be here.' Then Will adds, 'He looked for you though.'

'What do you mean?'

'He was looking around. As though imagining you here. It reminded me...'

'Of what?' asks Ben.

'Of how you'd look for Mike when you were little. First thing you'd look for when you came home from school, or anywhere.' Will sits on the stained sofa. 'Weird that Mike isn't the oldest now. He's a middle brother. Should you tell him? Or should I?'

Ben almost says that he doubts Mike will listen to Will but stops himself. He hasn't the heart to be cruel. He isn't angry at his dad anymore. Perhaps, in a curious twist of events, this genetic link could be the thing that unites the family. Perhaps Mike will also be able to forgive their dad.

'Maybe *I* should tell him,' says Ben.

The phone buzzes in his pocket. He pulls it out, clicks the message open. Esther, asking if he got home okay, saying she misses him already. He'll respond later when he can think what to say.

'You see many lions then?' asks Will.

'One or two.' Ben thinks of Lucy, her injury.

'Are they scary buggers?'

'Not really.' Ben feels lightheaded suddenly.

'Shall I order a takeaway while you shower?' asks Will.

'Okay.'

'And we can chat some more.'

'Maybe.'

Ben climbs the stairs and goes to his room. Aside from the bed having been stripped, it hasn't changed. He sits on the mattress. Closes his eyes. Remembers afternoons spent there with Andrew. Pushes the images away. That is not who they are now. Tomorrow he will go there, and hopefully Andrew will see him.

Ben takes *The Lion Tamer Who Lost* from his bag and turns to his letter at the back. He reads again the words: *I've thought a lot about maybe telling Dad the truth about us. Telling him he's got another son.* Andrew got there first. Even with distance, their thoughts are linked. And now it is out. They can be brothers. Andrew's wish will finally come true, how it always should have done.

Ben responds to Esther's text.

I'm home, I miss you too, I'll call tomorrow. X

He suddenly pictures Lucy disappearing into the darkness without looking back. He sends a message to Stig, asking after her.

If she's okay, he thinks, *then everything will be okay*.

After Ben finishes showering, Will calls up to say that the food has arrived.

Downstairs he finds his dad opening the containers. 'I got chicken curry and some prawn toast,' he says. 'Chips and rice, too. Come on, tuck in, lad.' He pauses, chip in hand. 'I'm Andrew's father, I know that, but I really don't think I'm Lola's ... No, listen. Don't say anything. You get a feeling about such things. When Andrew told me, it made sense. With hindsight, I felt I knew him that Sunday he came for lunch. But Lola. Trust me. She's not mine.'

'Mike may want a test, to prove it,' says Ben.

'I'd do it,' says Will. 'That's how sure I am.'

'Even if you're not, he may never forgive you.'

'No.'

'And when he finds out about Andrew, that might add to everything.'

Will nods. 'I'll take what comes.'

'I'll try and talk to him,' says Ben.

They eat at the kitchen table, the newspaper between them. Without speaking they solve the sudoku. Will still has the blue pencil he's always used for puzzles; it's just a stub now. Ben realises that he and his dad might never put all the numbers in the right squares like that, but they are in a better place. Theirs will always be a relationship where they'll force the numbers to fit. It will go wrong at times.

But when it's right, that will hopefully be enough.

44

Love Needs No Passport

Ben was sure that if he'd met his grandma as a stranger in a room full of other strangers, he'd still know she was his. He'd have felt it.

Andrew Fitzgerald, *The Lion Tamer Who Lost*

Standing at Andrew's door, holding a key from a lifetime ago, Ben pauses before knocking. He isn't sure what he'll say. How he will feel seeing him again after so long. He taps, gently at first. Waits. Nothing. Ben knocks a little harder. Still nothing. He turns the key over in his jacket pocket. Will he use it if there's no answer?

He tries knocking again.

The neighbour, Mrs Hardy, opens the door along the corridor. The smell of warm bread drifts out, taking Ben back to days spent in Andrew's flat, knowing what day of the week it was because of the different cooking smells. Bread on Wednesday. She hasn't changed her routine.

'Oh, hello,' she says. 'Andrew said you were in Zimbabwe.'

'Did he?' They must have talked about him.

'I asked where you were when I hadn't seen you in ages.'

'Do you know where Andrew is now?' asks Ben.

'No, sorry.' She has flour on her apron. To Ben's eyes it makes the shape of the African continent. 'He was in earlier. Heard his shower go. I knocked and gave him some quiche I made yesterday. I like trying to feed him up.'

Ben wonders if Andrew still works at Beverley's town library. As though sensing the query, Mrs Hardy says, 'He won't be at work. He gave that up a few months ago. Been dead busy with the book. And...'

'And what?' asks Ben.

'Well, he's been ill again, hasn't he? I think two jobs got to be too much.'

Ben puts a hand against the doorframe. Feels a wave of nausea rise. Though his dad mentioned Andrew looking unwell, Ben had clung to the thought that he had merely had low blood sugar, despite Andrew denying it was that.

'I ... well, I had an idea,' he says. 'What happened? Did he tell you?'

'I know he had cancer last year, but he said he'd gone into remission. He looked much better again. Was away with his book, doing tours and that. But then...'

'Then?'

'He started looking awful. He walked up the stairs so slowly the other day, I was right concerned. I said, you're not good, are you? He shook his head. Said it had come back.'

Ben feels faint.

'You okay?' Mrs Hardy moves towards him.

He nods. 'I will be. It's just...'

'You didn't know?'

'Not for sure.'

'Do you want to come in and sit down.' Mrs Hardy touches Ben's arm. 'I'll get you some cake and tea.'

'No, thank you. I'll let myself into Andrew's flat and wait there for him.'

'Sure?'

'Yes.'

For the first time in many months, Ben puts his key into the slot and opens Andrew's door. Mrs Hardy disappears into her flat, the smell of fresh bread still lingering. Ben enters the place he once loved as much as he did Zimbabwe. It is as though time hasn't passed. He goes into the narrow kitchen with cupboards lining one wall. Touches the fading I HEART PARIS fridge magnet. Andrew has a new 365-new-words-a-year calendar. Today's word is *sempiternal*. Ben leans closer to read the definition: eternal and unchanging, everlasting. He wonders if Andrew read it earlier. If he already knew what it meant. If he read it aloud as Ben has just done.

At the top is the lion postcard Ben sent from Zimbabwe. He unsticks it and reads the back: *I saw it and thought of us.*

The living room is unusually tidy. But it feels the same. A haven. There is one addition, and one absence. On the desk is stack of beautiful gold-spined paperbacks. *The Lion Tamer Who Lost*. Ben touches them, opens one and smells the new paper. He looks again at the dedication. *For Ben*. After a moment, he turns to the occasional table by the curtains.

The Wish Box isn't there.

Perhaps somewhere else? No, it never has been, and Ben can't imagine where it might be instead. He looks behind the curtains, on the window sill, behind the sofa. It isn't there.

Why?

He goes into the bedroom; the duvet is neatly pulled over the bed, and the window is open, letting a breeze move the curtains. He can smell Andrew. Picture him lying on top of the covers, reading. On the bedside table are small vials of pills next to glucose tablets and mini chocolate bars.

Ben sits on the bed with his head in his hands. He can't bear that Andrew is suffering. Why didn't he *tell* him? Andrew could have overlooked everything that happened and written to him. Could have let Ben *be* there. They are brothers after all. Ben realises with surprise that the feelings he has right now are in fact brotherly. His affection is protective, fraternal, profound. If Andrew were here now he would kiss his forehead, tuck him in, make sure he had everything he needed.

But where is he?

And where is the Wish Box?

If it were here, would he look at the current wish inside or respect Andrew's privacy as he has always done?

Ben's phone buzzes twice. He takes it out; there are two messages. He clicks on the first. It's Stig. Saying that Lucy is still doing fine. Her stitches are healing, and she has been resting and eating well. *Thank God.* Ben feels as if everything will be okay now. He clicks on Esther's message. She asks him to call her. He tells her he will do later, that he's just at the shop.

Ben goes back into the living room to wait there. After an hour, he decides to take a walk, call Esther, and then come back later. He heads towards the town centre. The June day is warm. Pink-and-white apple blossoms brighten his stroll. Café owners have set chairs out on the pavement and people fill them. He dials Esther's number and it only rings twice before she answers.

'It seems like forever since I saw you,' she says. 'How can it only be twenty-four hours?'

Ben can't believe it either. 'How fast you get used to being home. Are you okay? Your parents?'

'I told them last night. They were a bit shocked, which I totally get. But they're fine now. I said you'd come up soon and meet them. Got a doctor's appointment tomorrow.' She sighs. 'When will you be coming? I know you've only just got there, but you've no idea how much I miss you.'

'Soon,' says Ben. 'Just a few things to sort out here. Things I'll tell you about. But it's complicated over the...'

A smash engulfs Ben's *the* word, a sound like one he heard before, one he has never forgotten. One that was punctuated with glassy tinkles and car horns and squealing breaks. One that interrupted his walk with Jodie Cartwright. Led to Andrew. This one is softer and followed by swearing.

'Just a minute,' he says to Esther.

A car has pulled away from the kerb, perhaps without checking for oncoming traffic, and hit the bonnet of a passing cab. The taxi driver is assessing the damage. A young man is waving his arms and kicking the front tyre.

'Call you back in a tick,' says Ben.

He heads towards the cars, curious.

He remembers walking to the wreckage that day, right before he saw

Andrew in the cafe. Jodie had followed him, her heels out of time with his. Ben remembers the small boy, Jon, still strapped to his seat.

This accident though is minor.

The taxi's front is dented, and the other car scratched. Ben frowns. Music drifts from the cab: Andrea Bocelli. It is the driver who took them to the hospital when they got the results. What was his name? An unusual one. Bob Fracklehurst. That was it. He chatted nonstop. He was playing Andrea Bocelli then. Said he could enjoy his songs without knowing what the words meant because he could tell from the *way* Andrea sang them.

Ben has always resisted believing in fate; has always found logical explanation for coincidence. But now he shivers. In the back of the taxi is Andrew. Looking right at him. Pale, a little stunned, hair ruffled.

Ben goes to the car. Andrew winds the window down. Ben bends to speak to him.

'You always follow an accident,' he says.

Andrew smiles.

Ben smiles.

Bob Fracklehurst tells the man there's no need to swear.

'Thank God no one's hurt,' says Andrew.

'You sure you're okay?' asks Ben.

'Just got a bit of a jolt. I'm fine.' He pauses. 'You're home.'

'Yes.'

'When?'

'Yesterday.' Ben holds Andrew's gaze. 'I got there a few hours after you'd been.'

'You know.'

'Yes.'

'I *had* to tell him.'

'I understand,' says Ben softly.

'I saw your dad in the supermarket a while ago.' Andrew speaks slowly as though the memory exhausts him. 'I really wanted to speak to him. Then yesterday, when I woke up, I decided to go and tell him. I didn't want to cause trouble. Didn't want him to know about ... you know.'

Ben nods, wants to touch his cheek, say it will all be okay now.

Bob Fracklehurst comes to the car.

'Sorry about this,' he says to Andrew. 'Just going to exchange details and we'll be away. Do you want me to get another cab for you?'

'No,' says Andrew. 'I always allow extra time. I'll wait.'

Bob returns to the other driver.

'Where are you going?' Ben asks.

'Nowhere.'

'It must be somewhere. Andrew, I *know*. About the cancer. I was at your flat, saw Mrs Hardy.'

'I'm going to the hospital,' he admits.

'Let me come.'

'No.' Andrew is adamant.

'For God's sake!' Ben puts his forehead to the taxi roof. 'You don't understand. I get it now. I *understand*. I've moved on.' Ben pauses. Thinks of telling him about Esther, but that needs time, not a moment standing here on a pavement.

'It's just a simple check-up,' says Andrew. 'Maybe we can catch up tomorrow.'

'Are you just appleasing me?'

'*Appleasing*?'

Ben smiles. His mis-words are back. He doesn't even mind Andrew pointing it out.

'You know there's a word for that,' says Andrew.

'For what?'

'For your mis-words. It was on my word calendar on the fridge, about two weeks ago: *acyrologia*.' Andrew pauses, holds Ben's gaze. 'It means an improper use of a word.'

'Improper?' Ben says. 'No, it's all the *other* words that are improper.'

Andrew smiles.

'Maybe we can catch up tomorrow then?'

'Yes. This is just a boring check-up.' Andrew's cheeks are sunken, his eyes shadowy.

Ben feels terrible for berating him. He hesitates, then asks: 'Didn't the donation work?'.

'Oh, it did. I went into very early remission. I felt so much better. But it's quite common for this kind of leukaemia to return.'

'Can I donate my stem cells again then?' asks Ben.

'They found a matching donor. We're going to do it in a few weeks.'

'It's not mine though.' Ben feels sad.

'No,' says Andrew softly.

'But if it makes you better...'

'Do you know about the book?' Andrew's face lights up.

Ben nods. 'I saw it at the airport yesterday and read it on the journey home. It's beautiful.' He goes into his rucksack and takes it out.

'It's all thanks to you for entering it in that competition.'

'Here,' says Ben, handing him it.

'I've got loads of copies,' laughs Andrew.

'No. I wrote you a letter in the back. It will explain stuff.'

Andrew touches Ben's arm. The thrill this once gave is tempered. Not gone, but different. Warm. Intense. He takes the book.

'How was Zimbabwe? Was it what you imagined?'

'*Yes*,' says Ben. 'It's like another world out there. And the lions are nothing like the ones we saw in the circus that day. They're ... *real*. Huge and breathing and colourful. I rescued a lioness called Lucy.'

The phone in Ben's pocket buzzes. It is Esther. He doesn't answer, but sends a quick text saying something has come up and he'll ring tonight.

'Everything okay?' asks Andrew.

Ben nods. He has so many other things he wants to say.

'Isn't this weird?' is all he can come up with.

'I know. What are the chances?'

'Did you wish you'd see me today?' Ben asks.

Andrew smiles, but shakes his head.

'No new wishes?'

Andrew doesn't respond. Thinking of the Wish Box, Ben asks, 'Where were you before now?'

'What do you mean?'

'I was at your flat for an hour.'

'Just had some things to do in town. I signed a few of my novels in that little book shop up there.' Andrew looks at Ben. 'Then this.'

This. Them. Brought together, somehow, by a bigger hand than theirs.

Bob Fracklehurst returns to the cab, gets into the driver's seat. 'All done,' he says. 'That lad couldn't see that it was his fault, but no harm done. I've been in worse accidents. Ready to go?'

'You sure I can't come?' asks Ben.

'I'll be fine. We can talk tomorrow.'

'Shall I come after lunch?'

'Sure.'

Andrew smiles. Though his face is pale, orange sparks light his eyes for a moment. That family trait.

Ben leans a little closer. 'I loved that line near the end of the book,' he says.

'Which one?' asks Andrew.

'*Love goes with us – it is light and has easy-to-grip handles and needs no passport.*'

Andrew nods, his eyes glassy.

'You were with me the whole time,' says Ben. 'You became my brother out there.'

He kisses Andrew's forehead. Andrew closes his eyes.

'We can make this work,' Ben tells him. 'We *can*. You can have your family. Just read my letters in your book.'

Ben stands back and the taxi pulls away. He watches it leave. Waves. And unlike when he left on the bus that time long ago, Andrew turns and watches him too. He lifts his hand and waves. And even when the car is lost in the rest of the traffic, Ben imagines that Andrew's eyes still flash with gold.

Ben walks briskly home. The smell of the apple-tree blossoms is so English. The empty teacups at café tables are so English. The warmth that dies in moments at the arrival of a raincloud is so English.

Ben is home.

This is where he belongs.

45

Three Brothers

Nancy said, 'Let's play Cheaty Chess.' Ben shook his head, sad. 'It's all different now,' he said. 'We can't break the rules anymore.' So they did puzzles instead but Ben's heart wasn't in it.

Andrew Fitzgerald, *The Lion Tamer Who Lost*

Ben is back in Zimbabwe.

Standing on the hut's wooden decking at dawn, warm air tickles his bare legs and arms. The sun comes to life, turning the sky from ash into flame, the trees from shadow into textured browns. Far away, amidst the longer grass, is Lucy. She is the same colour as the sun. It's too early to hunt. She lies down, yawns and stretches, contented. Her back leg has healed fully.

The door opens behind Ben and he anticipates Simon – but it is Andrew. Though surprised, it feels to Ben like the most natural thing in the world that he is here.

'You're right,' says Andrew. He looks well. His cheeks have regained their colour, his hair its life, and both are as vibrant as the sky. 'This is just stunning.'

Ben is excited to enjoy his private view with him; to share ownership of the morning.

'I know,' he says. 'Wait until the sun gets a bit higher. The trees look like they're alight. Can you see Lucy over there?'

'Where?'

'There, in the grass.'

'No. Is she camouflaged? Maybe she's only visible to you?'

Ben frowns, looks harder, afraid he has imagined her. She rolls over as though to assure him of her existence.

'You can't see her?' he demands.

'Does it matter? *You* can.' Andrew sighs happily. 'Shall we go and get coffee? You can show me the rest of the place – the enclosures and the nurseries.'

Ben nods. 'What shall I tell everyone?' he asks.

'Say you invited your brother to see your favourite lion sanctuary.'

'I will,' smiles Ben.

'Don't forget me, will you?' says Andrew.

'Forget you? Why would I?'

Ben watches Lucy. She is sleeping now.

When he turns back to Andrew, he has gone.

'Andrew?'

Ben wakes with the word on his lips. Opens his eyes. He is home. In his small room; in England. It was a dream. But he can still feel Andrew's presence, still smell the faint whiff of lion shit and animal fur. He opens the window; freshly cut grass replaces the aroma. It is past nine already. The dream was so powerful that Ben is sure he was there; sure Andrew was there too. Maybe one day he will take him. For now, he's looking forward to going to the flat later.

Despite the lie-in, Ben is tired.

Last night he rang Esther and apologised for suddenly hanging up. He explained that there had been a minor car accident and he had known the passenger. They talked until late, her excitedly sharing plans for the baby – including a book of names she'd bought and ideas for the birth – while he listened and tried to enthuse.

But his mind was elsewhere.

He kept seeing Andrew's pale face. He knew it wasn't fair to Esther that he was preoccupied since they had got home. When she asked if he was still happy about the baby, he said absolutely, that he just had things to deal with at home, and he would explain when they were together again.

Now Ben goes for a shower. He hears his dad surface. He knows he was drinking last night, hiding it by putting vodka into a coffee mug. But Ben doesn't mind as much as he used to. It occurs to him that it wasn't so much the drinking as his behaviour that infuriated him. Now the truth about Andrew is out, and his dad – *their* dad – is accepting, Ben feels things might begin to heal.

He is still concerned about how Mike will take the news. Perhaps he should tell him, sooner rather than later. Is it fair that they all know, and Mike doesn't?

In the kitchen, Will smokes. 'Morning,' he says as Ben enters.

'Dad, I was thinking. I should go and see Kim and find out when Mike's next home. Doesn't he come every three months?'

'Six,' says Will. 'He might be home now. He left around the same time as you, remember.'

'It was a few weeks before me.' Ben switches the kettle on. 'He may have already been home. I'll ring her now.'

'Can't hurt,' says Will.

Ben finds her number on the notepad by the phone and dials. Mike answers.

Surprised, Ben says, 'Oh, it's you.'

'What kind of greeting is that?' laughs his brother.

'You're home,' says Ben.

'Only for three more days. When did you get back? I'd have come and seen you if I'd known, stranger.'

'Got back two days ago. How are you?'

'Okay.'

'And Lola?'

Ben feels bad that he hasn't thought much about her recently. He is going to be a dad at the end of the year. Is it a bad sign that he hasn't made more effort with his niece?

'She's great!' Mike speaks with obvious love. 'You wouldn't recognise her. She's sitting up, crawling. She gets everywhere. Come and see her today.' As though to prove her existence, Lola squeals in the background, and Mike laughs. 'There she goes!'

Ben pauses. 'Why don't you come here?'

Mike doesn't speak.

'Did you get Dad's letter?'

'I did.' He sighs. 'And I did think about coming over. I did. But ... I dunno. I'm still angry at times. Despite...'

'Despite what?' When Mike doesn't respond, Ben says, 'The thing is...'

'What?'

'I've got something to tell you.' Ben realises this is the understatement of the year.

'Okay. Is it good?'

'I don't know how to describe it,' admits Ben. 'Could you come now?'

In the background, Lola giggles. 'I suppose. For you. Is *he* there?'

'Yes.' Ben glances back to the kitchen, where their dad has opened the door and is standing in the sunlight. 'Surely you can't just ignore him forever?'

'I'll come,' says Mike, and hangs up.

Ben returns to the kitchen and tells his dad.

Will nods and walks up the garden path, where he remains until Mike turns up half an hour later. Affection floods Ben at the sight of his older brother. His hair is cut short for duty, but the stubble of beard is clue that he's been home a week or two. They hug. Will joins them from the garden and Mike eyes him, warily.

'How you been, lad?' asks Will.

'Yeah, good.' He looks at Ben. 'How was Zimbabwe?'

'Incredible. It was hard to leave.' They're making small talk, but greater things hang in the air between them. 'Do you want a coffee?'

'Go on then.' Mike sits at the table. 'Before you tell me your stuff, I've got something to say.'

'Okay.' Ben gets out three mugs.

Mike looks at their dad. 'I did a DNA test. Lola is mine. You're fucking lucky, Dad. If she hadn't been, I can't say what I'd have done. But I had to know. In the end, it drove me crazy. *Not* knowing is worse than knowing, even if it's bad.'

'I knew it would be so,' says Will.

'No, you didn't.' Mike hitches his voice up. 'You couldn't *know*.'

'I'm happy for you,' says Ben. 'Can't we all move on?'

Mike ignores the question. 'So, what's your news?'

'It's kind of … well, profound, in light of yours. It's about a test, too. But where do I start?' Ben pours water onto the coffee granules, stirs and hands one to Mike. Will opens the door and lights a cigarette. 'It's going to be quite a shock. So, the thing is … The news is…' Ben can't say it.

He suddenly sees Mike and him as kids. Sees them climbing trees and sharing sherbet dips and riding bikes in the cul-de-sac. Might another brother come between them?

Will takes over. 'I'm not Lola's dad,' he says. 'But I am a father again. I have another son.'

'What?' cries Mike. 'A baby? At your bloody age? Fuck. Don't you ever learn? It's so ridiculous it could be funny.'

'No, not a baby. He's older than you. It was a long time ago.'

'But how?' Mike shakes his head.

Will looks at Ben for help now.

'You never met my friend Andrew, did you?' says Ben. 'I stayed with him a while before I went to Zimbabwe. He got ill. Cancer. Anyway, he had no family for a stem-cell donation, so I offered. I felt so bad for him. And we were a perfect match.' Ben pauses. 'Because we're brothers.'

'I feel like I'm on one of those daytime shows where they do DNA tests live!' Mike shakes his head. 'Give us one of your cigs, Dad.'

'It blew my mind, too,' says Ben, 'the coincidence of it. But then in some ways it made sense.' He picks his words carefully. 'Andrew and I had a strong connection when we became mates. Now I know why. And is it so strange? His mother lived in the area. He does too. Weren't we going to cross paths at some point?'

'So, you were with his mother?' Mike looks at Will. 'When? Who is she?'

Will tells him the story of Anne, of their short time together.

'It was before Mum?'

'God, yes. Long before.'

Mike stubs his cigarette out in the ashtray on the table. He slowly shakes his head, exhales. 'I don't know what to say.'

'You don't have to say anything.' Ben joins him at the table. 'You don't have to *do* anything. But I wanted you to know before you went back to Afghanistan.' He pauses. 'You could meet him?'

Will nods. 'I think Ben wants to see him today. Go with him.'

Ben panics. He needs to see Andrew first, talk, prepare him. 'He's not well, Dad. He might need more warning. Tomorrow? How about then? If he's up to it.'

'I don't know,' says Mike. 'I think I need time to get my head around it. Fucking hell, Dad. Any more kids knocking about? I don't know whether to laugh or yell. You dirty old sod.'

Outside, an ice-cream van tune drifts closer.

'He looks like us,' says Ben.

'He does,' echoes Will.

'I'll meet him next time I'm home,' says Mike.

'Okay.' Ben clears their mugs away.

The phone rings in the other room. In the street, the ice-cream van song tinkles away too. Will goes into the lounge. Both sounds die at the same time. Ben runs the hot water and washes the mugs. Mike's phone buzzes and he responds to a text message. Ben realises that sharing his news about Esther and their baby might be too much right now. He can tell them both tomorrow. Let this news sink in first. Let things settle.

Now Ben's phone buzzes, too. He opens the message. Smiles. It's from Stig, saying Lucy is still doing well. It is a good sign.

Will comes back into the kitchen. His face is white.

'What is it?' asks Ben, drying his hands.

'That was the hospital.'

'The hospital?'

'It's Andrew,' says Will.

'Why are they ringing *you* about him?' Ben is indignant. 'Is it a hypo? They should ring *me*. I've always taken care of him.'

'They said he gave this number to them in the event of…'

'Of what?'

Will comes to Ben, puts his hand on his shoulder. 'Son, Andrew died this morning.'

46

Happiness

> *In the beginning a lioness entered the world and before she had a place in the family or a look at her surroundings or even a name – when she was still just first breath and blood – she knew she would never again be so absolutely free as she was then.*
>
> Andrew Fitzgerald, *The Lion Tamer Who Lost*

When Ben's mum died, he didn't have a mobile phone with her number in it. Back in 1994 only business people had them. He didn't have any way to contact her once she had gone. The only numbers were those in his head; the number of pills left in the vial on her bedside – twenty-nine; the number of cornflakes she hadn't eaten – one hundred and fifty-eight the hour before she died.

Ben can still call Andrew though. He can dial his mobile number, listen to it ring six times before hearing his voice.

Leave a message and I'll get back to you when I can.

Ben listens over and over and over, not even counting the times.

Leave a message and I'll get back to you when I can.

'Get back to me now,' he whispers.

It is dark. The phone's light is weak, like a clouded-over moon reflected in a dirty puddle. It must be almost morning. Ben has been sitting on his bed since maybe midnight. He isn't sure. Yesterday is a blur. He remembers little after the moment his dad came into the kitchen and said ... what were the words? Andrew is dead? Andrew has died? We've lost Andrew?

Ben only knows that he fell onto the kitchen tiles. Just as Andrew did that Sunday lunch. The next he knew was Mike's face looming over him, rough hands cradling him, and Will offering vodka. Ben's neck aches. Perhaps they helped him to the sofa. He recalls being there, head in his hands, vomit threatening to erupt. He recalls hasty calls being made around him: Mike to Kimberley, Will to someone.

Then Ben's mobile phone ringing and Will taking it, despite his insistence that it could be Andrew.

Was it Esther? Ben tries hard to put the call into its right place. Wasn't that the call from two days ago? No. Will's hazy face comes out of the blackness. He told Esther there had been a death. Ben can hear those words. Did Esther explain who she was? She must have done. She would have been confused, wondered who on earth Andrew was. What else did his dad say to her?

Didn't Esther text him yesterday?

Ben reluctantly clicks out of Andrew's number and finds her message. She sent two. One at 12.30 p.m.

So sad to hear about your brother Andrew. Wish I could be there with you. I'll come down tomorrow. Love you loads. xxx

No question about why Ben had never mentioned an Andrew. She probably knew that wasn't the moment to ask, but she must be wild with curiosity. It's too much for him to think of now. She sent another message at 3.44 p.m.

Thinking about you. Got a train booked for tomorrow. I'll be there at 3. xxx

Tomorrow. Isn't it tomorrow already?

Ben dials Andrew's number again and listens to it ringing.

Leave a message and I'll get back to you when I can.

Why didn't Ben call him when he first got back to England? Why didn't he just go there straightaway? Why the fuck did he *wait*?

Ben hasn't cried. He is dry; his heart feels tight, dehydrated. His legs ache. He recalls Andrew as though through a reverse telescope; he's distant, blurred. He sees him in the taxi yesterday – was it yesterday or the day before? – driving away. The time they shared so long ago isn't real. But the feelings are; this sadness that they'll never fulfil their role as brothers now.

Ben gets out of bed and goes to the window. Lazy light low in the sky heralds an early June dawn. It must be about four. He doesn't want a new day. He wants to go back. But to when? To when he met Andrew so he can change it and not go to the library that day? *No*. To when they did the test so they can change it and not do it? *No*. To yesterday so he could have gone first thing to Andrew's flat and been there when he...

How did Andrew die?

Did he ask Will that earlier?

Why won't his head clear?

He goes onto the landing, phone still in hand. He opens his dad's door and watches him snoring, flat on his back. In the other bedroom, Mike sleeps on the unmade bed, curled like a toddler, hands between his knees. He'll be used to sleeping rough. On his tours, he must have slept in far less comfortable places. Ben wants to curl beside him, like they did when camping as kids; he longs for that safety, that simplicity of childhood exhaustion after a day on their bikes.

But he goes downstairs, opens the back door and watches the sun climb over the trees in next-door's garden. The sight is not as vivid as the dawn viewed from his Zimbabwe hut, but the pain in his heart is. It is sharp, intense, as if one beat goes off kilter he'll choke. Ben realises he'll never take Andrew to the Liberty Lion project. He will never share the morning with him.

Ben takes out his phone again. He will never delete Andrew's number. Even when it rings out in the nowhere, when the account has been cancelled, Ben knows he won't have the heart to remove the digits from his list. He wonders how soon a phone contract gets cancelled when someone dies. If no one calls to do so, will it just end? When?

Because then there will be no more voice.

Leave a message and I'll get back to you when I can.

Ben doesn't know how long he stands watching the sunrise. When Mike puts a gentle hand on his shoulder, he starts.

'How are you doing?' he asks.

'I don't know.' This is the truth.

'Did you sleep?'

'No. I couldn't,' says Ben.

'I'll make coffee.' Mike switches the kettle on. 'This must be tough for you. You *knew* him. You were mates.' He pauses. 'For me, it's surreal. A brother I never met, and he's gone. It's terrible, sad, but ... well, for me it doesn't mean as much as it does for you.'

'You'd have liked him,' says Ben.

'If you did, yeah, I would've.'

'What happened?' ask Ben.

'What do you mean?'

'My head – it's cloudy. What did the hospital say? How did he...?'

'Oh. Dad said they told him that Andrew collapsed at home. Luckily his neighbour heard a crash and went in. She called an ambulance ... He died shortly after. It wasn't a hypo like you thought. It was the cancer. He must have already been pretty ill with it.'

Ben nods. So, there was nothing he could have done. Coke and biscuits would have made no difference. But it doesn't help. Now he feels wretched. But still there are no tears.

'I wonder what'll happen,' says Mike. 'From what Dad said, we're his only family. I think he told the hospital we would take care of whatever needs doing.'

'Good,' says Ben quietly.

'I'm supposed to be back in Afghanistan tomorrow but I'll see if I can delay.'

'Okay.'

Mike hands Ben a coffee, says, 'Can I do anything before I get a shower?'

'No. I'll just...' Ben doesn't know what the end of the sentence is.

'Who's this Esther?' asks his brother. 'Never mentioned her, you dark horse.'

He sips his drink. 'We met in Zimbabwe. She's ... we're...'

'Tell me another time. Dad said she's coming today.'

'Yeah, she said she'd get here at...' Ben feels sure it's this afternoon.

Moments after Mike goes for a shower, Will comes into the kitchen. As though this is any normal day, he lights a cigarette and stands at the sink. But Ben finds comfort in it. Then he feels sad that these are the familial moments that Andrew should have known, and never will.

'I dunno what to say.' Will inhales deeply.

'Should we be *doing* something?'

'The hospital will let us know. I said I'd take care of it all. It's the least I can do. He was my son and I met him twice.' Will looks at Ben. 'But at least you got to know him. At least he found us before...'

Ben nods. There is that.

Andrew got his wish before he died.

'This Esther sounds nice, lad.'

'She is.'

'You met over in Africa then?'

'Yeah.'

'I'm sure she'll make things a little easier for you when she gets here.'

Ben just feels guilty.

'I should go get some food in if we're going to have her overnight,' says Will.

'I'll go,' says Ben. 'I need some air.'

He showers when Mike is done. By the time he's dressed and ready to leave, it's ten-thirty. As he goes downstairs, someone knocks on the front door. The postman hands Ben a small parcel. He recognises the handwriting. Andrew's. How? He must have sent it *before*.

Ben feels a little sick.

'Be back soon,' he calls to his dad, and heads down the street.

He finds himself at the broken bench on the corner just before the main road. Sitting to avoid the missing slat, he holds the parcel but can't open it yet. The sun scorches his neck, impatient. Andrew's loopy script blurs.

Eventually he carefully opens the flap – the way his mum did when she wanted to keep the wrapping for another gift – and peers inside. A flash of silver, like a knowing wink.

The Wish Box.

Around it, is a letter. Ben closes his eyes for a moment. Then he takes out the paper, composes himself, and reads it aloud. He knows Andrew would want it no other way.

Dear Ben,

I gave this to Mrs Hardy-next-door to send to you if anything happened to me. So, if you're reading this, well, something has happened. Which is strange to write. I'm ill again. I thought about letting you know, but what would it serve? You'd only feel sad, want to do something, and I don't want that. I want you to enjoy Zimbabwe, not worry when there's no need.

I've thought so often about you. I hope you forgive me for refusing to see you when we found out. I've realised that if we'd found out we were brothers before we fell in love, I think we'd have been fine. Close. Brotherly. Affectionate. Time was at fault, not us. We found out too late. I was cruel to turn you away after the test, but I couldn't handle it. I knew you were young enough to find someone else. Which I wanted for you, even though it hurt like hell to think of.

I hope this letter never reaches you, that in years to come I ask Mrs Hardy to give it back to me. I hope I can one day tell Will who I am – perhaps with you by my side. I hope I can meet Mike. Are these hopes wishes? No. I only have one wish left to make, and that's in the Wish Box. That belongs there whether I give it to you myself or whether you receive this parcel. And if I'm not here anymore, I want this wish even more.

Andrew

Ben presses the letter to his chest, as though to permanently imprint the words there. He guesses Andrew must have written it a few weeks ago, before he decided to come to their dad's house and tell him the truth. If only Ben had known while he was away that Andrew was ill again. But what could he have done? Wouldn't some curious accident have occurred that brought Ben home to Andrew if it were *supposed* to happen?

Does he really believe this?

Yes. He thinks he does.

Ben folds the paper and puts it in his shirt pocket. Then he takes the Wish Box from the package, gently fingers the many ridges that are as familiar as the lines of Andrew's face. The wonky lid falls free, as always, clanking like the chains that first held Lucy. It lands on the grass. Inside is a single folded Post-it note.

Ben opens the yellow square. Again, he reads the words there aloud.

'I wish you happiness.'

He whispers them again. Hears Andrew's voice over his shoulder, echoing the wish. Ben knows what he means. He remembers the day they talked about happiness, in the hours before they got the test results.

'Happiness that lasts is much rarer,' Andrew said to him then. 'I think you need to be ... *honest*.'

Ben had insisted that he was going to tell his dad; said they should just get the test results and then he'd tell him about them.

'Then you'll be happy,' said Andrew. 'Because then you can really be yourself.'

I wish you happiness.

Ben finally cries. He sobs into the crook of his arm, the way children do when trying to be brave and hoping no one can see their tears. An old lady pushing a pink shopping trolley past the bench pauses, touches Ben's sleeve. He pulls back, embarrassed.

'Aw, lad,' she says. 'What's to do?'

'Nothing,' he chokes. 'I'm fine.'

'Must be summat. Best to get it all out.' She pats his head. Ben suddenly longs for his mum. 'My grandson's about your age and he always goes upstairs to cry. But I tell him, no need to hide it from me.' Seeing Ben is more composed now, she nods and moves on.

Ben watches her walk away, avoiding the cracks in the pavement.

I wish you happiness.

He knows what he must do.

47

Three Words

Ben told Nancy they were joined forever. 'Because you know my secret,' he said. 'About the lions.'

Andrew Fitzgerald, *The Lion Tamer Who Lost*

Ben is waiting in the station for Esther at three.

Her train arrives promptly. There is no delay, no overturned carriage or faulty track to interrupt their meeting. He hurries to help with her the bags. She's still tanned, and her hair is plaited. It may have only been days since they saw one another, but it feels as though it has been months. Ben half expects her pregnancy to be further on, her appearance to be different, more rounded. But she is the girl he saw every day in Africa.

The girl he has lied to.

His stomach turns over.

Esther is shy, kisses his cheek modestly.

'I'm sorry about your brother,' she says.

How much does she know? Ben realises she can only know what his dad does. He hugs her. The affection is genuine. She resists a little and can't look him fully in the eye.

'Shall we go somewhere quiet,' suggests Ben. 'I don't want to go home yet.'

'Whatever you want.'

They leave the shade of Paragon Station, and head for a sun-baked Queens Gardens. Ben finds a spot by the fountains and rows of colourful flowers that seem to compete with one another for attention.

Esther perches on the wall. She fans her face with a train ticket wallet, despite the occasional spray that cools them when the breeze blows their way.

'Not quite our rock in Zimbabwe, is it?' Ben says. 'Are you too hot? We can find shade. Or I'll go get you a drink…'

'Ben, it's okay, I'm fine.' She pauses. 'So, how are *you*?' Finally, she looks at him, her eyes watery.

Ben shrugs. He hurts, wants to say he's fine. But she deserves more, so much more. This isn't just about him.

'Not good,' he admits. 'I haven't slept since the hospital rang. My stomach feels like a cement mixer.'

'I guess Andrew was the *big thing* you couldn't tell me,' says Esther gently. 'The thing your dad had done that you couldn't forgive.'

'Yes. Andrew was why I was angry at him.' Ben realises that unless Esther knows what happened between them she won't fully understand why he was so secretive about it all. But she can *never* know that. He needs to make her think that it was all about his dad. 'My dad always had affairs, but I think I was angry that one of them meant I missed having one of my brothers all my life.'

'You only found out Andrew was your brother recently?'

Ben tells Esther about the test, omitting their real relationship back then.

'It wasn't myself I was angry for. It was Andrew. He was the one who missed out on a having a family. That's why I couldn't forgive my dad. I've learned since I got home that he didn't actually abandon Andrew's mother. He never even knew she was pregnant. I think he would have stayed if he'd known.'

A red ball lands at Esther's feet. She picks it up, smiles, and Ben sees vividly the future mother. The loving and patient parent she will be.

Moments later a little boy comes for it. 'Soz, miss,' he says, and returns to a game with his friends.

Esther looks back at Ben. Maybe, like he is, she is realising the reality; they will have their own child in just six months.

'Is that why you stayed with me when I found out I was pregnant?'

asks Esther. 'Because you thought your dad hadn't and you didn't want to be him?'

'*No*,' insists Ben.

'I know you've just had awful news, but I have to be honest with you, Ben.'

'Of course. Tell me.'

'I've been thinking the last few days. It's the first time I've had space from us since we met.' Esther fiddles with one pigtail. 'And I don't feel like you're all there. I mean, not that you're stupid, but not as into this relationship as I am. I've always felt it, but I just loved you so much I ignored it. Remember that day at the eclipse?'

'Of course,' says Ben.

'I said it was as though you were blocked. And that's how you seem. Half-hidden.' Esther pauses. 'You've never said you love me. I don't want you to ... if you don't ... but I guess I need to know *why*...'

Ben nods. This is the moment to be honest. But he can't speak. A stronger breeze gets up and spray wets them both. The boy with the red ball has lost it in the water and leans over the fountain wall. His mother comes and rescues him before he falls.

'Your silence says everything.' Esther's voice wavers.

'No, you don't understand.' Ben touches her face tenderly. 'It's not you. It's *never* been you. Fuck, this all sounds so clichéd. But I've been selfish. We got deeper and deeper into this. And I wanted to but ... I mean, I wanted to say...'

'What?' she asks softly.

'If I could love you, God, I would.'

'*If*?'

'Esther, I'm...' He closes his eyes for a moment. Then he says the words he should have said the first time she looked at him with interest. 'I'm gay.'

When she doesn't speak, he says, 'You don't realise, if I wasn't I'd be madly in love with you. You're my best friend. You've been my rock these last months. And I've fucked this up so badly. God, if I could...'

Esther starts to laugh. She covers her mouth, says sorry. Laughs some more. Then she stops. Shakes her head.

And looks desperately sad.

'Ben Roberts,' she says at last, 'I said you were full of secrets. And this is it. And it's so bloody obvious, it's ridiculous. I'm so stupid.'

'No, yo—'

'I should have known.' She shakes her head. 'But why the hell didn't you just *tell* me? Why sleep with me? Why not end it there? I don't get it.'

'My dad,' says Ben simply.

'Why?'

'I thought he'd disowned his brother for being gay years ago. It made sense – he's a total bigot. But I was wrong. It was because his brother had stolen from their mum.' Ben braces himself. Finds it hard to mention his mum when grief is so tight in his chest. 'Also, I promised my mum when she died that I'd make my dad happy. I thought he'd be miserable if I came out.'

'Oh, Ben.' Esther touches his arm. 'I want to be mad at you – I mean, *I am* for fuck's sake ... but, how can I? You're too bloody soft. Why didn't you tell me anyway? I'd never have shared it if you didn't want me to. We could have still been friends, great friends. Yeah, I'd have been sad not to *have* you ... and I'm heartbroken, I am...'

She begins to cry. Gets up.

'Oh shit, Esther,' Ben says gently.

'Just give me a minute.'

She heads away from him. He begins to follow but senses he should give her space.

After a while she returns and resumes her place.

'You okay?' asks Ben.

'No,' she admits. After a long pause, she says, 'When you're in love with someone you know doesn't love you the same they only haunt you more. You only want them more. Ben, that is how I've felt in the last two days being apart from you.'

Ben feels wretched. Maybe if he admits he was trying to put a sexual relationship with his own brother behind him by starting up with her it will somehow ease this mess. But he can never share that secret.

'I was messed up' is all he can say.

'It makes sense now. Your distance. Any excuse not to sleep with me.' Esther looks at him. Her eyes are still sad. 'But I'm in love with *you*, Ben Roberts. What am I supposed to do with that, eh?'

Ben knows so well about not being able to have the one person you want. He wants to say that with time, and with distance, it *is* possible to let that love change into the kind of love it is supposed to be.

'I may not love you in that way,' he says. 'But we're joined forever, aren't we?' He looks at her stomach. 'We'll do this together – be parents. I'll come to all the scans and stuff and be there at the birth, and for the next eighteen years. I'm not going anywhere.'

'But *how*? I live in Newcastle, you live here.' Esther sounds angry now. 'And we can't live together as a couple, can we? How's it all going to work?'

Ben realises how exhausted he is. He longs for a sugary drink.

'I could move up there. Live near to you. I'll do whatever makes it work.'

'For fuck's sake. Whatever makes it *work*?'

'Yes. I don't know what that is yet. But I'll do it.'

Perhaps realising how pale Ben looks, she says less angrily, 'Look, we don't have to figure it all out now. You have a lot to deal with first.'

'I'm sorry for lying to you,' he says. 'I had no right to mess with your life like that. To get you pregnant in such a dishonest way.'

'It is what it is.' She pauses. 'And I'm glad I'm pregnant.'

The fountain sprays them, like a blessing of baptismal water.

'So what now?' Ben asks.

'Right now?'

'Yes. Are you comfortable coming back to stay at my dad's?'

Esther shakes her head. 'I think I'll go home.'

'Home? But you just got here. You don't have t––'

'It's not a problem, I'll just get the next train back. I think that's best.

You're tired and you're going to have stuff to sort out. I need some time. You have to give me that, Ben.'

He nods.

'We can get together in a week or two, can't we?'

'Christ, what will you tell your family?' he asks.

'The truth,' she says. 'They're going to get to know you over the next eighteen years, aren't they?'

'I should have done that at the start,' says Ben.

'But then I wouldn't be having this baby, would I?' Esther adds softly, 'And I want her.'

'Her?'

'It's just an instinct.' Esther stretches, stands. 'Walk me to the station.'

Ben does. Her pink trainers match his pace. Their feet are in time, like his and Andrew's always were. He smiles.

The next train to Newcastle is in half an hour so they share a sandwich on the platform. When it arrives, Esther kisses Ben on the mouth as if she has forgotten.

'I'm sorry,' she says, embarrassed.

'Don't be.' He hugs her.

'Ben...'

'Yes?'

'Did you enjoy our time in Zimbabwe? Was that real?'

'Yes,' he says. 'That was one of the realest things that ever happened to me.'

When the train leaves, she waves.

And he waves back.

48

Sempiternal

The lioness let her cub go. She didn't want to. She knew what danger lurked in the shadows.

Andrew Fitzgerald, *The Lion Tamer Who Lost*

Andrew's funeral passes as any other; quietly, to a schedule, sun shining regardless. Ben has not been to many. His mum's passed in a blur. This one does, too. The salt-haired priest fakes intimate acquaintance with Andrew, reading his life facts from a sheet of paper: *He was a son, a brother, an uncle*. Ben realises everyone present is faking intimacy with Andrew. Only he knew him. Only his tears are real.

In the front pew, Will squeezes his arm. During the five days since Andrew's death, Ben has spent most of time in his room, surfacing only to eat or go for walks. Esther went home, and Ben returned from the station alone, telling his dad that they were taking some time apart until the funeral was done. If Will wondered what had really happened, he didn't ask.

'I'm here if you wanna talk, lad,' he said each time Ben went into the kitchen.

But Ben didn't know where to start.

Now he sits on one side of Ben, and Mike – who managed to extend his leave – sits on the other, quietly supportive. Kim is at home with Lola. Behind them are some of Andrew's friends, hastily located from an old address book, and his neighbour Mrs Hardy, who Ben spoke with at the start. He wonders if she ever knew about their true relationship, if she is now confused about Andrew being buried as Ben's brother. He would never ask her outright, and she was warm and pleasant to him earlier, but he feels uneasy at the thought that she might know. After this he will probably never see her again anyway.

That makes him sad, and he isn't sure why.

Halfway through, Ben spots Leo sitting at the back by the stone pillar. His heart stops. He turns quickly away, afraid to catch Leo's eye.

'Who's that?' Will asks Ben.

'Old friend of Andrew's.'

'Ah. One of *those* friends?'

'Dad. Seriously. Can you not?'

Ben feels sick. Leo must be wondering why the hell Andrew is being buried as his brother. He needs to keep him away from his family. Perhaps he will just slip away at the end; after all, he is sitting discreetly at the back. Ben's stomach turns over. He is glad that not many relatives are in attendance. Fewer questions to answer. Will and Ben agreed that the service should be modest, small, and not filled with nosy family members. There will be time for explanations later. For now, Andrew deserves a dignified send-off.

How dignified will it be if Leo is here to cause trouble?

But why would he be?

Still, Ben keeps his eyes on the coffin. On it is a colourful casket spray – pink roses, orchids and lilies – that was sent by Andrew's publisher, Tara, who rang with condolences last night. She said that now wasn't the time to discuss it fully, but Andrew's future royalties would be paid to the family as part of his will. Will said Ben should have it. But he couldn't think of money now. Didn't care about a penny of it.

Yesterday, there was a piece in the newspaper about Andrew's death. It described how he had recently achieved huge success with his third children's novel, *The Lion Tamer Who Lost*, only to lose his 'long and valiant fight with cancer'. The picture was one from his book tour, black and white, his face gaunt but eyes bright. Ben read the article numerous times at the kitchen table, touching the picture tenderly when his dad wasn't there.

'Even though you can tell he's ill,' he said, 'he looks so happy.'

Will nodded. 'I remember how passionate he was about his writing that Sunday.'

'He was. It was his life.'

Ben took the newspaper upstairs with him. Keeps it under his pillow.

The salt-haired priest concludes his sermon. No one has done a reading. Ben said to Will yesterday that he didn't think he'd be able to, even though there are a few lines in Andrew's novel he would have loved to have shared. Ben, Will and Mike, with three of the funeral home staff, carried the coffin from the hearse to the church earlier; now they must carry it out again.

They all stand.

Suddenly Ben doesn't know what to do with his hands; what does he usually do with them? He used to love holding Andrew's inside his. His left leg is slower than his right, limp, in the way, a burden. Which leg usually moves first when he walks? He can't recall. He cries without covering his face.

'Come on now, lad,' says his dad.

'Better out than in,' says Mike, gripping his shoulder. 'Isn't that what they say?'

'Yes, about farts,' mumbles Will.

Ben smiles through the tears.

At the graveside, the flowers wilt in the heat. Leo stands far away from the small group, eyes lowered, hands trembling. Ben's phone buzzes. He should have turned it off altogether. Stig has been ringing him the last few days, and he kept missing them. But the messages he left were good news. Lucy is continuing to improve. Her stitches are healing well, and she is apparently up and about like her old self. There is a part of Ben that is angry that Andrew did not recover so well. But it passes.

After the burial, when they all get into the cars, Ben tells his dad he won't be a moment and catches up with Leo on the path as he departs.

'Leo, *wait*,' he calls.

Leo turns. His weathered face is pale, his eyes sad.

'I had to...' Ben doesn't know what to say now.

'I just can't believe he's gone,' says Leo.

'I know. It was so...' Ben wants to say something about Andrew being his brother, to explain. But he can't find the right words.

'I know,' says Leo.

'Sorry.'

'I *know*,' he repeats. 'About you and Andrew. What happened.'

Ben has come to terms with Andrew being his brother, but Leo's words bring a surge of shame.

'How?' asks Ben, despite his sinking heart.

'I was at an awards ceremony in London with Andrew.' He pauses, admits, 'Not *with* him with him. But there as a competitor. He let it slip. I wouldn't let it go and, in the end, he told me about the test.'

'Oh.' Ben looks around, as though others might hear, but Mike and his dad are in the car.

'It was quite a shock,' says Leo.

'It was for *us*,' says Ben.

'I imagine so.'

'What will you do?'

'What do you mean?' asks Leo.

'Well, my family have no idea. They think we were mates. My dad doesn't even...'

'What?'

'Nothing,' sighs Ben.

'Doesn't know you're gay?' Leo shrugs. 'I wondered. You're only young. I didn't come out to my family until I was thirty. Hardest thing I ever did. My mum was fine. My dad ... well, he's okay now, but it took a while.'

'Shit.' Ben says this more to himself.

'Look,' says Leo. 'You guys didn't know when you ... you know. I'm not gonna say anything. At first, I admit I was like, wow, this could make a great story. I told Andrew that I might write something. But I know that was awful. I was insensitive. So I'm not going to. And I won't say anything more on it. I'm glad he found his family. I always felt for him being so alone.'

'Thanks.' There's not much more Ben can say.

'You'd better get back to your family,' says Leo. 'I'm glad you won't see me around and wonder how much I know or what I'll say. You can say hi. I'll say hi.'

Leo continues down the path. After a few steps, he turns, says, 'I hope you find a way to do it.'

'Do what?' asks Ben.

'Say those three words. To your family.'

As he returns to the car, Ben wonders if he can do it. Tell his dad. Tell Mike. He is tired of carrying it around, of worrying, of hiding, of secrets. Esther knows and that was hard enough. She rang him yesterday, wishing him well for the funeral, and she said she thought it was time to tell them.

'I had to say some really difficult words to my family last week,' she said. '*I'm pregnant*. Not the easiest thing to say when you're young and they hoped you'd do more with your life. And when you're now single...'

Ben wonders why he still dreads the idea of saying it. Now he knows that his dad didn't turn Uncle Jerry away, and that he wasn't bothered about Andrew, why do the three words get lodged in his throat.

Isn't it time to find the happiness Andrew wants him to have?

Ben gets in the car and it pulls away. There is no wake. No family gathering. It is over.

'Let's go to that pub,' says Ben.

'Which one, lad?' asks Will.

'Ye Olde Black Boy.'

The last time they were there, Ben confronted him about Kimberley. How long ago it seems.

'Yeah, let's,' agrees Mike.

'Can you drop us there?' Will asks the driver.

Returning to the pub near the river, with its wood panelling and tobacco-stained fixtures, Ben feels so much older now. Like he is coming back after a whole decade. Will buys the beer and they go into the darker back room. It's quiet, probably because it's midweek. They sit around a table, silent, sipping beer. The liquid warms Ben. He lets it in.

'Let's drink to Andrew,' says Mike eventually. 'A brother I never knew.' There's a hint of bitterness to the words, but Will ignores it.

'To Andrew,' says Ben, quietly.

'To Andrew,' says Will.

'He didn't even like beer,' says Ben, softly.

'No?' Will says. 'What the hell was wrong with him?'

'He wasn't much of a drinker.'

'Are we sure he was yours, Dad?' Mike is joking, not being cruel.

Ben looks around at them. 'I chose to come here now because...' He pales, sips his drink. 'Because last time we were here I didn't say *everything*.'

'Last time?' asks Mike.

'This is where I confronted Dad about Kimberley,' admits Ben.

'Oh.' Mike takes a huge swig of beer and feels around for his cigarettes.

'But I wasn't fully ... I mean ... I had other stuff I never said.'

'I had this feeling,' says Will. 'You seemed ... I dunno ... not yourself.'

Ben feels sick. He stands, legs wobbly. 'Give me a minute.'

He goes to the toilets. At the sink, he splashes cold water on his face. He looks at his phone. The message is from Stig. Lucy is going to go on the hunt again tonight. Ben smiles. For a split second, when he looks up, and into the mirror, Andrew is there too. Smiling. Eyes flashing gold. Ben turns but he is alone. No. He isn't. Not really. He never will be.

He goes back to the table.

'What is it?' asks Will, his face desperately concerned. '*Please* tell me you're not ill too, lad?'

'No, no, I'm fine. I'm not ill.'

'Well, did something happen in Zimbabwe? You had no appetite even before Andrew died. Son, I'm bloody worried.'

'No, it's nothing like that.' Ben takes another swig of beer. 'There's something else. God, I've thought and thought about how to say it.

The whole time I was away.' He pauses. 'Andrew knew something about me. He always said I should tell you. That I wouldn't truly be happy until I did.' Ben looks at Will. 'I almost did. Almost have. But ... Dad...'

Mike puts his glass down carefully. 'I think I know,' he says quietly.

'You do?'

'You *are* my brother, Ben.'

'Christ, what is it?' demands Will. 'I'm worried sick now.'

'You'll never know how hard this is,' says Ben. 'I thought it was something you'd disown me for. Thought the whole family would follow your lead. And I promised Mum before she died that I'd look after you all. Make you happy, Dad. I thought this would ruin everything.'

'Look, unless you've murdered someone, I can deal with owt, lad.' He adds, 'And even if you've killed some bugger, we can get past that too.'

It's just three words. *Say them.*

'Okay.' Ben closes his eyes. He opens them; says, 'I'm gay.'

Will laughs. 'Is that *it*?'

Ben is stunned. 'Yes. That's it.'

'Christ, we can deal with that.' Will swigs the rest of his beer. 'Jesus, I thought you were gonna say you were leaving again. Thank God you're not. There's a shirt-lifter comes in here on a Friday. He's a boring bastard but he does no harm to no one.'

Ben laughs. 'Dad, you're the most unbigoted bigot I know.'

'I'll drink to that,' says Mike.

'But Esther?' Will frowns. 'If you're ... you know...'

'Yes, that was something I thought might ... well, help me continue the lie. I thought I could be with her. I really did. It was stupid of me. She's the most incredible girl. She didn't deserve to be treated so badly, and I'll have to live with that.' Ben pauses. 'The thing is ... she's pregnant.'

'Bloody hell, lad. You don't waste your time!' Will looks pleased. 'What are you gonna do?'

'Be a dad,' says Ben. 'I guess we'll just ... work it out. Find a way. I'm gonna be there for them both.'

'I guess that's congratulations then, bro,' says Mike. 'Lola gets a cousin. Kimberley will be chuffed.'

'I'm going up to Newcastle in a few days,' says Ben. 'Going to meet Esther's family. It'll be tough facing them, but I guess it's what I deserve.'

'Look, I just wanna say…' Will raises his glass. 'I know I've been an arse. An idiot. Yes, worse,' he adds at Mike's glare. 'But I'm so proud of you. Of *both* of you.' This he says with a pointed glance at Ben. 'Can't say I won't be a dick again. Can't say I'll stop drinking. My love of it is a bit like your love of the fellas – can't help it or change it.'

Ben starts to interrupt, outraged at the comparison.

'I'm teasing, lad,' says Will. 'But, like you two, I am what I am. And I do love you.'

Neither of his sons says anything. After a while, Ben picks up the newspaper on the next table. He opens it at the sudoku puzzle.

'You wanna start or shall I?' he says.

The day after the pub, Ben goes to Andrew's flat. He stands at the dust-coated desk and touches the soft butterfly there. He knows it used to hang rigid in a frame, that Andrew's mum inherited it from her mother. Through his childhood, Andrew said he had touched the glass, hoping to rouse the sleeping creature. When his mum died, he smashed the frame and softened the butterfly under the tap.

Ben holds it in his open palm and watches it curl. He goes into the kitchen, touches the fading I HEART PARIS fridge magnet. The word on the 365-new-words-a-year calendar is still *sempiternal*. Andrew must have forgotten to tear off another day the morning he died. Maybe he liked the word. Ben reads the definition again: eternal and unchanging, everlasting. He takes both items from the fridge door.

Then he goes to the bedroom. He sits on the bed. He can smell Andrew. He closes his eyes and it is as though he's still here. They both had a fascination for numbers, a love of creatures that roamed free of gilt-edged frames and cages, and a wonderful difference of opinion over wishes. They ended up sharing DNA. Now Ben is the only one in their family who can share his memories, and he'll make sure they never forget him.

He leaves the flat with the little trinkets he wants to keep, knowing he will put them with the Wish Box and keep them forever.

49

Love Goes with Us

Because we all want to stay in the place we're loved.

Andrew Fitzgerald, *The Lion Tamer Who Lost*

Ben opens the book and recites the words.

The reading aloud he has done all his life is now perfectly right for this moment. He doesn't stumble over the sentences. Doesn't say any mis-words. He has read it so many times that he can almost repeat it from memory. But he likes to look at the pages, at the occasional pictures, and the tiny lion cub in the top corner of each page. He likes to have the book in his lap this way.

Ben reads *The Lion Tamer Who Lost* to his daughter.

Heidi lies contented in his arm. At two weeks, she's far too young to understand the words, but Ben learned in a parenting magazine that reading to a child from birth increases intelligence and creativity. So, in the soft orange light of her nursery, he has done this every night since they brought her home from the hospital.

He is staying at Esther's for these early weeks, and then he will visit every weekend. The thought of not being here every day is painful. Not seeing Heidi wake or seeing her feed or bathing her ... how will he do it? He knows he won't want to leave on a Sunday night and go back to Hull. He looks down at Heidi and smells the sweet odour of her forehead as though to fortify himself for the looming departure.

You've dealt with harder separations, Ben thinks. *And you keep Andrew alive simply by imagining him.*

Though he hasn't spoken to Esther about the idea yet, Ben has been thinking about using the money from Andrew's continuing royalties to open some kind of domestic animal sanctuary. Two film companies have expressed an interest in *The Lion Tamer Who Lost,* too, and if that happens Ben wants to do something Andrew would like with the income. What could be more fitting than opening somewhere that cares for animals between homes and then places them with their true families?

Ben could buy a venue up here, near Newcastle, and maybe live on the site. There is a lot to consider, but the idea won't leave his head. Maybe he and Esther could run it, and then take turns caring for their daughter. They could each still live their own lives. Esther can find a partner, as Ben often tells her she should feel free to do.

'I *will*,' Esther usually says. 'When I'm ready. I *just* had a bloody baby. And I'm...'

She never finishes that sentence but Ben knows what the end is. He sees the way she still looks at him. Maybe it will be better for them both when he isn't here all the time. He hates to think she is hurting still because of him.

'You'll find someone first, I reckon,' Esther says often to him.

But Ben doubts it. He once figured the odds of finding someone just like Andrew were zero. Maybe – if he wishes for it – he'll find another *somehow right*. Maybe you can get lucky twice in a lifetime.

Maybe getting lucky once is enough.

The baby sighs, as though impatient for her bedtime story. Ben smiles tenderly at his daughter, at her soft blonde wisps of hair, her pink cheeks. She squints the way newborns do when they're trying to focus. 'If you get bored of it, just say so. Maybe kick me, or cry or fart. You're good at that.'

She doesn't make a sound.

Esther puts her head around the door. 'You still reading? She'll be hungry soon, Ben.' She wears the fluffy white dressing gown he bought her; she looks tired, fragile as thin china, but pretty.

'We won't be long. I'll call you when she's hungry. Go, rest, Esther. She's probably gonna have us both up all night again.'

'Who needs sleep, eh?'

'Yeah, it's overrated.' Ben smiles. 'I just wanna sit and look at her all night anyway. She's sempiternal.'

'You *must* be tired. You're talking in those crazy wrong words again.'

'No, it's a real word. Means everlasting.'

'Nice.'

Esther disappears. Ben turns another page. It's Christmas Eve. Snow has failed to fall, but ice coats the outside surfaces with festive shine. There are gifts under the tree that Heidi's tiny fingers won't be able to open, that they will undo for her.

It suddenly occurs to Ben that exactly a year ago he was in a less cosy nursery with Lucy. He closes his eyes; he can still see the golden ripples of her damp fur, still smell the heat of animal. He remembers those long, sticky nights together; that curious intimacy where neither quite trusted the other, but some bond held them.

They were *somehow right* too.

The night Esther went into labour, Stig called. While Ben paced a hospital corridor, worried he was missing a new contraction or development, Stig told Ben that Lucy had been released. She was free. Untamed. Though her wilderness is still monitored by the project, the hope is that she will rear her own cubs, and that *they* will be truly free, and raised without any human contact at all.

Already emotional, Ben had cried at the news. He pictured the closing shot of the documentary he watched with his mum when he was a kid – the two lions walking off into the sunset.

'This is good,' Stig assured him. 'You did good. *She* did good.'

Ben thought of the circus, of those tired, toothless, balding lions. Lucy would never be whipped by a lion tamer. She would never submit to the instruction of a man with a chair.

'Think you'll come back and visit us?' asked Stig.

'I hope so. One day.'

Ben had hung up and returned to the labour suite, where nine hours later he watched his screaming, bloody daughter make her way into the world, too. He held her before anyone else. Though he had not done so with Lucy – and had had to form a bond with a three-month-old – this time he was there at the very start. He then carried Heidi, with skinny legs dangling from a blanket, from the midwife to a teary Esther.

Now Ben turns another page.

'Your mum's going to want you soon,' he whispers to Heidi.

It felt like the most natural thing to name her after his mum. Esther had no complaints, said she loved it. Will nodded when Ben told him, eyes watery.

'Shall we cheat a bit?' Ben says. 'You know the story anyway.'

He flicks through the book and finds the last page. It's his favourite. This paragraph is the one where he can most hear Andrew's voice. The one he can imagine Andrew typing. The one Andrew could never have known would be his final words.

'Okay, are you ready?' Ben asks.

He hopes that one day this book will be Heidi's childhood favourite.

Now she is asleep.

'Did I wear you out?' Ben smiles. 'No worries. I'll go it alone. So this is the bit where Book Ben – that's what Andrew always called him – has learned to walk again and is now all grown up. He wonders if the lions ever really came to his bedroom while he was ill all those years ago.'

Sometimes, Ben can hardly ever believe he was really in Zimbabwe.

It seems a million years ago.

And yet Andrew seems like only yesterday.

Heidi snorts suddenly, and Ben laughs.

'I know where this scene came from, you see,' he explains. 'I once told your Uncle Andrew about the first time I decided I wanted to go and help the lions in Africa. There was this documentary where the last shot was of two young lions lumbering into freedom against this dusty land and yellow sky.'

Ben is sure for a moment that he smells Andrew. It often happens, and is so powerful that he always turns, sure he'll be standing right behind him. No one there. The scent gone as soon as it began.

He looks back at Heidi.

In her, Andrew will go on. His mother will go on. Anne will go on. Ben pictures a scene so vivid it feels like a memory. He sees himself, perhaps ten years from now, and a little girl with hair like the angels in those Botticelli paintings standing on his feet while he clumsily dances.

'I know Andrew was thinking of what I told him when he wrote this ending.' Ben pauses. 'I guess you can understand why I like it so much? Listen, you stay asleep, and I'll try and do it right. Here we go...'

Ben reads the last page.

The lioness let her cub go. She didn't want to. She knew what danger lurked in the shadows. But she also knew that a lifetime without fight was a lifetime without purpose.

The cub ambled at first, like a newborn. All around, the horizon hummed with heat and gold. So many golds; sun, cub, sand, lioness, sun, savanna, cub, forever. The mother felt sad; her cub looked sad. Because we all want to stay in the place we're loved. But love goes with us – it is light and has easy-to-grip handles and needs no passport.

The mother knew this secret.

So she called out to her daughter – 'Run, run, run.'

The cub heard the words even when she was far away from her. She heard the words wherever she went. Because she had learned that when it seems like there is nothing, that's when you most appreciate everything. That you never dance alone, you are always dancing on the bigger feet of those who loved you first.

Acknowledgments

Thanks to Dean Wilson (Hull's fourth best poet and my first best), to my beloved sisters Grace and Claire, and to John Marrs (Northampton's Thomas Harris and Barbara Cartland rolled into one) for being my very first beta readers. You all brought something different, and equally helpful.

Thanks to Michael Mann, Liam Asplen, Julian Lugar and Paul Bennett for answering some of my probing questions as part of the research.

Thanks to StrangeDaze for the daze at WF – remember when this was a short story?

Thank you to Helen Jn Pierre (Cushion Lady!) and Dave the Cake Man for all your endless support. To Liz Robinson at Love Reading for absolutely everything. To Deirdre O'Brien and Nina Pottell for the reviews that made my year. To Anne Cater for your endless and eternal support. To Fiona Mills for interviewing me so many times, and Pete Mills for the interviews. To Carrie Martin for being my musical sidekick. To Janet Harrison for taking care of my very precious *How To Be Brave* notes. And to my new pal Mr Gravy, or Mart, or @laughinggravy on Twitter. Thank you for the incredible support all year!

Lots of love and thanks also to Mel Hewitt, Madeleine Black, Vicky Bramble, Sussi Louise Smith, Mary Picken, Sue Bond, Abby Fairbrother, Katherine at Bibliomaniac, Cath @whatcathyreadnext, Ann Bonny Book Reviews, Suspense Thrill, It's All About the Books, Steph's Book Blog, Shotsmag, DampPebbles, The Book Trail, Jaffa Reads Too, The Book Magnet, Hayley's Book Blog, Bloomin' Brilliant Books, Thoughts from a Highly Caffeinated Mind, Book Literati, Jo Robertson, If Only I Could Read Faster, Ali the Dragon Slayer, The Writing

Garnet, Anne Williams, Victoria Goldman, The Book Review Café, Blue Book Balloon, Portobello Book Blog, Liz Loves Books, Claire Knight, Noelle Holten, Short Book and Scribes, Books of all Kinds, Chocolate 'n' Waffles Blog, @WalesCrazy, Leah Moyse, Earl Grey and Cupcakes, Have Books Will Read, Karen at My Reading Corner, Susan Hampson, Beady Jan, Crime By The Book, Lisa Adamson, The Miss-tery, The Wrong Side of Forty, Rae Reads, Sue Featherstone, Emma Mitchell, Paige Turner, Trip Fiction, Hair Past a Freckle, Jen Med, Novel Gossip, Swirl and Thread, Follow the Hens, Joy Kluver, Ronnie Turner, Sharon Bairden, What Kathy Read Next, Novel Delights, The Quiet Knitter, Linda Hill, The Hazardous Hippo, Sarah Hardy, Mrs Bloggs' Books, Cheryl M-M's Book Blog, Over the Rainbow Book Blog, Janet Emson, Nat Marshall, and Tony Hill.

Always a shout out to #BeechsBitches – you all know who you are!

A big up to my Women of Words girls – Vicky, Cass, Lynda, Michelle and Julie – I love you all!

To the Newbald Book Group – the very best in Yorkshire. Home-made soup, bread, wine, and words – what more could anyone want?

Thanks to the Book Connectors on Facebook, where I learn so much from so many bloggers and readers.

Great thanks to the Prime Writers gang; my go-to place for writerly discussion and support!

I can't forget to mention THE Book Club (TBC) on Facebook, and Tracy Tits Fenton, who is a whirlwind of force in the book world, for the laughs, the recommendations, and the friends.

And last but DEFINITELY not least, in fact the MOST ... thank you again to my friend and publisher Karen Sullivan for believing in me, supporting me, and (ha ha) loving me! West Camel, you ain't bad either, and do a grand edit.